THE
HUNT BEGINS

THE WHEEL OF TIME™
BY ROBERT JORDAN

ROBERT JORDAN

THE HUNT BEGINS

Part One of
THE GREAT HUNT

Book Two of
The Wheel of Time™

A TOM DOHERTY ASSOCIATES BOOK
NEW YORK

THE HUNT BEGINS: Part One of the Great Hunt

Copyright © 1991 by Robert Jordan

Maps by Ellisa Mitchell
Interior ornament art by Matthew C. Nielsen and Ellisa Mitchell
Illustrations by Charles Keegan

The phrases "The Wheel of Time™" and "The Dragon Reborn™," and the snake-wheel symbol are trademarks of Robert Jordan.

A Starscape Book
Published by Tom Doherty Associates, LLC
175 Fifth Avenue
New York, NY 10010

www.starscapebooks.com

ISBN: 0-765-34843-8

First Starscape edition: January 2004

Printed in the United States of America

0 9 8 7 6 5 4 3 2 1

This book is dedicated to Lucinda Culpin, Al Dempsey, Tom Doherty, Susan England, Dick Gallen, Cathy Grooms, Marisa Grooms, Wilson and Janet Grooms, John Jarrold, the Johnson City Boys (Mike Leslie, Kenneth Loveless, James D. Lund, Paul R. Robinson), Karl Lundgren, William McDougal, the Montana Gang (Eldon Carter, Ray Grenfell, Ken Miller, Rod Moore, Dick Schmidt, Ray Sessions, Ed Wildey, Mike Wildey, and Sherman Williams), Charlie Moore, Louisa Cheves Popham Raoul, Ted and Sydney Rigney, Robert A. T. Scott, Bryan and Sharon Webb, and Heather Wood.

They came to my aid when God walked across the water and the true Eye of the World passed over my house.

—Robert Jordan
Charleston, SC
February 1990

CONTENTS

And it shall come to pass that what men made shall be shattered, and the Shadow shall lie across the Pattern of the Age, and the Dark One shall once more lay his hand upon the world of man. Women shall weep and men quail as the nations of the earth are rent like rotting cloth. Neither shall anything stand nor abide . . .

Yet one shall be born to face the Shadow, born once more as he was born before and shall be born again, time without end. The Dragon shall be Reborn, and there shall be wailing and gnashing of teeth at his rebirth. In sackcloth and ashes shall he clothe the people, and he shall break the world again by his coming, tearing apart all ties that bind. Like the unfettered dawn shall he blind us, and burn us, yet shall the Dragon Reborn confront the Shadow at the Last Battle, and his blood shall give us the Light. Let tears flow, O ye people of the world. Weep for your salvation.

— from ***The Karaethon Cycle:
The Prophecies of the Dragon,***
as translated by Ellaine Maris'idin Alshinn,
Chief Librarian at the Court of Arafel,
in the Year of Grace 231
of the New Era, the Third Age

PROLOGUE

In the Shadow

THE MAN WHO CALLED HIMSELF BORS, AT least in this place, sneered at the low murmuring that rolled around the vaulted chamber like the soft gabble of geese. His grimace was hidden by the black silk mask that covered his face, though, just-like the masks that covered the hundred other faces in the chamber. A hundred black masks, and a hundred pairs of eyes trying to see what lay behind them.

If one did not look too closely, the huge room could have been in a palace, with its tall marble fireplaces and its golden lamps hanging from the domed ceiling, its colorful tapestries and intricately patterned mosaic floor. If one did not look too closely. The fireplaces were cold, for one thing. Flames danced on logs as thick as a man's leg, but gave no heat. The walls behind the tapestries, the ceiling high above the lamps, were undressed stone, almost black. There were no windows, and only two doorways, one at either end of the room. It was as if someone had intended to give the semblance of a palace reception chamber but had not cared enough to bother with more than the outline and a few touches for detail.

Where the chamber was, the man who called himself Bors did not know, nor did he think any of the others knew. He did not like to think about where it might be. It was enough that he had been summoned. He did not like to think about that, either, but for such a summons, even he came.

He shifted his cloak, thankful that the fires were cold, else it would have been too hot for the black wool draping him to the floor. All his clothes were black. The bulky folds of the cloak hid the stoop he used to disguise his height, and bred confusion as to whether he was thin or thick. He was not the only one there enveloped in a tailor's span of cloth.

Silently he watched his companions. Patience had marked much of his life. Always, if he waited and watched long enough, someone made a mistake. Most of the men and women here might have had the same philosophy; they watched, and listened silently to those who had to speak. Some people could not bear waiting, or silence, and so gave away more than they knew.

Servants circulated through the guests, slender, golden-haired youths proffering wine with a bow and a wordless smile. Young men and young women alike, they wore tight white breeches and flowing white shirts. And male and female alike, they moved with disturbing grace. Each looked more than a mirror image of the others, the boys as handsome as the girls were beautiful. He doubted he could distinguish one from another, and he had an eye and a memory for faces.

A smiling, white-clad girl offered her tray of crystal goblets to him. He took one with no intention of drinking; it might appear untrusting—or worse, and either could be deadly here—if he refused altogether, but anything could be slipped into a drink. Surely some among his companions would have no objections to seeing the number of their rivals for power dwindle, whomever the unlucky ones happened to be.

Idly he wondered whether the servants would have to be disposed of after this meeting. *Servants hear everything.* As the serving girl straightened from her bow, his eye caught hers above that sweet smile. Blank eyes. Empty eyes. A doll's eyes. Eyes more dead than death.

He shivered as she moved gracefully away, and raised the goblet to his lips before he caught himself. It was not what had been done to the girl that chilled him. Rather, every time he thought he detected a weakness in those he now served, he found himself preceded, the supposed weakness cut out with a ruthless precision that left him amazed. And worried. The first rule of his life had always been to search for weakness, for every weakness was a chink where he could probe and pry and influence. If his current masters, his masters for the moment, had no weakness. . . .

Frowning behind his mask, he studied his companions. At least there was plenty of weakness there. Their nervousness betrayed them, even those who had sense enough to guard their tongues. A stiffness in the way this one held himself, a jerkiness in the way that one handled her skirts.

A good quarter of them, he estimated, had not bothered with disguise beyond the black masks. Their clothes told much. A woman standing before a gold-and-crimson wall hanging, speaking softly to a figure—impossible to say whether it was man or woman—cloaked and hooded in gray. She had obviously chosen the spot because the colors of the tapestry set off her garb. Doubly foolish to draw attention to herself, for her scarlet dress, cut low in the bodice to show too much flesh and high at the hem to display golden slippers, marked her from Illian, and a woman of wealth, perhaps even of noble blood.

Not far beyond the Illianer, another woman stood, alone and admirably silent. With a swan's neck and lustrous black hair falling in waves below her waist, she kept her back to the stone wall, observing everything. No nervousness there, only serene self-possession. Very admirable, that, but her coppery skin and her creamy, high-necked gown—leaving nothing but her hands uncovered, yet clinging and only just barely opaque, so that it hinted at everything and revealed nothing—marked her just as clearly of the first blood of Arad Doman. And unless the man who called himself Bors missed his guess entirely, the wide golden bracelet on her left wrist bore her House symbols. They would be for her own House; no Domani bloodborn would bend her stiff pride enough to wear the sigils of another House. Worse than foolishness.

A man in a high-collared, sky-blue Shienaran coat passed him with a wary, head-to-toe glance through the eyeholes of his mask. The man's carriage named him soldier; the set of his shoulders, the way his gaze never rested in one place for long, and the way his hand seemed ready to dart for a sword that was not there, all proclaimed it. The Shienaran wasted little time on the man who called himself Bors; stooped shoulders and a bent back held no threat.

The man who called himself Bors snorted as the Shienaran moved on, right hand clenching and eyes already studying elsewhere for danger. He could read them all, to class and country. Merchant and warrior, commoner and noble. From Kandor and Cairhien, Saldaea and Ghealdan. From every nation and nearly every people. His nose wrinkled in sudden disgust. Even a Tinker, in bright green breeches and a virulent yellow coat. *We can do without* those *come the Day.*

The disguised ones were no better, many of them, cloaked and shrouded as they were. He caught sight, under the edge of one dark robe, of the silver-worked boots of a High Lord of Tear, and under another a glimpse of golden lion-head spurs, worn only by high officers in the Andoran Queen's Guards. A slender fellow—slender even in a floor-dragging black robe and an anonymous gray cloak caught with a plain silver pin—watched from the shadows of his deep cowl. He could be anyone, from anywhere . . . except for the six-pointed star tattooed on the web between thumb and forefinger of his right hand. One of the Sea Folk then, and a look at his left hand would show the marks of his clan and line. The man who called himself Bors did not bother to try.

Suddenly his eyes narrowed, fixing on a woman enveloped in black till nothing showed but her fingers. On her right hand rested a gold ring in the shape of a serpent eating its own tail. Aes Sedai, or at least a woman trained in Tar Valon by Aes Sedai. None else would wear that ring. Either way made no difference to him. He looked away before she could notice his watching, and almost immediately he spotted another woman swathed from head to toe in black and wearing a Great Serpent ring. The two witches gave no sign that they knew each other. In the White Tower they sat like spiders in the middle of a web, pulling the strings that made kings and queens dance, meddling. *Curse them all to death eternal!* He realized that he was grinding his teeth. If numbers must dwindle— and they must, before the Day—there were some who would be missed even less than Tinkers.

A chime sounded, a single, shivering note that came from everywhere at once and cut off all other sounds like a knife.

The tall doors at the far end of the chamber swung open, and two Trollocs stepped into the room, spikes decorating the black mail that hung to their knees. Everyone shied back. Even the man who called himself Bors.

Head and shoulders taller than the tallest man there, they were a stomach-turning blend of man and animal, human faces twisted and altered. One had a heavy, pointed beak where his mouth and nose should have been, and feathers covered his head instead of hair. The other walked on hooves, his face pushed out in a hairy muzzle, and goat horns stuck up above his ears.

Ignoring the humans, the Trollocs turned back toward the door and bowed, servile and cringing. The feathers on the one lifted in a tight crest.

A Myrddraal stepped between them, and they fell to their knees. It was garbed in black that made the Trollocs' mail and the humans' masks seem bright, garments that hung still, without a ripple, as it moved with a viper's grace.

The man who called himself Bors felt his lips drawing back over his teeth, half snarl and half, he was shamed to admit even to himself, fear. It had its face uncovered. Its pasty pale face, a man's face, but eyeless as an egg, like a maggot in a grave.

The smooth white face swiveled, regarding them all one by one, it seemed. A visible shiver ran through them under that eyeless look. Thin, bloodless lips quirked in what might almost have been a smile as, one by one, the masked ones tried to press back into the crowd, milling to avoid that gaze. The Myrddraal's look shaped them into a semicircle facing the door.

The man who called himself Bors swallowed. *There will come a day, Halfman. When the Great Lord of the Dark comes again, he will choose his new Dreadlords, and you will cower before them. You will cower before men. Before me! Why doesn't it speak? Stop staring at me, and speak!*

"Your Master comes." The Myrddraal's voice rasped like a dry snake skin crumbling. "To your bellies, worms! Grovel, lest his brilliance blind and burn you!"

Rage filled the man who called himself Bors, at the tone as much as the words, but then the air above the Halfman shimmered, and the import drove home. *It can't be! It can't . . .!* The Trollocs were already on their bellies, writhing as if they wanted to burrow into the floor.

Without waiting to see if anyone else moved, the man who

called himself Bors dropped facedown, grunting as he bruised himself on the stone. Words sprang to his lips like a charm against danger—they were a charm, though a thin reed against what he feared—and he heard a hundred other voices, breathy with fear, speaking the same against the floor.

"The Great Lord of the Dark is my Master, and most heartily do I serve him to the last shred of my very soul." In the back of his mind a voice chattered with fear. *The Dark One and all the Forsaken are bound....* Shivering, he forced it to silence. He had abandoned that voice long since. "Lo, my Master is death's Master. Asking nothing do I serve against the Day of his coming, yes do I serve in the sure and certain hope of life everlasting." ... *bound in Shayol Ghul, bound by the Creator at the moment of creation. No, I serve a different master now.* "Surely the faithful shall be exalted in the land, exalted above the unbelievers, exalted above thrones, yet do I serve humbly against the Day of his Return." *The hand of the Creator shelters us all, and the Light protects us from the Shadow. No, no! A different master.* "Swift come the Day of Return. Swift come the Great Lord of the Dark to guide us and rule the world forever and ever."

The man who called himself Bors finished the creed panting, as if he had run ten miles. The rasp of breath all around told him he was not the only one.

"Rise. All of you, rise."

The mellifluous voice took him by surprise. Surely none of his companions, lying on their bellies with their masked faces pressed to the mosaic tiles, would have spoken, but it was not the voice he expected from. ... Cautiously, he raised his head enough to see with one eye.

The figure of a man floated in the air above the Myrddraal, the hem of his blood-red robe hanging a span over the Halfman's head. Masked in blood-red, too. Would the Great Lord of the Dark appear to them as a man? And masked, besides? Yet the Myrddraal, its very gaze fear, trembled and almost cowered where it stood in the figure's shadow. The man who called himself Bors grasped for an answer his mind could contain without splitting. One of the Forsaken, perhaps.

That thought was only a little less painful. Even so, it meant the Day of the Dark One's return must be close at hand if one of the Forsaken was free. The Forsaken, thirteen of the most powerful wielders of the One Power in an Age filled with powerful wielders, had been sealed up in Shayol Ghul along with the Dark One, sealed away from the world of men by the Dragon and the Hundred Companions. And the backblast of that sealing had tainted the male half of the True Source; and all the male Aes Sedai, those cursed wielders of the Power, went mad and broke the world, tore it apart like a pottery bowl smashed on rocks, ending the Age of Legends before they died, rotting while they still lived. A fitting death for Aes Sedai, to his mind. Too good for them. He regretted only that the women had been spared.

Slowly, painfully, he forced the panic to the back of his mind, confined it and held it tight though it screamed to get out. It was the best he could do. None of those on their bellies had risen, and only a few had even dared raise their heads.

"Rise." There was a snap in the red-masked figure's voice this time. He gestured with both hands. "Stand!"

The man who called himself Bors scrambled up awkwardly, but halfway to his feet, he hesitated. Those gesturing hands were horribly burned, crisscrossed by black fissures, the raw flesh between as red as the figure's robes. *Would the Dark One appear so? Or even one of the Forsaken?* The eyeholes of that blood-red mask swept slowly across him, and he straightened hastily. He thought he could feel the heat of an open furnace in that gaze.

The others obeyed the command with no more grace and no less fear in their rising. When all were on their feet, the floating figure spoke.

"I have been known by many names, but the one by which you shall know me is Ba'alzamon."

The man who called himself Bors clamped his teeth to keep them from chattering. Ba'alzamon. In the Trolloc tongue, it meant Heart of the Dark, and even unbelievers knew it was the Trolloc name for the Great Lord of the Dark. He Whose Name Must Not Be Uttered. Not the True Name, Shai'tan, but still forbidden. Among those gathered here, and others of their kind, to sully either with a human tongue was blasphemy. His breath whistled through his nostrils, and all around him he could hear others panting behind their masks. The servants were gone, and the Trollocs as well, though he had not seen them go.

"The place where you stand lies in the shadow of Shayol Ghul." More than one voice moaned at that; the man who called himself Bors was not sure his own was not among them. A touch of what might almost be called mockery entered Ba'alzamon's voice as he spread his arms wide. "Fear not, for the Day of your Master's rising upon the world is near at hand. The Day of Return draws nigh. Does it not tell you so that I am here, to be seen by you favored few among your brothers and sisters? Soon the Wheel of Time will be broken. Soon the Great Serpent will die, and with the power of that death, the death of Time itself, your Master will remake the world in his own image for this Age and for all Ages to come. And those who serve me, faithful and steadfast, will sit at my feet above the stars in the sky and rule the world of men forever. So have I promised, and so shall it be, without end. You shall live and rule forever."

A murmur of anticipation ran through the listeners, and some even took a step forward, toward the floating, crimson shape, their eyes lifted, rapturous. Even the man who called himself Bors felt the pull of that promise, the promise for which he had dealt away his soul a hundred times over.

"The Day of Return comes closer," Ba'alzamon said. "But there is much yet to do. Much to do."

The air to Ba'alzamon's left shimmered and thickened, and the figure of a young man hung there, a little lower than Ba'alzamon. The man who called himself Bors could not decide whether it was a living being or not. A country lad, by his clothes, with a light of mischief in his brown eyes and the hint of a smile on his lips, as if in memory or anticipation of a prank. The flesh looked warm, but the chest did not move with breath, the eyes did not blink.

The air to Ba'alzamon's right wavered as if with heat, and a second country-clad figure hung suspended a little below Ba'alzamon. A curly-haired youth, as heavily muscled as a blacksmith. And an oddity: a battle axe hung at his aide, a great, steel half-moon balanced by a thick spike. The man who called himself Bors suddenly leaned forward, intent on an even greater strangeness. A youth with yellow eyes.

For the third time air solidified into the shape of a young man, this time directly under Ba'alzamon's eye, almost at his feet. A tall fellow, with eyes now gray, now almost blue as the light took them, and dark, reddish hair. Another villager, or farmer. The man who called himself Bors gasped. Yet another thing out of the ordinary, though he wondered why he should expect anything to be ordinary here. A sword swung from the figure's belt, a sword with a bronze heron on the scabbard and another inset into the long, two-handed hilt. *A village boy with a heron-mark blade? Impossible! What can it mean? And a boy with yellow eyes.* He noticed the Myrddraal looking at the figures, trembling; and unless he misjudged entirely, its trembling was no longer fear, but hatred.

Dead silence had fallen, silence that Ba'alzamon let deepen before he spoke. "There is now one who walks the world, one who was and will be, but is not yet, the Dragon."

A startled murmur ran through his listeners.

"The Dragon Reborn! We are to kill him, Great Lord?" That from the Shienaran, hand grasping eagerly at his side where his sword would hang.

"Perhaps," Ba'alzamon said simply. "And perhaps not. Perhaps he can be turned to my use. Sooner or later it will be so, in this Age or another."

The man who called himself Bors blinked. *In this Age or another? I thought the Day of Return was near. What matter to me what happens in another Age if I grow old and die waiting in this one?* But Ba'alzamon was speaking again.

"Already a bend is forming in the Pattern, one of many points where he who will become the Dragon may be turned to my service. Must be turned! Better that he serve me alive than dead, but alive or dead, serve me he must and will! These three you must know, for each is a thread in the pattern *I* mean to weave, and it will be up to you to see that they are placed as I command. Study them well, that you will know them."

Abruptly all sound was gone. The man who called himself Bors shifted uneasily, and saw others doing the same. All but the Illianer woman, he realized. With her hands spread over her bosom as if to hide the rounded flesh she exposed, eyes wide, half frightened and half ecstatic, she was nodding eagerly as though to someone face-to-face with her. Sometimes she appeared to give a reply, but the man who called himself Bors heard not a word. Suddenly she arched backwards, trembling and rising on her toes. He could not see why she did not fall, unless something unseen held her. Then, just as abruptly, she settled back to her feet and nodded again, bowing, shivering. Even as she straightened, one of the women wearing a Great Serpent ring gave a start and began nodding.

So each of us hears his own instructions, and none hears another's. The man who called himself Bors muttered in frustration. If he knew what even one other was commanded, he might be able to use the knowledge to advantage, but this way. . . . Impatiently he waited for his turn, forgetting himself enough to stand straight.

One by one the gathering received their orders, each walled in silence yet still giving tantalizing clues, if only he could read them. The man of the Atha'an Miere, the Sea Folk, stiffening with reluctance as he nodded. The Shienaran, his stance bespeaking confusion even while he acquiesced. The second woman of Tar Valon giving a start, as of shock, ad the gray-swathed figure whose sex he could not determine shaking its head before falling to its knees and nodding vigorously. Some underwent the same convulsion as the Illianer woman, as if pain itself lifted them to toe tips.

"Bors."

The man who called himself Bors jerked as a red mask filled his eyes. He could still see the room, still see the floating shape of Ba'alzamon and the three figures before him, but at the same time all he could see was the red-masked face. Dizzy, he felt as if his skull were splitting open and his eyes were being pushed out of his head. For a moment he thought he could see flames through the eyeholes of the mask.

"Are you faithful . . . Bors?"

The hint of mocking in the name sent a chill down his backbone. "I am faithful, Great Lord. I cannot hide from you." *I am faithful! I swear it!*

"No, you cannot."

The certainty in Ba'alzamon's voice dried his mouth, but he forced himself to speak. "Command me, Great Lord, and I obey."

"Firstly, you are to return to Tarabon and continue your *good* works. In fact, I command you to redouble your efforts."

He stared at Ba'alzamon in puzzlement, but then fires flared again behind the mask, and he took the excuse of a bow to pull his eyes away. "As you command, Great Lord, so shall it be."

"Secondly, you will watch for the three young men, and have your followers watch. Be warned; they are dangerous."

The man who called himself Bors glanced at the figures floating in front of Ba'alzamon. *How can I do that? I can see them, but I can't see anything except* his *face.* His head felt about to burst. Sweat slicked his hands under his thin gloves, and his shirt clung to his back. "Dangerous, Great Lord? Farmboys? Is one of them the—"

"A sword is dangerous to the man at the point, but not to the man at the hilt. Unless the man holding the sword is a fool, or careless, or unskilled, in which case it is twice as dangerous to him as to anyone else. It is enough that I have told you to know them. It is enough that you obey me."

"As you command, Great Lord, so shall it be."

"Thirdly, regarding those who have landed at Toman Head, and the Domani. Of this you will speak to no one. When you return to Tarabon. . . ."

The man who called himself Bors realized as he listened that his mouth was sagging open. The instructions made no sense. *If I knew what some of the others were told, perhaps I could piece it together.*

Abruptly he felt his head grasped as though by a giant hand crushing his temples, felt himself being lifted, and the world blew apart in a thousand starbursts, each flash of the light becoming an image that fled across his mind or spun and dwindled into the distance before he could more than barely grasp it. An impossible sky of striated clouds, red and yellow and black, racing as if driven by the mightiest wind the world had ever seen. A woman—a girl?—dressed in white receded into blackness and vanished as soon as she appeared. A raven stared him in the eye, *knowing* him, and was gone. An armored man in a brutal helm, shaped and painted and gilded like some monstrous, poisonous insect, raised a sword and plunged to one side, beyond his view. A horn, curled and golden, came hurtling out of the far distance. One piercing note it sounded as it flashed toward him, tugging his soul. At the last instant it flashed into a blinding, golden ring of light that passed through him, chilling him beyond death. A wolf leaped from the shadows of lost sight and ripped out his throat. He could not scream. The torrent went on, drowning him, burying him. He could barely remember who he was, or what he was. The skies rained fire, and the moon and stars fell; rivers ran in blood, and the dead walked; the earth split open and fountained molten rock. . . .

The man who called himself Bors found himself half crouching in the chamber with the others, most watching him, all silent. Wherever he looked, up or down or in any direction, the masked face of Ba'alzamon overwhelmed his eyes. The images that had flooded into his mind were fading; he was sure many were already gone from memory. Hesitantly, he straightened, Ba'alzamon always before him.

"Great Lord, what—?"

"Some commands are too important to be known even by he who carries them out."

The man who called himself Bors bent almost double in his bow. "As you command, Great Lord," he whispered hoarsely, "so shall it be."

When he straightened, he was alone in silence once more. Another, the Tairen High Lord, nodded and bowed to someone none else saw. The man who called himself Bors put an unsteady hand to his brow, trying to hold on to something of what had burst through his mind, though he was not completely certain he wanted to remember. The last remnant flickered out, and suddenly he was wondering what it was that he was trying to recall. *I know there was something, but what? There* was *something! Wasn't there?* He rubbed his hands together, grimacing at the feel of sweat under his gloves, and turned his attention to the three figures hanging suspended before Ba'alzamon's floating form.

The muscular, curly-haired youth; the farmer with the sword; and the lad with the look of mischief on his face. Already, in his mind, the man who called himself Bors had named them the Blacksmith, the Swordsman, and the Trickster. *What is their place in the puzzle?* They must be important, or Ba'alzamon would not have made them the center of this gathering. But from his orders alone they could all die at any time, and he had to think that some of the others, at least, had orders as deadly for the three. *How important are they?* Blue eyes could mean the nobility of Andor—unlikely in those clothes—and there were Border-landers with light eyes, as well as some Tairens, not to mention a few from Ghealdan, and, of course. . . . No, no help there. But *yellow* eyes? *Who* are *they? What* are *they?*

He started at a touch on his arm, and looked around to find one of the white-clad servants, a young man, standing by his side. The others were back, too, more than before, one for each of the masked. He blinked. Ba'alzamon was gone. The Myrddraal was gone, too, and only rough stone was where the door it had used had been. The three figures still hung there, though. He felt as if they were staring at him.

"If it please you, my Lord Bors, I will show you to your room."

Avoiding those dead eyes, he glanced once more at the three figures, then followed. Uneasily he wondered how the youth had known what name to use. It was not until the strange carved doors closed behind him and they had walked a dozen paces that he realized he was alone in the corridor with the servant. His brows drew down suspiciously behind his mask, but before he could open his mouth, the servant spoke.

"The others are also being shown to their rooms, my Lord. If you please, my Lord? Time is short, and our Master is impatient."

The man who called himself Bors ground his teeth, both at the lack of information and at the implication of sameness between himself and the servant, but he followed in silence. Only a fool ranted at a servant, and worse, remembering the fellow's eyes, he was not sure it would do any good. *And how did he know what I was going to ask?* The servant smiled.

The man who called himself Bors did not feel at all comfortable until he was back in the room where he had waited on first arriving, and then not much. Even finding the seals on his saddlebags untouched was small comfort.

The servant stood in the hallway, not entering. "You may change to your own garments if you wish, my Lord. None will see you depart here, nor arrive at your destination, but it may be best to arrive already properly clothed. Someone will come soon to show you the way."

Untouched by any visible hand, the door swung shut:

The man who called himself Bors shivered in spite of himself. Hastily he undid the seals and buckles of his saddlebags and pulled out his usual cloak. In the back of his mind a small voice wondered if the promised power, even the immortality, was worth another meeting like this, but he laughed it down immediately. *For that much power, I would praise the Great Lord of the Dark under the Dome of Truth.* Remembering the commands given him by Ba'alzamon, he fingered the golden, flaring sun worked on the breast of the white cloak, and the red shepherd's crook behind the sun, symbol of his office in the world of men, and he almost laughed. There was work, great work, to be done in Tarabon, and on Almoth Plain.

THE
HUNT BEGINS

CHAPTER 1

The Flame of Tar Valon

THE WHEEL OF TIME TURNS, AND AGES COME and pass leaving memories that become legend, then fade to myth, and are long forgot when that Age comes again. In one Age, called the Third Age by some, an Age yet to come, an Age long past, a wind rose in the Mountains of Dhoom. The wind was not the beginning. There are neither beginnings nor endings to the turning of the Wheel of Time. But it was a beginning.

Born among black, knife-edged peaks, where death roamed the high passes yet hid from things still more dangerous, the wind blew south across the tangled forest of the Great Blight, a forest tainted and twisted by the touch of the Dark One. The sickly sweet smell of corruption faded by the time the wind crossed that invisible line men called the border of Shienar, where spring flowers hung thick in the trees. It should have been summer by now, but spring had been late in coming, and the land had run wild to catch up. New-come pale green bristled on every bush, and red new growth tipped every tree branch. The wind rippled farmers' fields like verdant ponds, solid with crops that almost seemed to creep upward visibly.

The smell of death was all but gone long before the wind reached the stone-walled town of Fal Dara on its hills, and whipped around a tower of the fortress in the very center of the town, a tower atop which two men seemed to dance. Hard-walled and high, Fal Dara, both keep and town, never taken, never betrayed. The wind moaned across wood-shingled rooftops, around tall stone chimneys and taller towers, moaned like a dirge.

Stripped to the waist, Rand al'Thor shivered at the wind's cold caress, and his fingers flexed on the long hilt of the practice sword he held. The hot sun had slicked his chest, and his dark, reddish hair clung to his head in a sweat-curled mat. A faint odor in the swirl of air made his nose twitch, but he did not connect the smell with the image of an old grave fresh-opened that flashed through his head. He was barely aware of odor or image at all; he strove to keep his mind empty, but the other man sharing the tower top with him kept intruding on the emptiness. Ten paces across, the tower top was, encircled by a chest-high, crenellated wall. Big enough and more not to feel crowded, except when shared with a Warder.

Young as he was, Rand was taller than most men, but Lan stood just as tall and more heavily muscled, if not quite so broad in the shoulders. A narrow band of braided leather held the Warder's long hair back from his face, a face that seemed made from stony planes and angles, a face unlined as if to belie the tinge of gray at his temples. Despite the heat and exertion, only a light coat of sweat glistened on his chest and arms. Rand searched Lan's icy blue eyes, hunting for some hint of what the other man intended. The Warder never seemed to blink, and the practice sword in his hands moved surely and smoothly as he flowed from one stance to another.

With a bundle of thin, loosely bound staves in place of a blade, the practice sword would make a loud clack when it struck anything, and leave a welt where it hit flesh. Rand knew all too well. Three thin red lines stung on his ribs, and another burned his shoulder. It had taken all his efforts not to wear more decorations. Lan bore not a mark.

As he had been taught, Rand formed a single flame in his mind and concentrated on it, tried to feed all emotion and passion into it, to form a void within himself, with even thought outside. Emptiness came. As was too often the case of late it was not a perfect emptiness; the flame still remained, or some sense of light sending ripples through the stillness. But it was enough, barely. The cool peace of the void crept over him, and he was one with the practice sword, with the smooth stones under his boots, even with Lan. All was one, and he moved without thought in a rhythm that matched the Warder's step for step and move for move.

The wind rose again, bringing the ringing of bells from the town. *Somebody's still celebrating that spring has finally come.* The extraneous thought fluttered through the void on waves of light, disturbing the emptiness, and as if the Warder could read Rand's mind, the practice sword whirled in Lan's hands.

For a long minute the swift *clack-clack-clack* of bundled lathes meeting filled the tower top. Rand made no effort to reach the other man; it was all he could do to keep the Warder's strikes from reaching him. Turning Lan's blows at the last possible moment, he was forced back. Lan's expression never changed; the practice sword seemed alive in his hands. Abruptly the Warder's swinging slash changed in mid-motion to a thrust. Caught by surprise, Rand stepped back, already wincing with the blow he knew he could not stop this time.

The wind howled across the tower . . . and trapped him. It was as if the air had suddenly jelled, holding him in a cocoon. Pushing him forward. Time and motion slowed; horrified, he watched

Lan's practice sword drift toward his chest. There was nothing slow or soft about the impact. His ribs creaked as if he had been struck with a hammer. He grunted, but the wind would not allow him to give way; it still carried him forward, instead. The lathes of Lan's practice sword flexed and bent—ever so slowly, it seemed to Rand—then shattered, sharp points oozing toward his heart, jagged lathes piercing his skin. Pain lanced through his body; his whole skin felt slashed. He burned as though the sun had flared to crisp him like bacon in a pan.

With a shout, he threw himself stumbling back, falling against the stone wall. Hand trembling, he touched the gashes on his chest and raised bloody fingers before his gray eyes in disbelief.

"And what was that fool move, sheepherder?" Lan grated. "You know better by now, or should unless you have forgotten everything I've tried to teach you. How badly are you—?" He cut off as Rand looked up at him.

"The wind." Rand's mouth was dry. "It—it pushed me! It. . . . It was solid as a wall!"

The Warder stared at him in silence, then offered a hand. Rand took it and let himself be pulled to his feet.

"Strange things can happen this close to the Blight," Lan said finally, but for all the flatness of the words he sounded troubled. That in itself was strange. Warders, those half-legendary warriors who served the Aes Sedai, seldom showed emotion, and Lan showed little even for a Warder. He tossed the shattered lathe sword aside and leaned against the wall where their real swords lay, out of the way of their practice.

"Not like that," Rand protested. He joined the other man, squatting with his back against the stone. That way the top of the wall was higher than his head, protection of a kind from the wind. If it was a wind. No wind had ever felt . . . solid . . . like that. "Peace! Maybe not even *in* the Blight."

"For someone like you. . . ." Lan shrugged as if that explained everything. "How long before you leave, sheepherder? A month since you said you were going, and I thought you'd be three weeks gone by now."

Rand stared up at him in surprise. *He's acting like nothing happened!* Frowning, he set down the practice sword and lifted his real sword to his knees, fingers running along the long, leather-wrapped hilt inset with a bronze heron. Another bronze heron stood on the scabbard, and yet another was scribed on the sheathed blade. It was still a little strange to him that he had a sword. Any sword, much less one with a blademaster's mark. He was a farmer from the Two Rivers, so far away, now. Maybe far away forever, now. He was a shepherd like his father—*I was a shepherd. What am I now?*—and his father had given him a heron-marked sword. *Tam is my father, no matter what anybody says.* He wished his own thoughts did not sound as if he was trying to convince himself.

Again Lan seemed to read his mind. "In the Borderlands, sheepherder, if a man has the raising of a child, that child is his, and none can say different."

Scowling, Rand ignored the Warder's words. It was no one's business but his own. "I want to learn how to use this. I need to." It had caused him problems, carrying a heron-marked sword. Not everybody knew what it meant, or even noticed it, but even so a heron-mark blade, especially in the hands of a youth barely old enough to be called a man, still attracted the wrong sort of attention. "I've been able to bluff sometimes, when I could not run, and I've been lucky, besides. But what happens when I can't run, and I can't bluff, and my luck runs out?"

"You could sell it," Lan said carefully. "That blade is rare even among heron-mark swords. It would fetch a pretty price."

"No!" It was an idea he had thought of more than once, but he rejected it now for the same reason he always had, and more fiercely for coming from someone else. *As long as I keep it, I have the right to call Tam father. He gave it to me, and it gives me the right.* "I thought any heron-mark blade was rare."

Lan gave him a sidelong look. "Tam didn't tell you, then? He must know. Perhaps he didn't believe. Many do not." He snatched up his own sword, almost the twin of Rand's except for the lack of herons, and whipped off the scabbard. The blade, slightly curved and single-edged, glittered silvery in the sunlight.

It was the sword of the kings of Malkier. Lan did not speak of it—he did not even like others to speak of it—but al'Lan Mandragoran was Lord of the Seven Towers, Lord of the Lakes, and uncrowned King of Malkier. The Seven Towers were broken now, and the Thousand Lakes the lair of unclean things. Malkier lay swallowed by the Great Blight, and of all the Malkieri lords, only one still lived.

Some said Lan had become a Warder, bonding himself to an Aes Sedai, so he could seek death in the Blight and join the rest of his blood. Rand had indeed seen Lan put himself in harm's way seemingly without regard for his own safety, but far beyond his own life and safety he held those of Moiraine, the Aes Sedai who held his bond. Rand did not think Lan would truly seek death while Moiraine lived.

Turning his blade in the light, Lan spoke. "In the War of the Shadow, the One Power itself was used as a weapon, and weapons were made with the One Power. Some weapons *used* the One Power, things that could destroy an entire city at one blow, lay waste to the land for leagues. Just as well those were all lost in the Breaking; just as well no one remembers the making of them. But there were simpler weapons, too, for those who would face Myrddraal, and worse things the Dreadlords made, blade to blade.

"With the One Power, Aes Sedai drew iron and other metals from the earth, smelted them, formed and wrought them. All with the Power. Swords, and other weapons, too. Many that survived the Breaking of the World were destroyed by men who feared and hated Aes Sedai work, and others have vanished with the years. Few remain, and few men truly know what they are. There have been legends of them, swollen tales of swords that seemed to have a power of their own. You've heard the gleemen's tales. The reality is enough. Blades that will not shatter or break, and never lose their edge. I've seen men sharpening them—playing at sharpening, as it were—but only because they could not believe a sword did not need it after use. All they ever did was wear away their oilstones.

"Those weapons the Aes Sedai made, and there will never be others. When it was done, war and Age ended together, with the world shattered, with more dead unburied than there were alive and those alive fleeing, trying to find some place, any place, of safety, with every second woman weeping because she'd never see husband or sons again; when it was done, the Aes Sedai who still lived swore they would never again make a weapon for one man to kill another. Every Aes Sedai swore it, and every woman of them since has kept that oath. Even the Red Ajah, and they care little what happens to any male.

"One of those swords, a plain soldier's sword"—with a faint grimace, almost sad, if the Warder could be said to show emotion, he slid the blade back into its sheath—"became something more. On the other hand, those made for lord-generals, with blades so hard no bladesmith could mark them, yet marked already with a heron, those blades became sought after."

Rand's hands jerked away from the sword propped on his knees. It toppled, and instinctively he grabbed it before it hit the floorstones. "You mean Aes Sedai made this? I thought you were talking about *your* sword."

"Not all heron-mark blades are Aes Sedai work. Few men handle a sword with the skill to be named blademaster and be awarded a heron-mark blade, but even so, not enough Aes Sedai blades remain for more than a handful to have one. Most come from master bladesmiths; the finest steel men can make, yet still wrought by a man's hands. But that one, sheepherder . . . that one could tell a tale of three thousand years and more."

"I can't get away from them," Rand said, "can I?" He balanced the sword in front of him on scabbard point; it looked no different than it had before he knew. "Aes Sedai work." *But Tam gave it to me. My* father *gave it to me.* He refused to think of how a Two Rivers shepherd had come by a heron-mark blade. There were dangerous currents in such thoughts, deeps he did not want to explore.

"Do you really want to get away, sheepherder? I'll ask again. Why are you not gone, then? The sword? In five years I could make you worthy of it, make you a blademaster. You have quick wrists, good balance, and you don't make the same mistake twice. But I do not have five years to give over to teaching you, and you do not have five years for learning. You have not even one year, and you know it. As it is, you will not stab yourself in the foot. You hold yourself as if the sword belongs at your waist, sheepherder, and most village bullies will sense it. But you've had that much almost since the day you put it on. So why are you still here?"

"Mat and Perrin are still here," Rand mumbled. "I don't want to leave before they do. I won't ever—I might not see them again for—for years, maybe." His head dropped back against the wall. "Blood and ashes! At least they just think I'm crazy not to go home with them. Half the time Nynaeve looks at me like I'm six years old and I've skinned my knee, and she's going to make it better; the other half she looks like she's seeing a stranger. One she might offend if she looks too closely, at that. She's a Wisdom, and besides that, I don't think she's ever been afraid of anything, but she. . . ." He shook his head. "And Egwene. Burn me! She knows why I have to go, but every time I mention it she looks at me, and I knot up inside and. . . ." He closed his eyes, pressing the sword hilt against his forehead as if he could press what he was thinking out of existence. "I wish. . . . I wish. . . ."

"You wish everything could be the way it was, sheepherder? Or you wish the girl would go with you instead of to Tar Valon? You think she'll give up becoming an Aes Sedai for a life of wandering? With you? If you put it to her in the right way, she might. Love is an odd thing." Lan sounded suddenly weary. "As odd a thing as there is."

"No." It was what he had been wishing, that she would want to go with him. He opened his eyes and squared his back and made his voice firm. "No, I wouldn't let her come with me if she did ask." He could not do that to her. *But Light, wouldn't it be sweet, just for a minute, if she said she wanted to?* "She gets muley stubborn if she thinks I'm trying to tell her what to do, but I can still protect her from that." He wished she were back home in Emond's Field, but all hope of that had gone the day Moiraine came to the Two Rivers. "Even if it means she does become an Aes Sedai!" The corner of his eye caught Lan's raised eyebrow, and he flushed.

"And that is all the reason? You want to spend as much time as you can with your friends from home before they go? That's why you're dragging your feet? You know what's sniffing at your heels."

Rand surged angrily to his feet. "All right, it's Moiraine! I wouldn't even be here if not for her, and she won't as much as talk to me."

"You'd be dead if not for her, sheepherder," Lan said flatly, but Rand rushed on.

"She tells me . . . tells me horrible things about myself"—his knuckles whitened on the sword. *That I'm going to go mad and die!*—"and then suddenly she won't even say two words to me. She acts as if I'm no different than the day she found me, and that smells wrong, too."

"You want her to treat yon like what you are?"

"No! I don't mean that. Burn me, I don't know what I mean half the time. I don't want that, and I'm scared of the other. Now she's gone off somewhere, vanished . . ."

"I told you she needs to be alone sometimes. It isn't for you, or anyone else, to question her actions."

". . . without telling anybody where she was going, or when she'd be back, or even if she would be back. She has to be able to tell me something to help me, Lan. Something. She has to. If she ever comes back."

"She's back, sheepherder. Last night. But I think she has told you all she can. Be satisfied. You've learned what you can from her." With a shake of his head, Lan's voice became brisk. "You certainly aren't learning anything standing there. Time for a little balance work. Go through Parting the Silk, beginning from Heron Wading in the Rushes. Remember that that Heron form is only for practicing balance. Anywhere but doing forms, it leaves you wide open; you can strike home from it, if you wait for the other man to move first, but you'll never avoid his blade."

"She *has* to be able to tell me something, Lan. That wind. It wasn't natural, and I don't care how close to the Blight we are."

"Heron Wading in the Rushes, sheepherder. And mind your wrists."

From the south came a faint peal of trumpets, a rolling fanfare slowly growing louder, accompanied by the steady *thrum-thrum-THRUM-thrum* of drums. For a moment Rand and Lan stared at each other, then the drums drew them to the tower wall to stare southward.

The city stood on high hills, the land around the city walls cleared to ankle height for a full mile in all directions, and the keep covered the highest hill of all. From the tower top, Rand had a clear view across the chimneys and roofs to the forest. The drummers appeared first from the trees, a dozen of them, drums

lifting as they stepped to their own beat, mallets whirling. Next
came trumpeters, long, shining horns raised, still calling the flour-
ish. At that distance Rand could not make out the huge, square
banner whipping in the wind behind them. Lan grunted, though;
the Warder had eyes like a snow eagle.

Rand glanced at him, but the Warder said nothing, his eyes
intent on the column emerging from the forest. Mounted men in
armor rode out of the trees, and women ahorseback, too. Then a
palanquin borne by horses, one before and one behind, its curtains
down, and more men on horseback. Ranks of men afoot, pikes rising above them like a bristle of long thorns, and archers with their
bows held slanted across their chests, all stepping to the drums.
The trumpets cried again. Like a singing serpent the column
wound its way toward Fal Dara.

The wind flapped the banner, taller than a man, straight out to
one side. As big as it was, it was close enough now for Rand to see
clearly. A swirl of colors that meant nothing to him, but at the
heart of it, a shape like a pure white teardrop. His breath froze in
his throat. The Flame of Tar Valon.

"Ingtar's with them." Lan sounded as if his thoughts were elsewhere. "Back from his hunting at last. Been gone long enough. I
wonder if he had any luck?"

"Aes Sedai," Rand whispered when he finally could. All those
women out there. . . . Moiraine was Aes Sedai, yes, but he had
traveled with her, and if he did not entirely trust her, at least he
knew her. Or thought he did. But she was only one. So many Aes
Sedai together, and coming like this, was something else again.
He cleared his throat; when he spoke, his voice grated. "Why so
many, Lan? Why any at all? And with drums and trumpets and a
banner to announce them."

Aes Sedai were respected in Shienar, at least by most people,
and the rest respectfully feared them, but Rand had been in places
where it was different, where there was only the fear, and often hate.

Where he had grown up, some men, as least, spoke of "Tar Valon witches" as they would speak of the Dark One. He tried to count the women, but they kept no ranks or order, moving their horses around to converse with one another or with whoever was in the palanquin. Goose bumps covered him. He had traveled with Moiraine, and met another Aes Sedai, and he had begun to think of himself as worldly. Nobody ever left the Two Rivers, or almost nobody, but he had. He had seen things no one back in the Two Rivers had ever laid eyes on, done things they had only dreamed of, if they had dreamed so far. He had seen a queen and met the Daughter-Heir of Andor, faced a Myrddraal and traveled the Ways, and none of it had prepared him for this moment.

"Why so many?" he whispered again.

"The Amyrlin Seat's come in person." Lan looked at him, his expression as hard and unreadable as a rock. "Your lessons are done, sheepherder." He paused then, and Rand almost thought there was sympathy on his face. That could not be, of course. "Better for you if you were a week gone." With that the Warder snatched up his shirt and disappeared down the ladder into the tower.

Rand worked his mouth, trying to get a little moisture. He stared at the column approaching Fal Dara as if it really were a snake, a deadly viper. The drums and trumpets sang, loud in his ears. The Amyrlin Seat, who ordered the Aes Sedai. *She's come because of me.* He could think of no other reason.

They knew things, had knowledge that could help him, he was sure. And he did not dare ask any of them. He was afraid they had come to gentle him. *And afraid they haven't, too,* he admitted reluctantly. *Light, I don't know which scares me more.*

"I didn't mean to channel the Power," he whispered. "It was an accident! Light, I don't want anything to do with it. I swear I'll never touch it again! I swear it!"

With a start, he realized that the Aes Sedai party was entering the city gates. The wind swirled up fiercely, chilling his sweat like droplets of ice, making the trumpets sound like sly laughter; he thought he could smell an opened grave, strong in the air. *My grave, if I keep standing here.*

Grabbing his shirt, he scrambled down the ladder and began to run.

CHAPTER 2

The Welcome

THE HALLS OF FAL DARA KEEP, THEIR smooth stone walls sparsely decorated with elegantly simple tapestries and painted screens, bustled with news of the Amyrlin Seat's imminent arrival. Servants in black-and-gold darted about their tasks, running to prepare rooms or carry orders to the kitchens, moaning that they could not have everything ready for so great a personage when they had had no warning. Dark-eyed warriors, their heads shaven except for a top-knot bound with a leather cord, did not run, but haste filled their steps and their faces shone with an excitement normally reserved for battle. Some of the men spoke as Rand hurried past.

"Ah, there you are, Rand al'Thor. Peace favor your sword. On your way to clean up? You'll want to look your best when you are presented to the Amyrlin Seat. She'll want to see you and your two friends as well as the women, you can count on it."

He trotted toward the broad stairs, wide enough for twenty men abreast, that led up to the men's apartments.

"The Amyrlin herself, come with no more warning than a pack peddler. Must be because of Moiraine Sedai and you southerners, eh? What else?"

The wide, iron-bound doors of the men's apartments stood open, and half jammed with top-knotted men buzzing with the Amyrlin's arrival.

"Ho, southlander! The Amyrlin's here. Come for you and your friends, I suppose. Peace, what honor for you! She seldom leaves Tar Valon, and she's never come to the Borderlands in my memory."

He fended them all off with a few words. He had to wash. Find a clean shirt. No time to talk. They thought they understood, and let him go. Not a one of them knew a thing except that he and his friends traveled in company with an Aes Sedai, that two of his friends were women who were going to Tar Valon to train as Aes Sedai, but their words stabbed at him as if they knew everything. *She's come for me.*

He dashed through the men's apartments, darted into the room he shared with Mat and Perrin . . . and froze, his jaw dropping in astonishment. The room was filled with women wearing the black-and-gold, all working purposefully. It was not a big room, and its windows, a pair of tall, narrow arrowslits looking down on one of the inner courtyards, did nothing to make it seem larger. Three beds on black-and-white tiled platforms, each with a chest at the foot, three plain chairs, a washstand by the door, and a tall, wide wardrobe crowded the room. The eight women in there seemed like fish in a basket.

The women barely glanced at him, and went right on clearing his clothes—and Mat's and Perrin's—out of the wardrobe and replacing them with new. Anything found in the pockets was put atop the chests, and the old clothes were bundled up carelessly, like rags.

"What are you doing?" he demanded when he caught his breath. "Those are my clothes!" One of the women sniffed and poked a finger through a tear in the sleeve of his only coat, then added it to the pile on the floor.

Another, a black-haired woman with a big ring of keys at her waist, set her eyes on him. That was Elansu, *shatayan* of the keep. He thought of the sharp-faced woman as a housekeeper, though the house she kept was a fortress and scores of servants did her bidding. "Moiraine Sedai said all of your clothes are worn out, and the Lady Amalisa had new made to give you. Just keep out of our way," she added firmly, "and we will be done the quicker." There were few men the *shatayan* could not bully into doing as she wished—some said even Lord Agelmar—and she plainly did not expect any trouble with one man young enough to be her son.

He swallowed what he had been going to say; there was no time for arguing. The Amyrlin Seat could be sending for him at any minute. "Honor to the Lady Amalisa for her gift," he managed, after the Shienaran way, "and honor to you, Elansu Shatayan. Please, convey my words to the Lady Amalisa, and tell her I said, heart and soul to serve." That ought to satisfy the Shienaran love of ceremony for both women. "But now if you'll pardon me, I want to change."

"That is well," Elansu said comfortably. "Moiraine Sedai said to remove all the old. Every stitch. Smallclothes, too." Several of the women eyed him sideways. None of them made a move toward the door.

He bit his cheek to keep from laughing hysterically. Many ways were different in Shienar from what he was used to, and there were some to which he would never become accustomed if he lived forever. He had taken to bathing in the small hours of the morning, when the big, tiled pools were empty of people, after he discovered that at any other time a woman might well climb into the water with him. It could be a scullion or the Lady Amalisa,

Lord Agelmar's sister herself—the baths were one place in Shienar where there was no rank—expecting him to scrub her back in return for the same favor, asking him why his face was so red, had he taken too much sun? They had soon learned to recognize his blushes for what they were, and not a woman in the keep but seemed fascinated by them.

I might be dead or worse in another hour, and they're waiting to see me blush! He cleared his throat. "If you'll wait outside, I will pass the rest out to you. On my honor."

One of the women gave a soft chortle, and even Elansu's lips twitched, but the *shatayan* nodded and directed the other women to gather up the bundles they had made. She was the last to leave, and she paused in the doorway to add, "The boots, too. Moiraine Sedai said everything."

He opened his mouth, then closed it again. His boots, at least, were certainly still good, made by Alwyn al'Van, the cobbler back in Emond's Field, and well broken in and comfortable. But if giving up his boots would make the *shatayan* leave him alone so he could go, he would give her the boots, and anything else she wanted. He had no time. "Yes. Yes, of course. On my honor." He pushed on the door, forcing her out.

Alone, he dropped onto his bed to tug off his boots—they *were* still good, a little worn, the leather cracked here and there, but still wearable and well broken-in to fit his feet—then hastily stripped off, piling everything atop the boots, and washed at the basin just as quickly. The water was cold; the water was always cold in the men's apartments.

The wardrobe had three wide doors carved in the simple Shienaran manner, suggesting more than showing a series of waterfalls and rocky pools. Pulling open the center door, he stared for a moment at what had replaced the few garments he had brought with him. A dozen high-collared coats of the finest wool and as well cut as any he had ever seen on a merchant's back or

a lord's, most embroidered like feastday clothes. A dozen! Three
shirts for every coat, both linen and silk, with wide sleeves and
tight cuffs. Two cloaks. Two, when he had made do with one at
a time all his life. One cloak was plain, stout wool and dark green,
the other deep blue with a stiff-standing collar embroidered in
gold with herons . . . and high on the left breast, where a lord
would wear his sign. . . .

His hand drifted to the cloak of its own accord. As if uncertain
what they would feel, his fingers brushed the stitching of a serpent
curled almost into a circle, but a serpent with four legs and a
lion's golden mane, scaled in crimson and gold, its feet each
tipped with five golden claws. His hand jerked back as if burned.
*Light help me! Was it Amalisa had this made, or Moiraine? How
many saw it? How many know what it is, what it means? Even one
is too many. Burn me, she's trying to get me killed. Bloody
Moiraine won't even talk to me, but now she's given me bloody
fine new clothes to die in!*

A rap at the door sent him leaping half out of his skin.

"Are you done?" came Elansu's voice. "Every stitch, now. Perhaps I had better. . . ." A creak as if she were trying the knob.

With a start Rand realized he was still naked. "I'm done," he
shouted. "Peace! Don't come in!" Hurriedly he gathered up what
he had been wearing, boots and all. "I'll bring them!" Hiding
behind the door, he opened it just wide enough to shove the bundle into the arms of the *shatayan*. "That's everything."

She tried to peer through the gap. "Are you sure? Moiraine
Sedai said everything. Perhaps I had better just look—"

"It's everything," he growled. "On my honor!" He shouldered
the door shut in her face, and heard laughter from the other side.

Muttering under his breath, he dressed hurriedly. He would not
put it past any of them to find some excuse to come bulling in anyway. The gray breeches were snugger than he was used to, but still
comfortable, and the shirt, with its billowy sleeves, was white

enough to satisfy any goodwife in Emond's Field on laundry day. The knee-high boots fit as if he had worn them a year. He hoped it was just a good cobbler, and not more Aes Sedai work.

All of these clothes would make a pack as big as he was. Yet, he had grown used to the comfort of clean shirts again, of not wearing the same breeches day after day until sweat and dirt made them as stiff as his boots, then wearing them still. He took his saddlebags from his chest and stuffed what he could into them, then reluctantly spread the fancy cloak out on the bed and piled a few more shirts and breeches on that. Folded with the dangerous sigil inside and tied with a cord looped so it could be slung on a shoulder, it looked not much different from the packs he had seen carried by other young men on the road.

A peal of trumpets rolled through the arrowslits, trumpets calling the fanfare from outside the walls, trumpets answering from the keep towers.

"I'll pick out the stitching when I get a chance," he muttered. He had seen women picking out embroidery when they had made a mistake or changed their mind on the pattern, and it did not look very hard.

The rest of the clothes—most of them, in fact—he stuffed back into the wardrobe. No need to leave evidence of flight to be found by the first person to poke a head in after he went.

Still frowning, he knelt beside his bed. The tiled platforms on which the beds rested were stoves, where a small fire damped down to burn all night could keep the bed warm through the worst night in a Shienaran winter. The nights were still cooler than he was used to this time of year, but blankets were enough for warmth now. Pulling open the firebox door, he took out a bundle he could not leave behind. He was glad Elansu had not thought anyone would keep clothes in there.

Setting the bundle atop the blankets, he untied one end and partially unfolded it. A gleeman's cloak, turned inside out to hide the hundreds of patches that covered it, patches in every size and color imaginable. The cloak itself was sound enough; the patches were a gleeman's badge. Had been a gleeman's badge.

Inside nestled two hard leather cases. The larger held a harp, which he never touched. *The harp was never meant for a farmer's clumsy fingers, boy.* The other, long and slim, contained the gold-and-silver chased flute he had used to earn his supper and bed more than once since leaving home. Thom Merrilin had taught him to play that flute, before the gleeman died. Rand could never touch it without remembering Thom, with his sharp blue eyes and his long white mustaches, shoving the bundled cloak into his hands and shouting for him to run. And then Thom had run himself, knives appearing magically in his hands as if he were performing, to face the Myrddraal that was coming to kill them.

With a shiver, he redid the bundle. "That's all over with." Thinking of the wind on the tower top, he added, "Strange things happen this close to the Blight." He was not sure he believed it, not the way Lan had apparently meant it. In any case, even without the Amyrlin Seat, it was past time for him to be gone from Fal Dara.

Shrugging into the coat he had kept out—it was a deep, dark green, and made him think of the forests at home, Tam's Westwood farm where he had grown up, and the Waterwood where he had learned to swim—he buckled the heron-mark sword to his waist and hung his quiver, bristling with arrows, on the other side. His unstrung bow stood propped in the corner with Mat's and Perrin's, the stave two hands taller than he was. He had made it himself since coming to Fal Dara, and besides him, only Lan and Perrin could draw it. Stuffing his blanketroll and his new cloak through the loops on his bundles, he slung the pair from his left shoulder, tossed his saddlebags atop the cords, and grabbed the bow. *Leave the sword-arm free,* he thought. *Make them think I'm dangerous. Maybe* somebody *will.*

Cracking the door revealed the hall all but empty; one liveried servant dashed by, but he never so much as glanced at Rand. As soon as the man's rapid footfalls faded, Rand slipped out into the corridor.

He tried to walk naturally, casually, but with saddlebags on his shoulder and bundles on his back, he knew he looked like what he was, a man setting out on a journey and not meaning to come back. The trumpets called again, sounding fainter here inside the keep.

He had a horse, a tall bay stallion, in the north stable, called the Lord's Stable, close by the salley gate that Lord Agelmar used when he went riding. Neither the Lord of Fal Dara nor any of his family would be riding today, though, and the stable might be empty except for the stableboys. There were two ways to reach the Lord's Stable from Rand's room. One would take him all the way around the keep, behind Lord Agelmar's private garden, then down the far side and through the farrier's smithy, likewise certainly empty now, to the stableyard. Time enough that way for orders to be given, for a search to start, before he reached his horse. The other was far shorter; first across the outer courtyard, where even now the Amyrlin Seat was arriving with another dozen or more Aes Sedai.

His skin prickled at the thought; he had had more than enough of Aes Sedai for any sane lifetime. One was too many. All the stories said it, and he knew it for fact. But he was not surprised when his feet took him toward the outer courtyard. He would never see legendary Tar Valon—he could not afford that risk, now or ever—but he might catch a glimpse of the Amyrlin Seat before he left. That would be as much as seeing a queen. *There can't be anything dangerous in just looking, from a distance. I'll keep moving and be gone before she ever knows I was there.*

He opened a heavy, iron-strapped door onto the outer courtyard and stepped out into silence. People forested the guardwalk atop every wall, top-knotted soldiers, and liveried servants, and menials still in their muck, all pressed together cheek by jowl, with children sitting on shoulders to look over their elders' heads or squeezing in to peer around waists and knees. Every archers' balcony was packed like a barrel of apples, and faces even showed in the narrow arrowslits in the walls. A thick mass of people bordered the courtyard like another wall. And all of them watched and waited in silence.

He pushed his way along the wall, in front of the smithies and fletchers' stalls that lined the court—Fal Dara was a fortress, not a palace, despite its size and grim grandeur, and everything about it served that end—apologizing quietly to the people he jostled. Some looked around with a frown, and a few gave a second stare to his saddlebags and bundles, but none broke the silence. Most did not even bother to look at who had bumped past them.

He could easily see over the heads of most of them, enough to make out clearly what was going on in the courtyard. Just inside the main gate, a line of men stood beside their horses, fifteen of them. No two wore the same kind of armor or carried the same sort of sword, and none looked like Lan, but Rand did not doubt they were Warders. Round faces, square faces, long faces, narrow faces, they all had the look, as if they saw things other men did not see, heard things other men did not hear. Standing at their ease, they looked as deadly as a pack of wolves. Only one other thing about them was alike. One and all they wore the color-shifting cloak he had first seen on Lan, the cloak that often seemed to fade into whatever was behind it. It did not make for easy watching or a still stomach, so many men in those cloaks.

A dozen paces in front of the Warders, a row of women stood by their horses' heads, the cowls of their cloaks thrown back. He could count them, now. Fourteen. Fourteen Aes Sedai. They must be. Tall and short, slender and plump, dark and fair, hair cut short or long, hanging loose down their backs or braided, their clothes were as different as the Warders' were, in as many cuts and colors as there were women. Yet they, too, had a sameness, one that was only obvious when they stood together like this. To a woman, they seemed ageless. From this distance he would have called them all young, but closer he knew they would be like Moiraine. Young-seeming yet not, smooth-skinned but with faces too mature for youth, eyes too knowing.

Closer? Fool! I'm too close already! Burn me, I should have gone the long way. He pressed on toward his goal, another iron-bound door at the far end of the court, but he could not stop looking.

Calmly the Aes Sedai ignored the onlookers and kept their attention on the curtained palanquin, now in the center of the courtyard. The horses bearing it held as still as if ostlers stood at their harness, but there was only one tall woman beside the palan-quin, her face an Aes Sedai's face, and she paid no mind to the horses. The staff she held upright before her with both hands was as tall as she, the gilded flame capping it standing above her eyes.

Lord Agelmar faced the palanquin from the far end of the court, bluff and square and face unreadable. His high-collared coat of dark blue bore the three running red foxes of the House Jagad as well as the stooping black hawk of Shienar. Beside him stood Ronan, age-withered but still tall; three foxes carved from red avatine topped the tall staff the *shambayan* bore. Ronan was Elansu's equal in ordering the keep, *shambayan* and *shatayan,* but Elansu left little for him except ceremonies and acting as Lord Agelmar's secretary. Both men's topknots were snow-white.

All of them—the Warders, the Aes Sedai, the Lord of Fal Dara, and his *shambayan*—stood as still as stone. The watching crowd seemed to hold its breath. Despite himself, Rand slowed.

Suddenly Ronan rapped his staff loudly three times on the broad paving stones, calling into the silence, "Who comes here? Who comes here? Who comes here?"

The woman beside the palanquin tapped her staff three times in reply. "The Watcher of the Seals. The Flame of Tar Valon. The Amyrlin Seat."

"Why should we watch?" Ronan demanded.

"For the hope of humankind," the tall woman replied.

"Against what do we guard?"

"The shadow at noon."

"How long shall we guard?"

"From rising sun to rising sun, so long as the Wheel of Time turns."

Agelmar bowed, his white topknot stirring in the breeze. "Fal Dara offers bread and salt and welcome. Well come is the Amyrlin Seat to Fal Dara, for here is the watch kept, here is the Pact maintained. Welcome."

The tall woman drew back the curtain of the palanquin, and the Amyrlin Seat stepped out. Dark-haired, ageless as all Aes Sedai were ageless, she ran her eyes over the assembled watchers as she straightened. Rand flinched when her gaze crossed him; he felt as if he had been touched. But her eyes passed on and came to rest on Lord Agelmar. A liveried servant knelt at her side with folded towels, steam still rising, on a silver tray. Formally, she wiped her hands and patted her face with a damp cloth. "I offer thanks for your welcome, my son. May the Light illumine House Jagad. May the Light illumine Fal Dara and all her people."

Agelmar bowed again. "You honor us, Mother." It did not sound odd, her calling him son or him calling her Mother, though comparing her smooth cheeks to his craggy face made him seem more like her father, or even grandfather. She had a presence that more than matched his. "House Jagad is yours. Fal Dara is yours."

Cheers rose on every side, crashing against the walls of the keep like breaking waves.

Shivering, Rand hurried toward the door to safety, careless of whom he bumped into now. *Just your bloody imagination. She doesn't even know who you are. Not yet. Blood and ashes, if she did.* . . . He did not want to think of what would have happened if she knew who he was, what he was. What would happen when she finally found out. He wondered if she had had anything to do with the wind atop the tower; Aes Sedai could do things like that. When he pushed through that door and slammed it shut behind him, muting the roar of welcome that still shook the courtyard, he heaved a relieved sigh.

The halls here were as empty as the others had been, and he all but ran. Out across a smaller courtyard, with a fountain splashing in the center, down yet another corridor and out into the flag-stoned stableyard. The Lord's Stable itself, built into the wall of the keep, stood tall and long, with big windows here inside the walls, and horses kept on two floors. The smithy across the court-yard stood silent, the farrier and his helpers gone to see the Welcome.

Tema, the leathery-faced head groom, met him at the wide doors with a deep bow, touching his forehead and then his heart. "Spirit and heart to serve, my Lord. How may Tema serve, my Lord?" No warrior's topknot here; Tema's hair sat on his head like an inverted gray bowl.

Rand sighed. "For the hundredth time, Tema, I am not a lord."

"As my Lord wishes." The groom's bow was even lower this time.

It was his name that caused the problem, and a similarity. Rand al'Thor. Al'Lan Mandragoran. For Lan, according to the custom of Malkier, the royal "al" named him King, though he never used it himself. For Rand, "al" was just a part of his name, though he had heard that once, long ago, before the Two Rivers was called the Two Rivers, it had meant "son of." Some of the servants in Fal Dara keep, though, had taken it to mean he was a king, too, or at least a prince. All of his argument to the contrary had only managed to demote him to lord. At least, he thought it had; he had never seen quite so much bowing and scraping, even with Lord Agelmar.

"I need Red saddled, Tema." He knew better than to offer to do it himself; Tema would not let Rand soil his hands. "I thought I'd spend a few days seeing the country around the town." Once he was on the big bay stallion's back, a few days would see him at the River Erinin, or across the border into Arafel. *They'll never find me then.*

The groom bent himself almost double, and stayed bent. "Forgive, my Lord," he whispered hoarsely. "Forgive, but Tema cannot obey."

Flushing with embarrassment, Rand took an anxious look around—there was no one else in sight—then grabbed the man's shoulder and pulled him upright. He might not be able to stop Tema and a few others from acting like this, but he could try to stop anyone else from seeing it. "Why not, Tema? Tema, look at me, please. Why not?"

"It is commanded, my Lord," Tema said, still whispering. He kept dropping his eyes, not afraid, but ashamed that he could not do what Rand asked. Shienarans took shame the way other people took being branded a thief. "No horse may leave this stable until the order is changed. Nor any stable in the keep, my Lord."

Rand had his mouth open to tell the man it was all right, but instead he licked his lips. "No horse from any stable?"

"Yes, my Lord. The order came down only a short time ago. Only moments." Tema's voice picked up strength. "All the gates are closed as well, my Lord. None may enter or leave without permission. Not even the city patrol, so Tema has been told."

Rand swallowed hard, but it did not lessen the feeling of fingers clutching his windpipe. "The order, Tema. It came from Lord Agelmar?"

"Of course, my Lord. Who else? Lord Agelmar did not speak the command to Tema, of course, nor even to the man who did speak to Tema, but, my Lord, who else could give such a command in Fal Dara?"

Who else? Rand jumped as the biggest bell in the keep bell tower let out a sonorous peal. The other bells joined in, then bells from the town.

"If Tema may be bold," the groom called above the reverberations, "my Lord must be very happy."

Rand had to shout back to be heard. "Happy? Why?"

"The Welcome is finished, my Lord." Tema's gesture took in the bell tower. "The Amyrlin Seat will be sending for my Lord, and my Lord's friends, to come to her, now."

Rand broke into a run. He just had time to see the surprise on Tema's face, and then he was gone. He did not care what Tema thought. *She will be sending for me now.*

CHAPTER 3

Friends and Enemies

R AND DID NOT RUN FAR, ONLY AS FAR AS THE sally gate around the corner from the stable. He slowed to a walk before he got there, trying to appear casual and unhurried.

The arched gate was closed tight. It was barely big enough for two men to ride through abreast, but like all the gates in the outer wall, it was covered with broad strips of black iron, and locked shut with a thick bar. Two guards stood before the gate in plain conical helmets and plate-and-mail armor, with long swords on their backs. Their golden surcoats bore the Black Hawk on the chest. He knew one of them slightly, Ragan. The scar from a Trolloc arrow made a white triangle against Ragan's dark cheek behind the bars of his face-guard. The puckered skin dimpled with a grin when he saw Rand.

"Peace favor you, Rand al'Thor." Ragan almost shouted to be

heard over the bells. "Do you intend to go hit rabbits over the head, or do you still insist that club is a bow?" The other guard shifted to stand more in front of the gate.

"Peace favor you, Ragan," Rand said, stopping in front of them. It was an effort to keep his voice calm. "You know it's a bow. You've seen me shoot it."

"No good from a horse," the other guard said sourly. Rand recognized him, now, with his deep-set, almost-black eyes that never seemed to blink. They peered from his helmet like twin caves inside another cave. He supposed there could be worse luck for him than Masema guarding the gate, but he was not sure how, short of a Red Aes Sedai. "It's too long," Masema added. "I can shoot three arrows with a horsebow while you loose one with that monster."

Rand forced a grin, as if he thought it was a joke. Masema had never made a joke in his hearing, nor laughed at one. Most of the men at Fal Dara accepted Rand; he trained with Lan, and Lord Agelmar had him at table, and most important of all, he had arrived at Fal Dara in company with Moiraine, an Aes Sedai. Some seemed unable to forget his being an outlander, though, barely saying two words to him, and then only if they had to. Masema was the worst of those.

"It's good enough for me," Rand said. "Speaking of rabbits, Ragan, how about letting me out? All this noise and bustle is too much for me. Better to be out hunting rabbits, even if I never see one."

Ragan half turned to look at his companion, and Rand's hopes began to lift. Ragan was an easygoing man, his manner belying his grim scar, and he seemed to like Rand. But Masema was already shaking his head. Ragan sighed. "It cannot be, Rand al'Thor." He gave a tiny nod toward Masema as if to explain. If it were up to him alone. . . . "No one is to leave without a written pass. Too bad you did not ask a few minutes ago. The command just came down to bar the gates."

"But why would Lord Agelmar want to keep *me* in?" Masema was eyeing the bundles on Rand's back, and his saddlebags. Rand tried to ignore him. "I'm his guest," he went on to Ragan. "By my honor, I could have left anytime these past weeks. Why would he mean this order for me? It is Lord Agelmar's order, isn't it?" Masema blinked at that, and his perpetual frown deepened; he almost appeared to forget Rand's packs.

Ragan laughed. "Who else could give such an order, Rand al'Thor? Of course, it was Uno who passed it to me, but whose order could it have been?"

Masema's eyes, fixed on Rand's face, did not blink. "I just want to go out by myself, that's all," Rand said. "I'll try one of the gardens, then. No rabbits, but at least there won't be a crowd. The Light illumine you, and peace favor you."

He walked away without waiting for an answering blessing, resolving not to go near any of the gardens on any account. *Burn me, once the ceremonies are done there could be Aes Sedai in any of them.* Aware of Masema's eyes on his back—he was sure it was Masema—he kept his pace normal.

Suddenly the bells stopped ringing, and he skipped a step. Minutes were passing. A great many of them. Time for the Amyrlin Seat to be shown to her chambers. Time for her to send for him, to start a search when he was not found. As soon as he was out of sight of the sally gate, he began to run again.

Near the barracks' kitchens, the Carters' Gate, where all the foodstuffs for the keep were brought in, stood closed and barred, behind a pair of soldiers. He hurried past, across the kitchen yard, as if he had never meant to stop.

The Dog Gate, at the back of the keep, just high enough and wide enough for one man on foot, had its guards, too. He turned around before they saw him. There were not many gates, even as big as the keep was, but if the Dog Gate was guarded, they all would be.

Perhaps he could find a length of rope. . . . He climbed one of the stairs to the top of the outer wall, to the wide parapet with its crenellated walls. It was not comfortable for him, being so high and exposed if that wind came again, but from there he could see across the tall chimneys and sharp roofs of the town all the way to the city wall. Even after nearly a month, the houses still looked odd to his Two Rivers eyes, eaves reaching almost to the ground as if the houses were all wood-shingled roof, and chimneys angled to let heavy snow slide past. A broad, paved square surrounded the keep, but only a hundred paces from the wall lay streets full of people going about their daily business, aproned shopkeepers out under the awnings in front of their shops, rough-clothed farmers in town to buy and sell, hawkers and tradesmen and townspeople gathered in knots, no doubt to talk about the surprise visit from the Amyrlin Seat. He could see carts and people flowing through one of the gates in the town wall. Apparently the guards there had no orders about stopping anyone.

He looked up at the nearest guardtower; one of the soldiers raised a gauntleted hand to him. With a bitter laugh, he waved back. Not a foot of the wall but was under the eyes of guards. Leaning through an embrasure, he peered down past the slots in the stone for setting hoardings, down the sheer expanse of stone to the drymoat far below. Twenty paces wide and ten deep, faced with stone polished slippery smooth. A low wall, slanted to give no hiding place, surrounded it to keep anyone from falling in by accident, and its bottom was a forest of razor-sharp spikes. Even with a rope to climb down and no guards watching, he could not cross that. What served to keep Trollocs out in the last extreme served just as well to keep him in.

Suddenly he felt weary to the bone, drained. The Amyrlin Seat was there, and there was no way out. No way out, and the Amyrlin Seat there. If she knew he was there, if she had sent the wind that had seized him, then she was already hunting him, hunting with an Aes Sedai's powers. Rabbits had more chance against his bow. He refused to give up, though. There were those who said Two Rivers folk could teach stones and give lessons to mules. When there was nothing else left, Two Rivers people hung on to their stubbornness.

Leaving the wall, he wandered through the keep. He paid no mind to where he went, so long as it was nowhere he would be expected. Not anywhere near his room, nor any of the stables, nor any gate—Masema might risk Uno's tongue to report him trying to leave—nor garden. All he could think of was keeping away from *any* Aes Sedai. Even Moiraine. She *knew* about him. Despite that, she had done nothing against him. *So far. So far as you know. What if she's changed her mind? Maybe she sent for the Amyrlin Seat.*

For a moment, feeling lost, he leaned against the corridor wall, the stone hard under his shoulder. Eyes blank, he stared at a distant nothing and saw things he did not want to see. *Gentled. Would it be so bad, to have it all over? Really over?* He closed his eyes, but he could still see himself, huddling like a rabbit with nowhere left to run, and Aes Sedai closing round him like ravens. *They almost always die soon after, men who've been gentled. They stop wanting to live.* He remembered Thom Merrilin's words too well to face that. With a brisk shake, he hurried on down the hall. No need to stay in one place until he was found. *How long till they find you anyway? You're like a sheep in a pen. How long?* He touched the sword hilt at his side. *No, not a sheep. Not for Aes Sedai or anybody else.* He felt a little foolish, but determined.

People were returning to their tasks. A din of voices and clattering pots filled the kitchen that lay nearest the Great Hall, where the Amyrlin Seat and her party would feast that night. Cooks and scullions and potboys all but ran at their work; the spit dogs trotted in their wicker wheels to turn the spitted meats. He made his way quickly through the heat and steam, through the smells of spices and cooking. No one spared him a second glance; they were all too busy.

The back halls, where the servants lived in small apartments, were stirring like a kicked antheap as men and women scurried to don their best livery. Children did their playing in corners, out of the way. Boys waved wooden swords, and girls played with carved dolls, some announcing that *hers* was the Amyrlin Seat. Most of the doors stood open, doorways blocked only by beaded curtains. Normally, that meant whoever lived there was open to visitors, but today it simply meant the residents were in a hurry. Even those who bowed to him did so with hardly a pause.

Would any of them hear, when they went to serve, that he was being sought, and speak of seeing him? Speak to an Aes Sedai and tell her where to find him? The eyes that he passed suddenly appeared to be studying him slyly, and to be weighing and considering behind his back. Even the children took on sharper looks in his mind's eye. He knew it was just his imagination—he was sure it was; it had to be—but when the servants' apartments were behind him, he felt as if he had escaped before a trap could spring shut.

Some places in the keep were empty of people, the folk who normally worked there released for the sudden holiday. The armorer's forge, with all the fires banked, the anvils silent. Silent. Cold. Lifeless. Yet somehow not empty. His skin prickled, and he spun on his heel. No one there. Just the big square tool chests and the quenching barrels full of oil. The hair on the back of his neck stirred, and he whipped round again. The hammers and tongs hung in their places on the wall. Angrily he stared around the big room. *There's nobody there. It's just my imagination. That wind, and the Amyrlin; that's enough to make me imagine things.*

Outside in the armorer's yard, the wind swirled up around him momentarily. Despite himself he jumped, thinking it meant to catch him. For a moment he smelled the faint odor of decay again, and heard someone behind him laughing slyly. Just for a moment. Frightened, he edged in a circle, peering warily. The yard, paved with rough stone, was empty except for him. *Just your bloody imagination!* He ran anyway, and behind him he thought he heard the laughter again, this time without the wind.

In the woodyard, the presence returned, the sense of someone there. The feel of eyes peering at him around tall piles of split firewood under the long sheds, darting glances over the stacks of seasoned planks and timbers waiting on the other side of the yard for the carpenter's shop, now closed up tight. He refused to look around, refused to think of how one set of eyes could move from place to place so fast, could cross the open yard from the firewood shed to the lumbershed without even a flicker of movement that he could see. He was sure it was one set of eyes. *Imagination. Or maybe I'm going crazy already.* He shivered. *Not yet. Light, please not yet.* Stiff-backed, he stalked across the woodyard, and the unseen watcher followed.

Down deep corridors lit only by a few rush torches, in storerooms filled with sacks of dried peas or beans, crowded with slatted racks heaped with wrinkled turnips and beets, or stacked with barrels of wine and casks of salted beef and kegs of ale, the eyes were always there, sometimes following him, sometimes waiting when he entered. He never heard a footstep but his own, never heard a door creak except when he opened and closed it, but the eyes were there. *Light, I* am *going crazy.*

Then he opened another storeroom door, and human voices, human laughter, drifted out to fill him with relief. There would be no unseen eye here. He went in.

Half the room was stacked to the ceiling with sacks of grain. In the other half a thick semicircle of men knelt in front of one of the bare walls. They all seemed to wear the leather jerkins and bowl-cut hair of menials. No warriors' topknots, no livery. No one who might betray him accidentally. *What about on purpose?* The rattle

of dice came through their soft murmurs, and somebody let out a
raucous laugh at the throw.

Loial was watching them dice, rubbing his chin thoughtfully
with a finger thicker than a big man's thumb, his head almost
reaching the rafters nearly two spans up. None of the dicers gave
him a glance. Ogier were not exactly common in the Borderlands,
or anywhere else, but they were known and accepted here, and
Loial had been in Fal Dara long enough to excite little comment.
The Ogier's dark, stiff-collared tunic was buttoned up to his neck
and flared below the waist over his high boots, and one of the big
pockets bulged and sagged with the weight of something. Books,
if Rand knew him. Even watching men gamble, Loial would not
be far from a book.

In spite of everything, Rand found himself grinning. Loial
often had that effect on him. The Ogier knew so much about some
things, so little about others, and he seemed to want to know
everything. Yet Rand could remember the first time he ever saw
Loial, with his tufted ears and his eyebrows that dangled like long
mustaches and his nose almost as wide as his face—saw him and
thought he was facing a Trolloc. It still shamed him. Ogier and
Trollocs. Myrddraal, and things from the dark corners of midnight
tales. Things out of stories and legends. That was how he had
thought of them before he left Emond's Field. But since leaving
home he had seen too many stories walking in the flesh ever to be
so sure again. Aes Sedai, and unseen watchers, and a wind that
caught and held. His smile faded.

"All the stories are real," he said softly.

Loial's ears twitched, and his head turned toward Rand. When
he saw who it was, the Ogier's face split in a grin, and he came
over. "Ah, there you are." His voice was a deep bumblebee rumble. "I did not see you at the Welcome. That was something I had
not seen before. Two things. The Shienaran Welcome, and the
Amyrlin Seat. She looks tired, don't you think? It cannot be easy,

being Amyrlin. Worse than being an Elder, I suppose." He paused, with a thoughtful look, but only for a breath. "Tell me, Rand, do you play at dice, too? They play a simpler game here, with only three dice. We use four in the *stedding*. They won't let me play, you know. They just say, 'Glory to the Builders,' and will not bet against me. I don't think that's fair, do you? The dice they use *are* rather small"—he frowned at one of his hands, big enough to cover a human head—"but I still think—"

Rand grabbed his arm and cut him off. *The Builders!* "Loial, Ogier built Fal Dara, didn't they? Do you know any way out except by the gates? A crawl hole. A drain pipe. Anything at all, if it's big enough for a man to wiggle through. Out of the wind would be good, too."

Loial gave a pained grimace, the ends of his eyebrows almost brushing his cheeks. "Rand, Ogier built Mafal Dadaranell, but that city was destroyed in the Trolloc Wars. This"—he touched the stone wall lightly with broad fingertips—"was built by men. I can sketch a plan of Mafal Dadaranell—I saw the maps, once, in an old book in Stedding Shangtai—but of Fal Dara, I know no more than you. It *is* well built, though, isn't it? Stark, but well made."

Rand slumped against the wall, squeezing his eyes shut. "I need a way out," he whispered. "The gates are barred, and they won't let anyone pass, but I need a way out."

"But why, Rand?" Loial said slowly. "No one here will hurt you. Are you all right? Rand?" Suddenly his voice rose. "Mat! Perrin! I think Rand is sick."

Rand opened his eyes to see his friends straightening up out of the knot of dicers. Mat Cauthon, long-limbed as a stork, wearing a half smile as if he saw something funny that no one else saw. Shaggy-haired Perrin Aybara, with heavy shoulders and thick arms from his work as a blacksmith's apprentice. They both still wore their Two Rivers garb, plain and sturdy, but travel-worn.

Mat tossed the dice back into the semicircle as he stepped out, and one of the men called, "Here, southlander, you can't quit while you're winning."

"Better than when I'm losing," Mat said with a laugh. Unconsciously he touched his coat at the waist, and Rand winced. Mat had a dagger with a ruby in its hilt under there, a dagger he was never without, a dagger he could not be without. It was a tainted blade, from the dead city of Shadar Logoth, tainted and twisted by an evil almost as bad as the Dark One, the evil that had killed Shadar Logoth two thousand years before, yet still lived among the abandoned ruins. That taint would kill Mat if he kept the dagger; it would kill him even faster if he put it aside. "You'll have another chance to win it back." Wry snorts from the kneeling men indicated they did not think there was much chance of that.

Perrin kept his eyes down as he followed Mat across to Rand. Perrin always kept his eyes down these days, and his shoulders sagged as if he carried a weight too heavy even for their width.

"What's the matter, Rand?" Mat asked. "You're as white as your shirt. Hey! Where did you get those clothes? You turning Shienaran? Maybe I'll buy myself a coat like that, and a fine shirt." He shook his coat pocket, producing a clink of coins. "I seem to have luck with the dice. I can hardly touch them without winning."

"You don't have to buy anything," Rand said tiredly. "Moiraine had all our clothes replaced. They're burned already for all I know, all but what you two are wearing. Elansu will probably be around to collect those, too, so I'd change fast if I were you, before she takes them off your back." Perrin still did not look up, but his cheeks turned red; Mat's grin deepened, though it looked forced. They too had had encounters in the baths, and only Mat tried to pretend it did not matter. "And I'm not sick. I just need to get out of here. The Amyrlin Seat is here. Lan said . . . he said with her here, it would have been better for me if I were gone a week. I need to leave, and all the gates are barred."

"He said that?" Mat frowned. "I don't understand. He'd never say *anything* against an Aes Sedai. Why now? Look, Rand, I don't like Aes Sedai any more than you do, but they aren't going to do anything to us." He lowered his voice to say that, and looked over his shoulder to see if any of the gamblers was listening. Feared the Aes Sedai might be, but in the Borderlands, they were far from being hated, and a disrespectful comment about them could land you in a fight, or worse. "Look at Moiraine. She isn't so bad, even if she is Aes Sedai. You're thinking like old Cenn Buie telling his tall tales back home, in the Winespring Inn. I mean, she hasn't hurt us, and they won't. Why would they?"

Perrin's eyes lifted. Yellow eyes, gleaming in the dim light like burnished gold. *Moiraine hasn't hurt us?* Rand thought. Perrin's eyes had been as deep a brown as Mat's when they left the Two Rivers. Rand had no idea how the change had come about—Perrin did not want to talk about it, or about very much of anything since it happened—but it had come at the same time as the slump in his shoulders, and a distance in his manner as if he felt alone even with friends around him. Perrin's eyes and Mat's dagger. Neither would have happened if they had not left Emond's Field, and it was Moiraine who had taken them away. He knew that was not fair. They would probably all be dead at Trollocs' hands, and a good part of Emond's Field as well, if she had not come to their village. But that did not make Perrin laugh the way he used to, or take the dagger from Mat's belt. *And me? If I was home and still alive, would I still be what I am now? At least I wouldn't be worrying about what the Aes Sedai are going to do to me.*

Mat was still looking at him quizzically, and Perrin had raised his head enough to stare from under his eyebrows. Loial waited patiently. Rand could not tell them why he had to stay away from the Amyrlin Seat. They did not know what he was. Lan knew, and Moiraine. And Egwene, and Nynaeve. He wished none of them knew, and most of all he wished Egwene did not, but at least Mat and Perrin—and Loial, too—believed he was still the same. He thought he would rather die than let them know, than see the hesitation and worry he sometimes caught in Egwene's eyes, and Nynaeve's, even when they were trying their best.

"Somebody's . . . watching me," he said finally. "Following me. Only. . . . Only, there's nobody there."

Perrin's head jerked up, and Mat licked his lips and whispered, "A Fade?"

"Of course not," Loial snorted. "How could one of the Eyeless enter Fal Dara, town or keep? By law, no one may hide his face inside the town walls, and the lamplighters are charged with keeping the streets lit at night so there isn't a shadow for a Myrddraal to hide in. It could not happen."

"Walls don't stop a Fade," Mat muttered. "Not when it wants to come in. I don't know as laws and lamps will do any better." He did not sound like someone who had half thought Fades were only gleemen's tales less than half a year before. He had seen too much, too.

"And there was the wind," Rand added. His voice hardly shook as he told what had happened on the tower top. Perrin's fists tightened until his knuckles cracked. "I just want to leave here," Rand finished. "I want to go south. Somewhere away. Just somewhere away."

"But if the gates are barred," Mat said, "how do we get out?"

Rand stared at him. "We?" He had to go alone. It would be dangerous for anyone near him, eventually. He would be dangerous, and even Moiraine could not tell him how long he had. "Mat, you know you have to go to Tar Valon with Moiraine. She said that's the only place you can be separated from that bloody dagger without dying. And you know what will happen if you keep it."

Mat touched his coat over the dagger, not seeming to realize what he was doing. " 'An Aes Sedai's gift is bait for a fish,' " he quoted. "Well, maybe I don't want to put the hook in my mouth.

Maybe whatever she wants to do in Tar Valon is worse than if I don't go at all. Maybe she's lying. 'The truth an Aes Sedai tells is never the truth you think it is.' "

"You have any more old sayings you want to rid yourself of?" Rand asked. " 'A south wind brings a warm g.est, a north wind an empty house'? 'A pig painted gold is still a pig'? What about, 'talk shears no sheep'? 'A fool's words are dust'?"

"Easy, Rand," Perrin said softly. "There is no need to be so rough."

"Isn't there? Maybe I don't want you two going with me, always hanging around, falling into trouble and expecting me to pull you out. You ever think of that? Burn me, did it ever occur to you I might be tired of always having you there whenever I turn around? Always there, and I'm tired of it." The hurt on Perrin's face cut him like a knife, but he pushed on relentlessly. "There are some here think I'm a lord. A lord. Maybe I like that. But look at you, dicing with stablehands. When I go, I go by myself. You two can go to Tar Valon or go hang yourselves, but I leave here alone."

Mat's face had gone stiff, and he clutched the dagger through his coat till his knuckles were white. "If that is how you want it," he said coldly. "I thought we were. . . . However you want it, al'Thor. But if I decide to leave at the same time you do, I'll go, and you can stand clear of me."

"Nobody is going anywhere," Perrin said, "if the gates are barred." He was staring at the floor again. Laughter rolled from the gamblers against the wall as someone lost.

"Go or stay," Loial said, "together or apart, it doesn't matter. You are all three *ta'veren.* Even I can see it, and I don't have that Talent, just by what happens around you. And Moiraine Sedai says it, too."

Mat threw up his hands. "No more, Loial. I don't want to hear about that anymore."

Loial shook his head. "Whether you hear it or not, it is still true. The Wheel of Time weaves the Pattern of the Age, using the lives of men for thread. And you three are *ta'veren,* centerpoints of the weaving."

"No more, Loial."

"For a time, the Wheel will bend the Pattern around you three, whatever you do. And whatever you do is more likely to be chosen by the Wheel than by you. *Ta'veren* pull history along behind them and shape the Pattern just by being, but the Wheel weaves *ta'veren* on a tighter line than other men. Wherever you go and whatever you do, until the Wheel chooses otherwise you will—"

"No more!" Mat shouted. The men dicing looked around, and he glared at them until they bent back to their game.

"I am sorry, Mat," Loial rumbled. "I know I talk too much, but I did not mean—"

"I am not staying here," Mat told the rafters, "with a big-mouthed Ogier and a fool whose head is too big for a hat. You coming, Perrin?" Perrin sighed, and glanced at Rand, then nodded.

Rand watched them go with a stick caught in his throat. *I must go alone. Light help me, I have to.*

Loial was staring after them, too, eyebrows drooping worriedly. "Rand, I really didn't mean to—"

Rand made his voice harsh. "What are you waiting for? Go on with them! I don't see why you're still here. You are no use to me if you don't know a way out. Go on! Go find your trees, and your precious groves, if they haven't all been cut down, and good riddance to them if they have."

Loial's eyes, as big as cups, looked surprised and hurt, at first, but slowly they tightened into what almost might be anger. Rand did not think it could be. Some of the old stories claimed Ogier were fierce, though they never said how, exactly, but Rand had never met anyone as gentle as Loial.

"If you wish it so, Rand al'Thor," Loial said stiffly. He gave a rigid bow and stalked away after Mat and Perrin.

Rand slumped against the stacked sacks of grain. *Well,* a voice in his head taunted, *you did it, didn't you. I had to,* he told it. *I will be dangerous just to be around. Blood and ashes, I'm going to go mad, and. . . . No! No, I won't! I will not use the Power, and then I won't go mad, and. . . . But I can't risk it. I can't, don't you see?* But the voice only laughed at him.

The gamblers were looking at him, he realized. All of them, still kneeling against the wall, had turned to stare at him. Shienarans of any class were almost always polite and correct, even to blood enemies, and Ogier were never any enemies of Shienar. Shock filled the gamblers' eyes. Their faces were blank, but their eyes said what he had done was wrong. Part of him thought they were right, and that drove their silent accusation deep. They only looked at him, but he stumbled out of the storeroom as if they were chasing him.

Numbly he went on through the storerooms, hunting a place to secrete himself until some traffic was allowed through the gates again. Then he could hide in the bottom of a victualer's cart, maybe. If they did not search the carts on the way out. If they did not search the storerooms, search the whole keep for him. Stubbornly he refused to think about that, stubbornly concentrated on finding a safe place. But every place he found—a hollow in a stack of grain sacks, a narrow alley along the wall behind some wine barrels, an abandoned storeroom half filled with empty crates and shadows—he could imagine searchers finding him there. He could imagine that unseen watcher, whoever it was—or whatever—finding him there, too. So he hunted on, thirsty and dusty and with cobwebs in his hair.

And then he came out into a dimly torch-lit corridor, and Egwene was creeping along it, pausing to peer into the storerooms she passed. Her dark hair, hanging to her waist, was caught back with a red ribbon, and she wore a goose-gray dress in the Shienaran fashion, trimmed in red. At the sight of her, sadness and loss rolled over him, worse than when he had chased Mat and Perrin and Loial away. He had grown up thinking he would marry Egwene one day; they both had. But now. . . .

She jumped when he popped out right in front of her, and her breath caught loudly, but what she said was, "So there you are. Mat and Perrin told me what you did. And Loial. I know what you're trying to do, Rand, and it is plain foolish." She crossed her arms under her breasts, and her big, dark eyes fixed him sternly. He always wondered how she managed to seem to be looking down at him—she did it at will—although she was only as tall as his chest, and two years younger besides.

"Good," he said. Her hair suddenly made him angry. He had never seen a grown woman with her hair unbraided until he left the Two Rivers. There, every girl waited eagerly for the Women's Circle of her village to say she was old enough to braid her hair. Egwene certainly had. And here she was with her hair loose except for a ribbon. *I want to go home and can't, and she can't wait to forget Emond's Field.* "You go away and leave me alone, too. You don't want to keep company with a shepherd anymore. There are plenty of Aes Sedai here for you to moon around, now. And don't tell any of them you saw me. They're after me, and I don't need you helping them."

Bright spots of color bloomed in her cheeks. "Do you think I would—"

He turned to walk away, and with a cry she threw herself at him, flung her arms around his legs. They both tumbled to the stone floor, his saddlebags and bundles flying. He grunted when he hit, sword hilt digging into his side, and again when she scrabbled up and plopped herself down on his back as if he were a chair. "My mother," she said firmly, "always told me the best way to learn to deal with a man was to learn to ride a mule. She said they have about equal brains most of the time. Sometimes the mule is smarter."

He raised his head to look over his shoulder at her. "Get off me, Egwene. Get off! Egwene, if you don't get off"—he lowered his voice ominously—"I'll do something to you. You know what I am." He added a glare for good measure.

Egwene sniffed. "You wouldn't, if you could. You would not hurt anybody. But you can't, anyway. I know you cannot channel the One Power whenever you want; it just happens, and you cannot control it. So you are not going to do anything to me or anybody else. I, on the other hand, have been taking lessons with Moiraine, so if you don't listen to some sense, Rand al'Thor, I might just set your breeches on fire. I can manage that much. You keep on as you are and see if I cannot." Suddenly, for just a moment, the torch nearest them on the wall flared up with a roar. She gave a squeak and stared at it, startled.

Twisting around, he grabbed her arm, pulled her off his back, and sat her against the wall. When he sat up himself, she was sitting there across from him, rubbing her arm furiously. "You really would have, wouldn't you?" he said angrily. "You're fooling with things you don't understand. You could have burned both of us to charcoal!"

"Men! When you cannot win an argument, you either run away or resort to force."

"Hold on there! Who tripped who? Who sat on who? And you threatened—tried!—to—" He raised both hands. "No, you don't. You do this to me all the time. Whenever you realize the argument isn't going the way you want, suddenly we are arguing about something else completely. Not this time."

"I am not arguing," she said calmly, "and I am not changing the subject, either. What is hiding except running away? And after you hide, you'll run away for true. And what about hurting Mat, and Perrin, and Loial? And me? I know why. You're afraid you will hurt somebody even worse if you let them stay near you. If you don't do what you shouldn't, then you do not have to worry about hurting anybody. All this running around and striking out, and you don't even know if there's a reason. Why should the Amyrlin, or any Aes Sedai but Moiraine, even know you exist?"

For a moment he stared at her. The longer she spent with Moiraine and Nynaeve, the more she took on their manner, at least when she wanted to. They were much alike at times, the Aes Sedai and the Wisdom, distant and knowing. It was disconcerting coming from Egwene. Finally he told her what Lan had said. "What else could he mean?"

Her hand froze on her arm, and she frowned with concentration. "Moiraine knows about you, and she hasn't done anything, so why should she now? But if Lan. . . ." Still frowning, she met his eyes. "The storerooms are the first place they will look. If they do look. Until we find out if they are looking, we need to put you somewhere they would never think of searching. I know. The dungeon."

He scrambled to his feet. "The dungeon!"

"Not in a cell, silly. I go there some evenings to visit Padan Fain. Nynaeve does, too. No one will think it odd if I go early today. In truth, with everybody looking to the Amyrlin, no one will even notice us."

"But, Moiraine. . . ."

"She doesn't go to the dungeons to question Master Fain. She has him brought to her. And she has not done that very much for weeks. Believe me, you will be safe there."

Still, he hesitated. Padan Fain. "Why do you visit the peddler, anyway? He's a Darkfriend, admitted out of his own mouth, and a bad one. Burn me, Egwene, he brought the Trollocs to Emond's Field! The Dark One's hound, he called himself, and he has been sniffing on my trail since Winternight."

"Well, he is safe behind iron bars now, Rand." It was her turn to hesitate, and she looked at him almost pleading. "Rand, he has brought his wagon into the Two Rivers every spring since before

I was born. He knows all the people I know, all the places. It's strange, but the longer he has been locked up, the easier in himself he has become. It's almost as if he is breaking free of the Dark One. He laughs again, and tells funny stories, about Emond's Field folk, and sometimes about places I never heard of before. Sometimes he is almost like his old self. I just like to talk to somebody about home."

Since I've been avoiding you, he thought, *and since Perrin's been avoiding everybody, and Mat's been spending all his time gambling and carousing.* "I shouldn't have kept to myself so much," he muttered, then sighed. "Well, if Moiraine thinks it's safe enough for you, I suppose it is safe enough for me. But there's no need for you to be mixed in it."

Egwene got to her feet and concentrated on brushing off her dress, avoiding his eye.

"Moiraine *has* said it's safe? Egwene?"

"Moiraine Sedai has never told me I could not visit Master Fain," she said carefully.

He stared at her, then burst out, "You never asked her. She doesn't know. Egwene, that's stupid. Padan Fain's a Darkfriend, and as bad as ever a Darkfriend was."

"He is locked in a cage," she said stiffly, "and I do not have to ask Moiraine's permission for everything I do. It is a little late for you to start worrying about doing what an Aes Sedai thinks, isn't it? Now, are you coming?"

"I can find the dungeon without you. They are looking for me, or will be, and it won't do you any good to be found with me."

"Without me," she said dryly, "you'll likely trip over your own feet and fall in the Amyrlin Seat's lap, then confess everything while trying to talk your way out of it."

"Blood and ashes, you ought to be in the Women's Circle back home. If men were all as fumble-footed and helpless as you seem to think, we'd never—"

"Are you going to stand here talking until they do find you? Pick up your things, Rand, and come with me." Not waiting for an answer, she spun around and started off down the hall. Muttering under his breath, he reluctantly obeyed.

There were few people—servants, mainly—in the back ways they took, but Rand had the feeling that they all took special notice of him. Not notice of a man burdened for a journey, but of *him,* Rand al'Thor in particular. He knew it was his imagination— he hoped it was—but even so, he felt no relief when they stopped in a passageway deep beneath the keep, before a tall door with a small iron grill set in it, as thickly strapped with iron as any in the outer wall. A clapper hung below the grill.

Through the grill Rand could see bare walls, and two top- knotted soldiers sitting bareheaded at a table with a lamp on it. One of the men was sharpening a dagger with long, slow strokes of a stone. His strokes never faltered when Egwene rapped with the clapper, a sharp clang of iron on iron. The other man, his face flat and sullen, looked at the door as if considering before he finally rose and came over. He was squat and stocky, barely tall enough to look through the cross-hatched bars.

"What do you want? Oh, it's you again, girl. Come to see your Darkfriend? Who's that?" He made no move to open the door.

"He's a friend of mine, Changu. He wants to see Master Fain, too."

The man studied Rand, his upper lip quivering back to bare teeth. Rand did not think it was supposed to be a smile. "Well," Changu said finally. "Well. Tall, aren't you? Tall. And fancy dressed for your kind. Somebody catch you young in the Eastern Marches and tame you?" He slammed back the bolts and yanked open the door. "Well, come in if you're coming." He took on a mocking tone. "Take care not to bump your head, my Lord."

There was no danger of that; the door was tall enough for Loial. Rand followed Egwene in, frowning and wondering if this

Changu meant to make some sort of trouble. He was the first rude Shienaran Rand had met; even Masema was only cold, not really rude. But the fellow just banged the door shut and rammed the heavy bolts home, then went to some shelves beyond the end of the table and took one of the lamps there. The other man never ceased stropping his knife, never even looked up from it. The room was bare except for the table and benches and shelves, with straw on the floor and another iron-bound door leading deeper in.

"You'll want some light, won't you," Changu said, "in there in the dark with your Darkfriend friend." He laughed, coarse and humorless, and lit the lamp. "He's waiting for you." He thrust the lamp at Egwene, and undid the inner door almost eagerly. "Waiting for you. In there, in the dark."

Rand paused uneasily at the blackness beyond, and Changu grinning behind, but Egwene caught his sleeve and pulled him in. The door slammed, almost catching his heel; the latch bars clanged shut. There was only the light of the lamp, a small pool around them in the darkness.

"Are you sure he'll let us out?" he asked. The man had never even looked at his sword or bow, he realized, never asked what was in his bundles. "They aren't very good guards. We could be here to break Fain free for all he knows."

"They know me better than that," she said, but she sounded troubled, and she added, "They seem worse every time I come. All the guards do. Meaner, and more sullen. Changu told jokes the first time I came, and Nidao never even speaks anymore. But I suppose working in a place like this can't give a man a light heart. Maybe it is just me. This place does not do my heart any good, either." Despite her words, she drew him confidently into the black. He kept his free hand on his sword.

The pale lamplight showed a wide hall with flat iron grills to either side, fronting stone-walled cells. Only two of the cells they passed held prisoners. The occupants sat up on their narrow cots as the light struck them, shielding their eyes with their hands, glaring between their fingers. Even with their faces hidden, Rand was sure they were glaring. Their eyes glittered in the lamplight.

"That one likes to drink and fight," Egwene murmured, indicating a burly fellow with sunken knuckles. "This time he wrecked the common room of an inn in the town single-handed, and hurt some men badly." The other prisoner wore a gold-embroidered coat with wide sleeves, and low, gleaming boots. "He tried to leave the city without settling his inn bill"—she sniffed loudly at that; her father was an innkeeper as well as Mayor of Emond's Field—"nor paying half a dozen shopkeepers and merchants what he owed."

The men snarled at them, guttural curses as bad as any Rand had heard from merchants' guards.

"They grow worse every day, too," she said in a tight voice, and quickened her step.

She was enough ahead of him when they reached Padan Fain's

cell, at the very end, that Rand was out of the light entirely. He stopped there, in the shadows behind her lamp.

Fain was sitting on his cot, leaning forward expectantly as if waiting, just as Changu had said. He was a bony, sharp-eyed man, with long arms and a big nose, even more gaunt now than Rand remembered. Not gaunt from the dungeon—the food here was the same as the servants ate, and not even the worst prisoner was shorted—but from what he had done before coming to Fal Dara.

The sight of him brought back memories Rand would just as soon have done without. Fain on the seat of his big peddler's wagon wheeling across the Wagon Bridge, arriving in Emond's Field the day of Winternight. And on Winternight the Trollocs came, killing and burning, hunting. Hunting three young men, Moiraine had said. *Hunting me, if they only knew it, and using Fain for their trail hound.*

Fain stood at Egwene's approach, not shielding his eyes or even blinking at the light. He smiled at her, a smile that touched only his lips, then raised his eyes above her head. Looking straight at Rand, hidden in the blackness behind the light, he pointed a long finger at him. "I feel you there, hiding, Rand al'Thor," he said, almost crooning. "You can't hide, not from me, and not from them. You thought it was over, did you not? But the battle's never done, al'Thor. They are coming for me, and they're coming for you, and the war goes on. Whether you live or die, it's never over for you. Never." Suddenly he began to chant.

> "Soon comes the day all shall be free.
> Even you, and even me.
> Soon comes the day all shall die.
> Surely you, but never I."

He let his arm fall, and his eyes rose to stare intently at an angle up into the darkness. A crooked grin twisting his mouth, he chuckled deep in his throat as if whatever he saw was amusing. "Mordeth knows more than all of you. Mordeth knows."

Egwene backed away from the cell until she reached Rand, and only the edge of the light touched the bars of Fain's cell. Darkness hid the peddler, but they could still hear his chuckles. Even unable to see him, Rand was sure Fain was still peering off at nothing.

With a shiver, he pried his fingers off his sword hilt. "Light!" he said hoarsely. "This is what you call being like he used to be?"

"Sometimes he's better, and sometimes worse." Egwene's. voice was unsteady. "This is worse—much worse than usual."

"What is he seeing, I wonder. He's mad, staring at a stone ceiling in the dark." *If the stone weren't there, he'd be looking straight at the women's apartments. Where Moiraine is, and the Amyrlin Seat.* He shivered again. "He's mad."

"This was not a good idea, Rand." Looking over her shoulder at the cell, she drew him away from it and lowered her voice as if afraid Fain might overhear. Fain's chuckles followed them. "Even if they don't look here, I cannot stay here with him like this, and I do not think you should, either. There is something about him today that. . . ." She drew a shaky breath. "There is one place even safer from search than here. I did not mention it before because it was easier to get you in here, but they will never look in the women's apartments. Never."

"The women's . . .! Egwene, Fain may be mad, but you're madder. You can't hide from hornets in a hornets' nest."

"What better place? What is the one part of the keep no man will enter without a woman's invitation, not even Lord Agelmar? What is the one place no one would ever think to look for a man?"

"What is the one place in the keep sure to be full of Aes Sedai? It is crazy, Egwene."

Poking at his bundles, she spoke as if it were all decided. "You must wrap your sword and bow in your cloak, and then it will look as if you are carrying things for me. It should not be too hard to find you a jerkin and a shirt that isn't so pretty. You will have to stoop, though."

"I told you, I won't do it."

"Since you're acting stubborn as a mule, you should take right to playing my beast of burden. Unless you would really rather stay down here with him."

Fain's laughing whisper came through the black shadows. "The battle's never done, al'Thor. Mordeth knows."

"I'd have a better chance jumping off the wall," Rand muttered. But he unslung his bundles and set about wrapping sword and bow and quiver as she had suggested.

In the darkness, Fain laughed. "It's never over, al'Thor. Never."

CHAPTER 4

Summoned

ALONE IN HER ROOMS IN THE WOMEN'S Apartments, Moiraine adjusted the shawl, embroidered with curling ivy and grapevines, on her shoulders and studied the effect in the tall frame mirror standing in a corner. Her large, dark eyes could appear as sharp as a hawk's when she was angry. They seemed to pierce the silvered glass, now. It was only happenstance that she had had the shawl in her saddlebags when she came to Fal Dara. With the blazing white Flame of Tar Valon centered on the wearer's back and long fringe colored to show her Ajah—Moiraine's was as blue as a morning sky—the shawls were seldom worn outside Tar Valon, and even there usually only inside the White Tower. Little in Tar Valon besides a meeting of the Hall of the Tower called for the formality of the shawls, and beyond the Shining Walls a sight of the Flame would send too many people running, to hide or perhaps to fetch the Children of the Light. A Whitecloak's arrow was as fatal to an Aes Sedai as to anyone else, and the Children were too wily to let an Aes Sedai see the bowman before the arrow struck, while she still might do something about it. Moiraine had certainly never expected to wear the shawl in Fal Dara. But for an audience with the Amyrlin, there were proprieties to observe.

She was slender and not at all tall, and smooth-cheeked Aes Sedai agelessness often made her appear younger than she was, but Moiraine had a commanding grace and calm presence that could dominate any gathering. A manner ingrained growing up in the Royal Palace of Cairhien had been heightened, not submerged, by still more years as an Aes Sedai. She knew she might need every bit of it today. Yet much of the calm was on the surface, today. *There must be trouble, or she would not have come herself,* she thought for at least the tenth time. But beyond that lay a thousand questions more. *What trouble, and who did she choose to accompany her? Why here? Why now? It cannot be allowed to go wrong now.*

The Great Serpent ring on her right hand caught the light dully as she touched the delicate golden chain fastened in her dark hair, which hung in waves to her shoulders. A small, clear blue stone dangled from the chain, in the middle of her forehead. Many in the White Tower knew of the tricks she could do using that stone as a focus. It was only a polished bit of blue crystal, just something a young girl had used in her first learning, with no one to guide her. That girl had remembered tales of *angreal* and even more powerful *sa'angreal*—those fabled remnants of the Age of Legends that allowed Aes Sedai to channel more of the One Power than any could safely handle unaided—remembered and thought some such focus was required to channel at all. Her sisters in the White Tower knew a few of her tricks, and suspected others, including some that did not exist, some that had shocked her when she learned of them. The things she did with the stone were simple and small, if occasionally useful; the kind a child would imagine. But if the wrong women had accompanied the Amyrlin, the crystal might put them off balance, because of the tales.

A rapid, insistent knocking came at the chamber door. No Shienaran would knock that way, not at anyone's door, but least of all hers. She remained looking into the mirror until her eyes stared back serenely, all thought hidden in their dark depths. She checked the soft leather pouch hanging at her belt. *Whatever troubles brought her out of Tar Valon, she will forget them when I lay this trouble before her.* A second thumping, even more vigorous than the first, sounded before she crossed the room and opened the door with a calm smile for the two women who had come for her.

She recognized them both. Dark-haired Anaiya in her blue-fringed shawl, and fair-haired Liandrin in her red. Liandrin, not only young-seeming but young and pretty, with a doll's face and a small, petulant mouth, had her hand raised to pound again. Her dark brows and darker eyes were a sharp contrast to the multitude of pale honey braids brushing her shoulders, but the combination was not uncommon in Tarabon. Both women were taller than Moiraine, though Liandrin by less than a hand.

Anaiya's blunt face broke into a smile as soon as Moiraine opened the door. That smile gave her the only beauty she would ever have, but it was enough; almost everyone felt comforted, safe and special, when Anaiya smiled at them. "The Light shine on you, Moiraine. It's good to see you again. Are you well? It has been so long."

"My heart is lighter for your presence, Anaiya." That was certainly true; it was good to know she had at least one friend among the Aes Sedai who had come to Fal Dara. "The Light illumine you."

Liandrin's mouth tightened, and she gave her shawl a twitch.

"The Amyrlin Seat, she requires your presence, Sister." Her voice was petulant, too, and cold-edged. Not for Moiraine's sake, or not solely; Liandrin always sounded dissatisfied with something. Frowning, she tried to look over Moiraine's shoulder into the room. "This chamber, it is warded. We cannot enter. Why do you ward against your sisters?"

"Against all," Moiraine replied smoothly. "Many of the serving women are curious about Aes Sedai, and I do not want them pawing through my rooms when I am not here. There was no need to make a distinction until now." She pulled the door shut behind her, leaving all three of them in the corridor. "Shall we go? We must not keep the Amyrlin waiting."

She started down the hallway with Anaiya chatting at her side. Liandrin stood for a moment staring at the door as if wondering what Moiraine was hiding, then hurried to join the others. She bracketed Moiraine, walking as stiffly as a guard. Anaiya merely walked, keeping company. Their slippered footsteps fell softly on thick-woven carpets with simple patterns.

Liveried women curtsied deeply as they passed, many more deeply than they would have for the Lord of Fal Dara himself. Aes Sedai, three together, and the Amyrlin Seat herself in the keep; it was more honor than any woman of the keep had ever expected in her lifetime. A few women of noble Houses were out in the halls, and they curtsied, too, which they most certainly would not have done for Lord Agelmar. Moiraine and Anaiya smiled and bowed their heads to acknowledge each reverence, from servant or noble equally. Liandrin ignored them all.

There were only women here, of course, no men. No Shienaran male above the age of ten would enter the women's rooms without permission or invitation, although a few small boys ran and played in the halls here. They knelt on one knee, awkwardly, when their sisters dropped deep curtsies. Now and then Anaiya smiled and ruffled a small head as she passed.

"This time, Moiraine," Anaiya said, "you have been gone from Tar Valon too long. Much too long. Tar Valon misses you. Your sisters miss you. And you are needed in the White Tower."

"Some of us must work in the world," Moiraine said gently. "I will leave the Hall of the Tower to you, Anaiya. Yet in Tar Valon, you hear more of what occurs in the world than I. Too often I out-run what happens where I was yesterday. What news have you?"

"Three more false Dragons." Liandrin bit the words off. "In Saldaea, Murandy, and Tear false Dragons ravage the land. The while, you Blues smile and talk of nothing, and try to hold on to the past." Anaiya raised an eyebrow, and Liandrin snapped her mouth shut with a sharp sniff.

"Three," Moiraine mused softly. For an instant her eyes gleamed, but she masked it quickly. "Three in the last two years, and now three more at once."

"As the others were, these will be dealt with also. This male vermin and any ragtag rabble who follow their banners."

Moiraine was almost amused by the certainty in Liandrin's voice. Almost. She was too aware of the realities, too aware of the possibilities. "Have a few months been enough for you to forget, Sister? The last false Dragon all but tore Ghealdan apart before his army, ragtag rabble or not, was defeated. Yes, Logain is in Tar Valon by now, gentled and safe, I suppose, but some of our sisters died to overpower him. Even one sister dead is more loss than we can bear, but Ghealdan's losses were much worse. The two before Logain could not channel, yet even so the people of Kandor and Arad Doman remember them well. Villages burned and men dead in battle. How easily can the world deal with three at one time? How many will flock to their banners? There has never been a shortage of followers for any man claiming to be the Dragon Reborn. How great will the wars be this time?"

"It isn't so grim as that," Anaiya said. "As far as we know, only the one in Saldaea can channel. He has not had time to attract many followers, and sisters should already be there to deal with him. The Tairens are harrying their false Dragon and his followers through Haddon Mirk, while the fellow in Murandy is already in chains." She gave a short, wondering laugh. "To think the Murandians, of all people, would deal with theirs so quickly. Ask, and they do not even call themselves Murandians, but Lugarders, or Inishlinni, or this or that lord's or lady's man. Yet for fear one of their neighbors would take the excuse to invade, the Murandians leaped on their false Dragon almost as soon as he opened his mouth to proclaim himself."

"Still," Moiraine said, "three at the same time cannot be ignored. Has any sister been able to do a Foretelling?" It was a slight chance—few Aes Sedai had manifested any part of that Talent, even the smallest part, in centuries—so she was not surprised when Anaiya shook her head. Not surprised, but a little relieved.

They reached a juncture of hallways at the same time as the Lady Amalisa. She dropped a full curtsy, bowing deep and spreading her pale green skirts wide. "Honor to Tar Valon," she murmured. "Honor to Aes Sedai."

The sister of the Lord of Fal Dara required more than a nod of the head. Moiraine took Amalisa's hands and drew her to her feet. "You honor us, Amalisa. Rise, Sister."

Amalisa straighted gracefully, with a flush on her face. She had never as much as been to Tar Valon, and to be called Sister by an Aes Sedai was heady even for someone of her rank. Short and of middle years, she had a dark, mature beauty, and the color in her cheeks set it off. "You honor me too greatly, Moiraine Sedai."

Moiraine smiled. "How long have we known each other, Amalisa? Must I now call you my Lady Amalisa, as if we had never sat over tea together?"

"Of course not." Amalisa smiled back. The strength evident in her brother's face was in hers, too, and no less for the softer line of cheek and jaw. There were those who said that as hard and renowned a fighter as Agelmar was, he was no better than an even match for his sister. "But with the Amyrlin Seat here. . . . When King Easar visits Fal Dara, in private I call him *Magami,* Little Uncle, as I did when I was a child and he gave me rides on his shoulder, but in public it must be different."

Anaiya *tsked.* "Sometimes formality is necessary, but men often make more of it than they must. Please, call me Anaiya, and I will call you Amalisa, if I may."

From the corner of her eye, Moiraine saw Egwene, far down the side hall, disappearing hurriedly around a corner. A stooped shape in a leather jerkin, head down and arms loaded with bundles, shambled at her heels. Moiraine permitted herself a small smile, quickly masked. *If the girl shows as much initiative in Tar Valon,* she thought wryly, *she will sit in the Amyrlin Seat one day. If she can learn to control that initiative. If there is an Amyrlin Seat left on which to sit.*

When she turned her attention back to the others, Liandrin was speaking.

". . . and I would welcome the chance to learn more of your land." She wore a smile, open and almost girlish, and her voice was friendly.

Moiraine schooled her face to stillness as Amalisa extended an invitation to join her and her ladies in her private garden, and Liandrin accepted warmly. Liandrin made few friends, and none outside the Red Ajah. *Certainly never outside the Aes Sedai. She would sooner make friends with a man, or a Trolloc.* Moiraine was not sure Liandrin saw much difference between men and Trollocs. She was not sure any of the Red Ajah did.

Anaiya explained that just now they must attend the Amyrlin Seat. "Of course," Amalisa said. "The Light illumine her, and the Creator shelter her. But later, then." She stood straight and bowed her head as they left her.

Moiraine studied Liandrin as they walked, never looking at her directly. The honey-haired Aes Sedai was staring straight ahead, rosebud lips pursed thoughtfully. She appeared to have forgotten Moiraine and Anaiya both. *What is she up to?*

Anaiya seemed not to have noticed anything out of the ordinary, but then she always managed to accept people both as they were and as they wanted to be. It constantly amazed Moiraine that Anaiya dealt as well as she did in the White Tower, but those who were devious always seemed to take her openness and honesty, her acceptance of everyone, an cunning devices. They were always caught completely off balance when she turned out to mean what she said and say what she meant. Too, she had a way of seeing to the heart of things. And of accepting what she saw. Now she blithely resumed speaking of the news.

"The word from Andor is both good and bad. The street riots in Caemlyn died down with the coming of spring, but there is still talk, too much talk, blaming the Queen, and Tar Valon as well, for the long winter. Morgase holds her throne less securely than she did last year, but she holds it still, and will so long as Gareth Bryne is Captain-General of the Queen's Guards. And the Lady Elayne, the Daughter-Heir, and her brother, the Lord Gawyn, have come safely to Tar Valon for their training. There was some fear in the White Tower that the custom would be broken."

"Not while Morgase has breath in her body," Moiraine said.

Liandrin gave a little start, as if she had just awakened. "Pray that she continues to have breath. The Daughter-Heir's party was followed to the River Erinin by the Children of the Light. To the very bridges to Tar Valon. More still camp outside Caemlyn, for the chance of mischief, and inside Caemlyn still are those who listen."

"Perhaps it is time Morgase learned a little caution," Anaiya sighed. "The world is becoming more dangerous every day, even for a queen. Perhaps especially for a queen. She was ever headstrong. I remember when she came to Tar Valon as a girl. She did not have the ability to become a full sister, and it rankled in her.

Sometimes I think she pushes her daughter because of that, whatever the girl chooses."

Moiraine sniffed disdainfully. "Elayne was born with the spark in her; it was not a matter of choosing. Morgase would not risk letting the girl die from lack of training if all the Whitecloaks in Amadicia were camped outside Caemlyn. She would command Gareth Byrne and the Queen's Guards to cut a path through them to Tar Valon, and Gareth Byrne would do it if he had to do it alone." *But she still must keep the full extent of the girl's potential secret. Would the people of Andor knowingly accept Elayne on the Lion Throne after Morgase if they knew? Not just a queen trained in Tar Valon according to custom, but a full Aes Sedai?* In all of recorded history there had been only a handful of queens with the right to be called Aes Sedai, and the few who let it be known had all lived to regret it. She felt a touch of sadness. But too much was afoot to spare aid, or even worry, for one land and one throne. "What else, Anaiya?"

"You must know that the Great Hunt of the Horn has been called in Illian, the first time in four hundred years. The Illianers say the Last Battle is coming"—Anaiya gave a little shiver, as well she might, but went on without a pause—"and the Horn of Valere must be found before the final battle against the Shadow. Men from every land are already gathering, all eager to be part of the legend, eager to find the Horn. Murandy and Altara are on their toes, of course, thinking it's all a mask for a move against one of them. That is probably why the Murandians caught their false Dragon so quickly. In any case, there will be a new lot of stories for the bards and gleemen to add to the cycle. The Light send it is only new stories."

"Perhaps not the stories they expect," Moiraine said. Liandrin looked at her sharply, and she kept her face still.

"I suppose not," Anaiya said placidly. "The stories they least expect will be exactly the ones they will add to the cycle. Beyond that, I have only rumor to offer. The Sea Folk are agitated, their ships flying from port to port with barely a pause. Sisters from the islands say the Coramoor, their Chosen One, is coming, but they won't say more. You know how closemouthed the Atha'an Miere are with outsiders about the Coramoor, and in this our sisters seem to think more as Sea Folk than Aes Sedai. The Aiel appear to be stirring, too, but no one knows why. No one ever knows with the Aiel. At least there is no evidence they mean to cross the Spine of the World again, thank the Light." She sighed and shook her head. "What I would not give for even one sister from among the Aiel. Just one. We know too little of them."

Moiraine laughed. "Sometimes I think you belong in the Brown Ajah, Anaiya."

"Almoth Plain," Liandrin said, and looked surprised that she had spoken.

"Now that truly *is* rumor, Sister," Anaiya said. "A few whispers heard as we were leaving Tar Valon. There may be fighting on Almoth Plain, and perhaps Toman Head, as well. I say, may be. The whispers were faint. Rumors of rumors. We left before we could hear more."

"It would have to be Tarabon and Arad Doman," Moiraine said, and shook her head. "They have squabbled over Almoth Plain for nearly three hundred years, but it has never come to open blows." She looked at Liandrin; Aes Sedai were supposed to throw off all their old loyalties to lands and rulers, but few did so completely. It was hard not to care for the land of your birth. "Why would they now—?"

"Enough of idle talk," the honey-haired woman broke in angrily. "For you, Moiraine, the Amyrlin waits." She took three quick strides ahead of the others and threw open one of a pair of tall doors. "For you, the Amyrlin will have no idle talk."

Unconsciously touching the pouch at her waist, Moiraine went past Liandrin through the doorway, with a nod as if the other woman were holding the door for her. She did not even smile at the white flash of anger on Liandrin's face. *What is the wretched girl up to?*

Brightly colored carpets covered the anteroom floor in layers, and the room was pleasantly furnished with chairs and cushioned benches and small tables, the wood simply worked or just polished. Brocaded curtains sided the tall arrowslits to make them seem more like windows. No fires burned in the fireplaces; the day was warm, and the Shienaran chill would not come until nightfall.

Fewer than half a dozen of the Aes Sedai who had accompanied the Amyrlin were there. Verin Mathwin and Serafelle, of the Brown Ajah, did not look up at Moiraine's entrance. Serafelle was intently reading an old book with a worn, faded leather cover, handling its tattered pages carefully, while plump Verin, sitting cross-legged beneath an arrowslit, held a small blossom up to the light and made notes and sketches in a precise hand in a book balanced on her knee. She had an open inkpot on the floor beside her, and a small pile of flowers on her lap. The Brown sisters concerned themselves with little beside seeking knowledge. Moiraine sometimes wondered if they were really aware of what was going on in the world, or even immediately around them.

The three other women already in the room turned, but they made no effort to approach Moiraine, only looked at her. One, a slender woman of the Yellow Ajah, she did not know; she spent too little time in Tar Valon to know all the Aes Sedai, although their numbers were no longer very great. She was acquainted with the two remaining, however. Carlinya was as pale of skin and cold of manner as the white fringe on her shawl, the exact opposite in every way of dark, fiery Alanna Mosvani, of the Green, but they both stood and stared at her without speaking, without expression. Alanna sharply snugged her shawl around her, but Carlinya made no move at all. The slender Yellow sister turned away with an air of regret.

"The Light illumine you all, Sisters," Moiraine said. No one answered. She was not sure Serafelle or Verin had even heard. *Where are the others?* There was no need for them all to be there—most would be resting in their rooms, freshing from the journey—but she was on edge now, all the questions she could not ask running through her head. None of it showed on her face.

The inner door opened, and Leane appeared, without her gilt-flamed staff. The Keeper of the Chronicles was as tall as most men, willowy and graceful, still beautiful, with coppery skin and short, dark hair. She wore a blue stole, a hand wide, instead of a shawl, for she sat in the Hall of the Tower, though as Keeper, not to represent her Ajah.

"There you are," she said briskly to Moiraine, and gestured to the door behind her. "Come, Sister. The Amyrlin Seat is waiting." She spoke naturally in a clipped, quick way that never changed, whether she was angry or joyful or excited. As Moiraine followed Leane in, she wondered what emotion the Keeper was feeling now. Leane pulled the door in behind them; it banged shut with something of the sound of a cell door closing.

The Amyrlin Seat herself sat behind a broad table in the middle of the carpet, and on the table rested a flattened cube of gold, the size of a travel chest and ornately worked with silver. The table was heavily built, its legs stout, but it seemed to squat under a weight two strong men would have had trouble lifting.

At the sight of the golden cube Moiraine had difficulty keeping her face unruffled. The last she had seen of it, it had been safely locked in Agelmar's strongroom. On learning of the Amyrlin Seat's arrival she had meant to tell her of it herself. That it was already in the Amyrlin's possession was a trifle, but a worrisome trifle. Events could be outpacing her.

She swept a deep curtsy and said formally, "As you called me, Mother, so have I come." The Amyrlin extended her hand, and Moiraine kissed her Great Serpent ring, no different from that of any other Aes Sedai. Rising, she made her tone more conversational, but not too much so. She was aware of the Keeper standing behind her, beside the door. "I hope you had a pleasant journey, Mother."

The Amyrlin had been born in Tear, of a simple fisherman's family, not a noble House, and her name was Siuan Sanche, though very few had used that name, or even thought of it, in the ten years since she had been raised from the Hall of the Tower. She was the Amyrlin Seat; that was the whole of it. The broad stole on her shoulders was striped in the colors of the seven Ajahs; the Amyrlin was of all Ajahs and of none. She was only of medium height, and handsome rather than beautiful, but her face held a strength that had been there before her elevation, the strength of the girl who had survived the streets of the Maule, Tear's port district, and her clear blue gaze had made kings and queens, and even the Captain Commander of the Children of the Light, drop their eyes. Her own eyes were strained, now, and there was a new tightness to her mouth.

"We called the winds to speed our vessels up the Erinin, Daughter, and even turned the currents to our aid." The Amyrlin's voice was deep, and sad. "I have seen the flooding we caused in villages along the river, and the Light only knows what we have done to the weather. We will not have endeared ourselves by the damage we've done and the crops we may have ruined. All to reach here as quickly as possible." Her eyes strayed to the ornate golden cube, and she half lifted a hand as if to touch it, but when she spoke it was to say, "Elaida is in Tar Valon, Daughter. She came with Elayne and Gawyn."

Moiraine was conscious of Leane standing to one side, quiet as always in the presence of the Amyrlin. But watching, and listening. "I am surprised, Mother," she said carefully. "This is no time for Morgase to be without Aes Sedai counsel." Morgase was one of the few rulers to openly admit to an Aes Sedai councilor; almost all had one, but few admitted it.

"Elaida insisted, Daughter, and queen or not, I doubt Morgase is a match for Elaida in a contest of wills. In any case, perhaps this time she did not wish to be. Elayne has potential. More than I have ever seen before. Already she shows progress. The Red sisters are swollen up like puff-fish with it. I don't think the girl leans to their way of thinking, but she is young, and there is no telling. Even if they don't manage to bend her, it will make little difference. Elayne could well be the most powerful Aes Sedai in a thousand years, and it is the Red Ajah who found her. They have gained much status in the Hall from the girl."

"I have two young women with me in Fal Dara, Mother," Moiraine said. "Both from the Two Rivers, where the blood of Manetheren still runs strong, though they do not even remember there was once a land called Manetheren. The old blood sings, Mother, and it sings loudly in the Two Rivers. Egwene, a village girl, is at least as strong as Elayne. I have seen the Daughter-Heir, and I know. As for the other, Nynaeve was the Wisdom in their village, yet she is little more than a girl herself. It says something of her that the women of her village chose her Wisdom at her age. Once she gains conscious control of what she now does without knowing, she will be as strong as any in Tar Valon. With training, she will shine like a bonfire beside the candles of Elayne and Egwene. And there is no chance these two will choose the Red. They are amused by men, exasperated by them, but they do like them. They will easily counter whatever influence the Red Ajah gains in the White Tower from finding Elayne."

The Amyrlin nodded as if it were all of no consequence. Moiraine's eyebrows lifted in surprise before she caught herself and smoothed her features. Those were the two main concerns in the Hall of the Tower, that fewer girls who could be trained to channel the One Power were found every year, or so it seemed, and that fewer of real power were found. Worse than the fear in those who blamed Aes Sedai for the Breaking of the World, worse than the hatred from the Children of the Light, worse even than the workings of Darkfriends, were the sheer dwindling of numbers and the lessening of abilities. The corridors of the White Tower were sparsely populated where once they had been crowded, and what could once be done easily with the One Power could now be done only with difficulty, or not at all.

"Elaida had another reason for coming to Tar Valon, Daughter. She sent the same message by six different pigeons to make sure I received it—and to whom else in Tar Valon she sent pigeons, I can only guess—then came herself. She told the Hall of the Tower that you are meddling with a young man who is *ta'veren,* and dangerous. He was in Caemlyn, she said, but when she found the inn where he had been staying, she discovered you had spirited him away."

"The people at that inn served us well and faithfully, Mother. If she harmed any of them. . . ." Moiraine could not keep the sharpness out of her voice, and she heard Leane shift. One did not speak to the Amyrlin Seat in that tone; not even a king on his throne did.

"You should know, Daughter," the Amyrlin said dryly, "that Elaida harms no one except those she considers dangerous. Darkfriends, or those poor fool men who try to channel the One Power. Or one who threatens Tar Valon. Everyone else who isn't Aes Sedai might as well be pieces on a stones board as far as she is concerned. Luckily for him, the innkeeper, one Master Gill as I remember, apparently thinks much of Aes Sedai, and so answered her questions to her satisfaction. Elaida actually spoke well of him. But she spoke more of the young man you took away with you. More dangerous than any man since Artur Hawkwing, she said. She has the Foretelling sometimes, you know, and her words carried weight with the Hall."

For Leane's sake, Moiraine made her voice as meek as she could. That was not very meek, but it was the best she could do. "I have three young men with me, Mother, but none of them is a king, and I doubt very much if any of them even dreams of uniting the world under one ruler. No one has dreamed Artur Hawkwing's dream since the War of the Hundred Years."

"Yes, Daughter. Village youths, so Lord Agelmar tells me. But one of them is *ta'veren*." The Amyrlin's eyes strayed to the flattened cube again. "It was put forward in the Hall that you should be sent into retreat for contemplation. This was proposed by one of the Sitters for the Green Ajah, with the other two nodding approval as she spoke."

Leane made a sound of disgust, or perhaps frustration. She always kept in the background when the Amyrlin Seat spoke, but Moiraine could understand the small interruption this time. The Green Ajah had been allied with the Blue for a thousand years; since Artur Hawkwing's time, they had all but spoken with one voice. "I have no desire to hoe vegetables in some remote village, Mother." *Nor will I, whatever the Hall of the Tower says.*

"It was further proposed, also by the Greens, that your care during your retreat should be given to the Red Ajah. The Red Sitters tried to appear surprised, but they looked like fisher-birds who knew the catch was unguarded." The Amyrlin sniffed. "The Reds professed reluctance to take custody of one not of their Ajah, but said they would accede to the wishes of the Hall."

Despite herself, Moiraine shivered. "That would be . . . most unpleasant, Mother." It would be worse than unpleasant, much worse; the Reds were never gentle. She put the thought of it firmly to one side, to deal with later. "Mother, I cannot understand this apparent alliance between the Greens and the Reds. Their beliefs, their attitudes toward men, their views of our very purposes as Aes Sedai, are completely opposite. A Red and a Green cannot even talk to each other without coming to shouts."

"Things change, Daughter. Four of the last five women raised Amyrlin have come from the Blue. Perhaps they feel that is too many, or that the Blue way of thinking no longer suffices in a world full of false Dragons. After a thousand years, many things change." The Amyrlin grimaced and spoke as if to herself. "Old walls weaken, and old barriers fall." She shook herself, and her voice firmed. "There was yet another proposal, one that still smells like week-old fish on the jetty. Since Leane is of the Blue Ajah and I came from the Blue, it was put forward that sending two sisters of the Blue with me on this journey would give the Blue four representatives. Proposed in the Hall, to my face, as if they were discussing repairing the drains. Two of the White Sisters stood against me, and two Green. The Yellow muttered among themselves, then would not speak for or against. One more saying nay, and your sisters Anaiya and Maigan would not be here. There was even some talk, open talk, that I should not leave the White Tower at all."

Moiraine felt a greater shock than on hearing that the Red Ajah wanted her in their hands. Whatever Ajah she came from, the Keeper of the Chronicles spoke only for the Amyrlin, and the Amyrlin spoke for all Aes Sedai and all Ajahs. That was the way it had always been, and no one had ever suggested otherwise, not in the darkest days of the Trolloc Wars, not when Artur Hawkwing's armies had penned every surviving Aes Sedai inside Tar Valon. Above all, the Amyrlin Seat was the Amyrlin Seat. Every Aes Sedai was pledged to obey her. No one could question what she did or where she chose to go. This proposal went against three thousand years of custom and law.

"Who would dare, Mother?"

The Amyrlin Seat's laugh was bitter. "Almost anyone, Daughter. Riots in Caemlyn. The Great Hunt called without any of us having a hint of it until the proclamation. False Dragons popping up like redbells after a rain. Nations fading, and more nobles playing at the Game of Houses than at any time since Artur Hawkwing cut all their plottings short. And worst of all, every one of us knows the Dark One is stirring again. Show me a sister who does not think the White Tower is losing its grip on events, and if she is not Brown Ajah, she is dead. Time may be growing short for all of us, Daughter. Sometimes I think I can almost feel it growing shorter."

"As you say, Mother, things change. But there are still worse perils outside the Shining Walls than within."

For a long moment the Amyrlin met Moiraine's gaze, then nodded slowly. "Leave us, Leane. I would talk to my Daughter Moiraine alone."

There was only a moment's hesitation before Leane said, "As you wish, Mother." Moiraine could feel her surprise. The Amyrlin gave few audiences without the Keeper present, especially not to a sister she had reason to chastise.

The door opened and closed behind Leane. She would not say a word in the anteroom of what had occurred inside, but the news that Moiraine was alone with the Amyrlin would spread through the Aes Sedai in Fal Dara like wildfire through a dry forest, and the speculation would begin.

As soon as the door closed the Amyrlin stood, and Moiraine felt a momentary tingle in her skin as the other woman channeled the One Power. For an instant, the Amyrlin Seat seemed to her to be surrounded by a nimbus of bright light.

"I don't know that any of the others have your old trick," the Amyrlin Seat said, lightly touching the blue stone on Moiraine's forehead with one finger, "but most of us have some small tricks remembered from childhood. In any event, no one can hear what we say now."

Suddenly she threw her arms around Moiraine, a warm hug between old friends; Moiraine hugged back as warmly.

"You are the only one, Moiraine, with whom I can remember who I was. Even Leane always acts as if I had *become* the stole and the staff, even when we are alone, as if we'd never giggled together as novices. Sometimes I wish we still were novices, you and I. Still innocent enough to see it all as a gleeman's tale come true, still innocent enough to think we would find men—they would be princes, remember, handsome and strong and gentle?—who could bear to live with women of an Aes Sedai's power. Still innocent enough to dream of the happy ending to the gleeman's tale, of living our lives as other women do, just with more than they."

"We are Aes Sedai, Siuan. We have our duty. Even if you and I had not been born to channel, would you give it up for a home and a husband, even a prince? I do not believe it. That is a village goodwife's dream. Not even the Greens go so far."

The Amyrlin stepped back. "No, I would not give it up. Most of the time, no. But there have been times I envied that village good-wife. At this moment, I almost do. Moiraine, if anyone, even Leane, discovers what we plan, we will both be stilled. And I can't say they would be wrong to do it."

CHAPTER 5

The Shadow in Shienar

STILLED. THE WORD SEEMED TO QUIVER IN the air, almost visible. When it was done to a man who could channel the Power, who must be stopped before madness drove him to the destruction of all around him, it was called gentling, but for Aes Sedai it was stilling. Stilled. No longer able to channel the flow of the One Power. Able to sense *saidar,* the female half of the True Source, but no longer having the ability to touch it. Remembering what was gone forever. So seldom had it been done that every novice was required to learn the name of each Aes Sedai since the Breaking of the World who had been stilled, and her crime, but none could think of it without a shudder. Women bore being stilled no better than men did being gentled.

Moiraine had known the risk from the first, and she knew it was necessary. That did not mean it was pleasant to dwell on. Her eyes narrowed, and only the gleam in them showed her anger, and her worry. "Leane would follow you to the slopes of Shayol Ghul, Siuan, and into the Pit of Doom. You cannot think she would betray you."

"No. But then, would she think it betrayal? Is it betrayal to betray a traitor? Do you never think of that?"

"Never. What we do, Siuan, is what must be done. We have both known it for nearly twenty years. The Wheel weaves as the Wheel wills, and you and I were chosen for this by the Pattern. We are a part of the Prophecies, and the Prophecies must be fulfilled. Must!"

"The Prophecies must be fulfilled. We were taught that they will be, and must be, and yet that fulfillment is treason to everything else we were taught. Some would say to everything we stand for." Rubbing her arms, the Amyrlin Seat walked over to peer through the narrow arrowslit at the garden below. She touched the curtains. "Here in the women's apartments they hang draperies to soften the rooms, and they plant beautiful gardens, but there is no part of this place not purpose-made for battle, death, and killing." She continued in the same pensive tone. "Only twice since the Breaking of the World has the Amyrlin Seat been stripped of stole and staff."

"Tetsuan, who betrayed Manetheren for jealousy of Ellisande's powers, and Bonwhin, who tried to use Artur Hawkwing for a puppet to control the world and so nearly destroyed Tar Valon."

The Amyrlin continued her study of the garden. "Both of the Red, and both replaced by Amyrlin from the Blue. The reason there has not been an Amyrlin chosen from the Red since Bonwhin, and the reason the Red Ajah will take any pretext to pull down an Amyrlin from the Blue, all wrapped neatly together. I have no wish to be the third to lose the stole and the staff, Moiraine. For you, of course, it would mean being stilled and put outside the Shining Walls."

"Elaida, for one, would never let me off so easily." Moiraine watched her friend's back intently. *Light, what has come over her? She has never been like this before. Where is her strength, her fire?* "But it will not come to that, Siuan."

The other woman went on as if she had not spoken. "For me, it would be different. Even stilled, an Amyrlin who has been pulled down cannot be allowed to wander about loose; she might be seen as a martyr, become a rallying point for opposition. Tetsuan and Bonwhin were kept in the White Tower as servants. Scullery maids, who could be pointed to as cautions as to what can happen to the mightiest. No one can rally around a woman who must scrub floors and pots all day. Pity her, yes, but not rally to her."

Eyes blazing, Moiraine leaned her fists on the table. "Look at me, Siuan. Look at me! Are you saying that you want to give up, after all these years, after all we have done? Give up, and let the world go? And all for fear of a switching for not getting the pots clean enough!" She put into it all the scorn she could summon, and was relieved when her friend spun to face her. The strength was still there, strained but still there. Those clear blue eyes were as hot with anger as her own.

"I remember which of the two of us squealed the loudest when we were switched as novices. You had lived a soft life in Cairhien, Moiraine. Not like working a fishing boat." Abruptly Siuan slapped the table with a loud crack. "No, I am not suggesting giving up, but neither do I propose to watch everything slide out of our hands *while I can do nothing!* Most of my troubles with the Hall stem from you. Even the Greens wonder why I haven't called you to the Tower and taught you a little discipline. Half the sisters with me think you should be handed over to the Reds, and if that happens, you will wish you were a novice again, with nothing worse to look forward to than a switching. Light! If any of them remember we were friends as novices, I'd be there beside you.

"We had a plan! A plan, Moiraine! Locate the boy and bring

him to Tar Valon, where we could hide him, keep him safe and guide him. Since you left the Tower, I have had only two messages from you. Two! I feel as if I'm trying to sail the Fingers of the Dragon in the dark. One message to say you were entering the Two Rivers, going to this village, this Emond's Field. Soon, I thought. He's found, and she'll have him in hand soon. Then word from Caemlyn to say you were coming to Shienar, to Fal Dara, not Tar Valon. Fal Dara, with the Blight almost close enough to touch. Fal Dara, where Trollocs raid and Myrddraal ride as near every day as makes no difference. Nearly twenty years of planning and searching, and you toss all our plans practically in the Dark One's face. Are you mad?"

Now that she had stirred life in the other woman, Moiraine returned to outward calm, herself. Calm, but firm insistence, too. "The Pattern pays no heed to human plans, Siuan. With all our scheming, we forgot what we were dealing with. *Ta'veren.* Elaida is wrong. Artur Paendrag Tanreall was never this strongly *ta'-veren.* The Wheel will weave the Pattern around this young man as *it* wills, whatever our plans."

The anger left Amyrlin's face, replaced by white-faced shock. "It sounds as if *you* are saying we might as well give up. Do *you* now suggest standing aside and watching the world burn?"

"No, Siuan. Never standing aside." *Yet the world will burn, Siuan, one way or another, whatever we do. You could never see that.* "But we must now realize that our plans are precarious things. We have even less control than we thought. Perhaps only a fingernail's grip. The winds of destiny are blowing, Siuan, and we must ride them where they take us."

The Amyrlin shivered as if she felt those winds icy on the back of her neck. Her hands went to the flattened cube of gold, blunt, capable fingers finding precise points in the complex designs. Cunningly balanced, the top lifted back to reveal a curled, golden horn nestled within a space designed to hold it. She lifted the instrument and traced the flowing silver script, in the Old Tongue, inlaid around the flaring mouth.

" 'The grave is no bar to my call,' " she translated, so softly she seemed to be speaking to herself. "The Horn of Valere, made to call dead heroes back from the grave. And prophecy said it would only be found just in time for the Last Battle." Abruptly she thrust the Horn back into its niche and closed the lid as if she could no longer bear the sight of it. "Agelmar pushed it into my hands as soon as the Welcome was done. He said he was afraid to go into his own strongroom any longer, with it there. The temptation was too great, he said. To sound the Horn himself and lead the host that answered its call north through the Blight to level Shayol Ghul itself and put an end to the Dark One. He burned with the ecstasy of glory, and it was that, he said, that told him it was not to be him, must not be him. He could not wait to be rid of it, yet he wanted it still."

Moiraine nodded. Agelmar was familiar with the Prophecy of the Horn; most who fought the Dark One were. " 'Let whosoever sounds me think not of glory, but only of salvation.' "

"Salvation." The Amyrlin laughed bitterly. "From the look in Agelmar's eyes, he didn't know whether he was giving away salvation or rejecting the condemnation of his own soul. He only knew he had to be rid of it before it burned him up. He has tried to keep it secret, but he says there are rumors in the keep already. I do not feel his temptation, yet the Horn still makes my skin crawl. He will have to take it back into his strongroom until I leave. I could not sleep with it even in the next room." She rubbed frown lines from her forehead and sighed. "And it was not to be found until just before the Last Battle. Can it be that close? I thought, hoped, we would have more time."

"The Karaethon Cycle."

"Yes, Moiraine. You do not have to remind me. I've lived with the Prophecies of the Dragon as long as you." The Amyrlin shook her head. "Never more than one false Dragon in a generation since the Breaking, and now three loose in the world at one time, and three more in the past two years. The Pattern demands a Dragon because the Pattern weaves toward Tarmon Gai'don. Sometimes doubt fills me, Moiraine." She said it musingly, as if wondering at it, and went on in the same tone. "What if Logain was the one? He could channel, before the Reds brought him to the White Tower, and we gentled him. So can Mazrim Taim, the man in Saldaea. What if it is him? There are sisters in Saldaea already; he may be taken by now. What if we have been wrong since the start? What happens if the Dragon Reborn is gentled before the Last Battle even begins? Even prophecy can fail if the one prophesied is slain or gentled. And then we face the Dark One naked to the storm."

"Neither of them is the one, Siuan. The Pattern does not demand *a* Dragon, but the one true Dragon. Until he proclaims himself, the Pattern will continue to throw up false Dragons, but after that there will be no others. If Logain or the other were the one, there would be no others."

" 'For he shall come like the breaking dawn, and shatter the world again with his coming, and make it anew.' Either we go naked in the storm, or cling to a protection that will scourge us. The Light help us all." The Amyrlin shook herself as if to throw off her own words. Her face was set, as though bracing for a blow. "You could never hide what you were thinking from me as you do from everyone else, Moiraine. You have more to tell me, and nothing good."

For answer Moiraine took the leather pouch from her belt and upended it, spilling the contents on the table. It appeared to be only a heap of fragmented pottery, shiny black and white.

The Amyrlin Seat touched one bit curiously, and her breath caught. *"Cuendillar."*

"Heartstone," Moiraine agreed. The making of *cuendillar* had been lost at the Breaking of the World, but what had been made of heartstone had survived the cataclysm. Even those objects swallowed by the earth or sunk in the sea had survived; they must have. No known force could break *cuendillar* once it was complete; even the One Power directed against heartstone only made it stronger. Except that some power *had* broken this.

The Amyrlin hastily assembled the pieces. What they formed was a disk the size of a man's hand, half blacker than pitch and half whiter than snow, the colors meeting along a sinuous line, unfaded by age. The ancient symbol of Aes Sedai, before the world was broken, when men and women wielded the Power together. Half of it was now called the Flame of Tar Valon; the other half was scrawled on doors, the Dragon's Fang, to accuse those within of evil. Only seven like it had been made; everything ever made of heartstone was recorded in the White Tower, and those seven were remembered above all. Siuan Sanche stared at it as she would have at a viper on her pillow.

"One of the seals on the Dark One's prison," she said finally, reluctantly. It was those seven seals over which the Amyrlin Seat was supposed to be Watcher. The secret hidden from the world, if the world ever thought of it, was that no Amyrlin Seat had known where any of the seals were since the Trolloc Wars.

"We know the Dark One is stirring, Siuan. We know his prison cannot stay sealed forever. Human work can never match the Creator's. We know he has touched the world again, even if, thank the Light, only indirectly. Darkfriends multiply, and what we called evil but ten years ago seems almost caprice compared with what now is done every day."

"If the seals are already breaking. . . . We may have no time at all."

"Little enough. But that little may be enough. It will have to be."

The Amyrlin touched the fractured seal, and her voice grew

tight, as if she were forcing herself to speak. "I saw the boy, you know, in the courtyard during the Welcome. It is one of my Talents, seeing *ta'veren.* A rare Talent these days, even more rare than *ta'veren,* and certainly not of much use. A tall boy, a fairly handsome young man. Not much different from any young man you might see in any town." She paused to draw breath. "Moiraine, he blazed like the sun. I've seldom been afraid in my life, but the sight of him made me afraid right down to my toes. I wanted to cower, to howl. I could barely speak. Agelmar thought I was angry with him, I said so little. That young man . . . he's the one we have sought these twenty years."

There was a hint of question in her voice. Moiraine answered it. "He is."

"Are you certain? Can he . . .? Can he . . . channel the One Power?"

Her mouth strained around the words, and Moiraine felt the tension, too, a twisting inside, a cold clutching at her heart. She kept her face smooth, though. "He can." A man wielding the One Power. That was a thing no Aes Sedai could contemplate without fear. It was a thing the whole world feared. *And I will loose it on the world.* "Rand al'Thor will stand before the world as the Dragon Reborn."

The Amyrlin shuddered. "Rand al'Thor. It does not sound like a name to inspire fear and set the world on fire." She gave another shiver and rubbed her arms briskly, but her eyes suddenly shone with a purposeful light. "If he is the one, then we truly may have time enough. But is he safe here? I have two Red sisters with me, and I can no longer answer for Green or Yellow, either. The Light consume me, I can't answer for any of them, not with this. Even Verin and Serafelle would leap on him the way they would a scarlet adder in a nursery."

"He is safe, for the moment."

The Amyrlin waited for her to say more. The silence stretched, until it was plain she would not. Finally the Amyrlin said, "You say our old plan is useless. What do you suggest now?"

"I have purposely let him think I no longer have any interest in him, that he may go where he pleases for all of me." She raised her hands as the Amyrlin opened her mouth. "It was necessary, Siuan. Rand al'Thor was raised in the Two Rivers, where Manetheren's stubborn blood flows in every vein, and his own blood is like rock beside clay compared to Manetheren's. He must be handled gently, or he will bolt in any direction but the one we want."

"Then we'll handle him like a newborn babe. We'll wrap him in swaddling clothes and play with his toes, if that's what you think we need. But to what immediate purpose?"

"His two friends, Matrim Cauthon and Perrin Aybara, are ripe to see the world before they sink back into the obscurity of the Two Rivers. If they can sink back; they are *ta'veren,* too, if lesser than he. I will induce them to carry the Horn of Valere to Illian." She hesitated, frowning. "There is . . . a problem with Mat. He carries a dagger from Shadar Logoth."

"Shadar Logoth! Light, why did you ever let them get near that place? Every stone of it is tainted. There isn't a pebble safe to carry away. Light help us, if Mordeth touched the boy. . . ." The Amyrlin sounded as though she were strangling. "If that happened, the world would be doomed."

"But it did not, Siuan. We do what we must from necessity, and it was necessary. I have done enough so that Mat will not infect others, but he had the dagger too long before I knew. The link is still there. I had thought I must take him to Tar Valon to cure it, but with so many sisters present, it might be done here. So long as there are a few you can trust not to see Darkfriends where there are none. You and I and two others will suffice, using my *angreal.*"

"Leane will do for one, and I can find another." Suddenly the

Amyrlin Seat gave a wry grin. "The Hall wants that *angreal* back, Moiraine. There are not very many of them left, and you are now considered . . . unreliable."

Moiraine smiled, but it did not touch her eyes. "They will think worse of me before I am done. Mat will leap at the chance to be so big a part of the legend of the Horn, and Perrin should not be hard to convince. He needs something to take his mind off his own troubles. Rand knows what he is—some of it, at least; a little— and he is afraid of it, naturally. He wants to go off somewhere alone, where he cannot hurt anyone. He says he will never wield the Power again, but he fears not being able to stop it."

"As well he might. Easier to give up drinking water."

"Exactly. And he wants to be free from Aes Sedai." Moiraine gave a small, mirthless smile. "Offered the chance to leave Aes Sedai behind and still stay with his friends a while longer, he should be as eager as Mat."

"But how is he leaving Aes Sedai behind? Surely you must travel with him. We can't lose him now, Moiraine."

"I cannot travel with him." *It is a long way from Fal Dara to Illian, but he has traveled almost as far already.* "He must be let off the leash for a time. There is no help for it. I have had all of their old clothes burned. There has been too much opportunity for some shred of what they were wearing to have fallen into the wrong hands. I will cleanse them before they leave; they will not even realize it has been done. There will be no chance they can be tracked that way, and the only other threat of that kind is locked away here in the dungeon." The Amyrlin, midway in nodding approval, gave her a questioning look, but she did not pause. "They will travel as safely as I can manage, Siuan. And when Rand needs me in Illian, I will be there, and I will see that it is he who presents the Horn to the Council of Nine and the Assemblage. I will see to everything in Illian. Siuan, the Illianers would follow the Dragon, or Ba'alzamon himself, if he came bearing the

Horn of Valere, and so will the greater part of those gathered for the Hunt. The true Dragon Reborn will not need to gather a following before nations move against him. He will begin with a nation around him and an army at his back."

The Amyrlin dropped back into her chair, but immediately leaned forward. She seemed caught between weariness and hope. "But *will* he proclaim himself? If he's afraid. . . . The Light knows he should be, Moiraine, but men who name themselves as the Dragon *want* the power. If he does not. . . ."

"I have the means to see him named Dragon whether he wills it or not. And even if I somehow fail, the Pattern itself will see him named Dragon whether he wills it or not. Remember, he is *ta'veren*, Siuan. He has no more control over his fate than a candle wick has over the flame."

The Amyrlin sighed. "It's risky, Moiraine. Risky. But my father used to say, 'Girl, if you won't take a chance, you'll never win a copper.' We have plans to make. Sit down; this won't be done quickly. I will send for wine and cheese."

Moiraine shook her head. "We have been closeted alone too long already. If any did try listening and found your Warding, they will be wondering already. It is not worth the risk. We can contrive another meeting tomorrow." *Besides, my dearest friend, I cannot tell you everything, and I cannot risk letting you know I am holding anything back.*

"I suppose you are right. But first thing in the morning. There's so much I have to know."

"The morning," Moiraine agreed. The Amyrlin rose, and they hugged again. "In the morning I will tell you everything you need to know."

Leane gave Moiraine a sharp look when she came out into the anteroom, then darted into the Amyrlin's chamber. Moiraine tried to put on a chastened face, as if she had endured one of the Amyrlin's infamous upbraidings—most women, however strong-willed, returned from those bigeyed and weak-kneed—but the expression was foreign to her. She looked more angry than anything else, which served much the same purpose. She was only vaguely aware of the other women in the outer room; she thought some had gone and others come since she went in, but she barely looked at them. The hour was growing late, and there was much to be done before the morning came. Much, before she spoke to the Amyrlin Seat again.

Quickening her step, she moved deeper into the keep.

THE COLUMN WOULD have made an impressive sight under the waxing moon, moving through the Tarabon night to the jangle of harness, had there been anyone to see it. A full two thousand Children of the Light, well mounted, in white tabards and cloaks, armor burnished, with their train of supply wagons, and farriers, and grooms with the strings of remounts. There were villages in this sparsely forested country, but they had left roads behind, and stayed clear of even farmers' crofts. They were to meet . . . someone . . . at a flyspeck village near the northern border of Tarabon, at the edge of Almoth Plain.

Geofram Bornhald, riding at the head of his men, wondered what it was all about. He remembered too well his interview with Pedron Niall, Lord Captain Commander of the Children of the Light, in Amador, but he had learned little there.

"We are alone, Geofram," the white-haired man had said. His voice was thin and reedy with age. "I remember giving you the oath . . . what . . . thirty-six years ago, it must be, now."

Bornhald straightened. "My Lord Captain Commander, may I ask why I was called back from Caemlyn, and with such urgency? A push, and Morgase could be toppled. There are Houses in Andor that see dealing with Tar Valon as we do, and they were ready to lay claim to the throne. I left Eamon Valda in charge, but he seemed intent on following the Daughter-Heir to Tar Valon.

I would not be surprised to learn the man has kidnapped the girl, or even attacked Tar Valon." And Dain, Bornhald's son, had arrived just before Bornhald was recalled. Dain was full of zeal. Too much zeal, sometimes. Enough to fall in blindly with whatever Valda proposed.

"Valda walks in the Light, Geofram. But you are the best battle commander among the Children. You will assemble a full legion, the best men you can find, and take them into Tarabon, avoiding any eyes attached to a tongue that may speak. Any such tongue must be silenced, if the eyes see."

Bornhald hesitated. Fifty Children together, or even a hundred, could enter any land without question, at least without open question, but an entire legion. . . . "Is it war, my Lord Captain Commander? There is talk in the streets. Wild rumors, mainly, about Artur Hawkwing's armies come back." The old man did not speak. "The King. . . ."

"Does not command the Children, Lord Captain Bornhald." For the first time there was a snap in the Lord Captain Commander's voice. "I do. Let the King sit in his palace and do what he does best. Nothing. You will be met at a village called Alcruna, and there you will receive your final orders. I expect your legion to ride in three days. Now go, Geofram. You have work to do."

Bornhald frowned. "Pardon, my Lord Captain Commander, but who will meet me? Why am I risking war with Tarabon?"

"You will be told what you must know when you reach Alcruna." The Lord Captain Commander suddenly looked more than his age. Absently he plucked at his white tunic, with the golden sunburst of the Children large on the chest. "There are forces at work beyond what you know, Geofram. Beyond what even you can know. Choose your men quickly. Now go. Ask me no more. And the Light ride with you."

Now Bornhald straightened in his saddle, working a knot out of his back. *I am getting old,* he thought. A day and a night in the saddle, with two pauses to water the horses, and he felt every gray hair on his head. He would not even have noticed a few years ago. *At least I have not killed any innocents.* He could be as hard on Darkfriends as any man sworn to the Light—Darkfriends must be destroyed before they pulled the whole world under the Shadow—but he wanted to be sure they *were* Darkfriends first. It had been difficult avoiding Taraboner eyes with so many men, even in the backcountry, but he had managed it. No tongues had needed to be silenced.

The scouts he had sent out came riding back, and behind them came more men in white cloaks, some carrying torches to ruin the night vision of everyone at the head of the column. With a muttered curse, Bornhald ordered a halt while he studied those who came to meet him.

Their cloaks bore the same golden sunburst on the breast as his, the same as every Child of the Light, and their leader even had golden knots of rank below it equivalent to Bornhald's. But behind their sunbursts were red shepherd's crooks. Questioners. With hot irons and pinchers and dripping water the Questioners pulled confession and repentance from Darkfriends, but there were those who said they decided guilt before ever they began. Geofram Bornhald was one who said it.

I have been sent here to meet Questioners?

"We have been waiting for you, Lord Captain Bornhald," the leader said in a harsh voice. He was a tall, hook-nosed man with the gleam of certainty in his eyes that every Questioner had. "You could have made better time. I am Einor Saren, second to Jaichim Carridin, who commands the Hand of the Light in Tarabon." The Hand of the Light—the Hand that dug out truth, so they said. They did not like the name Questioners. "There is a bridge at the village. Have your men move across. We will talk in the inn. It is surprisingly comfortable."

"I was told by the Lord Captain Commander himself to avoid all eyes."

"The village has been . . . pacified. Now move your men. *I* command, now. I have orders with the Lord Captain Commander's seal, if you doubt."

Bornhald suppressed the growl that rose in his throat. Pacified. He wondered if the bodies had been piled outside the village, or if they had been thrown into the river. It would be like the Questioners, cold enough to kill an entire village for secrecy and stupid enough to throw the bodies into the river to float downstream and trumpet their deed from Alcruna to Tanchico. "What I doubt is why I am in Tarabon with two thousand men, Questioner."

Saren's face tightened, but his voice remained harsh and demanding. "It is simple, Lord Captain. There are towns and villages across Almoth Plain with none in authority above a mayor or a Town Council. It is past time they were brought to the Light. There will be many Darkfriends in such places."

Bornhald's horse stamped. "Are you saying, Saren, that I've brought an entire legion across most of Tarabon in secrecy to root a few Darkfriends out of some grubby villages?"

"You are here to do as you are told, Bornhald. To do the work of the Light! Or are you sliding from the Light?" Saren's smile was a grimace. "If battle is what you seek, you may have your chance. The strangers have a great force on Toman Head, more than Tarabon and Arad Doman together may be able to hold, even if they can stop their own bickering long enough to work together. If the strangers break through, you will have all the fighting you can handle. The Taraboners claim the strangers are monsters, creatures of the Dark One. Some say they have Aes Sedai to fight for them. If they *are* Darkfriends, these strangers, they will have to be dealt with, too. In their turn."

For a moment, Bornhald stopped breathing. "Then the rumors are true. Artur Hawkwing's armies have returned."

"Strangers," Saren said flatly. He sounded as if he regretted having mentioned them. "Strangers, and probably Darkfriends, from wherever they came. That is all we know, and all you need to know. They do not concern you now. We are wasting time. Move your men across the river, Bornhald. I will give you your orders in the village." He whirled his horse and galloped back the way he had come, his torch-bearers riding at his heels.

Bornhald closed his eyes to hasten the return of his night sight. *We are being used like stones on a board.* "Byar!" He opened his eyes as his second appeared at his side, stiffening in his saddle before the Lord Captain. The gaunt-faced man had almost the Questioner's light in his eyes, but he was a good soldier despite. "There is a bridge ahead. Move the legion across the river and make camp. I will join you as soon as I can."

He gathered his reins and rode in the direction the Questioner had taken. *Stones on a board. But who is moving us? And why?*

AFTERNOON SHADOWS GAVE way to evening as Liandrin made her way through the women's apartments. Beyond the arrowslits, darkness grew and pressed on the light from the lamps in the corridor. Twilight was a troubled time for Liandrin of late, that and dawn. At dawn the day was born, just as twilight gave birth to night, but at dawn, night died, and at twilight, day. The Dark One's power was rooted in death; he gained power from death, and at those times she thought she could feel his power stirring. Something stirred in the half dark, at least. Something she almost thought she could catch if she turned quickly enough, something she was sure she could see if she looked hard enough.

Serving women in black-and-gold curtsied as she passed, but she did not respond. She kept her eyes fixed straight ahead, and did not see them.

At the door she sought, she paused for a quick glance up and down the hall. The only women in sight were servants; there were

no men, of course. She pushed open the door and went in without
knocking.

The outer room of the Lady Amalisa's chambers was brightly
lit, and a blazing fire on the hearth held back the chill of the Shienaran night. Amalisa and her ladies sat about the room, in chairs and
on the layered carpets, listening while one of their number, standing, read aloud to them. It was *The Dance of the Hawk and the
Hummingbird,* by Teven Aerwin, which purported to set forth the
proper conduct of men toward women and women toward men.
Liandrin's mouth tightened; she certainly had not read it, but she
had heard as much as she needed about it. Amalisa and her ladies
greeted each pronouncement with gales of laughter, falling against
each other and drumming their heels on the carpets like girls.

The reader was the first to become aware of Liandrin's presence. She cut off with a surprised widening of her eyes. The others turned to see what she was staring at, and silence replaced
laughter. All but Amalisa scrambled to their feet, hastily smooth-
ing hair and skirts.

The Lady Amalisa rose gracefully, with a smile. "You honor us
with your presence, Liandrin. This is a most pleasant surprise. I
did not expect you until tomorrow. I thought you would want to
rest after your long jour—"

Liandrin cut her off sharply, addressing the air. "I will speak to
the Lady Amalisa alone. All of you will leave. Now."

There was a moment of shocked silence, then the other women
made their goodbyes to Amalisa. One by one they curtsied to
Liandrin, but she did not acknowledge them. She continued to
stare straight ahead at nothing, but she saw them, and heard. Hon-
orifics offered with breathy unease at the Aes Sedai's mood. Eyes
falling when she ignored them. They squeezed past her to the
door, pressing back awkwardly so their skirts did not disturb hers.

As the door closed behind the last of them, Amalisa said,
"Liandrin, I do not underst—"

"Do you walk in the Light, my daughter?" There would be none of that foolishness of calling her sister here. The other woman was older by some years, but the ancient forms would be observed. However long they had been forgotten, it was time they were remembered.

As soon as the question was out of her mouth, though, Liandrin realized she had made a mistake. It was a question guaranteed to cause doubt and anxiety, coming from an Aes Sedai, but Amalisa's back stiffened, and her face hardened.

"That is an insult, Liandrin Sedai. I am Shienaran, of a noble House and the blood of soldiers. My line has fought the Shadow since before there *was* a Shienar, three thousand years without fail or a day's weakness."

Liandrin shifted her point of attack, but she did not retreat. Striding across the room, she took the leather-bound copy of *The Dance of the Hawk and the Hummingbird* from the mantelpiece and hefted it without looking at it. "In Shienar above other lands, my daughter, the Light must be precious, and the Shadow feared." Casually she threw the book into the fire. Flames leaped as if it were a log of fatwood, thundering as they licked up the chimney. In the same instant every lamp in the room flared, hissing, so fiercely did they burn, flooding the chamber with light. "Here above all. Here, so close to the cursed Blight, where corruption waits. Here, even one who thinks he walks in the Light may still be corrupted by the Shadow."

Beads of sweat glistened on Amalisa's forehead. The hand she had raised in protest for her book fell slowly to her side. Her features still held firm, but Liandrin saw her swallow, and her feet shift. "I do not understand, Liandrin Sedai. Is it the book? It is only foolishness."

There was a faint quaver in her voice. *Good.* Glass lamp mantles cracked as the flames leaped higher and hotter, lighting the room as bright as unsheltered noon. Amalisa stood as stiff as a post, her face tight as she tried not to squint.

"It is you who are foolish, my daughter. I care nothing for books. Here, men enter the Blight, and walk in its taint. In the very Shadow. Why wonder you that that taint may seep into them? Whether or not against their will, still it may seep. Why think you the Amyrlin Seat herself has come?"

"No." It was a gasp.

"Of the Red am I, my daughter," Liandrin said relentlessly. "I hunt all men corrupted."

"I don't understand."

"Not only those foul ones who try the One Power. All men corrupted. High and low do I hunt."

"I don't. . . ." Amalisa licked her lips unsteadily and made a visible effort to gather herself. "I do not understand, Liandrin Sedai. Please. . . ."

"High even before low."

"No!" As if some invisible support had vanished, Amalisa fell to her knees, and her head dropped. "Please, Liandrin Sedai, say you do not mean Agelmar. It cannot be him."

In that moment of doubt and confusion, Liandrin struck. She did not move, but lashed out with the One Power. Amalisa gasped and gave a jerk, as if she had been pricked with a needle, and Liandrin's petulant mouth perked in a smile.

This was her own special trick from childhood, the first learned of her abilities. It had been forbidden to her as soon as the Mistress of Novices discovered it, but to Liandrin that only meant one more thing she needed to conceal from those who were jealous of her.

She strode forward and pulled Amalisa's chin up. The metal that had stiffened her was still there, but it was baser metal now, malleable to the right pressures. Tears trickled from the corners of Amalisa's eyes, glistening on her cheeks. Liandrin let the fires die back to normal; there was no longer any need for such. She softened her words, but her voice was as unyielding as steel.

"Daughter, no one wants to see you and Agelmar thrown to the people as Darkfriends. I will help you, but you must help."

"H-help you?" Amalisa put her hands to her temples; she looked confused. "Please, Liandrin Sedai, I don't . . . understand. It is all so. . . . It's all. . . ."

It was not a perfect ability; Liandrin could not force anyone to do what she wanted—though she had tried; oh, how she had tried. But she could open them wide to her arguments, make them want to believe her, want more than anything to be convinced of her rightness.

"Obey, daughter. Obey, and answer my questions truthfully, and I promise that no one will speak of you and Agelmar as Darkfriends. You will not be dragged naked through the streets, to be flogged from the city if the people do not tear you to pieces first. I will not let this happen. You understand?"

"Yes, Liandrin Sedai, yes. I will do as you say and answer you truly."

Liandrin straightened, looking down at the other woman. The Lady Amalisa stayed as she was, kneeling, her face as open as a child's, a child waiting to be comforted and helped by someone wiser and stronger. There was a rightness about it to Liandrin. She had never understood why a simple bow or curtsy was sufficient for Aes Sedai when men and women knelt to kings and queens. *What queen has within her my power?* Her mouth twisted angrily, and Amalisa shivered.

"Be easy in yourself, my daughter. I have come to help you, not to punish. Only those who deserve it will be punished. Truth only, speak to me."

"I will, Liandrin Sedai. I will, I swear it by my House and honor."

"Moiraine came to Fal Dara with a Darkfriend."

Amalisa was too frightened to show surprise. "Oh, no, Liandrin Sedai. No. That man came later. He is in the dungeons now."

"Later, you say. But it is true that she speaks often with him? She is often in company with this Darkfriend? Alone?"

"S-sometimes, Liandrin Sedai. Only sometimes. She wishes to find out why he came here. Moiraine Sedai is—" Liandrin held up her hand sharply, and Amalisa swallowed whatever else she had been going to say.

"By three young men Moiraine was accompanied. This I *know*. Where are they? I have been to their rooms, and they are not to be found."

"I—I do not know, Liandrin Sedai. They seem nice boys. Surely you don't think they are Darkfriends."

"Not Darkfriends, no. Worse. By far more dangerous than Darkfriends, my daughter. The entire world is in danger from them. They must be found. You will command your servants to search the keep, and your ladies, and yourself. Every crack and cranny. To this, you will see personally. Personally! And to no one will you speak of it, save those I name. None else may know. None. From Fal Dara in secrecy these young men must be removed, and to Tar Valon taken. In utter secrecy."

"As you command, Liandrin Sedai. But I do not understand the need for secrecy. No one here will hinder Aes Sedai."

"Of the Black Ajah you have heard?"

Amalisa's eyes bulged, and she leaned back away from Liandrin, raising her hands as though to shield herself from a blow. "A v-vile rumor, Liandrin Sedai. V-vile. There are n-no Aes Sedai who s-serve the Dark One. I do not believe it. You must believe me! Under the Light, I s-swear I do not believe it. By my honor and my House, I swear. . . ."

Coolly Liandrin let her go on, watching the last remaining strength leach out of the other woman with her own silence. Aes Sedai had been known to become angry, very angry, with those who even mentioned the Black Ajah much less those who said they believed in its hidden existence. After this, with her will already weakened by that little childhood trick, Amalisa would be as clay in her hands. After one more blow.

"The Black Ajah is *real,* child. Real, and here within Fal Dara's walls." Amalisa knelt there, her mouth hanging open. The Black Ajah. Aes Sedai who were also Darkfriends. Almost as horrible to learn the Dark One himself walked Fal Dara keep. But Liandrin would not let up now. "Any Aes Sedai in the halls you pass, a Black sister could be. This I swear. I cannot tell you which they are, but my protection you can have. If in the Light you walk and me obey."

"I will," Amalisa whispered hoarsely. "I will. Please, Liandrin Sedai, please say you will protect my brother, and my ladies. . . ."

"Who deserves protection I will protect. Concern yourself with yourself, my daughter. And think only of what I have commanded of you. Only that. The fate of the world rides on this, my daughter. All else you must forget."

"Yes, Liandrin Sedai. Yes. Yes."

Liandrin turned and crossed the room, not looking back until she reached the door. Amalisa was still on her knees, still watching her anxiously. "Rise, my Lady Amalisa." Liandrin made her voice pleasant, with only a hint of the mocking she felt. *Sister, indeed! Not one day as a novice would she last. And power to command she* has. "Rise." Amalisa straightened in slow, stiff jerks, as if she had been bound hand and foot for hours. As she finally came upright, Liandrin said, the steel back in full strength, "And if you fail the world, if you fail me, that wretched Darkfriend in the dungeon will be your envy."

From the look on Amalisa's face, Liandrin did not think failure would come from any lack of effort on her part.

Pulling the door shut behind her, Liandrin suddenly felt a prickling across her skin. Breath catching, she whirled about, looking up and down the dimly lit hall. Empty. It was full night beyond the arrowslits. The hall was empty, yet she was sure there had been eyes on her. The vacant corridor, shadowy between the lamps on the walls, mocked her. She shrugged uneasily, then started down the hall determinedly. *Fancies take me. Nothing more.*

Full night already, and there was much to do before dawn. Her orders had been explicit.

Pɪᴛᴄʜ-ʙʟᴀᴄᴋɴᴇss ᴄᴏᴠᴇʀᴇᴅ ᴛʜᴇ dungeons whatever the hour, unless someone brought in a lantern, but Padan Fain sat on the edge of his cot, staring into the dark with a smile on his face. He could hear the other two prisoners grumbling in their sleep, muttering in nightmares. Padan Fain was waiting for something, something he had been awaiting for a long time. For too long. But not much longer.

The door to the outer guardroom opened, spilling in a flood of light, darkly outlining a figure in the doorway.

Fain stood. "You! Not who I expected." He stretched with a casualness he did not feel. Blood raced through his veins; he thought he could leap over the keep if he tried. "Surprises for everyone, eh? Well, come on. The night's getting old, and I want some sleep sometime."

As a lamp came into the cell chamber, Fain raised his head, grinning at something, unseen yet felt, beyond the dungeon's stone ceiling. "It isn't over yet," he whispered. "The battle's never over."

CHAPTER 6

Dark Prophecy

THE FARMHOUSE DOOR SHOOK UNDER FURIOUS blows from outside; the heavy bar across the door jumped in its brackets. Beyond the window next to the door moved the heavy-muzzled silhouette of a Trolloc. There were windows everywhere, and more shadowy shapes outside. Not shadowy enough, though. Rand could still make them out.

The windows, he thought desperately. He backed away from the door, clutching his sword before him in both hands. *Even if the door holds, they can break in the windows. Why aren't they trying the windows?*

With a deafening metallic screech, one of the brackets pulled partly away from the doorframe, hanging loose on nails ripped a finger's width out of the wood. The bar quivered from another blow, and the nails squealed again.

"We have to stop them!" Rand shouted. *Only we can't. We*

can't stop them. He looked around for a way to run, but there was only the one door. The room was a box. Only one door, and so many windows. "We have to do something. Something!"

"It's too late," Mat said. "Don't you understand?" His grin looked odd on a bloodless pale face, and the hilt of a dagger stood out from his chest, the ruby that capped it blazing as if it held fire. The gem had more life than his face. "It's too late for us to change anything."

"I've finally gotten rid of them," Perrin said, laughing. Blood streamed down his face like a flood of tears from his empty sockets. He held out red hands, trying to make Rand look at what he held. "I'm free, now. It's over."

"It's never over, al'Thor," Padan Fain cried, capering in the middle of the floor. "The battle's never done."

The door exploded in splinters, and Rand ducked away from the flying shards of wood. Two red-clad Aes Sedai stepped through, bowing their master in. A mask the color of dried blood covered Ba'alzamon's face, but Rand could see the flames of his eyes through the eyeslits; he could hear the roaring fires of Ba'alzamon's mouth.

"It is not yet done between us, al'Thor," Ba'alzamon said, and he and Fain spoke together as one, "For you, the battle is never done."

With a strangled gasp Rand sat up on the floor, clawing his way awake. It seemed he could still hear Fain's voice, as sharp as if the peddler were standing beside him. *It's never over. The battle's never done.*

Bleary-eyed, he looked around to convince himself that he was still hidden away where Egwene had left him, bedded down on a pallet in a corner of her room. The dim light of a single lamp suffused the room, and he was surprised to see Nynaeve, knitting in a rocking chair on the other side of the lone bed, its covers still in place. It was night outside.

Dark-eyed and slender, Nynaeve wore her hair in a fat braid, pulled over one shoulder and hanging almost to her waist. She had not given up on home. Her face was calm, and she seemed aware of nothing except her knitting as she rocked gently. The steady *click-click* of her knitting needles was the only sound. The rug silenced the rocking chair.

There had been nights of late when he had wished for a carpet on the cold stone floor of his room, but in Shienar men's rooms were always bare and stark. The walls here had two tapestries, mountain scenes with waterfalls, and flower-embroidered curtains alongside the arrowslits. Cut flowers, white morningstars, stood in a flat, round vase on the table by the bed, and more nodded in glazed white sconces on the walls. A tall mirror stood in a corner, and another hung over the washstand, with its blue-striped pitcher and bowl. He wondered why Egwene needed two mirrors; there was none in his room, and he did not miss it. There was only one lamp lit, but four more stood around the room, which was nearly as large as the one he shared with Mat and Perrin. Egwene had it alone.

Without looking up, Nynaeve said, "If you sleep in the afternoon, you can't expect to sleep at night."

He frowned, though she could not see it. At least, he thought she could not. She was only a few years older than he, but being Wisdom added fifty years of authority. "I needed a place to hide, and I was tired," he said, then quickly added, "I didn't just come here. Egwene invited me into the women's apartments."

Nynaeve lowered her knitting and gave him an amused smile. She was a pretty woman. That was something he would never have noticed back home; one just did not think of a Wisdom that way. "The Light help me, Rand, you are becoming more Shienaran every day. Invited into the women's apartments, indeed." She sniffed. "Any day now, you'll start talking about your honor, and asking peace to favor your sword." He colored, and hoped she did not notice in the dim light. She eyed his sword, its hilt sticking out of the long bundle beside him on the floor. He knew she did not approve of the sword, of any sword, but she said nothing about it for once. "Egwene told me why you need a place to hide. Don't worry. We will keep you hidden from the Amyrlin, or from any other Aes Sedai, if that is what you want."

She met his eyes and jerked hers away, but not before he saw her uneasiness. Her doubt. *That's right, I can channel the Power. A man wielding the One Power! You ought to be helping the Aes Sedai hunt me down and gentle me.*

Scowling, he straightened the leather jerkin Egwene had found for him and twisted around so he could lean back against the wall. "As soon as I can, I will hide in a cart, or sneak out. You won't have to hide me long." Nynaeve did not say anything; she fixed on her knitting, making an angry sound when she dropped a stitch. "Where is Egwene?"

She let the knitting fall onto her lap. "I don't know why I am even trying tonight. I can't keep track of my stitches for some reason. She has gone down to see Padan Fain. She thinks seeing faces he knows might help him."

"Mine certainly did not. She ought to stay away from him. He's dangerous."

"She wants to help him," Nynaeve said calmly. "Remember, she was training to be my assistant, and being a Wisdom is not all predicting the weather. Healing is part of it, too. Egwene has the desire to heal, the need to. And if Padan Fain is so dangerous, Moiraine would have said something."

He barked a laugh. "You didn't ask her. Egwene admitted it, and I can just see you asking permission for anything." Her raised eyebrow wiped the laugh off his face. He refused to apologize, though. They were a long way from home, and he did not see how she could go on being Wisdom of Emond's Field if she was going to Tar Valon. "Have they started to search for me, yet? Egwene is not sure they will, but Lan says the Amyrlin Seat is here because of me, and I think I'll take his opinion over hers."

For a moment Nynaeve did not answer. Instead she fussed with her skeins of yarn. Finally she said, "I am not sure. One of the serving women came a little while ago. To turn down the bed, she said. As if Egwene would be going to sleep already, with the feast for the Amyrlin tonight. I sent her away; she didn't see you."

"Nobody turns your bed down for you in the men's quarters." She gave him a level look, one that would have set him stammering a year ago. He shook his head. "They wouldn't use the maids to look for me, Nynaeve."

"When I went to the buttery for a cup of milk earlier, there were too many women in the halls. Those who are attending the feast should have been getting dressed, and the others should either have been helping them or getting ready to serve, or to. . . ." She frowned worriedly. "There's more than enough work for everybody with the Amyrlin here. And they were not just here in the women's apartments. I saw the Lady Amalisa herself coming out of a storeroom near the buttery with her face all over dust."

"That's ridiculous. Why would she be part of a search? Or any of the women, for that matter. They'd be using Lord Agelmar's soldiers, and the Warders. And the Aes Sedai. They must just be doing something for the feast. Burn me if I know what a Shien-aran feast takes."

"You are a woolhead, sometimes, Rand. The men I saw didn't know what the women were doing either. I heard some of them complaining about having to do all the work by themselves. I know it makes no sense that they were looking for you. None of the Aes Sedai seemed to be taking any interest. But Amalisa was not readying herself for the feast by dirtying her dress in a store-room. They were looking for something, something important. Even if she began right after I saw her, she would barely have time to bathe and change. Speaking of which, if Egwene doesn't come back soon, she'll have to choose between changing and being late."

For the first time, he realized that Nynaeve was not wearing the Two Rivers woolens he was used to. Her dress was pale blue silk, embroidered in snowdrop blossoms around the neck and down the sleeves. Each blossom centered on a small pearl, and her belt was tooled in silver, with a silver buckle set with pearls. He had never seen her in anything like that. Even feastday clothes back home might not match it.

"You're going to the feast?"

"Of course. Even if Moiraine had not said I should, I would never let her think I was. . . ." Her eyes lit up fiercely for a moment, and he knew what she meant. Nynaeve would never let anyone think she was afraid, even if she was. Certainly not Moiraine, and especially not Lan. He hoped she did not know he was aware of her feelings for the Warder.

After a moment her gaze softened as it fell on the sleeve of her dress. "The Lady Amalisa gave me this," she said so softly he wondered if she was speaking to herself. She stroked the silk with her fingers, outlining the embroidered flowers, smiling, lost in thought.

"It's very pretty on you, Nynaeve. You're pretty tonight." He winced as soon as he said it. Any Wisdom was touchy about her authority, but Nynaeve was touchier than most. The Women's Circle back home had always looked over her shoulder because she was young, and maybe because she was pretty, and her fights with the Mayor and the Village Council had been the stuff of stories.

She jerked her hand away from the embroidery and glared at him, brows lowering. He spoke quickly to forestall her.

"They can't keep the gates barred forever. Once they are opened, I will be gone, and the Aes Sedai will never find me. Perrin says there are places in the Black Hills and the Caralain Grass you can go for days without seeing a soul. Maybe—maybe I can figure out what to do about. . . ." He shrugged uncomfortably.

There was no need to say it, not to her. "And if I can't, there'll be no one to hurt."

Nynaeve was silent for a moment, then she said slowly, "I am not so sure, Rand. I can't say you look like more than another village boy to me, but Moiraine insists you are *ta'veren,* and I don't think she believes the Wheel is finished with you. The Dark One seems—"

"Shai'tan is dead," he said harshly, and abruptly the room seemed to lurch. He grabbed his head as waves of dizziness sloshed through him.

"You fool! You pure, blind, idiotic fool! Naming the Dark One, bringing his attention down on you! Don't you have enough trouble?"

"He's dead," Rand muttered, rubbing his head. He swallowed. The dizziness was already fading. "All right, all right. Ba'alzamon, if you want. But he's dead; I saw him die, saw him burn."

"And I wasn't watching you when the Dark One's eye fell on you just now? Don't tell me you felt nothing, or I'll box your ears; I saw your face."

"He's dead," Rand insisted. The unseen watcher flashed through his head, and the wind on the tower top. He shivered. "Strange things happen this close to the Blight."

"You *are* a fool, Rand al'Thor." She shook a fist at him. "I *would* box your ears for you if I thought it would knock any sense—"

The rest of her words were swallowed as bells crashed out ringing all over the keep.

He bounded to his feet. "That's an alarm! They're searching. . . ." *Name the Dark One, and his evil comes down on you.*

Nynaeve stood more slowly, shaking her head uneasily. "No, I don't think so. If they are searching for you, all the bells do is warn you. No, if it's an alarm, it is not for you."

"Then what?" He hurried to the nearest arrowslit and peered out.

Lights darted through the night-cloaked keep like fireflies, lamps and torches dashing here and there. Some went to the outer walls and towers, but most of those that he could see milled through the garden below and the one courtyard he could just glimpse part of. Whatever had caused the alarm was inside the keep. The bells fell silent, unmasking the shouts of men, but he could not make out what they were calling.

If it isn't for me. . . . "Egwene," he said suddenly. *If he's still alive, if there's any evil, it's supposed to come to me.*

Nynaeve turned from looking through another arrowslit. "What?"

"Egwene." He crossed the room in quick strides and snatched his sword and scabbard free of the bundle. *Light, it's supposed to hurt me, not her.* "She's in the dungeon with Fain. What if he's loose somehow?"

She caught him at the door, grabbing his arm. She was not as tall as his shoulder, but she held on like iron. "Don't be a worse goat-brained fool than you've already been, Rand al'Thor. Even if this doesn't have anything to do with you, the women are looking for something! Light, man, this is the women's apartments. There will be Aes Sedai out there in the halls, likely as not. Egwene will be all right. She was going to take Mat and Perrin with her. Even if she met trouble, they would look after her."

"What if she couldn't find them, Nynaeve? Egwene would never let that stop her. She would go alone, the same as you, and you know it. Light, I told her Fain is dangerous! Burn me, I told her!" Pulling free, he jerked open the door and dashed out. *Light burn me, it's supposed to hurt me!*

A woman screamed at the sight of him, in a laborer's coarse shirt and jerkin with a sword in his hand. Even invited, men did not go armed in the women's apartments unless the keep was under attack. Women filled the corridor, serving women in the black-and-gold, ladies of the keep in silks and laces, women in embroidered shawls with long fringes, all talking loudly at the same time, all demanding to know what was happening. Crying children clung to skirts everywhere. He plunged through them, dodging where he could, muttering apologies to those he shouldered aside, trying to ignore their startled stares.

One of the women in a shawl turned to go back into her room, and he saw the back of her shawl, saw the gleaming white teardrop in the middle of her back. Suddenly he recognized faces he had seen in the outer courtyard. Aes Sedai, staring at him in alarm, now.

"Who are you? What are you doing here?"

"Is the keep under attack? Answer me, man!"

"He's no soldier. Who is he? What's happening?"

"It's the young southland lord!"

"Someone stop him!"

Fear pushed his lips back, baring his teeth, but he kept moving, and tried to move faster.

Then a woman came out into the hall, face-to-face with him, and he stopped in spite of himself. He recognized that face above the rest; he thought he would remember it if he lived forever. The Amyrlin Seat. Her eyes widened at the sight of him, and she started back. Another Aes Sedai, the tall woman he had seen with the staff, put herself between him and the Amyrlin, shouting something at him that he could not make out over the increasing babble.

She knows. Light help me, she knows. Moiraine told her. Snarling, he ran on. *Light, just let me make sure Egwene's safe before they. . . .* He heard shouting behind him, but he did not listen.

There was enough turmoil around him out in the keep. Men running for the courtyards with swords in hand, never looking at him. Over the clamor of alarm bells, he could make out other noises, now. Shouts. Screams. Metal ringing on metal. He had just time to realize they were the sounds of battle—*Fighting? Inside*

Fal Dara?—when three Trollocs came dashing around a corner in front of him.

Hairy snouts distorted otherwise human faces, and one of them had ram's horns. They bared teeth, raising scythe-like swords as they sped toward him.

The hallway that had been full of running men a moment before was empty now except for the three Trollocs and himself. Caught by surprise, he unsheathed his sword awkwardly, tried Hummingbird Kisses the Honeyrose. Shaken at finding Trollocs in the heart of Fal Dara keep, he did the form so badly Lan would have stalked off in disgust. A bear-snouted Trolloc evaded it easily, bumping the other two off stride for just an instant.

Suddenly there were a dozen Shienarans rushing past him at the Trollocs, men half dressed in finery for the feast, but swords at the ready. The bear-snouted Trolloc snarled as it died, and its companions ran, pursued by shouting men waving steel. Shouts and screams filled the air from everywhere.

Egwene!

Rand turned deeper into the keep, running down halls empty of life, though now and again a dead Trolloc lay on the floor. Or a dead man.

Then he came to a crossing of corridors, and to his left was the tail end of a fight. Six top-knotted men lay bleeding and still, and a seventh was dying. The Myrddraal gave its sword an extra twist as it pulled the blade free of the man's belly, and the soldier screamed as he dropped his sword and fell. The Fade moved with viperous grace, the serpent illusion heightened by the armor of black, overlapping plates that covered its chest. It turned, and that pale, eyeless face studied Rand. It started toward him, smiling a bloodless smile, not hurrying. It had no need to hurry for one man alone.

He felt rooted where he stood; his tongue stuck to the roof of his mouth. The look of the Eyeless is fear. That was what they said along the Border. His hands shook as he raised his sword. He never even thought of assuming the void. *Light, it just killed seven armed soldiers together. Light, what am I going to do. Light!*

Abruptly the Myrddraal stopped, its smile gone.

"This one is mine, Rand." Rand gave a start as Ingtar stepped up beside him, dark and stocky in a yellow feastday coat, sword held in both hands. Ingtar's dark eyes never left the Fade's face; if the Shienaran felt the fear of that gaze, he gave no sign. "Try yourself on a Trolloc or two," he said softly, "before you face one of these."

"I was coming down to see if Egwene is safe. She was going to the dungeon to visit Fain, and—"

"Then go see to her."

Rand swallowed. "We'll take it together, Ingtar."

"You aren't ready for this. Go see to your girl. Go! You want Trollocs to find her unprotected?"

For a moment Rand hung there, undecided. The Fade had raised its sword, for Ingtar. A silent snarl twisted Ingtar's mouth, but Rand knew it was not fear. And Egwene could be alone in the dungeon with Fain, or worse. Still he felt ashamed as he ran for the stairs that led underground. He knew a Fade's look could make any man afraid, but Ingtar had conquered the dread. His stomach still felt knotted.

The corridors beneath the keep were silent, and feebly lit by flickering, far-spaced lamps on the walls. He slowed as he came closer to the dungeons, creeping as silently as he could on his toes. The grate of his boots on the bare stone seemed to fill his ears. The door to the dungeons stood cracked open a handbreadth. It should have been closed and bolted.

Staring at the door, he tried to swallow and could not. He opened his mouth to call out, then shut it again quickly. If Egwene was in there and in trouble, shouting would only warn whoever was endangering her. Or whatever. Taking a deep breath, he set himself.

In one motion he pushed the door wide open with the scabbard in his left hand and threw himself into the dungeon, tucking his shoulder under to roll through the straw covering the floor and come to his feet, spinning this way and that too quickly to get a clear picture of the room, looking desperately for anyone who might attack him, looking for Egwene. There was no one there.

His eyes fell on the table, and he stopped dead, breath and even thought freezing. On either side of the still-burning lamp, as if to make a centerpiece, sat the heads of the guards in two pools of blood. Their eyes stared at him, wide with fear, and their mouths gaped in a last scream no one could hear. Rand gagged and doubled over; his stomach heaved again and again as he vomited into the straw. Finally he managed to pull himself erect, scrubbing his mouth with his sleeve; his throat felt scraped raw.

Slowly he became aware of the rest of the room, only half seen and not taken in during his hasty search for an attacker. Bloody

lumps of flesh lay scattered through the straw. There was nothing
he could recognize as human except the two heads. Some of the
pieces looked chewed. *So that's what happened to the rest of their
bodies.* He was surprised at the calmness of his thoughts, almost
as if he had achieved the void without trying. It was the shock, he
knew vaguely.

He did not recognize either of the heads; the guards had been
changed since he was there earlier. He was glad for that. Knowing
who they were, even Changu, would have made it worse. Blood
covered the walls, too, but in scrawled letters, single words and
whole sentences splashed on every which way. Some were harsh
and angular, in a language he did not know, though he recognized
Trolloc script. Others he could read, and wished he could not.
Blasphemics and obscenities bad enough to make a stablehand or
a merchant's guard go pale.

"Egwene." Calmness vanished. Shoving his scabbard through
his belt, he snatched the lamp from the table, hardly noticing
when the heads toppled over. "Egwene! Where are you?"

He started toward the inner door, took two steps, and stopped,
staring. The words on the door, dark and glistening wetly in the
light of his lamp, were plain enough.

WE WILL MEET AGAIN ON TOMAN HEAD.
IT IS NEVER OVER, AL'THOR.

His sword dropped from a hand suddenly numb. Never taking
his eyes off the door, he bent to pick it up. Instead he grabbed a
handful of straw and began scrubbing furiously at the words on
the door. Panting, he scrubbed until it was all one bloody smear,
but he could not stop.

"What do you do?"

At the sharp voice behind him, he whirled, stooping to seize his
sword.

A woman stood in the outer doorway, back stiff with outrage. Her hair was like pale gold, in a dozen or more braids, but her eyes were dark, and sharp on his face. She looked not much older than he, and pretty in a sulky way, but there was a tightness to her mouth he did not like. Then he saw the shawl she had wrapped tightly around her, with its long, red fringe.

Aes Sedai. And Light help me, she's Red Ajah. "I. . . . I was just. . . . It's filthy stuff. Vile."

"Everything must be left exactly as it is for us to examine. Touch nothing." She took a step forward, peering at him, and he took one back. "Yes. Yes, as I thought. One of those with Moiraine. What do you have to do with this?" Her gesture took in the heads on the table and the bloody scrawl on the walls.

For a minute he goggled at her. "Me? Nothing! I came down here to find. . . . Egwene!"

He turned to open the inner door, and the Aes Sedai shouted, "No! You will answer me!"

Suddenly it was all he could do to stand up, to keep holding the lamp and his sword. Icy cold squeezed at him from all sides. His head felt caught in a frozen vise; he could barely breathe for the pressure on his chest.

"Answer me, boy. Tell me your name."

Involuntarily he grunted, trying to answer against the chill that seemed to be pressing his face back into his skull, constricting his chest like frozen iron bands. He clenched his jaws to keep the sound in. Painfully he rolled his eyes to glare at her through a blur of tears. *The Light burn you, Aes Sedai! I won't say a word, the Shadow take you!*

"Answer me, boy! Now!"

Frozen needles pierced his brain with agony, grated into his bones. The void formed inside him before he even realized he had thought of it, but it could not hold out the pain. Dimly he sensed light and warmth somewhere in the distance. It flickered queasily, but the light was warm, and he was cold. Distant beyond knowing, but somehow just within reach. *Light, so cold. I have to reach . . . what? She's killing me. I have to reach it, or she'll kill me.* Desperately he stretched toward the light.

"What is going on here?"

Abruptly the cold and the pressure and the needles vanished. His knees sagged, but he forced them stiff. He would not fall to his knees; he would not give her the satisfaction. The void was gone, too, as suddenly as it had come. *She* was *trying to kill me.* Panting, he raised his head. Moiraine stood in the doorway.

"I asked what is going on here, Liandrin," she said.

"I found this boy here," the Red Aes Sedai replied calmly. "The guards are murdered, and here he is. One of yours. And what are you doing here, Moiraine? The battle is above, not here."

"I could ask the same of you, Liandrin." Moiraine looked around the room with only a slight tightening of her mouth for the charnel. "Why *are* you here?"

Rand turned away from them, awkwardly shoved back the bolts on the inner door and pulled it open. "Egwene came down here," he announced for anyone who cared, and went in, holding his lamp high. His knees kept wanting to give way; he was not sure how he stayed on his feet, only that he had to find Egwene. "Egwene!"

A hollow gurgle and a thrashing sound came from his right, and he thrust the lamp that way. The prisoner in the fancy coat was sagging against the iron grille of his cell, his belt looped around the bars and then around his neck. As Rand looked, he gave one last kick, scraping across the straw-covered floor, and was still, tongue and eyes bulging out of a face gone almost black. His knees almost touched the floor; he could have stood anytime he wanted to.

Shivering, Rand peered into the next cell. The big man with the sunken knuckles huddled in the back of his cell, eyes as wide as they could open. At the sight of Rand, he screamed and twisted around, clawing frantically at the stone wall.

"I won't hurt you," Rand called. The man kept on screaming and digging. His hands were bloody, and his scrabblings streaked across dark, conjealed smears. This was not his first attempt to dig through the stone with his bare hands.

Rand turned away, relieved that his stomach was already empty. But there was nothing he could do for either of them. "Egwene!"

His light finally reached the end of the cells. The door to Fain's cell stood open, and the cell was empty, but it was the two shapes on the stone in front of the cell that made Rand leap forward and drop to his knees between them.

Egwene and Mat lay sprawled bonelessly, unconscious . . . or dead. With a flood of relief he saw their chests rise and fall. There did not seem to be a mark on either of them.

"Egwene? Mat?" Setting the sword down, he shook Egwene gently. "Egwene?" She did not open her eyes. "Moiraine! Egwene's hurt! And Mat!" Mat's breathing sounded labored, and his face was deathly pale. Rand felt almost like crying. *It was supposed to hurt me. I named the Dark One. Me!*

"Do not move them." Moiraine did not sound upset, or even surprised.

The chamber was suddenly flooded with light as the two Aes Sedai entered. Each balanced a glowing ball of cool light, floating in the air above her hand.

Liandrin marched straight down the middle of the wide hall, holding her skirts up out of the straw with her free hand, but Moiraine paused to look at the two prisoners before following. "There is nothing to do for the one," she said, "and the other can wait."

Liandrin reached Rand first and began to bend toward Egwene, but Moiraine darted in ahead of her and laid her free hand on Egwene's head. Liandrin straightened with a grimace.

"She is not badly hurt," Moiraine said after a moment. "She was struck here." She traced an area on the side of Egwene's head, covered by her hair; Rand could see nothing different about it. "That is the only injury she has taken. She will be all right."

Rand looked from one Aes Sedai to the other. "What about Mat?" Liandrin arched an eyebrow at him and turned to watch Moiraine with a wry expression.

"Be quiet," Moiraine said. Fingers still lying on the area where she said Egwene had been hit, she closed her eyes. Egwene murmured and stirred, then lay still.

"Is she . . .?"

"She is sleeping, Rand. She will be well, but she must sleep." Moiraine shifted to Mat, but here she only touched him for a moment before drawing back. "This is more serious," she said softly. She fumbled at Mat's waist, pulling his coat open, and made an angry sound. "The dagger is gone."

"What dagger?" Liandrin asked.

Voices suddenly came from the outer room, men exclaiming in disgust and anger.

"In here," Moiraine called. "Bring two litters. Quickly." Someone in the outer room raised a cry for litters.

"Fain is gone," Rand said.

The two Aes Sedai looked at him. He could read nothing on their faces. Their eyes glittered in the light.

"So I see," Moiraine said in a flat voice.

"I told her not to come. I told her he was dangerous."

"When I came," Liandrin said in a cold voice, "he was destroying the writing in the outer chamber."

He shifted uneasily on his knees. The Aes Sedai's eyes seemed alike, now. Measuring and weighing him, cool and terrible.

"It—it was filth," he said. "Just filth." They still looked at him, not speaking. "You don't think I. . . . Moiraine, you can't think I had anything to do with—with what happened out there." *Light, did I? I named the Dark One.*

She did not answer, and he felt a chill that was not lessened by men rushing in with torches and lamps. Moiraine and Liandrin let their glowing balls wink out. The lamps and torches did not give as much light; shadows sprang up in the depths of the cells. Men with litters hurried to the figures lying on the floor. Ingtar led them. His topknot almost quivered with anger, and he looked eager to find something on which to use his sword.

"So the Darkfriend is gone, too," he growled. "Well, it's the least of what has happened this night."

"The least even here," Moiraine said sharply. She directed the men putting Egwene and Mat on the litters. "The girl is to be taken to her room. She needs a woman to watch in case she wakes in the night. She may be frightened, but more than anything else she needs sleep, now. The boy. . . ." She touched Mat as two men lifted his litter, and pulled her hand back quickly. "Take him to the Amyrlin Seat's chambers. Find the Amyrlin wherever she is, and tell her he is there. Tell her his name is Matrim Cauthon. I will join her as soon as I am able."

"The Amyrlin!" Liandrin exclaimed. "You think to have the Amyrlin as Healer for your—your pet? You are mad, Moiraine."

"The Amyrlin Seat," Moiraine said calmly, "does not share your Red Ajah prejudices, Liandrin. She will Heal a man without need of a special use for him. Go ahead," she told the litter bearers.

Liandrin watched them leave, Moiraine and the men carrying Mat and Egwene, then turned to stare at Rand. He tried to ignore her. He concentrated on scabbarding his sword and brushing off the straw that clung to his shirt and breeches. When he raised his head, though, she was still studying him, her face as blank as ice. Saying nothing, she turned to consider the other men thoughtfully. One held the body of the hanged man up while another worked to unfasten the belt. Ingtar and the others waited respectfully. With a last glance at Rand, she left, head held like a queen.

"A hard woman," Ingtar muttered, then seemed surprised that he had spoken. "What happened here, Rand al'Thor?"

Rand shook his head. "I don't know, except that Fain escaped somehow. And hurt Egwene and Mat doing it. I saw the guardroom"—he shuddered—"but in here. . . . Whatever it was, Ingtar, it scared that fellow bad enough that he hung himself. I think the other one's gone mad from seeing it."

"We are all going mad tonight."

"The Fade . . . you killed it?"

"No!" Ingtar slammed his sword into its sheath; the hilt stuck up above his right shoulder. He seemed angry and ashamed at the same time. "It's out of the keep by now, along with the rest of what we could not kill."

"At least you're alive, Ingtar. That Fade killed seven men!"

"Alive? Is that so important?" Suddenly Ingtar's face was no longer angry, but tired and full of pain. "We had it in our hands. In our hands! And we lost it, Rand. Lost it!" He sounded as if he could not believe what he was saying.

"Lost what?" Rand asked.

"The Horn! The Horn of Valere. It's gone, chest and all."

"But it was in the strongroom."

"The strongroom was looted," Ingtar said wearily. "They did not take much, except for the Horn. What they could stuff in their pockets. I wish they had taken everything else and left that. Ronan is dead, and the watchmen he had guarding the strongroom." His voice became quiet. "When I was a boy, Ronan held Jehaan Tower with twenty men against a thousand Trollocs. He did not go down easily, though. The old man had blood on his dagger. No man can ask more than that." He was silent for a moment. "They came in through the Dog Gate, and left the same way. We put an end to fifty or more, but too many escaped. Trollocs! We've never before had Trollocs inside the keep. Never!"

"How could they get in through the Dog Gate, Ingtar? One man could stop a hundred there. And all the gates were barred." He shifted uneasily, remembering why. "The guards would not have opened it to let anybody in."

"Their throats were cut," Ingtar said. "Both good men, and yet they were butchered like pigs. It was done from inside. Someone killed them, then opened the gate. Someone who could get close to them without suspicion. Someone they knew."

Rand looked at the empty cell where Padan Fain had been. "But that means. . . ."

"Yes. There are Darkfriends inside Fal Dara. Or were. We will soon know if that's the case. Kajin is checking now to see if anyone is missing. Peace! Treachery in Fal Dara keep!" Scowling, he looked around the dungeon, at the men waiting for him. They all had swords, worn over feastday clothes, and some had helmets. "We aren't doing any good here. Out! Everyone!" Rand joined the withdrawal. Ingtar tapped Rand's jerkin. "What is this? Have you decided to become a stableman?"

"It's a long story," Rand said. "Too long to tell here. Maybe some other time." *Maybe never, if I'm lucky. Maybe I can escape in all this confusion. No, I can't. Not until I know Egwene's all right. And Mat. Light, what will happen to him without the dagger?* "I suppose Lord Agelmar's doubled the guard on all the gates."

"Tripled," Ingtar said in tones of satisfaction. "No one will pass those gates, from inside or out. As soon as Lord Agelmar heard what had happened, he ordered that no one was to be allowed to leave the keep without his personal permission."

As soon as he heard . . . ? "Ingtar, what about before? What about the earlier order keeping everyone in?"

"Earlier order? What earlier order? Rand, the keep was not closed until Lord Agelmar heard of this. Someone told you wrong."

Rand shook his head slowly. Neither Ragan nor Tema would have made up something like that. And even if the Amyrlin Seat had given the order, Ingtar would have to know of it. *So who? And how?* He glanced sideways at Ingtar, wondering if the Shienaran was lying. *You really* are *going mad if you suspect Ingtar.*

They were in the dungeon guardroom, now. The severed heads and the pieces of the guards had been removed, though there were still red smears on the table and damp patches in the straw to show where they had been. Two Aes Sedai were there, placid-looking women with brown-fringed shawls, studying the words scrawled on the walls, careless of what their skirts dragged through in the straw. Each had an inkpot in a writing-case hung at her belt and was making notes in a small book with a pen. They never even glanced at the men trooping through.

"Look here, Verin," one of them said, pointing to a section of stone covered with lines of Trolloc script. "This looks interesting."

The other hurried over, picking up reddish stains on her skirt. "Yes, I see. A much better hand than the rest. Not a Trolloc. Very interesting." She began writing in her book, looking up every so often to read the angular letters on the wall.

Rand hurried out. Even if they had not been Aes Sedai, he would not have wanted to remain in the same room with anyone who thought reading Trolloc script written in human blood was "interesting."

Ingtar and his men stalked on ahead, intent on their duties. Rand dawdled, wondering where he could go now. Getting back into the women's apartments would not be easy without Egwene to help. *Light, let her be all right. Moiraine* said *she'd be all right.*

Lan found him before he reached the first stairs leading up. "You can go back to your room, if you want, sheepherder. Moiraine had your things fetched from Egwene's room and taken to yours."

"How did she know . . .?"

"Moiraine knows a great many things, sheepherder. You should understand that by now. You had better watch yourself. The women are all talking about you running through the halls, waving a sword. Staring down the Amyrlin, so they say."

"Light! I am sorry they're angry, Lan, but I *was* invited in. And when I heard the alarm . . . burn me, Egwene was down here!"

Lan pursed his lips thoughtfully; it was the only expression on his face. "Oh, they're not angry, exactly. Though most of them think you need a strong hand to settle you down some. Fascinated is more like it. Even the Lady Amalisa can't stop asking questions about you. Some of them are starting to believe the servants' tales. They think you're a prince in disguise, sheepherder. Not a bad thing. There is an old saying here in the Borderlands: 'Better to have one woman on your side than ten men.' The way they are talking among themselves, they're trying to decide whose daughter is strong enough to handle you. If you don't watch your step, sheepherder, you will find yourself married into a Shienaran House before you realize what has happened." Suddenly he burst out laughing; it looked odd, like a rock laughing. "Running through the halls of the women's apartments in the middle of the night, wearing a laborer's jerkin and waving a sword. If they don't have you flogged, at the very least they'll talk about you for years. They have never seen a male as peculiar as you. Whatever wife they chose for you, she'd probably have you the head of your own House in ten years, and have you thinking you had done it yourself, besides. It is too bad you have to leave."

Rand had been gaping at the Warder, but now he growled, "I have been trying. The gates are guarded, and no one can leave. I tried while it was still daylight. I couldn't even take Red out of the stable."

"No matter, now. Moiraine sent me to tell you. You can leave anytime you want to. Even right now. Moiraine had Agelmar exempt you from the order."

"Why now, and not earlier? Why couldn't I leave before? Was

she the one who had the gates barred then? Ingtar said he knew
nothing about any order to keep people in before tonight."

Rand thought the Warder looked troubled, but all he said was,
"When someone gives you a horse, sheepherder, don't complain
that it isn't as fast as you'd like."

"What about Egwene? And Mat? Are they really all right? I
can't leave until I know they're all right."

"The girl is fine. She'll wake in the morning, and probably not
even remember what happened. Blows to the head are like that."

"What about Mat?"

"The choice is up to you, sheepherder. You can leave now, or
tomorrow, or next week. It's up to you." He walked away, leaving
Rand standing there in the corridor deep under Fal Dara keep.

CHAPTER 7

Blood Calls Blood

As the litter carrying Mat left the Amyr-lin Seat's chambers, Moiraine carefully rewrapped the *angreal*—a small, age-darkened ivory carving of a woman in flowing robes—in a square of silk and put it back into her pouch. Working together with other Aes Sedai, merging their abilities, channeling the flow of the One Power to a single task, was tiring work under the best conditions, even with the aid of an *angreal,* and working through the night without sleep was not the best conditions. And the work they had done on the boy had not been easy.

Leane directed the litter bearers out with sharp gestures and a few crisp words. The two men kept ducking their heads, nervous at being around so many Aes Sedai at once, and one of them the Amyrlin herself, never mind that the Aes Sedai had been using the Power. They had waited in the corridor, squatting against the wall while the work was done, and they were anxious to be gone from the women's apartments. Mat lay with his eyes closed and his face pale, but his chest rose and fell in the even rhythm of a deep sleep.

How will this affect matters? Moiraine wondered. *He is not necessary with the Horn gone, and yet. . . .*

The door closed behind Leane and the litter bearers, and the Amyrlin drew an unsteady breath. "A nasty business that. Nasty." Her face was smooth, but she rubbed her hands together as if she wanted to wash them.

"But quite interesting," Verin said. She had been the fourth Aes Sedai the Amyrlin had chosen for the work. "It is too bad we do not have the dagger so the Healing could be complete. For all we did tonight, he will not live long. Months, perhaps, at best." The three Aes Sedai were alone in the Amyrlin's chambers. Beyond the arrowslits dawn pearled the sky.

"But he will have those months, now," Moiraine said sharply. "And if it can be retrieved, the link can still be broken." *If it can be retrieved. Yes, of course.*

"It can still be broken," Verin agreed. She was a plump, square-faced woman, and even with the Aes Sedai gift of agelessness, there was a touch of gray in her brown hair. That was her only sign of age, but for an Aes Sedai it meant she was very old indeed. Her voice held steady, though, matching her smooth cheeks. "He has been linked to the dagger a long time, however, as a thing like that must be reckoned. And he will be linked longer yet, whether it is found or not. He may already be changed beyond the reach of full Healing, even if no longer enough to contaminate others. Such a small thing, that dagger," she mused, "but it will corrupt whoever carries it long enough. He who carries it will in turn corrupt those who come in contact with him, and they will corrupt still others, and the hatred and suspicion that destroyed Shadar Logoth, every man and woman's hand turned against every other, will be loose in the world again. I wonder how many people it can taint in, say, a year. It should be possible to calculate a reasonable approximation."

Moiraine gave the Brown sister a wry look. *Another danger confronts us, and she sounds as if it is a puzzle in a book. Light, the Browns truly are* not *aware of the world at all.* "Then we must find the dagger, Sister. Agelmar is sending men to hunt those who took the Horn and slew his oath-men, the same who took the dagger. If one is found, the other will be."

Verin nodded, but frowned at the same time. "Yet, even if it is found, who can return it safely? Whoever touches it risks the taint if they handle it long. Perhaps in a chest, well wrapped and padded, but it would still be dangerous to those nearby for any great time. Without the dagger itself to study, we cannot be sure how much it must be shielded. But you saw it and more, Moiraine. You dealt with it, enough for that young man to survive carrying it and to stop him infecting others. You must have a good idea of how strong its influence is."

"There is one," Moiraine said, "who can retrieve the dagger without being harmed by it. One whom we have shielded and buffered against that taint as much as anyone can be. Mat Cauthon."

The Amyrlin nodded. "Yes, of course. He can do it. If he lives long enough. The Light only knows how far it will be carried before Agelmar's men find it. If they do find it. And if the boy dies first . . . well, if the dagger is loose that long, we have another worry." She rubbed her eyes tiredly. "I think we must find this Padan Fain, too. Why is this Darkfriend important enough for them to risk what they did to rescue him? Much easier for them just to steal the Horn. Still risky as a winter gale in the Sea of Storms, coming into the very keep like that, but they compounded their risk to free this Darkfriend. If the Lurks think he is that important"—she paused, and Moiraine knew she was wondering if it truly was still only the Myrddraal giving commands—"then so must we."

"He must be found," Moiraine agreed, hoping that none of the urgency she felt showed, "but it is likely he will be found with the Horn."

"As you say, Daughter." The Amyrlin pressed fingers to her lips to stifle a yawn. "And now, Verin, if you will excuse me, I will just say a few words to Moiraine and then sleep a little. I suppose Agelmar will insist on feasting tonight since last night was spoiled. Your help was invaluable, Daughter. Please remember, say nothing of the nature of the boy's hurt to anyone. There are some of your sisters who would see the Shadow in him instead of a thing men made on their own."

There was no need to name the Red Ajah. And perhaps, Moiraine thought, the Reds were no longer the only ones of whom it was necessary to be wary.

"I will say nothing, of course, Mother." Verin bowed, but made no move toward the door. "I thought you might wish to see this, Mother." She pulled a small notebook, bound in soft, brown leather, from her belt. "What was written on the walls in the dungeon. There were few problems with translation. Most was the usual—blasphemy and boasting; Trollocs seem to know little else—but there was one part done in a better hand. An educated Darkfriend, or perhaps a Myrddraal. It could be only taunting, yet it has the form of poetry, or song, and the sound of prophecy. We know little of prophecies from the Shadow, Mother."

The Amyrlin hesitated only a moment before nodding. Prophecies from the Shadow, dark prophecies, had an unfortunate way of being fulfilled as well as prophecies from the Light. "Read it to me."

Verin ruffled through the pages, then cleared her throat and began in a calm, level voice.

"Daughter of the Night, she walks again.
The ancient war, she yet fights.

Her new lover she seeks, who shall serve her and die,
    yet serve still.
Who shall stand against her coming?
The Shining Walls shall kneel.
Blood feeds blood.
Blood calls blood.
Blood is, and blood was, and blood shall ever be.

The man who channels stands alone.
He gives his friends for sacrifice.
Two roads before him, one to death beyond dying,
    one to life eternal.
Which will he choose? Which will he choose?
What hand shelters? What hand slays?
Blood feeds blood.
Blood calls blood.
Blood is, and blood was, and blood shall ever be.

Luc came to the Mountains of Dhoom.
Isam waited in the high passes.
The hunt is now begun. The Shadow's hounds now
    course, and kill.
One did live, and one did die, but both are.
The Time of Change has come.
Blood feeds blood.
Blood calls blood.
Blood is, and blood was, and blood shall ever be.

The Watchers wait on Toman's Head.
The seed of the Hammer burns the ancient tree.
Death shall sow, and summer burn, before the Great
    Lord comes.

Death shall reap, and bodies fail, before the Great
   Lord comes.
Again the seed slays ancient wrong, before the Great
   Lord comes.
Now the Great Lord comes.
Now the Great Lord comes.
Blood feeds blood.
Blood calls blood.
Blood is, and blood was, and blood shall ever be.
Now the Great Lord comes."

There was a long silence when she finished.

Finally the Amyrlin said, "Who else has seen this, Daughter? Who knows of it?"

"Only Serafelle, Mother. As soon as we had copied it down, I had men scrub the walls. They didn't question; they were eager to be rid of it."

The Amyrlin nodded. "Good. Too many in the Borderlands can puzzle out Trolloc script. No need to give them something else to worry over. They have enough."

"What do you make of it?" Moiraine asked Verin in a careful voice. "Is it prophecy, do you think?"

Verin tilted her head, peering at her notes in thought. "Possibly. It has the form of some of the few dark prophecies we know. And parts of it are clear enough. It could still be only a taunt, though." She rested a finger on one line. " 'Daughter of the Night, she walks again.' That can only mean Lanfear is loose again. Or someone wants us to think she is."

"That would be something to worry us, Daughter," the Amyrlin Seat said, "if it were true. But the Forsaken are still bound." She glanced at Moiraine, looking troubled for an instant before she schooled her features. "Even if the seals *are* weakening, the Forsaken are still bound."

Lanfear. In the Old Tongue, Daughter of the Night. Nowhere was her real name recorded, but that was the name she had taken for herself, unlike most of the Forsaken, who had been named by those they betrayed. Some said she had really been the most powerful of the Forsaken, next to Ishamael, the Betrayer of Hope, but had kept her powers hidden. Too little was left from that time for any scholar to say for certain.

"With all the false Dragons that are appearing, it is not surprising someone would try to bring Lanfear into it." Moiraine's voice was as unruffled as her face, but inside herself she roiled. Only one thing for certain was known of Lanfear beside the name: before she went over to the Shadow, before Lews Therin Telamon met Ilyena, Lanfear had been his lover. *A complication we do not need.*

The Amyrlin Seat frowned as if she had had the same thought, but Verin nodded as if it were all just words. "Other names are clear, too, Mother. Lord Luc, of course, was brother to Tigraine, then the Daughter-Heir of Andor, and he vanished in the Blight. Who Isam is, or what he has to do with Luc, I do not know, however."

"We will find out what we need to know in time," Moiraine said smoothly. "There is no proof as yet that this is prophecy." She knew the name. Isam had been the son of Breyan, wife of Lain Mandragoran, whose attempt to seize the throne of Malkier for her husband had brought the Trolloc hordes crashing down. Breyan and her infant son had both vanished when the Trollocs overran Malkier. And Isam had been blood kin to Lan. *Or is blood kin? I must keep this from him, until I know how he will react. Until we are away from the Blight. If he thought Isam were alive. . . .*

" 'The Watchers wait on Toman Head,' " Verin went on. "There are a few who still cling to the old belief that the armies Artur Hawkwing sent across the Aryth Ocean will return one day, though after all this time. . . ." She gave a disdainful sniff. "The Do Miere A'vron, the Watchers Over the Waves, still have a . . . community is the best word, I suppose . . . on Toman Head, at

Falme. And one of the old names for Artur Hawkwing was Hammer of the Light."

"Are you suggesting, Daughter," the Amyrlin Seat said, "that Artur Hawkwing's armies, or rather their descendants, might actually return after a thousand years?"

"There are rumors of war on Almoth Plain and Toman Head," Moiraine said slowly. "And Hawkwing sent two of his sons, as well as armies. If they did survive in whatever lands they found, there could well be many descendants of Hawkwing. Or none."

The Amyrlin gave Moiraine a guarded look, obviously wishing they were alone so she could demand to know what Moiraine was up to. Moiraine made a soothing gesture, and her old friend grimaced at her.

Verin, with her nose still buried in her notes, noticed none of it. "I don't know, Mother. I doubt it, though. We know nothing at all of those lands Artur Hawkwing set out to conquer. It's too bad the Sea Folk refuse to cross the Aryth Ocean. They say the Islands of the Dead lie on the other side. I wish I knew what they meant by that, but that accursed Sea Folk closemouthedness. . . ." She sighed, still not raising her head. "All we have is one reference to 'lands under the Shadow, beyond the setting sun, beyond the Aryth Ocean, where the Armies of Night reign.' Nothing there to tell us if the armies Hawkwing sent were enough by themselves to defeat these 'Armies of the Night,' or even to survive Hawkwing's death. Once the War of the Hundred Years started, everyone was too intent on carving out their own part of Hawkwing's empire to spare a thought for his armies across the sea. It seems to me, Mother, that if their descendants still lived, and if they ever intended to return, they would not have waited so long."

"Then you believe it is not prophecy, Daughter?"

"Now, 'the ancient tree,'" Verin said, immersed in her own thoughts. "There have always been rumors—no more than that—that while the nation of Almoth still lived, they had a branch of

Avendesora, perhaps even a living sapling. And the banner of Almoth was 'blue for the sky above, black for the earth below, with the spreading Tree of Life to join them.' Of course, Taraboners call themselves the Tree of Man, and claim to be descended from rulers and nobles in the Age of Legends. And Domani claim descent from those who made the Tree of Life in the Age of Legends. There are other possibilities, but you will note, Mother, that at least three center around Almoth Plain and Toman Head."

The Amyrlin's voice became deceptively gentle. "Will you make up your mind, Daughter? If Artur Hawkwing's seed is *not* returning, then this is not prophecy and it doesn't matter a rotted fish head what ancient tree is meant."

"I can only give you what I know, Mother," Verin said, looking up from her notes, "and leave the decision in your hands. I believe the last of Artur Hawkwing's foreign armies died long ago, but because I believe it does not make it so. The Time of Change, of course, refers to the end of an Age, and the Great Lord—"

The Amyrlin slapped the tabletop like a thunderclap. "I know very well who the Great Lord is, Daughter. I think you had better go now." She took a deep breath, and took hold of herself visibly. "Go, Verin. I do not want to become angry with you. I do not want to forget who it was had the cooks leave sweetcakes out at night when I was a novice."

"Mother," Moiraine said, "there is nothing in this to suggest prophecy. Anyone with a little wit and a little knowledge could put together as much, and no one has ever said Myrddraal do not have a sly wit."

"And of course," Verin said calmly, "the man who channels must be one of the three young men traveling with you, Moiraine."

Moiraine stared in shock. *Not aware of the world? I am a fool.* Before she realized what she was doing, she had reached out to the pulsing glow she always felt there waiting, to the True Source. The One Power surged along her veins, charging her with energy, muting the sheen of Power from the Amyrlin Seat as she did the same. Moiraine had never before even thought of wielding the Power against another Aes Sedai. *We live in perilous times, and the world hangs in the balance, and what must be done, must be done. It must. Oh, Verin, why did you have to put your nose in where it does not belong?*

Verin closed her book and slipped it back behind her belt, then looked from one woman to the other. She could not but be aware of the nimbus surrounding each of them, the light that came from touching the True Source. Only someone trained in channeling herself could see the glow, but there was no chance of any Aes Sedai missing it in another woman.

A hint of satisfaction settled on Verin's face, but no sign that she realized she had hurled a lightning bolt. She only looked as if she had found another piece that fit in a puzzle. "Yes, I thought it must be so. Moiraine could not do this alone, and who better to help than her girlhood friend who used to sneak down with her to snitch sweetcakes." She blinked. "Forgive me, Mother. I should not have said that."

"Verin, Verin." The Amyrlin shook her head wonderingly. "You accuse your sister—and me?—of. . . . I won't even say it. And you are worried that you've spoken too familiarly to the Amyrlin Seat? You bore a hole in the boat and worry that it's raining. Think what you are suggesting, Daughter."

It is too late for that, Siuan, Moiraine thought. *If we had not panicked and reached for the Source, perhaps then. . . . But she is sure, now.* "Why are you telling us this, Verin?" she said aloud. "If you believe what you say, you should be telling it to the other sisters, to the Reds in particular."

Verin's eyes widened in surprise. "Yes. Yes, I suppose I should. I hadn't thought of that. But then, if I did, you would be stilled, Moiraine, and you, Mother, and the man gentled. No one has ever recorded the progression in a man who wields the Power. When does the madness come, exactly, and how does it take him? How quickly does it grow? Can he still function with his body rotting around him? For how long? Unless he is gentled, what will happen to the young man, whichever he is, will happen whether or not I am there to put down the answers. If he is watched and guided, we should be able to keep some record with reasonable safety, for a time, at least. And, too, there is *The Karaethon Cycle.*" She calmly returned their startled looks. "I assume, Mother, that he *is* the Dragon Reborn? I cannot believe you would do this—leave walking free a man who can channel—unless he was the Dragon."

She thinks only of the knowledge, Moiraine thought wonderingly. *The culmination of the direst prophecy the world knows, perhaps the end of the world, and she cares only about the knowledge. But she is still dangerous, for that.*

"Who else knows of this?" The Amyrlin's voice was faint, but still sharp. "Serafelle, I suppose. Who else, Verin?"

"No one, Mother. Serafelle is not really interested in anything that someone hasn't already set down in a book, preferably as long ago as possible. She thinks there are enough old books and manuscripts and fragments scattered about, lost or forgotten, to equal ten times what we have gathered in Tar Valon. She feels certain there is enough of the old knowledge still there to be found for—"

"Enough, Sister," Moiraine said. She loosed her hold on the True Source, and after a moment felt the Amyrlin do the same. It was always a loss to feel the Power draining away, like blood and life pouring from an open wound. A part of her wanted to hold on, but unlike some of her sisters, she made it a point of self-discipline not to grow too fond of the feeling. "Sit down, Verin, and tell us what you know and how you found it out. Leave out nothing."

As Verin took a chair—with a look to the Amyrlin for permission to sit in her presence—Moiraine watched her sadly.

"It is unlikely," Verin began, "that anyone who hasn't studied the old records thoroughly would notice anything except that you were behaving oddly. Forgive me, Mother. It was nearly twenty years ago, with Tar Valon besieged, that I had my first clue, and that was only. . . ."

Light help me, Verin, how I loved you for those sweetcakes, and for your bosom to weep on. But I will do what I must do. I will. I must.

PERRIN PEERED AROUND the corner at the retreating back of the Aes Sedai. She smelled of lavender soap, though most would not have scented it even close up. As soon as she turned out of sight, he hurried for the infirmary door. He had already tried to see Mat once, and that Aes Sedai—Leane, he had heard somebody call her—had nearly snapped his head off without even looking around to see who he was. He felt uneasy around Aes Sedai, especially if they started looking at his eyes.

Pausing at the door to listen—he could hear no footsteps down the corridor either way, and nothing on the other side of the door—he went in and closed it softly behind him.

The infirmary was a long room with white walls, and the entrances to archers' balconies at either end let in lots of light. Mat was in one of the narrow beds that lined the walls. After last night, Perrin had expected most of the beds to have men in them, but in a moment he realized the keep was full of Aes Sedai. The only thing an Aes Sedai could not cure by Healing was death. To him, the room smelled of sickness anyway.

Perrin grimaced when he thought of that. Mat lay still, eyes closed, hands unmoving atop his blankets. He looked exhausted. Not sick really, but as if he had worked three days in the fields and only now laid down to rest. He smelled . . . wrong, though. It was nothing Perrin could put a name to. Just wrong.

Perrin sat down carefully on the bed next to Mat's. He always did things carefully. He was bigger than most people, and had been bigger than the other boys as long as he could remember. He had had to be careful so he would not hurt someone accidentally, or break things. Now it was second nature to him. He liked to think things through, too, and sometimes talk them over with somebody. *With Rand thinking he's a lord, I can't talk to him, and Mat certainly isn't going to have much to say.*

He had gone into one of the gardens the night before, to think things through. The memory still made him a little ashamed. If he had not gone, he would have been in his room to go with Egwene and Mat, and maybe he could have kept them from being hurt. More likely, he knew, he would be in one of these beds, like Mat, or dead, but that did not change the way he felt. Still, he had gone to the garden, and it was nothing to do with the Trolloc attack that was worrying him now.

Serving women had found him sitting there in the dark, and one of the Lady Amalisa's attendants, the Lady Timora. As soon as they came upon him, Timora sent one of the others running, and he had heard her say, "Find Liandrin Sedai! Quickly!"

They had stood there watching him as if they had thought he might vanish in a puff of smoke like a gleeman. That had been when the first alarm bell rang, and everybody in the keep started running.

"Liandrin," he muttered now. "Red Ajah. About all they do is hunt for men who channel. You don't think she believes I'm one of those, do you?" Mat did not answer, of course. Perrin rubbed his nose ruefully. "Now I'm talking to myself. I don't need that on top of everything else."

Mat's eyelids fluttered. "Who . . .? Perrin? What happened?" His eyes did not open all the way, and his voice sounded as if he were still mostly asleep.

"Don't you remember, Mat?"

"Remember?" Mat sleepily raised a hand toward his face, then let it fall again with a sigh. His eyes began to drift shut. "Remember Egwene. Asked me . . . go down . . . see Fain." He laughed, and it turned into a yawn. "She didn't ask. Told me. . . . Don't know what happened after. . . ." He smacked his lips, and resumed the deep, even breathing of sleep.

Perrin leaped to his feet as his ears caught the sound of approaching footsteps, but there was nowhere to go. He was still standing there beside Mat's bed when the door opened and Leane came in. She stopped, put her fists on her hips, and looked him slowly up and down. She was nearly as tall as he was.

"Now you," she said, in tones quiet yet brisk, "are almost a pretty enough boy to make me wish I was a Green. Almost. But if you've disturbed my patient . . . well, I dealt with brothers almost as big as you before I went to the Tower, so you needn't think those shoulders will help you any."

Perrin cleared his throat. Half the time he did not understand what women meant when they said things. *Not like Rand. He always knows what to say to the girls.* He realized he was scowling and wiped it away. He did not want to think about Rand, but he certainly did not want to upset an Aes Sedai, especially one who was beginning to tap her foot impatiently. "Ah . . . I didn't disturb him. He's still sleeping. See?"

"So he is. A good thing for you. Now, what are you doing in here? I remember chasing you out once; you needn't think I don't."

"I only wanted to know how he is."

She hesitated. "He is sleeping is how he is. And in a few hours, he will get out of that bed, and you'll think there was never anything wrong with him."

The pause made his hackles rise. She was lying, somehow. Aes Sedai never lied, but they did not always tell the truth, either. He was not certain what was going on—Liandrin looking for him, Leane lying to him—but he thought it was time he got away from Aes Sedai. There was nothing he could do for Mat.

"Thank you," he said. "I'd better let him sleep, then. Excuse me."

He tried to slide around her to the door, but suddenly her hands shot out and grabbed his face, tilting it down so she could peer into his eyes. Something seemed to pass through him, a warm ripple that started at the top of his head and went to his feet, then came back again. He pulled his head out of her hands.

"You're as healthy as a young wild animal," she said, pursing her lips. "But if you were born with those eyes, I am a Whitecloak."

"They're the only eyes I ever had," he growled. He felt a little abashed, speaking to an Aes Sedai in that tone, but he was as surprised as she when he took her gently by the arms and lifted her to one side, setting her down again out of his way. As they stared at each other, he wondered if his eyes were as wide with shock as hers. "Excuse me," he said again, and all but ran.

My eyes. My Light-cursed eyes! The morning sunlight caught his eyes, and they glinted like burnished gold.

Rand twisted on his bed, trying to find a comfortable position on the thin mattress. Sunlight streamed through the arrowslits, painting the bare stone walls. He had not slept during the remainder of the night, and tired as he was, he was sure he could not sleep now. The leather jerkin lay on the floor between his bed and the wall, but aside from that he was fully dressed, even to his new boots. His sword stood propped beside the bed, and his bow and quiver rested in a corner across the bundled cloaks.

He could not rid himself of the feeling that he should take the chance Moiraine had given him and leave immediately. The urge had been with him all night. Three times he had risen to go. Twice he had gone as far as opening the door. The halls had been empty except for a few servants doing late chores; the way had been clear. But he had to know.

Perrin came in, head down and yawning, and Rand sat up. "How is Egwene? And Mat?"

"She's asleep, so they tell me. They wouldn't let me into the women's apartments to see her. Mat is—" Suddenly Perrin scowled at the floor. "If you're so interested, why haven't you gone to see him yourself? I thought you were not interested in us anymore. You said you weren't." He pulled open his door of the wardrobe and began rummaging for a clean shirt.

"I did go to the infirmary, Perrin. There was an Aes Sedai there, that tall one who's always with the Amyrlin Seat. She said Mat was asleep, and I was in the way, and I could come back some other time. She sounded like Master Thane ordering the men at the mill. You know how Master Thane is, all full of snap and do it right the first time, and do it right now."

Perrin did not answer. He just shucked off his coat and pulled his shirt off over his head.

Rand studied his friend's back for a moment, then dug up a laugh. "You want to hear something? You know what she said to me? The Aes Sedai in the infirmary, I mean. You saw how tall she is. As tall as most men. A hand taller, and she could almost look me in the eyes. Well, she stared me up and down, and then she muttered, 'Tall, aren't you? Where were you when I was sixteen? Or even thirty?' And then she laughed, as if it was all a joke. What do you think of that?"

Perrin finished tugging on a clean shirt and gave him a sidelong look. With his burly shoulders and thick curls, he made Rand think of a hurt bear. A bear that did not understand why had he been hurt.

"Perrin, I'm—"

"If you want to make jokes with Aes Sedai," Perrin broke in, "that's up to you. My Lord." He began stuffing his shirttail into his breeches. "I don't spend much time being—witty; is that the word?—witty with Aes Sedai. But then, I'm only a clumsy blacksmith, and I might be in somebody's way. My Lord." Snatching his coat from the floor, he started for the door.

"Burn me, Perrin, I'm sorry. I was afraid, and I thought I was in trouble—maybe I was; maybe I still am, I don't know—and I didn't want you and Mat to be in it with me. Light, all the women were looking for me last night. I think that's part of the trouble I'm in. I think so. And Liandrin. . . . She. . . ." He threw up his hands. "Perrin, believe me, you don't want any part of this."

Perrin had stopped, but he stood facing the door and only turned his head enough for Rand to see one golden eye. "Looking for you? Maybe they were looking for all of us."

"No, they were looking for me. I wish they hadn't been, but I know better."

Perrin shook his head. "Liandrin wanted me, anyway, I know. I heard."

Rand frowned. "Why would she . . .? It doesn't change anything. Look, I opened my mouth and said what I shouldn't. I did not mean it, Perrin. Now, please, would you tell me about Mat?"

"He's asleep. Leane—that's the Aes Sedai—said he would be on his feet in a few hours." He shrugged uncomfortably. "I think she was lying. I know Aes Sedai never lie, not so you can catch them, but she was lying, or keeping something back." He paused, looking at Rand sideways. "You didn't mean all that? We will leave here together? You, and me, and Mat?"

"I can't, Perrin. I can't tell you why, but I really do have to go by myse—Perrin, wait!"

The door slammed behind his friend.

Rand fell back on the bed. "I can't tell you," he muttered. He pounded his fist on the side of the bed. "I can't." *But you can go now,* a voice said in the back of his head. *Egwene's going to be all right, and Mat will be up and around in an hour or two. You can go now. Before Moiraine changes her mind.*

He started to sit up when a pounding on the door made him leap to his feet. If it was Perrin come back, he would not knock. The pounding came again.

"Who is it?"

Lan strode in, pushing the door to behind him with his boot heel. As usual, he wore his sword over a plain coat of green that was nearly invisible in the woods. This time, though, he had a wide, golden cord tied high around his left arm, the fringed ends hanging almost to his elbow. On the knot was pinned a golden crane in flight, the symbol of Malkier.

"The Amyrlin Seat wants you, sheepherder. You can't go like that. Out of that shirt and brush your hair. You look like a haystack." He jerked open the wardrobe and began pawing through the clothes Rand meant to leave behind.

Rand stood stiff where he was; he felt as though he had been hit in the head with a hammer. He had expected it, of course, in a way, but he had been sure he would be gone before the summons came. *She knows. Light, I'm sure of it.* "What do you mean, she wants me? I'm leaving, Lan. You were right. I am going to the stable right now, get my horse, and leave."

"You should have done that last night." The Warder tossed a white silk shirt onto the bed. "No one refuses an audience with the Amyrlin Seat, sheepherder. Not the Lord Captain Commander of the Whitecloaks himself. Pedron Niall might spend the trip planning how to kill her, if he could do it and get away, but he would come." He turned around with one of the high-collared coats in his hands and held it up. "This one will do." Tangled, long-thorned briars climbed each red sleeve in a thick, gold-embroidered line, and ran around each cuff. Golden herons stood on the collars, which were edged with gold. "The color is right, too." He seemed to be amused at something, or satisfied. "Come on, sheepherder. Change your shirt. Move."

Reluctantly Rand pulled the coarse wool workman's shirt over his head. "I'll feel a fool," he muttered. "A silk shirt! I never wore a silk shirt in my life. And I never wore so fancy a coat, either, even on a feastday." *Light, if Perrin sees me in that . . . Burn me, after all that fool talk about being a lord, if he sees me in that, he'll never listen to reason.*

"You can't go before the Amyrlin Seat dressed like a groom fresh out of the stables, sheepherder. Let me see your boots. They'll do. Well, get on with it, get on with it. You don't keep the Amyrlin waiting. Wear your sword."

"My sword!" The silk shirt over his head muffled Rand's yelp. He yanked it the rest of the way on. "In the women's apartments? Lan, if I go for an audience with the Amyrlin Seat—the Amyrlin Seat!—wearing a sword, she'll—"

"Do nothing," Lan cut him off dryly. "If the Amyrlin is afraid of you—and it's smarter for you to think she isn't, because I don't know anything that could frighten that woman—it won't be for a sword. Now remember, you kneel when you go before her. One knee only, mind," he added sharply. "You're not some merchant caught giving short weight. Maybe you had better practice it."

"I know how, I think. I saw how the Queen's Guards knelt to Queen Morgase."

The ghost of a smile touched the Warder's lips. "Yes, you do it just as they did. That will give them something to think about."

Rand frowned. "Why are you telling me this, Lan? You're a Warder. You're acting as if you are on my side."

"I am on your side, sheepherder. A little. Enough to help you a bit." The Warder's face was stone, and sympathetic words sounded strange in that rough voice. "What training you've had, I gave you, and I'll not have you groveling and sniveling. The Wheel weaves us all into the Pattern as it wills. You have less freedom about it than most, but by the Light, you can still face it on your feet. You remember who the Amyrlin Seat is, sheepherder, and you show her proper respect, but you do what I tell you, and you look her in the eye. Well, don't stand there gaping. Tuck in your shirt."

Rand shut his mouth and tucked in his shirt. *Remember who she is? Burn me, what I wouldn't give to forget who she is!*

Lan kept up a running flow of instructions while Rand shrugged into the red coat and buckled on his sword. What to say and to whom, and what not to say. What to do, and what not. How to move, even. He was not sure he could remember it all—most of it sounded odd, and easy to forget—and he was sure whatever he forgot would be just the thing to make the Aes Sedai angry with him. *If they aren't already. If Moiraine told the Amyrlin Seat, who else did she tell?*

"Lan, why can't I just leave the way I planned? By the time she knew I was not coming, I'd be a league outside the walls and galloping."

"And she'd have trackers after you before you had gone two. What the Amyrlin wants, sheepherder, she gets." He adjusted Rand's sword belt so the heavy buckle was centered. "What I do is the best I can for you. Believe it."

"But why all this? What does it mean? Why do I put my hand over my heart if the Amyrlin Seat stands up? Why refuse anything but water—not that I want to eat a meal with her—then dribble some on the floor and say 'The land thirsts'? And if she asks how old I am, why tell her how long it is since I was given the sword? I don't understand half of what you've told me."

"Three drops, sheepherder, don't pour it. You *sprinkle* three drops only. You can understand later so long as you remember now. Think of it as upholding custom. The Amyrlin will do with you as she must. If you believe you can avoid it, then you believe you can fly to the moon like Lenn. You can't escape, but maybe you can hold your own for a while, and perhaps you can keep your pride, at least. The Light burn me, I am probably wasting my time, but I've nothing better to do. Hold still." From his pocket the Warder produced a long length of wide, fringed golden cord and tied it around Rand's left arm in a complicated knot. On the knot he fastened a red-enameled pin, an eagle with its wings spread. "I had that made to give you, and now is as good a time as any. That will make them think." There was no doubt about it, now. The Warder was smiling.

Rand looked down at the pin worriedly. *Caldazar*. The Red Eagle of Manetheren. "A thorn to the Dark One's foot," he murmured, "and a bramble to his hand." He looked at the Warder. "Manetheren's long dead and forgotten, Lan. It's just a name in a book, now. There is only the Two Rivers. Whatever else I am, I'm a shepherd and a farmer. That's all."

"Well, the sword that could not be broken was shattered in the end, sheepherder, but it fought the Shadow to the last. There is one rule, above all others, for being a man. Whatever comes, face it on your feet. Now, are you ready? The Amyrlin Seat waits."

With a cold knot in the pit of his belly, Rand followed the Warder into the hall.

CHAPTER 8

The Dragon Reborn

RAND WALKED STIFF-LEGGED AND NERVOUS at first, beside the Warder. *Face it on your feet.* It was easy for Lan to say. He had not been summoned by the Amyrlin Seat. He was not wondering if he would be gentled before the day was done, or worse. Rand felt as if he had something caught in his throat; he could not swallow, and he wanted to, badly.

The corridors bustled with people, servants going about their morning chores, warriors wearing swords over lounging robes. A few young boys carrying small practice swords stayed near their elders, imitating the way they walked. No sign remained of the fighting, but an air of alertness clung even to the children. Grown men looked like cats waiting for a pack of rats.

Ingtar gave Rand and Lan a peculiar look, almost troubled, opening his mouth, then saying nothing as they passed him. Kajin, tall and lean and sallow, pumped his fists over his head and shouted, *"Tai'shar Malkier! Tai'shar Manetheren!"* True blood of Malkier. True blood of Manetheren.

Rand jumped. *Light, why did he say that? Don't be a fool,* he told himself. *They all know about Manetheren here. They know every old story, if it has fighting in it. Burn me, I have to take a rein on myself.*

Lan raised his fists in reply. *"Tai'shar Shienar!"*

If he made a run for it, could he lose himself in the crowd long enough to reach his horse? *If she sends trackers after me. . . .* With every step he grew more tense.

As they approached the women's apartments, Lan suddenly snapped, "Cat Crosses the Courtyard!"

Startled, Rand instinctively assumed the walking stance as he had been taught, back straight but every muscle loose, as if he hung from a wire at the top of his head. It was a relaxed, almost arrogant, saunter. Relaxed on the outside; he certainly did not feel it inside. He had no time to wonder what he was doing. They rounded the last corridor in step with each other.

The women at the entrance to the women's apartments looked up calmly as they came closer. Some sat behind slanted tables, checking large ledgers and sometimes making an entry. Others were knitting, or working with needle and embroidery hoop. Ladies in silks kept this watch, as well as women in livery. The arched doors stood open, unguarded except for the women. No more was needed. No Shienaran man would enter uninvited, but any Shienaran man stood ready to defend that door if needed, and he would be aghast at the need.

Rand's stomach churned, harsh and acid. *They'll take one look at our swords and turn us away. Well, that's what I want, isn't it? If they turn us back, maybe I can still get away. If they don't call the guards down on us.* He clung to the stance Lan had given him as he would have to a floating branch in a flood; holding it was the only thing that kept him from turning tail and running.

One of the Lady Amalisa's attendants, Nisura, a round-faced woman, put aside her embroidery and stood as they came to a stop. Her eyes flickered across their swords, and her mouth tightened, but she did not mention them. All the women stopped what they were doing to watch, silent and intent.

"Honor to you both," Nisura said, bowing her head slightly. She glanced at Rand, so quickly he was almost not sure he had seen it; it reminded him of what Perrin had said. "The Amyrlin Seat awaits you." She motioned, and two other ladies—not servants; they were being honored—stepped forward for escorts. The women bowed, a hair more than Nisura had, and motioned them through the archway. They both gave Rand a sidelong glance, then did not look at him again.

Were they looking for all of us, or just me? Why all of us?

Inside, they got the looks Rand expected—two men in the women's apartments where men were rare—and their swords caused more than one raised eyebrow, but none of the women spoke. The two men left knots of conversation in their path, soft murmurs too low for Rand to make out. Lan strode along as if he did not even notice. Rand kept pace behind their escorts and wished he could hear.

And then they reached the Amyrlin Seat's chambers, with three Aes Sedai in the hall outside the door. The tall Aes Sedai, Leane, held her golden-flamed staff. Rand did not know the other two, one of the White Ajah and one Yellow by their fringe. He remembered their faces, though, staring at him as he had run through these same halls. Smooth Aes Sedai faces, with knowing eyes. They studied him with arched eyebrows and pursed lips. The women who had brought Lan and Rand curtsied, handing them over to the Aes Sedai.

Leane looked Rand over with a slight smile. Despite the smile, her voice had a snap to it. "What have you brought the Amyrlin Seat today, Lan Gaidin? A young lion? Better you don't let any

Greens see this one, or one of them will bond him before he can take a breath. Greens like to bond them young."

Rand wondered if it was really possible to sweat inside your skin. He felt as if he was. He wanted to look at Lan, but he remembered this part of the Warder's instructions. "I am Rand al'Thor, son of Tam al'Thor, of the Two Rivers, which once was Manetheren. As I have been summoned by the Amyrlin Seat, Leane Sedai, so do I come. I stand ready." He was surprised that his voice did not shake once.

Leane blinked, and her smile faded to a thoughtful look. "This is supposed to be a shepherd, Lan Gaidin? He was not so sure of himself this morning."

"He is a man, Leane Sedai," Lan said firmly, "no more, and no less. We are what we are."

The Aes Sedai shook her head. "The world grows stranger every day. I suppose the blacksmith will wear a crown and speak in High Chant. Wait here." She vanished inside to announce them.

She was only gone a few moments, but Rand was uncomfortably aware of the eyes of the remaining Aes Sedai. He tried to return their gaze levelly, the way Lan had told him to, and they put their heads together, whispering. *What are they saying? What do they know? Light, are they going to gentle me? Was that what Lan meant about facing whatever comes?*

Leane returned, motioning Rand to go in. When Lan started to follow, she thrust her staff across his chest, stopping him. "Not you, Lan Gaidin. Moiraine Sedai has a task for you: Your lion cub will be safe enough by himself."

The door swung shut behind Rand, but not before he heard Lan's voice, fierce and strong, but low for his ear alone. *"Tai'shar Manetheren!"*

Moiraine sat to one side of the room, and one of the Brown Aes Sedai he had seen in the dungeon sat to the other, but it was the woman in the tall chair behind the wide table who held his eyes.

The curtains had been partially drawn over the arrowslits, but the gaps let in enough light behind her to make her face hard to see clearly. He still recognized her, though. The Amyrlin Seat.

Quickly he dropped to one knee, left hand on sword hilt, right fist pressed to the patterned rug, and bowed his head. "As you have summoned me, Mother, so have I come. I stand ready." He lifted his head in time to see her eyebrows rise.

"Do you now, boy?" She sounded almost amused. And something else he could not make out. She certainly did not look amused. "Stand up, boy, and let me have a look at you."

He straightened and tried to keep his face relaxed. It was an effort not to clench his hands. *Three Aes Sedai. How many does it take to gentle a man? They sent a dozen or more after Logain. Would Moiraine do that to me?* He met the Amyrlin Seat's look eye to eye. She did not blink.

"Sit, boy," she said finally, gesturing to a ladder-back chair that had been pulled around squarely in front of the table. "This will not be short, I fear."

"Thank you, Mother." He bowed his head, then, as Lan had told him, glanced at the chair and touched his sword. "By your leave, Mother, I will stand. The watch is not done."

The Amyrlin Seat made an exasperated sound and looked at Moiraine. "Have you let Lan at him, Daughter? This will be difficult enough without him picking up Warder ways."

"Lan has been teaching all the boys, Mother," Moiraine replied calmly. "He has spent a little more time with this one than the others because he carries a sword."

The Brown Aes Sedai shifted on her chair. "The Gaidin are stiff-necked and proud, Mother, but useful. I would not be without Tomas, as you would not lose Alric. I have even heard a few Reds say they sometimes wish for a Warder. And the Greens, of course. . . ."

The three Aes Sedai were all ignoring him, now. "This sword," the Amyrlin Seat said. "It appears to be a heron-mark blade. How did he come by that, Moiraine?"

"Tam al'Thor left the Two Rivers as a boy, Mother. He joined the army of Illian, and served in the Whitecloak War and the last two wars with Tear. In time he rose to be a blademaster and the Second Captain of the Companions. After the Aiel War, Tam al'Thor returned to the Two Rivers with a wife from Caemlyn and an infant boy. It would have saved much, had I known this earlier, but I know it now."

Rand stared as Moiraine. He knew Tam had left the Two Rivers and come back with an outlander wife and the sword, but the rest. . . . *Where did you learn all that? Not in Emond's Field. Unless Nynaeve told you more than she's ever told me. An infant boy. She doesn't say his son. But I am.*

"Against Tear." The Amyrlin Seat frowned slightly. "Well, there was blame enough on both sides in those wars. Fool men who would rather fight than talk. Can you tell if the blade is authentic, Verin?"

"There are tests, Mother."

"Then take it and test it, Daughter."

The three women were not even looking at him. Rand stepped back, gripping the hilt hard. "My father gave this sword to me," he said angrily. "Nobody is taking it from me." It was only then that he realized Verin had not moved from her chair. He looked at them in confusion, trying to recover his equilibrium.

"So," the Amyrlin Seat said, "you have some fire in you besides whatever Lan put in. Good. You will need it."

"I am what I am, Mother," he managed smoothly enough. "I stand ready for what comes."

The Amyrlin Seat grimaced. "Lan *has* been at you. Listen to me, boy. In a few hours, Ingtar will leave to find the stolen Horn. Your friend, Mat, will go with him. I expect that your other friend—Perrin?—will go, also. Do you wish to accompany them?"

"Mat and Perrin are going? Why?" Belatedly he remembered to add a respectful, "Mother."

"You know of the dagger your friend carried?" A twist of her mouth showed what she thought of the dagger. "That was taken, too. Unless it is found, the link between him and the blade cannot be broken completely, and he will die. You can ride with them, if you want. Or you can stay here. No doubt Lord Agelmar will let you remain as a guest as long as you wish. I will be leaving today, as well. Moiraine Sedai will accompany me, and so will Egwene and Nynaeve, so you will stay alone, if you stay. The choice is yours."

Rand stared at her. *She is saying I can go as I want. Is that what she brought me here for? Mat is dying!* He glanced at Moiraine, sitting impassively with her hands folded in her lap. She looked as if nothing in the world could concern her less than where he went. *Which way are you trying to push me, Aes Sedai? Burn me, but I'll go another. But if Mat's dying. . . . I can't abandon him. Light, how are we going to find that dagger?*

"You do not have to make the choice now," the Amyrlin said. She did not seem to care, either. "But you will have to choose before Ingtar leaves."

"I will ride with Ingtar, Mother."

The Amyrlin Seat nodded absently. "Now that that is dealt with, we can move on to important matters. I know you can channel, boy. What do you know?"

Rand's mouth fell open. Caught up in worrying about Mat, her casual words hit him like a swinging barn door. All of Lan's advice and instructions went spinning. He stared at her, licking his lips. It was one thing to think she knew, entirely another to find out she really did. The sweat finally seeped out on his forehead.

She leaned forward in her seat, waiting for his answer, but he had the feeling she wanted to lean back. He remembered what Lan had said. *If she's afraid of you. . . .* He wanted to laugh. If *she* was afraid of *him*.

"No, I can't. I mean . . . I didn't do it on purpose. It just happened. I don't want to—to channel the Power. I won't ever do it again. I swear it."

"You don't want to," the Amyrlin Seat said. "Well, that's wise of you. And foolish, too. Some can be taught to channel; most cannot. A few, though, have the seed in them at birth. Sooner or later, they wield the One Power whether they want to or not, as surely as roe makes fish. You will continue to channel, boy. You can't help it. And you had better *learn* to channel, learn to control it, or you will not live long enough to go mad. The One Power kills those who cannot control its flow."

"How am I supposed to learn?" he demanded. Moiraine and Verin just sat there, unruffled, watching him. *Like spiders.* "How? Moiraine claims she can't teach me anything, and I don't know how to learn, or what. I don't want to, anyway. I want to stop. Can't you understand that? To stop!"

"I told you the truth, Rand," Moiraine said. She sounded as if they were having a pleasant conversation. "Those who could teach you, the male Aes Sedai, are three thousand years dead. No Aes Sedai living can teach you to touch *saidin* any more than you could learn to touch *saidar*. A bird cannot teach a fish to fly, nor a fish teach a bird to swim."

"I have always thought that was a bad saying," Verin said suddenly. "There are birds that dive and swim. And in the Sea of Storms are fish that fly, with long fins that stretch out as wide as your outstretched arms, and beaks like swords that can pierce. . . ." Her words trailed off and she became flustered. Moiraine and the Amyrlin Seat were staring at her without expression.

Rand took the interruption to try to regain some control of himself. As Tam had taught him long ago, he formed a single flame in his mind and fed his fears into it, seeking emptiness, the stillness of the void. The flame seemed to grow until it enveloped everything, until it was too large to contain or imagine any longer. With that it was gone, leaving in its place a sense of peace. At its edges, emotions still flickered, fear and anger like black blotches, but the void held. Thought skimmed across its surface like pebbles across ice. The Aes Sedai's attention was only off him for a moment, but when they turned back his face was calm.

"Why are you talking to me like this, Mother?" he asked. "You should be gentling me."

The Amyrlin Seat frowned and turned to Moiraine. "Did Lan teach him this?"

"No, Mother. He had it from Tam al'Thor."

"Why?" Rand demanded again.

The Amyrlin Seat looked him straight in the eye and said, "Because you are the Dragon Reborn."

The void rocked. The world rocked. Everything seemed to spin around him. He concentrated on nothing, and the emptiness returned, the world steadied. "No, Mother. I can channel, the Light help me, but I am not Raolin Darksbane, nor Guaire Amalasan, nor Yurian Stonebow. You can gentle me, or kill me, or let me go, but I will not be a tame false Dragon on a Tar Valon leash."

He heard Verin gasp, and the Amyrlin's eyes widened, a gaze as hard as blue rock. It did not affect him; it slid off the void within.

"Where did you hear those names?" the Amyrlin demanded. "Who told you Tar Valon pulls the lines on *any* false Dragon?"

"A friend, Mother," he said. "A gleeman. His name was Thom Merrilin. He's dead, now." Moiraine made a sound, and he glanced at her. She claimed Thom was not dead, but she had never offered any proof, and he could not see how any man could survive grappling hand-to-hand with a Fade. The thought was extraneous, and it faded away. There was only the void and the oneness now.

"You are not a false Dragon," the Amyrlin said firmly. "You are the true Dragon Reborn."

"I am a shepherd from the Two Rivers, Mother."

"Daughter, tell him the story. A *true* story, boy. Listen well."

Moiraine began speaking. Rand kept his eyes on the Amyrlin's face, but he heard.

"Nearly twenty years ago the Aiel crossed the Spine of the World, the Dragonwall, the only time they have ever done so. They ravaged through Cairhien, destroyed every army sent against them, burned the city of Cairhien itself, and fought all the way to Tar Valon. It was winter and snowing, but cold or heat mean little to an Aiel. The final battle, the last that counted, was fought outside the Shining Walls, in the shadow of Dragonmount. In three days and three nights of fighting, the Aiel were turned back. Or rather they turned back, for they had done what they came to do, which was to kill King Laman of Cairhien, for his sin against the Tree. It is then that my story begins. And yours."

They came over the Dragonwall like a flood. All the way to the Shining Walls. Rand waited for the memories to fade, but it was Tam's voice he heard, Tam sick and raving, pulling up secrets from his past. The voice clung outside the void, clamoring to get in.

"I was one of the Accepted, then," Moiraine said, "as was our Mother, the Amyrlin Seat. We were soon to be raised to sisterhood, and that night we stood attendance on the then Amyrlin. Her Keeper of the Chronicles, Gitara Moroso, was there. Every other full sister in Tar Valon was out Healing as many wounded as she could find, even the Reds. It was dawn. The fire on the hearth could not keep the cold out. The snow had finally stopped, and in the Amyrlin's chambers in the White Tower we could smell the smoke of outlying villages burned in the fighting."

Battles are always hot, even in the snow. Had to get away from the stink of death. Tam's delirious voice clawed at the empty calm inside Rand. The void trembled and shrank, steadied, then wavered again. The Amyrlin's eyes bored at him. He felt sweat on

his face again. "It was all a fever-dream," he said. "He was sick."
He raised his voice. "My name is Rand al'Thor. I am a shepherd.
My father is Tam al'Thor, and my mother was—"

Moiraine had paused for him, but now her unchanging voice
cut him off, soft and relentless. "*The Karaethon Cycle,* the
Prophecies of the Dragon, says that the Dragon will be reborn on
the slopes of Dragonmount, where he died during the Breaking of
the World. Gitara Sedai had the Foretelling sometimes. She was
old, her hair as white as the snow outside, but when she had the
Foretelling, it was strong. The morning light through the windows
was strengthening as I handed her a cup of tea. The Amyrlin Seat
asked me what news there was from the field of battle. And Gitara
Sedai started up out of her chair, her arms and legs rigid, trembling, her face as if she looked into the Pit of Doom at Shayol
Ghul, and she cried out, 'He is born again! I feel him! The Dragon
takes his first breath on the slope of Dragonmount! He is coming!
He is coming! Light help us! Light help the world! He lies in the
snow and cries like the thunder! He burns like the sun!' And she
fell forward into my arms, dead."

*Slope of the mountain. Heard a baby cry. Gave birth there
alone, before she died. Child blue with the cold.* Rand tried to
force Tam's voice away. The void grew smaller. "A fever-dream,"
he gasped. *I couldn't leave a child.* "I was born in the Two
Rivers." *Always knew you wanted children, Kari.* He pulled his
eyes away from the Amyrlin's gaze. He tried to force the void to
hold. He knew that was not the way, but it was collapsing in him.
Yes, lass. Rand is a good name. "I—am—Rand—al'Thor!" His
legs trembled.

"And so we knew the Dragon was Reborn," Moiraine went on.
"The Amyrlin swore us to secrecy, we two, for she knew not all
the sisters would see the Rebirth as it must be seen. She set us to
searching. There were many fatherless children after that battle.
Too many. But we found a story, that one man had found an infant

on the mountain. That was all. A man and an infant boy. So we searched on. For years we searched, finding other clues, poring over the Prophecies. 'He will be of the ancient blood, and raised by the old blood.' That was one; there were others. But there are many places where the old blood, descended from the Age of Legends, remains strong. Then, in the Two Rivers, where the old blood of Manetheren seethes still like a river in flood, in Emond's Field, I found three boys whose name-days were within weeks of the battle at Dragonmount. And one of them can channel. Did you think Trollocs came after you just because you are *ta'veren?* You are the Dragon Reborn."

Rand's knees gave way; he dropped to a squat, hands slapping the rug to catch himself from falling on his face. The void was gone, the stillness shattered. He raised his head, and they were looking at him, the three Aes Sedai. Their faces were serene, smooth as unruffled ponds, but their eyes did not blink. "My father is Tam al'Thor, and I was born. . . ." They stared at him, unmoving. *They're lying. I am not . . . what they say! Some way, somehow, they're lying, trying to use me.* "I will not be used by you."

"An anchor is not demeaned by being used to hold a boat," the Amyrlin said. "You were made for a purpose, Rand al'Thor. 'When the winds of Tarmon Gai'don scour the earth, he will face the Shadow and bring forth Light again in the world.' The Prophecies must be fulfilled, or the Dark One will break free and remake the world in his image. The Last Battle is coming, and you were born to unite mankind and lead them against the Dark One."

"Ba'alzamon is dead," Rand said hoarsely, and the Amyrlin snorted like a stablehand.

"If you believe that, you are as much a fool as the Domani. Many there believe he is dead, or say they do, but I notice they still won't risk naming him. The Dark One lives, and he is breaking free. You will face the Dark One. It is your destiny."

It is your destiny. He had heard that before, in a dream that had maybe not been entirely a dream. He wondered what the Amyrlin would say if she knew Ba'alzamon had spoken to him in dreams. *That's done with. Ba'alzamon is dead. I saw him die.*

Suddenly it came to him that he was crouching like a toad, huddling under their eyes. He tried to form the void again, but voices whirled through his head, sweeping away every effort. *It is your destiny. Babe lying in the snow. You are the Dragon Reborn. Ba'alzamon is dead. Rand is a good name, Kari. I will not be used!* Drawing on his own native stubbornness, he forced himself back upright. *Face it on your feet. You can keep your pride, at least.* The three Aes Sedai watched with no expression.

"What. . . ." With an effort he steadied his voice. "What are you going to do to me?"

"Nothing," the Amyrlin said, and he blinked. It was not the answer he had expected, the one he had feared. "You say you want to accompany your friend with Ingtar, and you may. I have not marked you out in any way. Some of the sisters may know you are *ta'veren,* but no more. Only we three know who you truly are. Your friend Perrin will be brought to me, as you were, and I will visit your other friend in the infirmary. You may go as you will, without fear that we will set the Red sisters on you."

Who you truly are. Anger flared up in him, hot and corrosive. He forced it to stay inside, hidden. "Why?"

"The Prophecies must be fulfilled. We let you walk free, knowing what you are, because otherwise the world we know will die, and the Dark One will cover the earth with fire and death. Mark me, not all Aes Sedai feel the same. There are some here in Fal Dara who would strike you down if they knew a tenth of what you are, and feel no more remorse than for gutting a fish. But then, there are men who've no doubt laughed with you who would do the same, if they knew. Have a care, Rand al'Thor, Dragon Reborn."

He looked at each of them in turn. *Your Prophecies are no part of me.* They returned his gaze so calmly it was hard to believe they were trying to convince him he was the most hated, the most feared man in the history of the world. He had gone right through fear and come out the other side in some place cold. Anger was all that kept him warm. They could gentle him, or burn him to a crisp where he stood, and he no longer cared.

A part of Lan's instructions came back to him. Left hand on the hilt, he twisted the sword behind him, catching the scabbard in his right, then bowed, arms straight. "By your leave, Mother, may I depart this place?"

"I give you leave to go, my son."

Straightening, he stood there a moment longer. "I will not be used," he told them. There was a long silence as he turned and left.

THE SILENCE STRETCHED on in the room after Rand left until it was broken by a long breath from the Amyrlin. "I cannot make myself like what we just did," she said. "It was necessary, but. . . . Did it work, Daughters?"

Moiraine shook her head, just the slightest movement. "I do not know. But it *was* necessary, and is."

"Necessary," Verin agreed. She touched her forehead, then peered at the dampness on her fingers. "He is strong. And as stubborn as you said, Moiraine. Much stronger than I expected. We may have to gentle him after all before. . . ." Her eyes widened. "But we cannot, can we? The Prophecies. The Light forgive us for what we are loosing on the world."

"The Prophecies," Moiraine said, nodding. "Afterwards, we will do as we must. As we do now."

"As we must," the Amyrlin said. "Yes. But when he learns to channel, the Light help us all."

The silence returned.

THERE WAS A storm coming. Nynaeve felt it. A big storm, worse than she had ever seen. She could listen to the wind, and hear what the weather would be. All Wisdoms claimed to be able to do that, though many could not. Nynaeve had felt more comfortable with the ability before learning it was a manifestation of the Power. Any woman who could listen to the wind could channel, though most were probably as she had been, unaware of what she was doing, getting it only in fits and starts.

This time, though, something was wrong. Outside, the morning sun was a golden ball in a clear blue sky, and birds sang in the gardens, but that was not it. There would have been nothing to listening to the wind if she could not foretell the weather before the signs were visible. There was something wrong with the feeling this time, something not quite the way it usually was. The storm felt distant, too far off for her to feel at all. Yet it felt as if the sky above should have been pouring down rain, and snow, and hail, all at the same time, with winds howling to shake the stones of the keep. And she could feel the good weather, too, lasting for days yet, but that was muted under the other.

A bluefinch perched in an arrowslit like a mockery of her weather sense, peering into the hallway. When it saw her, it vanished in a flash of blue and white feathers.

She stared at the spot where the bird had been. *There is a storm, and there isn't. It means something. But what?*

Far down the hall full of women and small children she saw Rand striding away, his escort of women half running to keep up. Nynaeve nodded firmly. If there was a storm that was not a storm, he would be the center of it. Gathering her skirts, she hurried after him.

Women with whom she had grown friendly since coming to Fal Dara tried to speak to her; they knew Rand had come with her and that they were both from the Two Rivers, and they wanted to know why the Amyrlin had summoned him. *The Amyrlin Seat!* Ice in the pit of her belly, she broke into a run, but before she left the women's apartments, she had lost him around too many corners and beyond too many people.

"Which way did he go?" she asked Nisura. There was no need to say who. She heard Rand's name in the conversation of the other women clustered around the arched doors.

"I don't know, Nynaeve. He came out as fast as if he had Heartsbane himself at his heels. As well he might, coming here with a sword at his belt. The Dark One should be the least of his worries after that. What is the world coming to? And him presented to the Amyrlin in her chambers, no less. Tell me, Nynaeve, is he really a prince in your land?" The other women stopped talking and leaned closer to listen.

Nynaeve was not sure what she answered. Something that made them let her go on. She hurried away from the women's apartments, head swiveling at every crossing corridor to look for him, fists clenched. *Light, what have they done to him? I should have gotten him away from Moiraine somehow, the Light blind her. I'm his Wisdom.*

Are you, a small voice taunted. *You've abandoned Emond's Field to fend for itself. Can you still call yourself their Wisdom?*

I did not abandon them, she told herself fiercely. *I brought Mavra Mallen up from Deven Ride to look after matters till I get back. She can deal well enough with the Mayor and the Village Council, and she gets on well with the Women's Circle.*

Mavra will have to get back to her own village. No village can do without its Wisdom for long. Nynaeve cringed inside. She had been gone months from Emond's Field.

"I am the Wisdom of Emond's Field!" she said aloud.

A liveried servant carrying a bolt of cloth blinked at her, then bowed low before scurrying off. By his face he was eager to be anywhere else.

Blushing, Nynaeve looked around to see if anyone had noticed. There were only a few men in the hall, engrossed in their own conversations, and some women in black-and-gold going about their business, giving her a bow or curtsy as she passed. She had

had that argument with herself a hundred times before, but this was the first time it had come to talking to herself out loud. She muttered under her breath, then pressed her lips firmly together when she realized what she was doing.

She was finally beginning to realize her search was futile when she came on Lan, his back to her, looking down on the outer courtyard through an arrowslit. The noise from the courtyard was all horses and men, neighing and shouting. So intent was Lan that he did not, for once, seem to hear her. She hated the fact that she could never sneak up on him, however softly she stepped. She had been accounted good at woodscraft back in Emond's Field, though it was not a skill in which many women took any interest.

She stopped in her tracks, pressing her hands to her stomach to quiet a flutter. *I ought to dose myself with rannel and sheepstongue root,* she thought sourly. It was the mixture she gave anyone who moped about and claimed they were sick, or behaved like a goose. Rannel and sheepstongue root would perk you up a little, and did no harm, but mainly it tasted horrible, and the taste lasted all day. It was a perfect cure for acting the fool.

Safe from his eyes, she studied the length of him, leaning against the stone and fingering his chin as he studied what was going on below. *He's too tall, for one thing, and old enough to be my father, for another. A man with a face like that would have to be cruel. No, he's not that. Never that.* And he was a king. His land was destroyed while he was a child, and he would not claim a crown, but he was a king, for that. *What would a king want with a village woman? He's a Warder, too. Bonded to Moiraine. She has his loyalty to death, and ties closer than any lover, and she has him. She has everything I want, the Light burn her!*

He turned from the arrowslit, and she whirled to go.

"Nynaeve." His voice caught and held her like a noose. "I wanted to speak to you alone. You always seem to be in the women's apartments, or in company."

It took an effort to face him, but she was sure her features were calm when she looked up at him. "I'm looking for Rand." She was not about to admit to avoiding him. "We said all we need to say long ago, you and I. I shamed myself—which I will not do again—and you told me to go away."

"I never said—" He took a deep breath. "I told you I had nothing to offer for brideprice but widow's clothes. Not a gift any man could give a woman. Not a man who can call himself a man."

"I understand," she said coolly. "In any case, a king does not give gifts to village women. And this village woman would not take them. Have you seen Rand? I need to talk to him. He was to see the Amyrlin. Do you know what she wanted with him?"

His eyes blazed like blue ice in the sun. She stiffened her legs to keep from stepping back, and met him glare for glare.

"The Dark One take Rand al'Thor and the Amyrlin Seat both," he grated, pressing something into her hand. "I will make you a gift and you will take it if I have to chain it around your neck."

She pulled her eyes away from his. He had a stare like a blue-eyed hawk when he was angry. In her hand was a signet ring, heavy gold and worn with age, almost large enough for both her thumbs to fit through. On it, a crane flew above a lance and crown, all carefully wrought in detail. Her breath caught. The ring of Malkieri kings. Forgetting to glare, she lifted her face. "I cannot take this, Lan."

He shrugged in an offhand way. "It is nothing. Old, and useless, now. But there are those who would know it when they saw it. Show that, and you will have guestright, and help if you need it, from any lord in the Borderlands. Show it to a Warder, and he will give aid, or carry a message to me. Send it to me, or a message marked with it, and I will come to you, without delay and without fail. This I swear."

Her vision blurred at the edges. *If I cry now, I will kill myself.* "I can't. . . . I do not want a gift from you, al'Lan Mandragoran. Here, take it."

He fended off her attempts to give the ring back to him. His hand enveloped hers, gentle but firm as a shackle. "Then take it for my sake, as a favor to me. Or throw it away, if it displeases you. I've no better use for it." He brushed her cheek with a finger, and she gave a start. "I must go now, Nynaeve *mashiara*. The Amyrlin wishes to leave before midday, and there is much yet to be done. Perhaps we will have time to talk on the journey to Tar Valon." He turned and was gone, striding down the hall.

Nynaeve touched her cheek. She could still feel where he had touched her. *Mashiara.* Beloved of heart and soul, it meant, but a love lost, too. Lost beyond regaining. *Fool woman! Stop acting like a girl with her hair still not braided. It's no use letting him make you feel. . . .*

Clutching the ring tightly, she turned around, and jumped when she found herself face-to-face with Moiraine. "How long have you been there?" she demanded.

"Not long enough to hear anything I should not have," the Aes

Sedai replied smoothly. "We *will* be leaving soon. I heard that. You must see to your packing."

Leaving. It had not penetrated when Lan said it. "I will have to say goodbye to the boys," she muttered, then gave Moiraine a sharp look. "What have you done to Rand? He was taken to the Amyrlin. Why? Did you tell her about—about . . .?" She could not say it. He was from her own village, and she was just enough older than he to have looked after him a time or two when he was little, but she could not even think about what he had become without her stomach twisting.

"The Amyrlin will be seeing all three, Nynaeve. *Ta'veren* are not so common that she would miss the chance to see three together in one placc. Perhaps she will give them a few words of encouragement, since they are riding with Ingtar to hunt those who stole the Horn. They will be leaving about the time we do, so you had better hurry with any farewells."

Nynaeve dashed to the nearest arrowslit and peered down at the outer courtyard. Horses were everywhere, pack animals and saddle horses, and men hurrying about them, calling to each other. The only clear space was where the Amyrlin's palanquin stood, its paired horses waiting patiently without any attendants. Some of the Warders were out there, looking over their mounts, and on the other side of the courtyard, Ingtar stood with a knot of Shienarans around him in armor. Sometimes a Warder or one of Ingtar's men crossed the paving stones to exchange a word.

"I should have gotten the boys away from you," she said, still looking out. *Egwene, too, if I could do it without killing her. Light, why did she have to be born with this cursed ability?* "I should have taken them back home."

"They are more than old enough to be off apron strings," Moiraine said dryly. "And you know very well why you could never do that. For one of them, at least. Besides, it would mean leaving Egwene to go to Tar Valon alone. Or have you decided to forgo Tar Valon yourself? If your own use of the Power is not schooled, you will never be able to use it against me."

Nynaeve spun to face the Aes Sedai, her jaw dropping. She could not help it. "I don't know what you are talking about."

"Did you think I did not know, child? Well, as you wish it. I take it that you *are* coming to Tar Valon? Yes, I thought so."

Nynaeve wanted to hit her, to knock away the brief smile that flashed across the Aes Sedai's face. Aes Sedai had not been able to wield power openly since the Breaking, much less the One Power, but they plotted and manipulated, pulled strings like puppetmasters, used thrones and nations like stones on a stones board. *She wants to use me, too, somehow. If a king or a queen, why not a Wisdom? Just the way she's using Rand. I'm no child, Aes Sedai.*

"What are you doing with Rand, now? Have you not used him enough? I don't know why you have not had him gentled, now the Amyrlin's here with all those other Aes Sedai, but you must have a reason. It must be some plot you're hatching. If the Amyrlin knew what you were up to, I wager she'd—"

Moiraine cut her off. "What possible interest could the Amyrlin have in a shepherd? Of course, if he were brought to her attention in the wrong way, he might be gentled, or even killed. He is what he is, after all. And there is considerable anger about last night. Everyone is looking for whom to blame." The Aes Sedai fell silent, and let the silence stretch. Nynaeve stared at her, grinding her teeth.

"Yes," Moiraine said finally, "much better to let a sleeping lion sleep. Best you see to your packing, now." She moved off in the direction Lan had gone, seeming to glide across the floor.

Grimacing, Nynaeve swung her fist back against the wall; the ring dug at her palm. She opened her hand to look at it. The ring seemed to heat her anger, focus her hate. *I* will *learn. You think because you know, you can escape me. But I will learn better than you think, and I will pull you down for what you've done. For what you've done to Mat, and to Perrin. For Rand, the Light help him and the Creator shelter him. Especially for Rand.* Her hand closed around the heavy circlet of gold. *And for me.*

EGWENE WATCHED THE liveried maid folding her dresses into a leather-covered travel chest, still a little uncomfortable, even after nearly a month's practice, with someone else doing what she could very well have done herself. They were such beautiful dresses, all gifts from the Lady Amalisa, just like the gray silk riding dress she wore, though that was plain except for a few white morningstar blossoms worked on the breast. Many of the dresses were much more elaborate. Any one of them would shine at Sunday, or at Bel Tine. She sighed, remembering that she would be in Tar Valon for the next Sunday, not Emond's Field. From the little Moiraine had told her of novice training—almost nothing, really—she expected she might not be home for Bel Tine, in the spring, or even the Sunday after that.

Nynaeve put her head into the room. "Are you ready?" She came the rest of the way in. "We must be down in the courtyard soon." She wore a riding dress, too, in blue silk with red lovers-knots on the bosom. Another gift from Amalisa.

"Nearly, Nynaeve. I am almost sorry to be going. I don't suppose we'll have many chances in Tar Valon to wear the nice dresses Amalisa gave us." She gave an abrupt laugh. "Still, Wisdom, I won't miss being able to bathe without looking over my shoulder the whole time."

"Much better to bathe alone," Nynaeve said briskly. Her face did not change, but after a moment her cheeks colored.

Egwene smiled. *She's thinking about Lan.* It was still odd to think of Nynaeve, the Wisdom, mooning after a man. She did not think it would be wise to put it to Nynaeve in quite that way, but of late, sometimes the Wisdom acted as strangely as any girl who had set her heart on a particular man. *And one who doesn't have*

enough sense to be worthy of her, at that. She loves him, and I can
see he loves her, so why can't he have sense enough to speak up?

"I don't think you should call me Wisdom any longer," Nynaeve said suddenly.

Egwene blinked. It was not required, exactly, and Nynaeve never insisted on it unless she was angry, or being formal, but this. . . . "Why ever not?"

"You are a woman, now." Nynaeve glanced at her unbraided hair, and Egwene resisted the urge to hurriedly twist it into a semblance of a braid. Aes Sedai wore their hair any way they wanted, but wearing hers loose had become a symbol of starting on a new life. "You are a woman," Nynaeve repeated firmly. "We are two women, a long way from Emond's Field, and it will be longer still before we see home again. It will be better if you simply call me Nynaeve."

"We will see home again, Nynaeve. We will."

"Don't try to comfort the Wisdom, girl," Nynaeve said gruffly, but she smiled.

There was a knock as the door, but before Egwene could open it, Nisura came in, agitation all over her face. "Egwene, that young man of yours is trying to come into the women's apartments." She sounded scandalized. "And wearing a sword. Just because the Amyrlin let him enter that way. . . . Lord Rand should know better. He is causing an uproar. Egwene, you must speak to him."

"Lord Rand," Nynaeve snorted. "That young man is growing too big for his breeches. When I get my hands on him, I'll lord him."

Egwene put a hand on Nynaeve's arm. "Let me speak to him, Nynaeve. Alone."

"Oh, very well. The best of men are not much better than housebroken." Nynaeve paused, and added half to herself, "But then, the best of them are worth the trouble of housebreaking."

Egwene shook her head as she followed Nisura into the hall.

Even half a year before, Nynaeve would never have added the second part. *But she'll never housebreak Lan.* Her thoughts turned to Rand. Causing an uproar, was he? "Housebreak him?" she muttered. "If he hasn't learned manners by this time, I'll skin him alive."

"Sometimes that is what it takes," Nisura said, walking quickly. "Men are never more than half-civilized until they're wedded." She gave Egwene a sidelong glance. "Do you intend to marry Lord Rand? I do not mean to pry, but you are going to the White Tower, and Aes Sedai seldom wed—none but some of the Green Ajah, that I've ever heard, and not many of them—and. . . ."

Egwene could supply the rest. She had heard the talk in the women's apartments about a suitable wife for Rand. At first it had caused stabs of jealousy, and anger. He had been all but promised to her since they were children. But she was going to be an Aes Sedai, and he was what he was. A man who could channel. She could marry him. And watch him go mad, watch him die. The only way to stop it would be to have him gentled. *I can't do that to him. I can't!* "I do not know," she said sadly.

Nisura nodded. "No one will poach where you have a claim, but you are going to the Tower, and he will make a good husband. Once he has been trained. There he is."

The women gathered around the entrance to the women's apartments, both inside and out, were all watching three men in the hallway outside. Rand, with his sword buckled over his red coat, was being confronted by Agelmar and Kajin. Neither of them wore a sword; even after what had happened in the night, these were still the women's apartments. Egwene stopped at the back of the crowd.

"You understand why you cannot go in," Agelmar was saying. "I know that things are different in Andor, but you do understand?"

"I didn't try to go in." Rand sounded as if he had explained all this more than once already. "I told the Lady Nisura I wanted to see Egwene, and she said Egwene was busy, and I'd have to wait. All I did was shout for her from the door. I did not try to enter. You'd have thought I was naming the Dark One, the way they all started in on me."

"Women have their own ways," Kajin said. He was tall for a Shienaran, almost as tall as Rand, lanky and sallow. His topknot was black as pitch. "They set the rules for the women's apartments, and we abide by them even when they are foolish." A number of eyebrows were raised among the women, and he hastily cleared his throat. "You must send a message in if you wish to speak to one of the women, but it will be delivered when they choose, and until it is, you must wait. That is our custom."

"I have to see her," Rand said stubbornly. "We're leaving soon. Not soon enough for me, but I still have to see Egwene. We will get the Horn of Valere and the dagger back, and that will be the end of it. The end of it. But I want to see her before I go." Egwene frowned; he sounded odd.

"No need to be so fierce," Kajin said. "You and Ingtar will find the Horn, or not. And if not, then another will retrieve it. The Wheel weaves as the Wheel wills, and we are but threads in the Pattern."

"Do not let the Horn seize you, Rand," Agelmar said. "It can take hold of a man—I know how it can—and that is not the way. A man must seek duty, not glory. What will happen, will happen. If the Horn of Valere is meant to be sounded for the Light, then it will be."

"Here is your Egwene," Kajin said, spotting her.

Agelmar looked around, and nodded when he saw her with Nisura. "I will leave you in her hands, Rand al'Thor. Remember, here, her words are law, not yours. Lady Nisura, do not be too hard on him. He only wished to see his young woman, and he does not know our ways."

Egwene followed Nisura as the Shienaran woman threaded her way through the watching women. Nisura inclined her head briefly to Agelmar and Kajin; she pointedly did not include Rand. Her voice was tight. "Lord Agelmar. Lord Kajin. He should know this much of our ways by now, but he is too big to spank, so I will let Egwene deal with him."

Agelmar gave Rand a fatherly pat on the shoulder. "You see. You will speak with her, if not exactly in the way you wished. Come, Kajin. We have much to see to yet. The Amyrlin still insists on. . . ." His voice trailed away as he and the other man left. Rand stood there, looking at Egwene.

The women were still watching, Egwene realized. Watching her as well as Rand. Waiting to see what she would do. *So I'm supposed to deal with him, am I?* Yet she felt her heart going out to him. His hair needed brushing. His face showed anger, defiance, and weariness. "Walk with me," she told him. A murmur started up behind them as he walked down the hall beside her, away from the women's apartments. Rand seemed to be struggling with himself, hunting for what to say.

"I've heard about your . . . exploits," she said finally. "Running through the women's apartments last night with a sword. Wearing a sword to an audience with the Amyrlin Seat." He still said nothing, only walked along frowning at the floor. "She didn't . . . hurt you, did she?" She could not make herself ask if he had been gentled; he looked anything but gentle, but she had no idea what a man looked like afterwards.

He gave a jerk. "No. She didn't. . . . Egwene, the Amyrlin. . . ." He shook his head. "She didn't hurt me."

She had the feeling he had been going to say something else entirely. Usually she could ferret out whatever he wanted to hide from her, but when he really wanted to be stubborn, she could more easily dig a brick out of a wall with her fingernails. By the set of his jaw, he was at his most stubborn right now.

"What did she want with you, Rand?"

"Nothing important. *Ta'veren*. She wanted to see *ta'veren*." His face softened as he looked down at her. "What about you, Egwene? Are you all right? Moiraine said you would be, but you were so still. I thought you were dead, at first."

"Well, I'm not." She laughed. She could not remember anything that had happened after she had asked Mat to go to the dungeons with her, not until waking in her own bed that morning. From what she had heard of the night, she was almost glad she could not remember. "Moiraine said she would have left me a headache for being foolish if she could have Healed the rest and not that, but she couldn't."

"I told you Fain was dangerous," he muttered. "I told you, but you wouldn't listen."

"If that's the way you are going to talk," she said firmly, "I will give you back to Nisura. She won't talk to you the way I am. The last man who tried to push his way into the women's apartments spent a month up to his elbows in soapy water, helping with the women's laundry, and he was only trying to find his betrothed and make up an argument. At least he knew enough not to wear his sword. The Light knows what they'd do to you."

"Everybody wants to do something to me," he growled. "Everybody wants to use me for something. Well, I won't be used. Once we find the Horn, and Mat's dagger, I'll never be used again."

With an exasperated grunt, she caught his shoulders and made him face her. She glared up at him. "If you don't start talking sense, Rand al'Thor, I swear I will box your ears."

"Now you sound like Nynaeve." He laughed. As he looked down at her, though, his laughter faded. "I suppose—I suppose I'll never see you again. I know you have to go to Tar Valon. I know that. And you'll become an Aes Sedai. I am done with Aes Sedai, Egwene. I won't be a puppet for them, not for Moiraine, or any of them."

He looked so lost she wanted to put his head on her shoulder, and so stubborn she really did want to box his ears. "Listen to me, you great ox. I *am* going to be an Aes Sedai, and I'll find a way to help you. I will."

"The next time you see me, you will likely want to gentle me."

She looked around hastily; they were alone in their stretch of the hall. "If you don't watch your tongue, I will not be able to help you. Do you want everyone to know?"

"Too many know already," he said. "Egwene, I wish things were different, but they aren't. I wish. . . . Take care of yourself. And promise me you won't choose the Red Ajah."

Tears blurred her vision as she threw her arms around him. "You take care of yourself," she said fiercely into his chest. "If you don't, I'll—I'll. . . ." She thought she heard him murmur, "I love you," and then he was firmly unwrapping her arms, gently moving her away from him. He turned and strode away from her, almost running.

She jumped when Nisura touched her arm. "He looks as if you set him a task he won't enjoy. But you mustn't let him see you cry over it. That negates the purpose. Come. Nynaeve wants you."

Scrubbing her cheeks, Egwene followed the other woman. *Take care of yourself, you wool-headed lummox. Light, take care of him.*

CHAPTER 9

Leavetakings

THE OUTER COURTYARD WAS IN ORDERED TUR-
moil when Rand finally reached it with his saddlebags
and the bundle containing the harp and flute. The sun
climbed toward midday. Men hurried around the horses, tugging
at saddle girths and pack harness, voices raised. Others darted
with last-minute additions to the packsaddles, or water for the
men working, or dashed off to fetch something just remembered.
But everyone seemed to know exactly what they were doing and
where they were going. The guardwalks and archers' balconies
were crowded again, and excitement crackled in the morning air.
Hooves clattered on the paving stones. One of the packhorses
began kicking, and stablemen ran to calm it. The smell of horses
hung thick. Rand's cloak tried to flap in the breeze that rippled the
swooping-hawk banners on the towers, but his bow, slung across
his back, held it down.

From outside the open gates came the sounds of the Amyrlin's pikemen and archers forming up in the square. They had marched around from a side gate. One of the trumpeters tested his horn.

Some of the Warders glanced at Rand as he walked across the courtyard; a few raised eyebrows when they saw the heron-mark sword, but none spoke. Half wore the cloaks that were so queasy-making to look at. Mandarb, Lan's stallion, was there, tall, and black, and fierce-eyed, but the man himself was not, and none of the Aes Sedai, none of the women, were in evidence yet either. Moiraine's white mare, Aldieb, stepped daintily beside the stallion.

Rand's bay stallion was with the other group on the far side of the courtyard, with Ingtar, and a bannerman holding Ingtar's Gray Owl banner, and twenty other armored men with lances tipped with two feet of steel, all mounted already. The bars of their helmets covered their faces, and golden surcoats with the Black Hawk on the chest hid their plate-and-mail. Only Ingtar's helmet had a crest, a crescent moon above his brow, points up. Rand recognized some of the men. Rough-tongued Uno, with a long scar down his face and only one eye. Ragan and Masema. Others who had exchanged a word, or played a game of stones. Ragan waved to him, and Uno nodded, but Masema was not the only one who gave him a cold stare and turned away. Their packhorses stood placidly, tails swishing.

The big bay danced as Rand tied his saddlebags and bundle behind the high-cantled saddle. He put his foot in the stirrup and murmured, "Easy, Red," as he swung into the saddle, but he let the stallion frisk away some of his stable-bound energy.

To Rand's surprise, Loial appeared from the direction of the stables, riding to join them. The Ogier's hairy-fetlocked mount was as big and heavy as a prime Dhurran stallion. Beside it, all the other animals looked the size of Bela, but with Loial in the saddle, the horse seemed almost a pony.

Loial carried no weapon that Rand could see; he had never heard of any Ogier using a weapon. Their *stedding* were protection enough. And Loial had his own priorities, his own ideas of what was needed for a journey. The pockets of his long coat had a telltale bulge, and his saddlebags showed the square imprints of books.

The Ogier stopped his horse a little way off and looked at Rand, his tufted ears twitching uncertainly.

"I didn't know you were coming," Rand said. "I'd think you would have had enough of traveling with us. This time there's no telling how long it will be, or where we will end up."

Loial's ears lifted a little. "There was no telling when I first met you, either. Besides, what held then, holds now. I can't let the chance pass to see history actually weave itself around *ta'veren*. And to help find the Horn. . . ."

Mat and Perrin rode up behind Loial and paused. Mat looked a little tired around the eyes, but his face wore a bloom of health.

"Mat," Rand said, "I'm sorry for what I said. Perrin, I didn't mean it. I was being stupid."

Mat only glanced at him, then shook his head and mouthed something to Perrin that Rand could not hear. Mat had only his bow and quiver, but Perrin also wore his axe at his belt, with its big half-moon blade balanced by a thick spike.

"Mat? Perrin? Really, I didn't—" They rode on toward Ingtar.

"That is not a coat for traveling, Rand," Loial said.

Rand glanced down at the golden thorns climbing his crimson sleeve and grimaced. *Small wonder Mat and Perrin still think I'm putting on airs.* On returning to his room he had found everything already packed and sent on. All of the plain coats he had been given were on the packhorses, so the servants said; every coat left in the wardrobe was at least as ornate as the one he wore. His saddlebags held nothing in the way of clothes but a few shirts, some wool stockings, and a spare pair of breeches. At least he had removed the golden cord from his sleeve, though he had the red eagle pin in his pocket. Lan had means it for a gift, after all.

"I'll change when we stop tonight," he muttered. He took a deep breath. "Loial, I said things to you I should not have, and I hope you'll forgive me. You have every right to hold them against me, but I hope you won't."

Loial grinned, and his ears stood up. He moved his horse closer. "I say things I should not all the time. The Elders always said I spoke an hour before I thought."

Suddenly Lan was at Rand's stirrup, in his gray-green scaled armor that would make him all but disappear in forest or darkness. "I need to talk to you, sheepherder." He looked at Loial. "Alone, if you please, Builder." Loial nodded and moved his big horse away.

"I don't know if I should listen to you," Rand told the Warder. "These fancy clothes, and all those things you told me, they didn't help much."

"When you can't win a big victory, sheepherder, learn to settle for the small ones. If you made them think of you as something more than a farmboy who'll be easy to handle, then you won a small victory. Now be quiet and listen. I've only time for one last lesson, the hardest. Sheathing the Sword."

"You've spent an hour every morning making me do nothing but draw this bloody sword and put it back in the scabbard. Standing, sitting, lying down. I think I can manage to get it back in the sheath without cutting myself."

"I said listen, sheepherder," the Warder growled. "There will come a time when you must achieve a goal at all costs. It may come in attack or in defense. And the only way will be to allow the sword to be sheathed in your own body."

"That's crazy," Rand said. "Why would I ever—?"

The Warder cut him off. "You will know when it comes, sheepherder, when the price is worth the gain, and there is no other choice left to you. That is called Sheathing the Sword. Remember it."

The Amyrlin appeared, striding across the crowded courtyard

with Leane and her staff, and Lord Agelmar at her shoulder. Even in a green velvet coat, the Lord of Fal Dara did not look out of place among so many armored men. There was still no sign of the other Aes Sedai. As they went by, Rand caught part of their conversation.

"But, Mother," Agelmar was protesting, "you've had no time to rest from the journey here. Stay at least a few days more. I promise you a feast tonight such as you could hardly get in Tar Valon."

The Amyrlin shook her head without breaking stride. "I cannot, Agelmar. You know I would if I could. I had never planned to remain long, and matters urgently require my presence in the White Tower. I should be there now."

"Mother, it shames me that you come one day and leave the next. I swear to you, there will be no repetition of last night. I have tripled the guard on the city gates as well as the keep. I have tumblers in from the town, and a bard coming from Mos Shirare. Why, King Easar will be on his way from Fal Moran. I sent word as soon as. . . ."

Their voices faded as they crossed the courtyard, swallowed up by the din of preparation. The Amyrlin never as much as glanced in Rand's direction.

When Rand looked down, the Warder was gone, and nowhere to be seen. Loial brought his horse back to Rand's side. "That is a hard man to catch and hold, isn't he, Rand? He's not here, then he's here, then he's gone, and you don't see him coming or going."

Sheathing the Sword. Rand shivered. *Warders must all be crazy.*

The Warder the Amyrlin was speaking to suddenly sprang into his saddle. He was at a dead gallop before he reached the widestanding gates. She stood watching him go, and her stance seemed to urge him to go faster.

"Where is he headed in such a hurry?" Rand wondered aloud.

"I heard," Loial said, "that she was sending someone out today, all the way to Arad Doman. There is word of some sort of trouble on Almoth Plain, and the Amyrlin Seat wants to know exactly what. What I don't understand is, why now? From what I hear, the rumors of this trouble came from Tar Valon with the Aes Sedai."

Rand felt cold. Egwene's father had a big map back at home, a map Rand had pored over more than once, dreaming before he found out what the dreams were like when they came true. It was old, that map, showing some lands and nations the merchants from outside said no longer existed, but Almoth Plain was marked, butting against Toman Head. *We will meet again on Toman Head.* It was all the way across the world he knew, on the Aryth Ocean. "It has nothing to do with us," he whispered. "Nothing to do with me."

Loial appeared not to have heard. Rubbing the side of his nose with a finger like a sausage, the Ogier was still peering at the gate where the Warder had vanished. "If she wanted to know, why not send someone before she left Tar Valon? But you humans are always sudden and excitable, always jumping around and shouting." His ears stiffened with embarrassment. "I *am* sorry, Rand. You see what I mean about speaking before I think. I'm rash and excitable sometimes myself, as you know."

Rand laughed. It was a weak laugh, but it felt good to have something to laugh at. "Maybe if we lived as long as you Ogier, we'd be more settled." Loial was ninety years old; by Ogier standards, not old enough by ten years to be outside the *stedding* alone. That he had gone anyway was proof, he maintained, of his rashness. If Loial was an excitable Ogier, Rand thought most of them must be made of stone.

"Perhaps so," Loial mused, "but you humans do so much with your lives. We do nothing but huddle in our *stedding.* Planting the groves, and even the building, were all done before the Long Exile ended." It was the groves Loial held dear, not the cities men remembered the Ogier for building. It was the groves, planted to remind Ogier Builders of the *stedding,* that Loial had left his home to see. "Since we found our way back to the *stedding,* we. . . ." His words trailed off as the Amyrlin approached.

Ingtar and the other men shifted in their saddles, preparing to dismount and kneel, but she motioned them to stay as they were. Leane stood at her shoulder, and Agelmar a pace back. From his glum face, he appeared to have given up trying to convince her to remain longer.

The Amyrlin looked at them one by one before she spoke. Her gaze stayed on Rand no longer than on any other.

"Peace favor your sword, Lord Ingtar," she said finally. "Glory to the Builders, Loial Kiseran."

"You honor us, Mother. May peace favor Tar Valon." Ingtar bowed in his saddle, and the other Shienarans did, too.

"All honor to Tar Valon," Loial said, bowing.

Only Rand, and his two friends on the other side of the party, stayed upright. He wondered what she had said to them. Leane's frown took in all three of them, and Agelmar's eyes widened, but the Amyrlin took no notice.

"You ride to find the Horn of Valere," she said, "and the hope of the world rides with you. The Horn cannot be left in the wrong hands, especially in Darkfriend hands. Those who come to answer its call, will come whoever blows it, and they are bound to the Horn, not to the Light."

There was a stir among the listening men. Everyone believed that those heroes called back from the grave would fight for the Light. If they could fight for the Shadow, instead. . . .

The Amyrlin went on, but Rand was no longer listening. The watcher was back. The hair stirred on the back of his neck. He peered up at the packed archers' balconies overlooking the court-yard, at the rows of people jammed along the guardwalks atop the walls. Somewhere among them was the set of eyes that had followed him unseen. The gaze clung to him like dirty oil. *It can't be a Fade, not here. Then who? Or what?* He twisted in his saddle, pulling Red around, searching. The bay began to dance again.

Suddenly something flashed across in front of Rand's face. A man passing behind the Amyrlin cried out and fell, a black-fletched arrow jutting from his side. The Amyrlin stood calmly looking at a rent in her sleeve; blood slowly stained the gray silk.

A woman screamed, and abruptly the courtyard rang with cries and shouts. The people on the walls milled furiously, and every man in the courtyard had his sword out. Even Rand, he was surprised to realize.

Agelmar shook his blade at the sky. "Find him!" he roared. "Bring him to me!" His face went from red to white when he saw the blood on the Amyrlin's sleeve. He fell to his knees, head bowed. "Forgive, Mother. I have failed your safety. I am ashamed."

"Nonsense, Agelmar," the Amyrlin said. "Leane, stop fussing over me and see to that man. I've cut myself worse than this more than once cleaning fish, and he needs help now. Agelmar, stand up. Stand up, Lord of Fal Dara. You have not failed me, and you have no reason for shame. Last year in the White Tower, with my own guards at every gate and Warders all around me, a man with a knife came within five steps of me. A Whitecloak, no doubt, though I've no proof. Please stand up, or I will be shamed." As Agelmar slowly rose, she fingered her sliced sleeve. "A poor shot for a Whitecloak bowman, or even a Darkfriend." Her eyes flickered up to touch Rand's. "If it was at me he aimed." Her gaze was gone before he could read anything on her face, but he suddenly wanted to dismount and hide.

It wasn't aimed at her, and she knows it.

Leane straightened from where she had been kneeling. Someone had laid a cloak over the face of the man who had taken the arrow. "He is dead, Mother." She sounded tired. "He was dead when he struck the ground. Even if I had been at his side. . . ."

"You did what you could, Daughter. Death cannot be Healed."

Agelmar moved closer. "Mother, if there are Whitecloak killers about, or Darkfriends, you must allow me to send men with you. As far as the river, at least. I could not live if harm came to you in Shienar. Please, return to the women's apartments. I will see them guarded with my life until you are ready to travel."

"Be at ease," she told him. "This scratch will not delay me a moment. Yes, yes, I will gladly accept your men as far as the river, if you insist. But I will not let this delay Lord Ingtar a moment, either. Every heartbeat counts until the Horn is found again. Your leave, Lord Agelmar, to order your oathmen?"

He bowed his head in assent. At that moment he would have given her Fal Dara had she asked.

The Amyrlin turned back to Ingtar and the men gathered behind him. She did not look at Rand again. He was surprised to see her smile suddenly.

"I wager Illian does not give its Great Hunt of the Horn so rousing a send-off," she said. "But yours is the true Great Hunt. You are few, so you may travel quickly, yet enough to do what you must. I charge you, Lord Ingtar of House Shinowa, I charge all of you, find the Horn of Valere, and let nothing bar your way."

Ingtar whipped his sword from his back and kissed the blade. "By my life and soul, by my House and honor, I swear it, Mother."

"Then ride."

Ingtar swung his horse toward the gate.

Rand dug his heels into Red's flanks and galloped after the column already disappearing through the gates.

Unaware of what had occurred within, the Amyrlin's pikemen and archers stood walling a path from the gates to the city proper, the Flame of Tar Valon on their chests. Her drummers and trumpeters waited near the gates, ready to fall in when she left. Behind the rows of armored men, people packed the square in front of the keep. Some cheered Ingtar's banner, and others no doubt thought this was the start of the Amyrlin Seat's departure. A swelling roar followed Rand across the square.

He caught up with Ingtar where low-eaved houses and shops stood to either side, and more people thickly lined the stone-paved street. Some of them cheered, too. Mat and Perrin had been riding at the head of the column with Ingtar and Loial, but the two of them fell back when Rand joined them. *How am I ever going to apologize if they won't stay near me long enough for me to say anything? Burn me, he doesn't look like he's dying.*

"Changu and Nidao are gone," Ingtar said abruptly. He sounded cold and angry, but shaken, too. "We counted every head in the keep, alive or dead, last night and again this morning. They are the only ones not accounted for."

"Changu was on guard in the dungeon yesterday," Rand said slowly.

"And Nidao. They had the second watch. They always stayed together, even if they had to trade or do extra duty for it. They were not on guard when it happened, but. . . . They fought at Tarwin's Gap, a month gone, and saved Lord Agelmar when his horse went down with Trollocs all around him. Now this. Darkfriends." He drew a deep breath. "Everything is breaking apart."

A man on horseback forced his way through the throng lining the street and joined in behind Ingtar. He was a townsman, by his clothes, lean, with a lined face and graying hair cut long. A bundle and waterbottles were lashed behind his saddle, and a short-bladed sword and a notched sword-breaker hung at his belt, along with a cudgel.

Ingtar noticed Rand's glances. "This is Hurin, our sniffer. There was no need to let the Aes Sedai know about him. Not that what he does is wrong, you understand. The King keeps a sniffer in Fal Moran, and there's another in Ankor Dail. It's just that Aes Sedai seldom like what they do not understand, and with him being a man. . . . It's nothing to do with the Power, of course. Aaaah! You tell him, Hurin."

"Yes, Lord Ingtar," the man said. He bowed low to Rand from his saddle. "Honor to serve, my Lord."

"Call me Rand." Rand stuck out his hand, and after a moment Hurin grinned and took it.

"As you wish, my Lord Rand. Lord Ingtar and Lord Kajin don't mind a man's ways—and Lord Agelmar, of course—but they say in the town you're an outland prince from the south, and some outland lords are strict for every man in his place."

"I'm not a lord." *At least I'll get away from that, now.* "Just Rand."

Hurin blinked. "As you wish, my Lor—ah—Rand. I'm a sniffer, you see. Been one four years this Sunday. I never heard of such a thing before then, but I hear there's a few others like me. It started slow, catching bad smells where nobody else smelled anything, and it grew. Took a whole year before I realized what it was. I could smell violence, the killing and the hurting. Smell where it happened. Smell the trail of those who did it. Every trail's different, so there's no chance of mixing them up. Lord Ingtar heard of it, and took me in his service, to serve the King's justice."

"You can smell violence?" Rand said. He could not help looking at the man's nose. Is was an ordinary nose, not large, not small. "You mean you can really follow somebody who, say, killed another man? By smell?"

"I can that, my Lor—ah—Rand. It fades with time, but the worse the violence, the longer it lasts. Aiie, I can smell a battlefield ten years old, though the trails of the men who were there are gone. Up near the Blight, the trails of the Trollocs almost never fade. Not much to a Trolloc but killing and hurting. A fight in a tavern, though, with maybe a broken arm . . . that smell's gone in hours."

"I can see where you wouldn't want Aes Sedai to find out."

"Ah, Lord Ingtar was right about the Aes Sedai, the Light illumine them—ah—Rand. There was one in Cairhien once—Brown Ajah, but I swear I thought she was Red before she let me go— she kept me a month trying to find out how I do it. She didn't like not knowing. She kept muttering, 'Is it old come again, or new?' and staring at me until you would have thought I *was* using the One Power. Almost had me doubting myself. But I haven't gone mad, and I don't *do* anything. I just smell it."

Rand could not help remembering Moiraine. *Old barriers weaken. There is something of dissolution and change about our time. Old things walk again, and new things are born. We may live to see the end of an Age.* He shivered. "So we'll track those who took the Horn with your nose."

Ingtar nodded. Hurin grinned proudly, and said, "We will that—ah—Rand. I followed a murderer to Cairhien, once, and another all the way to Maradon, to bring them back for the King's justice." His grin faded, and he looked troubled. "This is the worst ever, though. Murder smells bad, and the trail of a murderer stinks with it, but this. . . ." His nose wrinkled. "There were men in it last night. Darkfriends, must be, but you can't tell a Darkfriend by smell. What I'll follow is the Trollocs, and the Halfmen. And something even worse." He trailed off, frowning and muttering to himself, but Rand could hear it. "Something even worse, the Light help me."

They reached the city gates, and just beyond the walls Hurin lifted his face to the breeze. His nostrils flared, then he gave a snort of disgust. "That way, my Lord Ingtar." He pointed south.

Ingtar looked surprised. "Not toward the Blight?"

"No, Lord Ingtar. Faugh!" Hurin wiped his mouth on his sleeve. "I can almost taste them. South, they went."

"She was right, then, the Amyrlin Seat," Ingtar said slowly. "A great and wise woman, who deserves better than me to serve her. Take the trail, Hurin."

Rand turned and peered back through the gates, up the street to the keep. He hoped Egwene was all right. *Nynaeve will look after her. Maybe it's better this way, like a clean cut, too quick to hurt till after it's done.*

He rode after Ingtar and the Gray Owl banner, south. The wind was making up, and cold against his back despite the sun. He thought he heard laughter in it, faint and mocking.

THE WAXING MOON lit the humid, night-dark streets of Illian, which still rang with celebration left over from daylight. In only a few more days, the Great Hunt of the Horn would be sent forth with pomp and ceremony that tradition claimed dated to the Age of Legends. The festivities for the Hunters had blended into the Feast of Teven, with its famed contests and prizes for gleemen. The greatest prize of all, as always, would go for the best telling of *The Great Hunt of the Horn*.

Tonight the gleemen entertained in the palaces and mansions of the city, where the great and mighty disported themselves, and the Hunters come from every nation to ride out and find, if not the Horn of Valere itself, at least immortality in song and story. They would have music and dancing, and fans and ices to dispel the year's first real heat, but carnival filled the streets, too, in the moon-bright muggy night. Every day was a carnival, until the Hunt departed, and every night.

People ran past Bayle Domon in masks and costumes bizarre and fanciful, many showing too much flesh. Shouting and singing they ran, a half dozen together, then scattered pairs giggling and clutching each other, then twenty in a' raucous knot. Fireworks crackled in the sky, gold and silver bursts against the black. There were almost as many Illuminators in the city as there were gleemen.

Domon spared little thought for fireworks, or for the Hunt. He was on his way to meet men he thought might be trying to kill him.

He crossed the Bridge of Flowers, over one of the city's many canals, into the Perfumed Quarter, the port district of Illian. The canal smelled of too many chamber pots, with never a sign that there had ever been flowers near the bridge. The quarter smelled of hemp and pitch from the shipyards and docks, and sour harbor mud, all of it made fiercer by heated air that seemed nearly damp enough to drink. Domon breathed heavily; every time he returned from the northcountry he found himself surprised, for all he had been born there, at the early summer heat in Illian.

In one hand he carried a stout cudgel, and the other hand rested on the hilt of the short sword he had often used in defending the decks of his river trader from brigands. No few footpads stalked these nights of revelry, where the pickings were rich and most were deep in wine.

Yet he was a broad, muscular man, and none of those out for a catch of gold thought him rich enough, in his plain-cut coat, to risk his size and his cudgel. The few who caught a clear glimpse of him, when he passed through light spilling from a window, edged back till he was well past. Dark hair that hung to his shoulders and a long beard that left his upper lip bare framed a round face, but that face had never been soft, and now it was set as grimly as if he meant to batter his way through a wall. He had men to meet, and he was not happy about it.

More revelers ran past singing off-key, wine mangling their words. *"The Horn of Valere," my aged grandmother!* Domon thought glumly. *It be my ship I do want to hang on to. And my life, Fortune prick me.*

He pushed into an inn, under a sign of a big, white-striped badger dancing on its hind legs with a man carrying a silver shovel. Easing the Badger, it was called, though not even Nieda Sidoro, the innkeeper, knew what the name meant; there had always been an inn of the name in Illian.

The common room, with sawdust on the floor and a musician

softly strumming a twelve-stringed bittern in one of the Sea Folk's sad songs, was well lighted and quiet. Nieda allowed no commotion in her place, and her nephew, Bili, was big enough to carry a man out with either hand. Sailors, dockworkers, and warehousemen came to the Badger for a drink and maybe a little talk, for a game of stones or darts. The room was half full now; even men who liked quiet had been lured out by carnival. The talk was soft, but Domon caught mentions of the Hunt, and of the false Dragon the Murandians had taken, and of the one the Tairens were chasing through Haddon Mirk. There seemed to be some question whether it would be preferable to see the false Dragon die, or the Tairens.

Domon grimaced. *False Dragons! Fortune prick me, there be no place safe these days.* But he had no real care for false Dragons, any more than for the Hunt.

The stout proprietress, with her hair rolled at the back of her head, was wiping a mug, keeping a sharp eye on her establishment. She did not stop what she was doing, or even look at him, really, but her left eyelid drooped, and her eyes slanted toward three men at a table in the corner. They were quiet even for the Badger, almost somber, and their bell-shaped velvet caps and dark coats, embroidered across the chest in bars of silver and scarlet and gold, stood out among the plain dress of the other patrons.

Domon sighed and took a table in a corner by himself. *Cairhienin, this time.* He took a mug of brown ale from a serving girl and drew a long swallow. When he lowered the mug, the three men in striped coats were standing beside his table. He made an unobtrusive gesture, to let Nieda know that he did not need Bili.

"Captain Domon?" They were all three nondescript, but there was an air about the speaker that made Domon take him for their leader. They did not appear to be armed; despite their fine clothes, they looked as if they did not need to be. There were hard eyes in those so very ordinary faces. "Captain Bayle Domon, of the *Spray?*"

Domon gave a short nod, and the three sat down without waiting for an invitation. The same man did the talking; the other two just watched, hardly blinking. *Guards,* Domon thought, *for all their fine clothes. Who do he be to have a pair of guards to look over him?*

"Captain Domon, we have a personage who must be brought from Mayene to Illian."

"*Spray* be a river craft," Domon cut him off. "Her draft be shallow, and she has no the keel for deep water." It was not exactly true, but close enough for landsmen. *At least it be a change from Tear. They be getting smarter.*

The man seemed unperturbed at the interruption. "We had heard you were giving up the river trade."

"Maybe I do, and maybe no. I have no decided." He had, though. He would not go back upriver, back to the Borderlands, for all the silk shipped in Tairen bottoms. Saldaean furs and ice peppers were not worth it, and it had nothing to do with the false Dragon he had heard of there. But he wondered again how anyone knew. He had not spoken of it to anyone, yet the others had known, too.

"You can coast to Mayene easily enough. Surely, Captain, you would be willing to sail along the shoreline for a thousand gold marks."

Despite himself, Domon goggled. It was four times the last offer, and that had been enough to make a man's jaw drop. "Who do you want me to fetch for that? The First of Mayene herself? Has Tear finally forced her all the way out, then?"

"You need no names, Captain." The man set a large leather pouch on the table, and a sealed parchment. The pouch clinked heavily as he pushed them across the table. The big red wax circle holding the folded parchment shut bore the many-rayed Rising Sun of Cairhien. "Two hundred on account. For a thousand marks,

I think you need no names. Give that, seal unbroken, to the Port Captain of Mayene, and he will give you three hundred more, and your passenger. I will hand over the remainder when your passenger is delivered here. So long as you have made no effort to discover that personage's identity."

Domon drew a deep breath. *Fortune, it be worth the voyage if there be never another penny beyond what be in that sack.* And a thousand was more money than he would clear in three years. He suspected that if he probed a little more, there would be other hints, just hints, that the voyage involved hidden dealings between Illian's Council of Nine and the First of Mayene. The First's city-state was a province of Tear in all but name, and she would no doubt like Illian's aid. And there were many in Illian who said it was time for another war, that Tear was taking more than a fair share of the trade on the Sea of Storms. A likely net to snare him, if he had not seen three like it in the past month.

He reached to take the pouch, and the man who had done all the talking caught his wrist. Domon glared at him, but he looked back undisturbed.

"You must sail as soon as possible, Captain."

"At first light," Domon growled, and the man nodded and released his hold.

"At first light, then, Captain Domon. Remember, discretion keeps a man alive to spend his money."

Domon watched the three of them leave, then stared sourly at the pouch and the parchment on the table in front of him. Someone wanted him to go east. Tear or Mayene, it did not matter so long as he went east. He thought he knew who wanted it. *And then again, I have no a clue to them.* Who could know who was a Darkfriend? But he knew that Darkfriends had been after him since before he left Marabon to come back downriver. Darkfriends and Trollocs. Of that, he was sure. The real question, the one he had not even a glimmer of an answer for, was why?

"Trouble, Bayle?" Nieda asked. "You do look as if you had seen a Trolloc." She giggled, an improbable sound from a woman her size. Like most people who had never been to the Borderlands, Nieda did not believe in Trollocs. He had tried telling her the truth of it; she enjoyed his stories, and thought they were all lies. She did not believe in snow, either.

"No trouble, Nieda." He untied the pouch, dug a coin out without looking, and tossed it to her. "Drinks for everyone till that do run out, then I'll give you another."

Nieda looked at the coin in surprise. "A Tar Valon mark! Do you be trading with the witches now, Bayle?"

"No," he said hoarsely. "That I do not!"

She bit the coin, then quickly snugged it away behind her broad belt. "Well, it be gold for that. And I suspect the witches be no so bad as some make them out, anyway. I'd no say so much to many men. I know a money changer who do handle such. You'll no have to give me another, with as few as be here tonight. More ale for you, Bayle?"

He nodded numbly, though his mug was still almost full, and she trundled off. She was a friend, and would not speak of what she had seen. He sat staring at the leather pouch. Another mug was brought before he could make himself open it enough to look at the coins inside. He stirred them with a callused finger. Gold marks glittered up at him in the lamplight, every one of them bearing the damning Flame of Tar Valon. Hurriedly he tied the bag. Dangerous coins. One or two might pass, but so many would say to most people exactly what Nieda thought. There were Children of the Light in the city, and although there was no law in Illian against dealing with Aes Sedai, he would never make it to a magistrate if the Whitecloaks heard of this. These men had made sure he would not simply take the gold and stay in Illian.

While he was sitting there worrying, Yarin Maeldan, his brooding, stork-like second on *Spray,* came into the Badger with his brows pulled down to his long nose and stood over the captain's table. "Carn's dead, Captain."

Domon stared at him, frowning. Three others of his men had already been killed, one each time he refused a commission that would take him east. The magistrates had done nothing; the streets were dangerous at night, they said, and sailors a rough and quarrelsome lot. Magistrates seldom troubled themselves with what happened in the Perfumed Quarter, as long as no respectable citizens were injured.

"But this time I did accept them," he muttered.

"'Tisn't all, Captain," Yarin said. "They worked Carn with knives, like they wanted him to tell them something. And some more men tried to sneak aboard *Spray* not an hour gone. The dock watch ran them off. Third time in ten days, and I never knew wharf rats to be so persistent. They like to let an alarm die down before they try again. And somebody tossed my room at the Silver Dolphin last night. Took some silver, so I'd think it was thieves, but they left that belt buckle of mine, the one set with garnets and moonstones, lying right out in plain sight. What's going on, Captain? The men are afraid, and I'm a little nervous myself."

Domon reared to his feet. "Roust the crew, Yarin. Find them and tell them *Spray* sails as soon as there do be men enough aboard to handle her." Stuffing the parchment into his coat pocket, he snatched up the bag of gold and pushed his second out the door ahead of him. "Roust them, Yarin, for I'll leave any man who no makes it, standing on the quay as he is."

Domon gave Yarin a shove to start him running, then stalked off toward the docks. Even footpads who heard the clinking of the pouch he carried steered clear of him, for he walked now like a man going to do murder.

There were already crewmen scrambling aboard *Spray* when he arrived, and more running barefoot down the stone quay. They did not know what he feared was pursuing him, or even that anything did pursue him, but they knew he made good profits, and after the Illianer way, he gave shares to the crew.

Spray was eighty feet long, with two masts, and broad in the beam, with room for deck cargo as well as in the holds. Despite what Domon had told the Cairhienin—if they had been Cairhienin—he thought she could stand the open water. The Sea of Storms was quieter in the summer.

"She'll have to," he muttered, and strode below to his cabin.

He tossed the sack of gold on his bed, built neatly against the hull like everything else in the stern cabin, and dug out the parchment. Lighting a lantern, hanging in its swivel from the overhead, he studied the sealed document, turning it as if he could read what was inside without opening it. A rap on the door made him frown. "Come."

Yarin stuck his head in. "They're all aboard but three I couldn't find, Captain. But I've spread the word through every tavern, hell, and crib in the quarter. They'll be aboard before it's light enough to start upriver."

"*Spray* do sail now. To sea." Domon cut off Yarin's protests about light and tides, and *Spray* not being built for the open sea. "Now! *Spray* can clear the bars at dead low tide. You've no forgotten how to sail by the stars, have you? Take her out, Yarin. Take her out now, and come back to me when we be beyond the breakwater."

His second hesitated—Domon never let a tricky bit of sailing pass without him on deck giving orders, and taking *Spray* out in the night would be all of that, shallow draft or no—then nodded and vanished. In moments the sounds of Yarin shouting orders and bare feet thumping on the decks overhead penetrated Domon's cabin. He ignored them, even when the ship lurched, catching the tide.

Finally he lifted the mantle of the lantern and stuck a knife into the flame. Smoke curled up as oil burned off the blade, but before the metal could turn red, he pushed charts out of the way and pressed the parchment flat on his desk, working the hot steel slowly under the sealing wax. The top fold lifted.

It was a simple document, without preamble or salutation, and it made sweat break out on his forehead.

The bearer of this is a Darkfriend wanted in Cairhien for murders and other foul crimes, least among them, theft from Our Person. We call upon you to seize this man and all things found in his keeping, to the smallest. Our representative will come to carry away what he has stolen from Us. Let all he possesses, save what We claim, go to you as reward for taking him. Let the vile miscreant himself be hanged immediately, that his Shadow-spawned villainy no longer taint the Light.

> *Sealed by Our Hand*
> *Galldrian su Riatin Rie*
> *King of Cairhien*
> *Defender of the Dragonwall*

In thin red wax below the signature were impressed the Rising Sun seal of Cairhien and the Five Stars of House Riatin.

"Defender of the Dragonwall, my aged grandmother," Domon croaked. "Fine right the man do have to call himself that any longer."

He examined the seals and signature minutely, holding the document close to the lamp, with his nose all but brushing the parchment, but he could find no flaw in the one, and for the other, he had no idea what Galldrian's hand looked like. If it was not the King himself who had signed it, he suspected that whoever had had made a good imitation of Galldrian's scrawl. In any case, it made no real difference. In Tear, the letter would be instantly damning in the hands of an Illianer. Or in Mayene, with Tairen influence so strong. There was no war now, and men from either port came and went freely, but there was as little love for Illianers in Tear as the other way round. Especially with an excuse like this.

For a moment he thought of putting the parchment into the lantern's flame—it was a dangerous thing to have, in Tear or Illian or anywhere he could imagine—but finally he tucked it carefully into a secret cubbyhole behind his desk, concealed by a panel only he knew how to open.

"My possessions, eh?"

He collected old things, as much as he could living on shipboard. What he could not buy, because it was too expensive or too large, he collected by seeing and remembering. All those remnants of times gone, those wonders scattered around the world that had first pulled him aboard a ship as boy. He had added four to his collection in Maradon this last trip, and it had been then that the Darkfriend pursuit began. And Trollocs, too, for a time. He had heard that Whitebridge had been burned to the ground right after he sailed from there, and there had been rumors of Myrddraal as well as Trollocs. It was that, all of it together, that had first convinced him he was not imagining things, that had had him on guard when that first odd commission was offered, too much money for a simple voyage to Tear, and a thin tale for a reason.

Digging into his chest, he set out on the desk what he had bought in Maradon. A lightstick, left from the Age of Legends, or so it was said. Certainly no one knew the making of them any longer. Expensive, that, and rarer than an honest magistrate. It looked like a plain glass rod, thicker than his thumb and not quite as long as his forearm, but when held in the hand it glowed as brightly as a lantern. Lightsticks shattered like glass, too; he had nearly lost *Spray* in the fire caused by the first he had owned. A small, age-dark ivory carving of a man holding a sword. The fellow who sold it claimed if you held it long enough you started to feel warm. Domon never had, and neither had any of the crew he let hold it, but it was old, and that was enough for Domon. The skull of a cat as big as a lion, and so old it was turned to stone. But no lion had ever had fangs, almost tusks, a foot long. And a thick disk the size of a man's hand, half white and half black, a sinuous line separating the colors. The shopkeeper in Maradon had said it was from the Age of Legends, thinking he lied, but Domon had haggled only a little before paying, because he recognized what the shopkeeper did not: the ancient symbol of Aes Sedai from before the Breaking of the World. Not a safe thing to have, precisely, but neither a thing to be passed up by a man with a fascination for the old.

And it was heartstone. The shopkeeper had never dared add that to what he thought were lies. No riverfront shopkeeper in Maradon could afford even one piece of *cuendillar.*

The disk felt hard and smooth in his hand, and not at all valuable except for its age, but he was afraid it was what his pursuers were after. Lightsticks, and ivory carvings, and even bones turned to stone, he had seen other times, other places. Yet even knowing what they wanted—if he did know—he still had no idea why, and he could no longer be sure who his pursuers were. Tar Valon marks, and an ancient Aes Sedai symbol. He scrubbed a hand across his lips; the taste of fear lay bitter on his tongue.

A knock at the door. He set the disk down and pulled an unrolled chart over what lay on his desk. "Come."

Yarin entered. "We're beyond the breakwater, Captain."

Domon felt a flash of surprise, then anger with himself. He should never have gotten so engrossed that he failed to feel *Spray* lifting on the swells. "Make west, Yarin. See to it."

"Ebou Dar, Captain?"

No far enough. No by five hundred leagues. "We'll put in long enough for me to get charts and top the water barrels, then we do sail west."

"West, Captain? Tremalking? The Sea Folk are tight with any traders but their own."

"The Aryth Ocean, Yarin. Plenty of trade between Tarabon and Arad Doman, and hardly a Taraboner or Domani bottom to worry about. They do no like the sea, I have heard. And all those small towns on Toman Head, every one holding itself free of any nation at all. We can even pick up Saldaean furs and ice peppers brought down to Bandar Eban."

Yarin shook his head slowly. He always looked at the dark side, but he was a good sailor. "Furs and peppers'll cost more there than running upriver for them, Captain. And I hear there's some kind of war. If Tarabon and Arad Doman are fighting, there may be no trade. I doubt we'll make much off the towns on Toman Head alone, even if they are safe. Falme's the largest, and it is not big."

"The Taraboners and the Domani have always squabbled over Almoth Plain and Toman Head. Even if it has come to blows this time, a careful man can always find trade. West, Yarin."

When Yarin had gone topside, Domon quickly added the black-and-white disk to the cubbyhole, and stowed the rest back in the bottom of his chest. *Darkfriends or Aes Sedai, I'll no run the way they want me. Fortune prick me, I'll no.*

Feeling safe for the first time in months, Domon went on deck as *Spray* heeled to catch the wind and put her bow west into the night-dark sea.

CHAPTER 10

The Hunt Begins

INGTAR SET A FAST PACE FOR THE BEGINNING of a long journey, fast enough that Rand worried a little about the horses. The animals could keep up the trot for hours, but there was still most of the day ahead, and likely days more beyond that. The way Ingtar's face was set, though, Rand thought he might intend to catch those who had stolen the Horn in the first day, in the first hour. Remembering his voice when he swore his oath to the Amyrlin Seat, Rand would not have been surprised. He kept his mouth shut, though. It was Lord Ingtar's command; as friendly as he had been to Rand, he still would not appreciate a shepherd giving advice.

Hurin rode a pace behind Ingtar, but it was the sniffer who led them south, pointing the way for Ingtar. The land was rolling, forested hills, thick with fir and leatherleaf and oak, but the path Hurin set led almost straight as an arrow, never wavering except to go around a few of the taller hills, where the way was clearly quicker around than over. The Gray Owl banner rippled in the wind.

Rand tried to ride with Mat and Perrin, but when Rand let his horse drop back to them, Mat nudged Perrin, and Perrin reluctantly galloped to the head of the column with Mat. Telling himself there was no point riding at the back by himself, Rand rode back to the front. They fell to the rear again, Mat again urging Perrin.

Burn them. I only want to apologize. He felt alone. It did not help that he knew it was his own fault.

Atop one hill, Uno dismounted to examine ground churned by hooves. He poked at some horse droppings and grunted. "Bloody well moving fast, my Lord." He had a voice that sounded as if he were shouting when he was just speaking. "We've not made up an hour on them. Burn me, we may have lost a flaming hour. They'll kill their bloody horses, the way they're going." He fingered a hoofed track. "No horse, that. Bloody Trolloc. Some flaming goat feet over there."

"We will catch them," Ingtar said grimly.

"Our horses, my Lord. Does no good to ride them into the bloody ground before we do catch up, my Lord. Even if they do kill their horses, bloody Trollocs can keep going longer than horses."

"We will catch them. Mount, Uno."

Uno looked at Rand with his one eye, then shrugged and climbed into his saddle. Ingtar took them down the far slope at a run, half sliding all the way to the bottom, and galloped up the next.

Why did he look at me that way, Rand wondered. Uno was one of those who had never shown much friendliness toward him. It was not like Masema's open dislike; Uno was not friendly with anyone except a few veterans as grizzled as himself. *Surely he doesn't believe that tale about me being a lord.*

Uno spent his time studying the country ahead, but when he caught Rand looking at him, he gave back stare for stare, and never said a word. It did not mean much. He would stare Ingtar in the eye, too. That was Uno's way.

The path chosen by the Darkfriends—*And what else,* Rand wondered; Hurin kept muttering about "something worse"—who had stolen the Horn never came close to any village. Rand saw villages, from one hilltop to another, with a mile or more of up-and-down country between, but there was never one close enough to make out the people in the streets. Or close enough for those people to make out a party heading south. There were farms, too, with low-eaved houses and tall barns and smoking chimneys, on hilltops and on hillsides and in the bottoms, but never one close enough for the farmer to have seen their quarry.

Eventually even Ingtar had to realize that the horses could not keep on as they were going. Rand heard muttered curses, and Ingtar pounded his thigh with a gauntleted fist, but finally he ordered everyone to dismount. They trotted, leading their horses, uphill and down, for a mile, then mounted and rode again. Then it was down again and trot. Trot a mile, then ride a mile. Trot, then ride.

Rand was surprised to see Loial grinning when they were down on the ground, toiling up a hill. The Ogier had been uneasy about riding and horses when they first met, preferring to trust to his own feet, but Rand thought he had long gotten over that.

"Do you like to run, Rand?" Loial laughed. "I do. I was the fastest in Stedding Shangtai. I outran a horse, once."

Rand only shook his head. He did not want to waste breath on talk. He looked for Mat and Perrin, but they were still at the back, too many men between for Rand to make them out. He wondered how the Shienarans could manage this in their armor. Not a one of them slowed or voiced a complaint. Uno did not even look as if he were breaking a sweat, and the bannerman never let the Gray Owl waver.

It was a quick pace, but twilight began to close without any sight of those they hunted except their tracks. At last, reluctantly, Ingtar called a halt to make camp for the night in the forest. The Shienarans went about getting fires started and setting picket-lines for the horses with a smooth economy of effort born of long experience. Ingtar posted six guards, in pairs, for the first watch.

Rand's first order of business was finding his bundle in the wicker panniers from the packhorses. It was not hard—there were few personal bundles among the supplies—but when he had it open, he let out a shout that brought every man in the camp erect with sword in hand.

Ingtar came running. "What is it? Peace, did someone get through? I did not hear the guards."

"It's these coats," Rand growled, still staring at what he had unpacked. One coat was black, embroidered with silver thread, the other white worked in gold. Both had herons on the collars, and both were at least as ornate as the scarlet coat he was wearing. "The servants told me I had two good, serviceable coats in here. Look at them!"

Ingtar sheathed his sword over his shoulder. The other men began to settle back down. "Well, they are serviceable."

"I can't wear these. I can't go around dressed like this all the time."

"You can wear them. A coat's a coat. I understand Moiraine Sedai herself saw to your packing. Maybe Aes Sedai do not exactly understand what a man wears in the field." Ingtar grinned. "After we catch these Trollocs, perhaps we'll have a feast. You will be dressed for it, at least, even if the rest of us are not." He strolled back to where the cook fires were already burning.

Rand had not moved since Ingtar mentioned Moiraine. He stared at the coats. *What is she doing? Whatever it is, I will not be used.* He bundled everything together again and stuffed the bundle back into the pannier. *I can always go naked,* he thought bitterly.

Shienarans took turns at the cooking when they were in the field, and Masema was stirring the kettle when Rand returned to the fires. The smell of a stew made from turnips, onions, and dried meat settled over the camp. Ingtar was served first, and then Uno, but everyone else stood in line however they happened to come. Masema slopped a big ladle of stew on Rand's plate; Rand stepped back quickly to keep from getting the overflow on his coat, and made room for the next man while sucking a burned thumb. Masema stared at him, with a fixed grin that never reached his eyes. Until Uno stepped up and cuffed him.

"We didn't bloody bring enough for you to be spilling it on the flaming ground." The one-eyed man looked at Rand and left. Masema rubbed his ear, but his glare followed Rand.

Rand went to join Ingtar and Loial, sitting on the ground under a spreading oak. Ingtar had his helmet off, on the ground beside him, but otherwise he was fully armored. Mat and Perrin were already there, eating hungrily. Mat gave a broad sneer at Rand's coat, but Perrin barely looked up, golden eyes shining in the half-light from the fires, before bending back to his plate.

At least they didn't leave this time.

He sat cross-legged on the other side of Ingtar from them. "I wish I knew why Uno keeps looking at me. It's probably this bloody coat."

Ingtar paused thoughtfully around a mouthful of stew. Finally he said, "Uno no doubt wonders if you are worthy of a heron-mark blade." Mat snorted loudly, but Ingtar went on unperturbed. "Do not let Uno upset you. He would treat Lord Agelmar like a raw recruit if he could. Well, perhaps not Agelmar, but anyone else. He has a tongue like a file, but he gives good advice. He should; he's been campaigning since before I was born. Listen to his advice, don't mind his tongue, and you will do all right with Uno."

"I thought he was like Masema." Rand shoveled stew into his

mouth. It was too hot, but he gulped it down. They had not eaten since leaving Fal Dara, and he had been too worried to eat that morning. His stomach rumbled, reminding him it was past time. He wondered if telling Masema he liked the food would help. "Masema acts like he hates me, and I don't understand it."

"Masema served three years in the Eastern Marches," Ingtar said. "At Ankor Dail, against the Aiel." He stirred his stew with his spoon, frowning. "I ask no questions, mind. If Lan Dai Shan and Moiraine Sedai want to say you are from Andor, from the Two Rivers, then you are. But Masema can't get the look of the Aiel out of his head, and when he sees you. . . ." He shrugged. "I ask no questions."

Rand dropped his spoon in the plate with a sigh. "Everybody thinks I'm somebody I am not. I am from the Two Rivers, Ingtar. I grew tabac with—with my father, and tended his sheep. That is what I am. A farmer and shepherd from the Two Rivers."

"He's from the Two Rivers," Mat said scornfully. "I grew up with him, though you'd never know it now. You put this Aiel nonsense in his head on top of what's already there, and the Light knows what we'll have. An Aiel lord, maybe."

"No," Loial said, "he has the look. You remember, Rand, I remarked on it once, though I thought it was just because I didn't know you humans well enough then. Remember? 'Till shade is gone, till water is gone, into the Shadow with teeth bared, screaming defiance with the last breath, to spit in Sightblinder's eye on the Last Day.' You remember, Rand."

Rand stared at his plate. *Wrap a* shoufa *around your head, and you would be the image of an Aielman.* That had been Gawyn, brother to Elayne, the Daughter-Heir of Andor. *Everybody thinks I'm somebody I'm not.*

"What was that?" Mat asked. "About spitting in the Dark One's eye."

"That's how long the Aiel say they'll fight," Ingtar said, "and

I don't doubt they will. Except for peddlers and gleemen, Aiel divide the world in two. Aiel, and enemies. They changed that for Cairhien five hundred years ago, for some reason no one but an Aiel could understand, but I do not think they will ever do so again."

"I suppose not," Loial sighed. "But they do let the Tuatha'an, the Traveling People, cross the Waste. And they don't see Ogier as enemies, either, though I doubt any of us would want to go out into the Waste. Aiel come to Stedding Shangtai sometimes to trade for sung wood. A hard people, though."

Ingtar nodded. "I wish I had some as hard. Half as hard."

"Is that a joke?" Mat laughed. "If I ran a mile wearing all the iron you're wearing, I would fall down and sleep a week. You've done it mile after mile all day."

"Aiel are hard," Ingtar said. "Man and woman, hard. I've fought them, and I know. They will run fifty miles, and fight a battle at the end of it. They're death walking, with any weapon or none. Except a sword. They will not touch a sword, for some reason. Or ride a horse, not that they need to. If you have a sword, and the Aielman has his bare hands, it is an even fight. If you're good. They herd cattle and goats where you or I would die of thirst before the day was done. They dig their villages into huge rock spires out in the Waste. They've been there since the Breaking, near enough. Artur Hawkwing tried to dig them out and was bloodied, the only major defeats he ever suffered. By day the air in the Aiel Waste shimmers with heat, and by night it freezes. And an Aiel will give you that blue-eyed stare and tell you there is no place on earth he would rather be. He won't be lying, either. If they ever tried to come out, we would be hard-pressed to stop them. The Aiel War lasted three years, and that was only four out of thirteen clans."

"Gray eyes from his mother doesn't make him an Aiel," Mat said.

Ingtar shrugged. "As I said, I ask no questions."

When Rand finally settled down for the night, his head hummed with unwanted thoughts. *Image of an Aielman. Moiraine Sedai wants to say you're from the Two Rivers. Aiel ravaged all the way to Tar Valon. Born on the slopes of Dragonmount. The Dragon Reborn.*

"I will not be used," he muttered, but sleep was a long time coming.

Ingtar broke camp before the sun was up in the morning. They had breakfasted and were riding south while the clouds in the east were still red with sunrise to come and dew still hung on the leaves. This time Ingtar put out scouts, and though the pace was hard, it was no longer horse-killing. Rand thought maybe Ingtar had realized they were not going to do it all in a day. The trail still led south, Hurin said. Until, two hours after the sun rose, one of the scouts came galloping back.

"Abandoned camp ahead, my Lord. Just on that hilltop there. Must have been at least thirty or forty of them there last night, my Lord."

Ingtar put spurs to horse as if he had been told the Darkfriends were still there, and Rand had to keep pace or be trampled by the Shienarans who galloped up the hill behind him.

There was not much to see. The cold ashes of campfires, well hidden in the trees, with what looked like the remnants of a meal tossed in them. A refuse heap too near the fires and already buzzing with flies.

Ingtar kept the others back, and dismounted to walk through the campsite with Uno, examining the ground. Hurin rode the circumference of the site, sniffing. Rand sat his stallion with the other men; he had no desire for any closer look at a place where Trollocs and Darkfriends had camped. And a Fade. *And something worse.*

Mat scrambled up the hill afoot and stalked into the campsite.

"Is this what a Darkfriend camp looks like? Smells a bit, but I can't say it looks any different from anybody else's." He kicked at one of the ash heaps, knocking out a piece of burned bone, and stooped to pick it up. "What do Darkfriends eat? Doesn't look like a sheep bone, or a cow."

"There was murder done here," Hurin said mournfully. He scrubbed at his nose with a kerchief. "Worse than murder."

"There were Trollocs here," Ingtar said, looking straight at Mat. "I suppose they got hungry, and the Darkfriends were handy." Mat dropped the blackened bone; he looked as if he were going to be sick.

"They are not going south any longer, my Lord," Hurin said. That took everyone's attention. He pointed back, to the northeast. "Maybe they've decided to break for the Blight after all. Go around us. Maybe they were just trying to put us off by coming south." He did not sound as if he believed it. He sounded puzzled.

"Whatever they were trying," Ingtar snarled, "I'll have them now. Mount!"

Little more than an hour later, though, Hurin drew rein. "They changed again, my Lord. South again. And they killed someone else here."

There were no ashes there, in the gap between two hills, but a few minutes' search found the body. A man curled up and stuffed under some bushes. The back of his head was smashed in, and his eyes still bulged with the force of the blow. No one recognized him, though he was wearing Shienaran clothes.

"We'll waste no time burying Darkfriends," Ingtar growled. "We ride south." He suited his own words almost before they were out of his mouth.

The day was the same as the day before had been, though. Uno studied tracks and droppings, and said they had gained a little ground on their quarry. Twilight came with no sight of Trollocs or Darkfriends, and the next morning there was another abandoned camp—and another murder done, so Hurin said—and another change of direction, this time to the northwest. Less than two hours on that track found another body, a man with his skull split open by an axe, and another change of direction. South again. Again gaining ground, by Uno's reading of the tracks. Again seeing nothing but distant farms until nightfall. And the next day was the same, changes in direction, murders and all. And the next.

Every day brought them a little closer behind their prey, but Ingtar fumed. He suggested cutting straight across when the trail changed direction of a morning—surely they would come on the trail heading south again, and gain more time—and before anyone could speak, he said it was a bad idea, in case this once the men they hunted did not turn south. He urged everyone to greater speed, to start earlier and ride till full dark. He reminded them of the charge the Amyrlin Seat had given them, to recover the Horn of Valere, and let nothing bar their way. He spoke of the glory they would have, their names remembered in story and history, in gleemen's tales and bards' songs, the men who found the Horn. He talked as if he could not stop, and he stared down the trail they followed as if his hope of the Light lay at the end of it. Even Uno began to look at him askance.

And so they came to the River Erinin.

I⊤ COULD NOT properly be called a village at all, to Rand's mind. He sat his horse among the trees, peering up at half a dozen small houses with wood-shingled roofs and eaves almost to the ground, on a hilltop overlooking the river beneath the morning sun. Few people passed this way. It was only a few hours since they had broken camp, but past time for them to have found the remains of the Darkfriends' resting place if the pattern held. They had seen nothing of the sort, however.

The river itself was not much like the mighty Erinin of story, here so far toward its source in the Spine of the World. Perhaps sixty paces of swift water to the far bank, lined with trees, and a barge-like ferry on a thick rope spanning the distance. The ferry sat snugged against the other side.

For once the trail had led straight to human habitation. Straight to the houses on the hill. No one moved on the single dirt street around which the dwellings clustered.

"Ambush, my Lord?" Uno said softly.

Ingtar gave the necessary orders, and the Shienarans unlimbered their lances, sweeping around to encircle the houses. At a hand signal from Ingtar they galloped between the houses from four directions, thundering in with eyes searching, lances ready, dust rising under their hooves. Nothing moved but them. They drew rein, and the dust began to settle.

Rand returned to his quiver the arrow he had nocked, and slung his bow on his back again. Mat and Perrin did the same. Loial and Hurin had just waited there where Ingtar had left them, watching uneasily.

Ingtar waved, and Rand and the others rode up to join the Shienarans.

"I don't like the smell of this place," Perrin muttered as they came among the houses. Hurin gave him a look, and he stared back until Hurin dropped his eyes. "It smells wrong."

"Bloody Darkfriends and Trollocs went straight through, my Lord," Uno said, pointing to a few tracks not chopped to pieces by the Shienarans. "Straight through to the goatkissing ferry, which they bloody left on the other side. Blood and bloody ashes! We're flaming lucky they didn't cut it adrift."

"Where are the people?" Loial asked.

Doors stood open, curtains flapped at open windows, but no one had come out for all the thunder of hooves.

"Search the houses," Ingtar commanded. Men dismounted and ran to comply, but they came back shaking their heads.

"They're just gone, my Lord," Uno said. "Just bloody gone,

burn me. Like they'd picked up and decided to flaming walk away in the middle of the bloody day." He stopped suddenly, pointing urgently to a house behind Ingtar. "There's a woman at that window. How I bloody missed her. . . ." He was running for the house before anyone else could move.

"Don't frighten her!" Ingtar shouted. "Uno, we need information. The Light blind you, Uno, don't frighten her!" The one-eyed man disappeared through the open door. Ingtar raised his voice again. "We will not harm you, good lady. We are Lord Agelmar's oathmen, from Fal Dara. Do not be afraid! We will not harm you."

A window at the top of the house flew up, and Uno stuck his head out, staring around wildly. With an oath he pulled back. Thumps and clatters marked his passage back, as if he were kicking things in frustration. Finally he appeared from the doorway.

"Gone, my Lord. But she was there. A woman in a white dress, at the window. I saw her. I even thought I saw her inside, for a moment, but then she was gone, and. . . ." He took a deep breath. "The house is empty, my Lord." It was a measure of his agitation that he did not curse.

"Curtains," Mat muttered. "He's jumping at bloody curtains." Uno gave him a sharp look, then returned to his horse.

"Where did they go?" Rand asked Loial. "Do you think they ran off when the Darkfriends came?" *And Trollocs, and a Myrddraal. And Hurin's something worse. Smart people, if they ran as hard as they could.*

"I fear the Darkfriends took them, Rand," Loial said slowly. He grimaced, almost a snarl with his broad nose like a snout. "For the Trollocs." Rand swallowed and wished he had not asked; it was never pleasant to think on how Trollocs fed.

"Whatever was done here," Ingtar said, "our Darkfriends did it. Hurin, was there violence here? Killing? Hurin!"

The sniffer gave a start in his saddle and looked around wildly. He had been staring across the river. "Violence, my Lord? Yes.

Killing, no. Or not exactly." He glanced sideways at Perrin. "I've never smelled anything exactly like it before, my Lord. But there was hurting done."

"Is there any doubt they crossed over? Have they doubled back again?"

"They crossed, my Lord." Hurin looked uneasily at the far bank. "They crossed. What they did on the other side, though. . . ." He shrugged.

Ingtar nodded. "Uno, I want that ferry back on this side. And I want the other side scouted before we cross. Just because there was no ambush here doesn't mean there will not be one when we are split by the river. That ferry does not look big enough to carry us all in one trip. See to it."

Uno bowed, and in moments Ragan and Masema were helping each other out of their armor. Stripped down to breechclouts, with a dagger stuck behind in the small of the back, they trotted to the river on horse-men's bowed legs and waded in, beginning to work their way hand over hand along the thick rope along which the ferry ran. The cable sagged enough in the middle to put them in the river to their waists, and the current was strong, pulling them downstream, yet in less time than Rand expected they were hauling themselves over the slatted sides of the ferry. Drawing their daggers, they disappeared into the trees.

After what seemed like forever, the two men reappeared and began pulling the ferry slowly across. The barge butted against the bank below the village, and Masema tied it off while Ragan trotted up to where Ingtar waited. His face was pale, the arrow scar on his cheek sharp, and he sounded shaken.

"The far bank. . . . There is no ambush on the far bank, my Lord, but. . . ." He bowed deeply, still wet and shivering from his excursion. "My Lord, you must see for yourself. The big stone-oak, fifty paces south from the landing. I cannot say the words. You must see it yourself."

Ingtar frowned, looking from Ragan to the other bank. Finally, he said, "You have done well, Ragan. Both of you have." His voice became more brisk. "Find these men something to dry themselves on from the houses, Uno. And see if anybody left water on for tea. Put something hot into them, if you can. Then bring the second file and the pack animals over." He turned to Rand. "Well, are you ready to see the south bank of the Erinin?" He did not wait for an answer, but rode down to the ferry with Hurin and half the lancers.

Rand hesitated only a moment before following. Loial went with him. To his surprise, Perrin rode down ahead of them, looking grim. Some of the lancers, making gruff jokes, dismounted to haul on the rope and walk the ferry over.

Mat waited until the last minute, when one of the Shienarans was untying the ferry, before he kicked his horse and crowded aboard. "I have to come sooner or later, don't I?" he said, breathless, to no one in particular. "I have to find it."

Rand shook his head. With Mat looking as healthy as he ever had, he had almost forgotten why he was along. *To find the dagger. Let Ingtar have the Horn. I just want the dagger for Mat.* "We will find it, Mat."

Mat scowled at him—with a sneering glance for his fine red coat—and turned away. Rand sighed.

"It will all come right, Rand," Loial said quietly. "Somehow, it will."

The current took the ferry as it was hauled out from the bank, tugging it against the cable with a sharp creak. The lancers were odd ferrymen, walking the deck in helmets and armor, with swords on their backs, but they took the ferry out into the river well enough.

"This is how we left home," Perrin said suddenly. "At Taren Ferry. The ferrymen's boots clunking on the deck, and the water gurgling around the ferry. This is how we left. It will be worse, this time."

"How can it be worse?" Rand asked. Perrin did not answer. He searched the far bank, and his golden eyes almost seemed to shine, but not with eagerness.

After a minute, Mat asked, "How can it be worse?"

"It will be. I can smell it," was all Perrin would say. Hurin eyed him nervously, but then Hurin seemed to be eyeing everything nervously since they had left Fal Dara.

The ferry bumped against the south bank with a hollow thud of stout planks against hard clay, almost under overhanging trees, and the Shienarans who had been hauling on the rope mounted their horses, except for two Ingtar told to take the ferry back over for the others. The rest followed Ingtar up the bank.

"Fifty paces to a big stoneoak," Ingtar said as they rode into the trees. He sounded too matter-of-fact. If Ragan could not speak of it. . . . Some of the soldiers eased the swords on their backs, and held their lances ready.

At first Rand thought the figures hanging by their arms from the thick gray limbs of the stoneoak were scarecrows. Crimson scarecrows. Then he recognized the two faces. Changu, and the other man who had been on guard with him. Nidao. Eyes staring, teeth bared in a rictus of pain. They had lived a long time after it began.

Perrin made a sound in his throat, nearly a growl.

"As bad as ever I've seen, my Lord," Hurin said faintly. "As bad as ever I've smelled, excepting the dungeon at Fal Dara that night."

Frantically Rand sought the void. The flame seemed to get in the way, the queasy light fluttering in time with his convulsive swallows, but he pushed on until he had wrapped himself in emptiness. The queasiness pulsed in the void with him, though. Not outside, for once, but inside. *No wonder, looking at this.* The thought skittered across the void like a drop of water on a hot griddle. *What happened to them?*

"Skinned alive," he heard someone behind him say, and the

sounds of somebody else retching. He thought it was Mat, but it was all far away from him, inside the void. But that nauseous flickering was in there, too. He thought he might throw up himself.

"Cut them down," Ingtar said harshly. He hesitated a moment, then added, "Bury them. We cannot be sure they were Darkfriends. They could have been taken prisoner. They could have been. Let them know the last embrace of the mother, at least." Men rode forward gingerly with knives; even for battle-hardened Shienarans it was no easy task, cutting down the flayed corpses of men they knew.

"Are you all right, Rand?" Ingtar said. "I am not used to this either."

"I . . . am all right, Ingtar." Rand let the void vanish. He felt less sick without it; his stomach still curdled, but it was better. Ingtar nodded and turned his horse so he could watch the men working.

The burial was simple. Two holes dug in the ground, and the bodies laid in as the rest of the Shienarans watched in silence. The grave diggers began shoveling earth into the graves with no more ado.

Rand was shocked, but Loial explained softly. "Shienarans believe we all came from earth, and must return to earth. They never use coffins or shrouds, and the bodies are never clothed. The earth must hold the body. The last embrace of the mother, they call it. And there are never any words except 'The Light shine on you, and the Creator shelter you. The last embrace of the mother welcome you home.' " Loial sighed and shook his huge head. "I do not think anyone will say them this time. No matter what Ingtar says, Rand, there cannot be much doubt that Changu and Nidao slew the guards at the Dog Gate and let the Darkfriends into the keep. It had to be they who were responsible for all of it."

"Then who shot the arrow at—at the Amyrlin?" Rand swallowed. *Who shot at me?* Loial said nothing.

Uno arrived with the rest of the men and the packhorses as the last earth was being shoveled onto the graves. Someone told him what they had found, and the one-eyed man spat. "Goat-kissing Trollocs do that along the Blight, sometimes. When they want to shake your bloody nerve, or flaming warn you not to follow. Burn me if it works here, either."

Before they rode away, Ingtar paused on his horse beside the unmarked graves, two mounds of bare earth that looked too small to hold men. After a moment he said, "The Light shine on you, and the Creator shelter you. The last embrace of the mother welcome you home." When he raised his head, he looked at each man in turn. There was no expression on any face, least of all on Ingtar's. "They saved Lord Agelmar at Tarwin's Gap," he said. Several of the lancers nodded. Ingtar turned his horse. "Which way, Hurin?"

"South, my Lord."

"Take the trail! We hunt!"

The forest soon gave way to gently rolling flatland, sometimes crossed by a shallow stream that had dug itself a high-banked channel, with never more than a low rise or a squat hill that barely deserved the name. Perfect country for the horses. Ingtar took advantage of it, setting a steady, ground-covering pace. Occasionally Rand saw what might have been a farmhouse in the distance, and once what he thought was a village, with smoke rising from chimneys a few miles off and something flashing white in the sun, but the land near them stayed empty of human life, long swathes of grass dotted with brush and occasional trees, with now and again a small thicket, never more than a hundred paces across.

Ingtar put out scouts, two men riding ahead, in sight only when they topped an occasional rise. He had a silver whistle hanging around his neck to call them back if Hurin said the trail had veered, but it did not. South. Always south.

"We will reach the field of Talidar in three or four days at this rate," Ingtar said as they rode. "Artur Hawkwing's greatest single victory, when the Halfmen led the Trollocs out of the Blight against him. Six days and nights, it lasted, and when it was done, the Trollocs fled back into the Blight and never dared challenge him again. He raised a monument there to his victory, a spire a hundred spans high. He would not let them put his own name on it, but rather the names of every man who fell, and a golden sun at the top, symbol that there the Light had triumphed over the Shadow."

"I would like to see that," Loial said. "I have never heard of this monument."

Ingtar was silent for a moment, and when he spoke his voice was quiet. "It is not there any longer, Builder. When Hawkwing died, the ones who fought over his empire could not bear to leave a monument to a victory of his, even if it did not mention his name. There's nothing left but the mound where it stood. In three or four days we can see that, at least." His tone did not allow much conversation afterwards.

With the sun hanging golden overhead, they passed a structure, square and made of plastered brick, less than a mile from their path. It was not tall, no more than two stories still standing anywhere he saw, but it covered a good hide of ground. An air of long abandonment hung about it, roofs gone except for a few stretches of dark tile clinging to bits of rafter, most of the once-white plaster fallen to bare the dark, weathered brick beneath, walls fallen to show courtyards and decaying chambers inside. Brush, and even trees, grew in the cracks of what had once been courtyards.

"A manor house," Ingtar explained. The little humor he had regained seemed to fade as he looked at the structure. "When Harad Dakar still stood, I expect the manorman farmed this land for a league around. Orchards, maybe. The Hardani loved their orchards."

"Harad Dakar?" Rand said, and Ingtar snorted.

"Does no one learn history any longer? Harad Dakar, the capital city of Hardan, which nation this once was that we are riding across."

"I've seen an old map," Rand replied in a tight voice. "I know about the nations that aren't there anymore. Maredo, and Goaban, and Caralain. But there wasn't any Hardan on it."

"There were once others that are gone now, too," Loial said. "Mar Haddon, which is now Haddon Mirk, and Almoth. Kintara. The War of the Hundred Years cut Artur Hawkwing's empire into many nations, large and small. The small were gobbled up by the large, or else united, like Altara and Murandy. Forced together would be a better word than united, I suppose."

"So what happened to them?" Mat demanded. Rand had not noticed Perrin and Mat ride up to join them. They had been at the rear, as far from Rand al'Thor as they could get, the last he had seen.

"They could not hold together," the Ogier replied. "Crops failed, or trade failed. People failed. Something failed in each case, and the nation dwindled. Often neighboring countries absorbed the land, when the nations were gone, but they never lasted, those annexations. In time, the land truly was abandoned. Some villages hang on here and there, but mostly they have all gone to wilderness. It is nearly three hundred years since Harad Dakar was finally abandoned, but even before that it was a shell, with a king who could not control what happened inside the city walls. Harad Dakar itself is completely gone now, I understand. All the towns and cities of Hardan are gone, the stone carted away by farmers and villagers for their own use. Most of the farms and villages made with it are gone, too. So I read, and I've seen nothing to change it."

"It was quite a quarry, Harad Dakar, for almost a hundred years," Ingtar said bitterly. "The people left, finally, and then the city was hauled away, stone by stone. All faded away, and what has not gone is fading. Everything, everywhere, fading. There is hardly a nation that truly controls the land it claims on a map, and there is hardly a land that claims today on a map what it did even a hundred years ago. When the War of the Hundred Years ended, a man rode from one nation into another without end from the Blight to the Sea of Storms. Now we can ride through wilderness claimed by no nation for almost the whole of the land. We in the Borderlands have our battle with the Blight to keep us strong, and whole. Perhaps they did not have what they needed to keep them strong. You say they failed, Builder? Yes, they failed, and what nation standing whole today will fail tomorrow? We are being swept away, humankind. Swept away like flotsam on a flood. How long until there is nothing left but the Borderlands? How long before we, too, go under, and there is nothing left but Trollocs and Myrddraal all the way to the Sea of Storms?"

There was a shocked silence. Not even Mat broke it. Ingtar rode lost in his own dark thoughts.

After a time the scouts came galloping back, straight in the saddles, lances erect against the sky. "A village ahead, my Lord. We were not seen, but it lies directly in our line of march."

Ingtar shook himself out of his brown study, but did not speak until they had reached the crest of a low ridge looking down on the village, and then it was only to command a halt while he dug a looking glass from his saddlebags and raised it to peer at the village.

Rand studied the village with interest. It was as big as Emond's Field, though that was not very big compared to some of the towns he had seen since leaving the Two Rivers, much less the cities. The houses were all low and plastered with white clay, and they appeared to have grass growing on sloping roofs. A dozen windmills, scattered through the village, turned lazily, their long, cloth-covered arms flashing white in the sun. A low wall encircled the village, grassy dirt and chest high, and outside that was a wide ditch with sharpened stakes thick in the bottom. There was no gate in the one opening he could see in the wall, but he supposed it could be blocked easily enough with a cart or wagon. He could not see any people.

"Not even a dog in sight," Ingtar said, returning the looking glass to his saddlebags. "Are you sure they did not see you?" he asked the scouts.

"Not unless they have the Dark One's own luck, my Lord," one of the men replied. "We never crested the rise. We didn't see anyone moving then either, my Lord."

Ingtar nodded. "The trail, Hurin?"

Hurin drew a deep breath. "Toward the village, my Lord. Straight to it, as near as I can tell from here."

"Watch sharp," Ingtar commanded, gathering his reins. "And

do not believe that they're friendly just because they smile. If there is anyone there." He led them down toward the village at a slow walk, and reached up to loosen his sword in its scabbard.

Rand heard the sounds of others behind him doing the same. After a moment, he eased his, too. Trying to stay alive was not the same as trying to be a hero, he decided.

"You think these people would help Darkfriends?" Perrin asked Ingtar. The Shienaran was slow in answering.

"They have no great love for Shienarans," he said finally. "They think we should protect them. Us, or the Cairhienin. Cairhien did claim this land, once the last King of Hardan died. All the way to the Erinin, they claimed it. They could not hold it, though. They gave up the claim nearly a hundred years ago. The few people who still live here don't have to worry about Trollocs this far south, but there are plenty of human brigands. That's why they have the wall, and the ditch. All their villages do. Their fields will be hidden in hollows around here, but no one will live outside the wall. They would swear fealty to any king who would give them his protection, but we have all we can do against the Trollocs. They do not love us for it, though." As they reached the opening in the low wall, he added again, "Watch sharp!"

All the streets led toward a village square, but there was no one in the streets, no one peering from a window. Not even a dog moved, not so much as a chicken. Nothing living. Open doors swung, creaking in the wind, counterpoint to the rhythmic squeak of the windmills. The horses' hooves sounded loud on the packed dirt of the street.

"Like at the ferry," Hurin muttered, "but different." He rode hunched in his saddle, head down as if he were trying to hide behind his own shoulders. "Violence done, but . . . I don't know. It was bad here. It smells bad."

"Uno," Ingtar said, "take one file and search the houses. If you find anyone, bring them to me in the square. Do not frighten them this time, though. I want answers, not people running for their lives." He led the other soldiers toward the center of the village as Uno got his ten dismounted.

Rand hesitated, looking around. The creaking doors, the squealing windmills, the horses' hooves, all made too much noise, as if there were not another sound in the world. He scanned the houses. The curtains in an open window beat against the outside of the house. They all seemed lifeless. With a sigh he got down and walked to the nearest house, then stopped, staring at the door.

It's just a door. What are you afraid of? He wished he did not feel as if there was something waiting on the other side. He pushed it open.

Inside was a tidy room. Or had been. The table was set for a meal, ladder-back chairs gathered around, some plates already served. A few flies buzzed above bowls of turnips and peas, and more crawled on a cold roast sitting in its own congealed grease. There was a slice half carved from the roast, the fork still standing stuck in the meat and the carving knife lying partway in the platter as if dropped. Rand stepped inside.

Blink.

A smiling, bald-headed man in rough clothes laid a slice of meat on a plate held by a woman with a worn face. She was smiling, too, though. She added peas and turnips to the plate and passed it to one of the children lining the table. There were half a dozen children, boys and girls, from nearly grown down to barely tall enough to look over the table. The woman said something, and the girl taking the plate from her laughed. The man started to cut another slice.

Suddenly another girl screamed, pointing at the door to the street. The man dropped the carving knife and whirled, then he screamed, too, face tight with horror, and snatched up a child. The woman grabbed another, and motioned desperately to the others, her mouth working frantically, silently. They all scrabbled toward a door in the back of the room.

That door burst open, and—

Blink.

Rand could not move. The flies buzzing over the table sounded louder. His breath made a cloud in front of his mouth.

Blink.

Rand struggled, but his muscles seemed frozen. The room was colder; he wanted to shiver, but he could not move even that much. Flies crawled all over the table. He groped for the void. The sour light was there, but he did not care. He had to—

The room was freezing. *So cold.* Flies blackened the table; the walls were a shifting mass of flies, the floor, the ceiling, all black with them. They crawled on Rand, covering him, crawled over his face, his eyes, into his nose, his mouth. *Light, help me. Cold.* The flies buzzed like thunder. *Cold.* It penetrated the void, mocking the emptiness, encasing him in ice. Desperately he reached for the flickering light. His stomach twisted, but the light was warm. Warm. Hot. He was hot.

Suddenly he was tearing at . . . something. He did not know what, or how. Cobwebs made of steel. Moonbeams carved from stone. They crumbled at his touch, but he knew he had not touched anything. They shriveled and melted with the heat that surged through him, heat like a forge fire, heat like the world burning, heat like—

It was gone. Panting, he looked around with wide eyes. A few flies lay on the half-carved roast, in the platter. Dead flies. *Six flies. Only six.* There were more in the bowls, half a dozen tiny black specks among the cold vegetables. All dead. He staggered out into the street.

Mat was just coming out of a house across the street, shaking his head. "Nobody there," he told Perrin, still on his horse. "It looks like they just got up in the middle of supper and walked away."

A shout came from the square.

"They've found something," Perrin said, digging his heels into his horse's flanks. Mat scrambled into his saddle and galloped after him.

Rand mounted Red more slowly; the stallion shied as if feeling his unease. He glanced at the houses as he rode slowly toward the square, but he could not make himself look at them for long. *Mat went in one, and nothing happened to him.* He resolved not to set foot inside another house in that village no matter what. Booting Red, he quickened his pace.

Everyone was standing like statues in front of a large building with wide double doors. Rand did not think it could be an inn; there was no sign, for one thing. Perhaps a village meeting place. He joined the silent circle, and stared along with the rest.

There was a man spread-eagled across the doors with thick spikes through wrists and shoulders. More spikes had been driven into his eyes to hold his head up. Dark, dried blood made fans down his cheeks. Scuff marks on the wood behind his boots showed that he had been alive when it was done. When it began, anyway.

Rand's breath caught. Not a man. Those black clothes, blacker than black, had never been worn by any human. The wind flapped an end of the cloak caught behind the body—which it did not always, he knew too well; the wind did not always touch those clothes—but there had never been any eyes in that pale, bloodless face.

"Myrddraal," he breathed, and it was as if his speaking released all the others. They began to move again, and breathe.

"Who," Mat began, and had to stop to swallow. "Who could do this to a Fade?" His voice squeaked at the end.

"I don't know," Ingtar said. "I do not know." He looked around, examining faces, or perhaps counting to be sure everyone was there. "And I do not think we will learn anything here. We ride. Mount! Hurin, find the trail out of this place."

"Yes, my Lord. Yes. With pleasure. That way, my Lord. They're still heading south."

They rode away leaving the dead Myrddraal where it hung, the wind stirring its black cloak. Hurin was first beyond the wall, not waiting on Ingtar for a change, but Rand came close behind him.

CHAPTER 11

Glimmers of the Pattern

FOR ONCE, INGTAR CALLED A HALT TO THE day's march with the sun still golden above the horizon. The toughened Shienarans were feeling the effects of what they had seen in the village. Ingtar had not stopped so early before, and the campsite he chose had the look of a place that could be defended. It was a deep hollow, almost round, and big enough to hold all the men and horses comfortably. A sparse thicket of scrub oak and leatherleaf covered the outer slopes. The rim itself stood more than high enough to hide anyone in the campsite even without the trees. The height nearly passed for a hill, in that country.

"All I'm bloody saying," he heard Uno tell Ragan as they dismounted, "is that I bloody saw her, burn you. Just before we found the goat-kissing Halfman. The same flaming woman as at the flaming ferry. She was there, and then she bloody wasn't. You say what you bloody want to, but you watch how you flaming say it, or I'll bloody skin you myself, and burn the goat-kissing hide, you sheep-gutted milk-drinker."

Rand paused with one foot on the ground and the other still in the stirrup. *The same woman? But there wasn't any woman at the ferry, just some curtains blowing in the wind. And she couldn't have gotten to that village ahead of us if there had been.* The village. . . .

He shied away from the thought. Even more than the Fade nailed to the door, he wanted to forget that room, and the flies, and the people who were there and not there. The Halfman had been real—everybody had seen that—but the room. . . . *Maybe I'm finally going mad.* He wished Moiraine was there to talk to. *Wishing for an Aes Sedai. You* are *a fool. You're well out of that, now stay out. But am I out? What happened there?*

"Packhorses and supplies in the middle," Ingtar commanded as the lancers went about setting up camp. "Rub the horses down, then saddle them again in case we must move quickly. Every man sleeps by his mount, and there'll be no fires tonight. Watch changes every two hours. Uno, I want scouts out, as far as they can ride and return before dark. I want to know what is out there."

He's feeling it, Rand thought. *It isn't just some Darkfriends and a few Trollocs and maybe a Fade anymore.* Just some Darkfriends and a few Trollocs, and maybe a Fade! Even a few days before there would not have been any "just" about it. Even in the Borderlands, even with the Blight less than a day's ride, Darkfriends and Trollocs and Myrddraal had been bad enough for a nightmare, then. Before he had seen a Myrddraal nailed to a door. *What in the Light could have done* that? *What not in the Light?* Before he had walked into a room where a family had had their supper and their laughter cut off. *I must have imagined it. I must have.* Even in his own head he did not sound very convincing. He had not imagined the wind on the tower top, or the Amyrlin saying—

"Rand?" He jumped as Ingtar spoke at his shoulder. "Are you going to stay all night with one foot in the stirrup?"

Rand put his other foot on the ground. "Ingtar, what happened back at that village?"

"Trollocs took them. The same as the people at the ferry. That is what happened. The Fade. . . ." Ingtar shrugged and stared down at a flat, canvas-wrapped bundle, large and square, in his arms; he stared at it as if he saw hidden secrets he would rather not know. "The Trollocs took them for food. They do it in villages and farms near the Blight, too, sometimes, if a raid gets past the border towers in the night. Sometimes we get the people back, and sometimes not. Sometimes we get them back and almost wish we hadn't. Trollocs don't always kill before they start butchering. And Halfmen like to have their . . . fun. That's worse than what the Trollocs do." His voice was as steady as if he were talking of every day, and perhaps he was, for a Shienaran soldier.

Rand took a deep breath to steady his stomach. "The Fade back there didn't have any fun, Ingtar. What could nail a Myrddraal to a door, alive?"

Ingtar hesitated, shaking his head, then pushed the big bundle at Rand. "Here. Moiraine Sedai told me to give you this at the first camp south of the Erinin. I don't know what is in it, but she said you would need it. She said to tell you to take care of it; your life may depend on it."

Rand took it reluctantly; his skin prickled at the touch of the canvas. There was something soft inside. Cloth, maybe. He held it gingerly. *He doesn't want to think about the Myrddraal either. What happened in that room?* He realized suddenly that for him, the Fade, or even that room, was preferable to thinking about what Moiraine might have sent him.

"I was told to tell you at the same time that if anything happens to me, the lances will follow you."

"Me!" Rand gasped, forgetting the bundle and everything else.

Ingtar met his incredulous stare with a calm nod. "That's crazy! I've never led anything but a flock of sheep, Ingtar. They would not follow me anyway. Besides, Moiraine can't tell you who your second is. It's Uno."

"Uno and I were called to Lord Agelmar the morning we left. Moiraine Sedai was there, but it was Lord Agelmar who told me. You are second, Rand."

"But why, Ingtar? Why?" Moiraine's hand was bright and clear in it, hers and the Amyrlin's, pushing him along the path they had chosen, but he had to ask.

The Shienaran looked as if he did not understand it either, but he was a soldier, used to odd commands in the endless war along the Blight. "I heard rumors from the women's apartments that you were really a. . . ." He spread gauntleted hands. "No matter. I know you deny it. Just as you deny the look of your own face. Moiraine Sedai says you're a shepherd, but I never saw a shepherd with a heron-mark blade. No matter. I'll not claim I would have chosen you myself, but I think you have it in you to do what is needed. You will do your duty, if it comes to it."

Rand wanted to say it was no duty of his, but instead he said, "Uno knows about this. Who else, Ingtar?"

"All the lances. When we Shienarans ride, every man knows who is next in line if the man in command falls. A chain unbroken right down to the last man left, even if he's nothing but a horse-holder. That way, you see, even if he *is* the last man, he is not just a straggler running and trying to stay alive. He has the command, and duty calls him to do what must be done. If I go to the last embrace of the mother, the duty is yours. You will find the Horn, and you will take it where it belongs. You will." There was a peculiar emphasis in Ingtar's last words.

The bundle in Rand's arms seemed to weigh ten stone. *Light, she could be a hundred leagues off, and she still reaches out and tugs the leash. This way, Rand. That way. You're the Dragon*

Reborn, Rand. "I don't want the duty, Ingtar. I will not take it. Light, I'm just a shepherd! Why won't anybody believe that?"

"You will do your duty, Rand. When the man at the top of the chain fails, everything below him falls apart. Too much is falling apart. Too much already. Peace favor your sword, Rand al'Thor."

"Ingtar, I—" But Ingtar was walking away, calling to see if Uno had the scouts out yet.

Rand stared at the bundle in his arms and licked his lips. He was afraid he knew what was in it. He wanted to look, yet he wanted to throw it in a fire without opening it; he thought he might, if he could be sure it would burn without anyone seeing what was inside, if he could be sure what was inside would burn at all. But he could not look there, where other eyes than his might see.

He glanced around the camp. The Shienarans were unloading the pack animals, some already handing out a cold supper of dried meat and flatbread. Mat and Perrin tended their horses, and Loial sat on a stone reading a book, with his long-stemmed pipe clenched between his teeth and a wisp of smoke curling above his head. Gripping the bundle as if afraid he might drop it, Rand sneaked into the trees.

He knelt in a small clearing sheltered by thick-foliaged branches and set the bundle on the ground. For a time he just stared at it. *She wouldn't have. She couldn't.* A small voice answered, *Oh, yes, she could. She could and would.* Finally he set about untying the small knots in the cords that bound it. Neat knots, tied with a precision that spoke loudly of Moiraine's own hand; no servant had done this for her. She would not have dared let any servant see.

When he had the last cord unfastened, he opened out what was folded inside with hands that felt numb, then stared at it, his mouth full of dust. It was all of one piece, neither woven, nor dyed, nor painted. A banner, white as snow, big enough to be seen the length of a field of battle. And across it marched a rippling figure like a serpent scaled in gold and crimson, but a serpent with four scaled legs, each tipped with five golden claws, a serpent with eyes like the sun and a golden lion's mane. He had seen it once before, and Moiraine had told him what it was. The banner of Lews Therin Telamon, Lews Therin Kinslayer, in the War of the Shadow. The banner of the Dragon.

"Look at that! Look what he's got, now!" Mat burst into the clearing. Perrin came after him more slowly. "First fancy coats," Mat snarled, "and now a banner! We'll hear no end of lording it now, with—" Mat got close enough to see the banner clearly, and his jaw dropped. "Light!" He stumbled back a step. "Burn me!" He had been there, too, when Moiraine named the banner. So had Perrin.

Anger boiled up in Rand, anger at Moiraine and the Amyrlin Seat, pushing him, pulling him. He snatched up the banner in both hands and shook it at Mat, words boiling out uncontrollably. "That's right! The Dragon's banner!" Mat took another step back. "Moiraine wants me to be a puppet on Tar Valon strings, a false Dragon for the Aes Sedai. She's going to push it down my throat whatever I want. But—I—will—not—be—used!"

Mat had backed up against a tree trunk. "A false Dragon?" He swallowed. "You? That . . . that's crazy."

Perrin had not retreated. He squatted down with his thick arms on his knees and studied Rand with those bright golden eyes. In the evening shadows they seemed to shine. "If the Aes Sedai want you for a false Dragon. . . ." He paused, frowning, thinking things through. Finally, he said quietly, "Rand, can you channel?" Mat gave a strangled gasp.

Rand let the banner drop; he hesitated only a moment before nodding wearily. "I did not ask for it. I don't want it. But. . . . But I do not think I know how to stop it." The room with the flies came back unbidden to his mind. "I don't think they'll let me stop."

"Burn me!" Mat breathed. "Blood and bloody ashes! They'll kill us, you know. All of us. Perrin and me as well as you. If Ingtar and the others find out, they will cut our bloody throats for Darkfriends. Light, they'll probably think we were part of stealing the Horn, and killing those people in Fal Dara."

"Shut up, Mat," Perrin said calmly.

"Don't tell me to shut up. If Ingtar doesn't kill us, Rand will go mad and do it for him. Burn me! Burn me!" Mat slid down the tree to sit on the ground. "Why didn't they gentle you? If the Aes Sedai know, why didn't they gentle you? I never heard of them letting a man who can wield the Power just walk away."

"They don't all know," Rand sighed. "The Amyrlin—"

"The Amyrlin Seat! *She* knows? Light, no wonder she looked at me so strange."

"—and Moiraine told me I'm the Dragon Reborn, and then they said I could go wherever I wanted. Don't you see, Mat? They are trying to use me."

"Doesn't change you being able to channel," Mat muttered. "If I were you, I'd be halfway to the Aryth Ocean by now. And I would not stop until I found someplace where there were no Aes Sedai, and never likely to be any. And no people. I mean . . . well. . . ."

"Shut up, Mat," Perrin said. "Why *are* you here, Rand? The longer you stay around people, the more likely it is somebody will find out and send for Aes Sedai. Aes Sedai who *won't* tell you to go on about your business." He paused, scratching his head over that. "And Mat's right about Ingtar. I don't doubt he would name you Darkfriend and kill you. Kill all of us, maybe. He seems to like you, but he'd still do it, I think. A false Dragon? So would the others. Masema wouldn't need that much excuse, for you. So why aren't you gone?"

Rand shrugged. "I was going, but first the Amyrlin came, and then the Horn was stolen, and the dagger, and Moiraine said Mat was dying, and. . . . Light, I thought I could stay with you until we found the dagger, at least; I thought I could help with that. Maybe I was wrong."

"You came because of the dagger?" Mat said quietly. He rubbed his nose and grimaced. "I never thought of that. I never thought you wanted to. . . . Aaaah! Are you feeling all right? I mean, you aren't going mad already, are you?"

Rand dug a pebble out of the ground and threw it at him.

"Ouch!" Mat rubbed his arm. "I was just asking. I mean, all those fancy clothes, and all that talk about being a lord. Well, that isn't exactly right in the head."

"I was trying to get rid of you, fool! I was afraid I'd go mad and hurt you." His eyes dropped to the banner, and his voice lowered. "I will, eventually, if I don't stop it. Light, I don't know how to stop it."

"That is what I'm afraid of," Mat said, standing. "No offense, Rand, but I think I will just sleep as far away from you as I can, if you don't mind. That's if you are staying. I heard about a fellow who could channel, once. A merchant's guard told me. Before the Red Ajah found him, he woke one morning, and his whole village was smashed flat. All the houses, all the people, everything but the bed he was sleeping in, like a mountain had rolled over them."

Perrin said, "In that case, Mat, you should sleep cheek by jowl with him."

"I may be a fool, but I intend to be a live fool." Mat hesitated, looking sideways at Rand. "Look, I know you came along to help me, and I am grateful. I really am. But you just are not the same anymore. You understand that, don't you?" He waited as if he expected an answer. None came. Finally he vanished into the trees, back toward the camp.

"What about you?" Rand asked.

Perrin shook his head, shaggy curls swinging. "I don't know, Rand. You are the same, but then again, you aren't. A man channeling; my mother used to frighten me with that, when I was little. I just do not know." He stretched out his hand and touched a corner of the banner. "I think I would burn this, or bury it, if I were you. Then I'd run so far, so fast, no Aes Sedai would ever find me. Mat was right about that." He stood up, squinting at the western sky, beginning to turn red with the sinking sun. "Time to get back to the camp. You think on what I said, Rand. I'd run. But maybe you can't run. Think of that, too." His yellow eyes seemed to look inward, and he sounded tired. "Sometimes you can't run." Then he was gone, too.

Rand knelt there, staring at the banner spread out on the ground. "Well, sometimes you *can* run," he muttered. "Only, maybe she gave me this to make me run. Maybe she has something waiting for me, if I run. I won't do what she wants. I won't. I'll bury it right here. But she said my life may depend on it, and Aes Sedai never lie so you can see it. . . ." Suddenly his shoulders shook with silent laughter. "Now I'm talking to myself. Maybe I *am* going mad already."

When he returned to the camp, he carried the banner wrapped in the canvas once more, tied with knots less neat than Moiraine's had been.

The light had begun to fail and the shadow of the rim covered half the hollow. The soldiers were settling in, all with their horses by their sides, lances propped to hand. Mat and Perrin were bedding down alongside their horses. Rand gave them a sad look, then fetched Red, standing where he had been left with his reins dangling, and went to the other side of the hollow, where Hurin had joined Loial. The Ogier had given over reading and was examining the half-buried stone on which he had been sitting, tracing something on the stone with the long stem of his pipe.

Hurin stood and gave Rand something just short of a bow. "Hope you don't mind me making my bed here, Lord—uh—Rand. I was just listening to the Builder here."

"There you are, Rand," Loial said. "You know, I think this stone was worked once. See, it's weathered, but it looks as if it was a column of some kind. And there are markings, also. I can't quite make them out, but they look familiar, somehow."

"Maybe you'll be able to see them better in the morning," Rand said. He pulled the saddlebags from Red. "I'll be glad of your company, Hurin." *I'm glad of anybody's company who isn't afraid of me. How much longer can I have it, though?*

He shifted everything into one side of the saddlebags—spare shirts and breeches and woolen stockings, sewing kit, tinder box, tin plate and cup, a greenwood box with knife and fork and spoon, a packet of dried meat and flat-bread for emergency rations, and all the other traveler's necessaries—then stuffed the canvas-wrapped banner into the empty pocket. It bulged, the straps barely reaching the buckles, but then, the other side bulged now, too. It would do.

Loial and Hurin seemed to sense his mood, leaving him in silence while he stripped saddle and bridle from Red, rubbed the big bay down with tufts of grass torn from the ground, then resaddled him. Rand refused their offer of food; he did not think he could have stomached the best meal he had ever seen just then. All three of them made their beds there beside the stone, a simple matter of a blanket folded for a pillow and cloak to cover.

The camp was silent now, but Rand lay awake past the fall of full dark. His mind darted back and forth. The banner. *What is she trying to make me do?* The village. *What could kill a Fade like that?* Worst of all, the house in the village. *Did it really happen? Am I going mad already? Do I run, or do I stay? I have to stay. I have to help Mat find the dagger.*

An exhausted sleep finally came, and with sleep, unbidden, the void surrounded him, flickering with an uneasy glow that disturbed his dreams.

* * *

PADAN FAIN STARED northward out into the night, past the only fire in his camp, smiling a fixed smile that never touched his eyes. He still thought of himself as Padan Fain—Padan Fain was the core of him—but he had been changed, and he knew it. He knew many things, now, more than any of his old masters could suspect. He had been a Darkfriend long years before Ba'alzamon summoned him and set him on the track of the three young men from Emond's Field, distilling what he knew of them, distilling him, and feeding the essence back so that he could *feel* them, *smell* where they had been, follow wherever they ran. Especially the one. A part of him still cringed, remembering what Ba'alzamon had done to him, but it was a small part, hidden, suppressed. He was changed. Following the three had led him into Shadar Logoth. He had not wanted to go, but he had had to obey. Then. And in Shadar Logoth. . . .

Fain drew a deep breath and fingered the ruby-hilted dagger at his belt. That had come from Shadar Logoth, too. It was the only weapon he carried, the only one he needed; it felt like a part of him. He was whole within himself, now. That was all that mattered.

He cast a glance to either side of his fire. The twelve Dark-friends who were left, their once-fine clothes now rumpled and dirty, huddled in the darkness to one side, staring not at the fire, but at him. On the other squatted his Trollocs, twenty in number, the all-too-human eyes in those animal-twisted men's faces following his every move like mice watching a cat.

It had been a struggle at first, waking each morning to find himself not completely whole, to find the Myrddraal back in command, raging and demanding they go north, to the Blight, to Shayol Ghul. But bit by bit those mornings of weakness grew shorter, until. . . . He remembered the feel of the hammer in his hand, driving the spikes in, and he smiled; this time it did touch his eyes, with the joy of sweet memory.

Weeping from the dark caught his ear, and his smile faded. *I*

should never have let the Trollocs take so many. An entire village
to slow them down. If those few houses at the ferry had not been
deserted, perhaps. . . . But Trollocs were greedy by nature, and in
the euphoria of watching the Myrddraal die, he had not paid attention as he should.

He glanced at the Trollocs. Any one of them was nearly twice
as tall as he, strong enough to break him to flinders with one hand,
yet they edged back, still crouching. "Kill them. All. You may
feed, but then make a pile of everything that remains—for our
friends to find. Put the heads on top. Neatly, now." He laughed,
and cut it off short. "Go!"

The Trollocs scrambled away, drawing scythe-like swords and
raising spiked axes. In moments shrieks and bellows rose from
where the villagers were bound. Pleas for mercy and children's
screams were cut off by solid thuds and unpleasant squishing
noises, like melons being broken.

Fain turned his back on the cacophony to look at his Dark-friends. They were his, too, body and soul. Such souls as they had left. Every one of them was mired as deeply as he had been, before he found his way out. Every one with nowhere to go except to follow him. Their eyes clung to him, fearful, pleading. "You think they will grow hungry again before we find another village or a farm? They may. You think I will be letting them have some more of you? Well, perhaps one or two. There aren't any more horses to spare."

"The others were only commoners," one woman managed in an unsteady voice. Dirt streaked her face above a finely cut dress that marked her as a merchant, and wealthy. Smears stained the good gray cloth, and a long tear marred her skirt. "They were peasants. We have served—*I* have served—"

Fain cut her off, his easy tone making his words all the harder. "What are you, to me? Less than peasants. Herd cattle for the Trollocs, perhaps? If you want to live, cattle, you must be useful."

The woman's face broke. She sobbed, and suddenly all the rest were babbling, telling him how useful they were, men and women who had had influence and position before they were called to ful-fill their oaths at Fal Dara. They spilled out the names of impor-tant, powerful people whom they knew in the Borderlands, in Cairhien, and other lands. They babbled of the knowledge they alone had of this land or that, of political situations, alliances, intrigues, all the things they could tell him if he let them serve him. The noise of them blended with the sounds of the Trollocs' slaughter and fit right in.

Fain ignored all of it—he had no fear of turning his back on them, not since they had seen the Fade dealt with—and went to his prize. Kneeling, he ran his hands over the ornate, golden chest, feeling the power locked inside. He had to have a Trolloc carry it—he did not trust the humans enough to load it on a horse and packsaddle; some dreams of power might be strong enough to overcome even fear of him, but Trollocs never dreamed of anything except killing—and he had not yet puzzled out how to open it. But that would come. Everything would come. Everything.

Unsheathing the dagger, he laid it atop the chest before settling himself down beside the fire. That blade was a better guard than Trolloc or human. They had all seen what happened when he used it, once; none would come within a span of that bared blade without his command, and then reluctantly.

Lying there in his blankets, he stared northward. He could not feel al'Thor, now; the distance between them was too great. Or perhaps al'Thor was doing his vanishing trick. Sometimes, in the keep, the boy had suddenly vanished from Fain's senses. He did not know how, but always al'Thor came back, just as suddenly as he had gone. He would come back this time, too.

"This time you come to me, Rand al'Thor. Before, I followed you like a dog driven on the trail, but now you follow me." His laughter was a cackle that even he knew was mad, but he did not care. Madness was a part of him, too. "Come to me, al'Thor. The dance is not even begun yet. We'll dance on Toman Head, and I'll be free of you. I'll see you dead at last."

CHAPTER 12

Woven in the Pattern

EGWENE HURRIED AFTER NYNAEVE TOWARD the knot of Aes Sedai around the Amyrlin Seat's horse-borne palanquin, her desire to know what had caused the turmoil in Fal Dara keep outweighing even her worry over Rand. He was beyond her reach, for the moment. Bela, her shaggy mare, was with the Aes Sedai's horses, and Nynaeve's mount, too.

The Warders, hands on sword hilts and eyes searching everywhere, made a steel circle around the Aes Sedai and the palanquin. They were an island of relative calm in the courtyard, where Shienaran soldiers still ran amid the keep's horrified inhabitants. Egwene pushed in beside Nynaeve—the two of them all but ignored after a single sharp glance from the Warders; all knew they would be leaving with the Amyrlin—and caught enough in the crowd's murmurs to learn of an arrow that had flashed seemingly from nowhere and a bowman yet uncaught.

Egwene stopped, wide-eyed, too shocked even to think that she was surrounded by Aes Sedai. An attempt on the life of the Amyrlin Seat. It went beyond thinking of.

The Amyrlin sat in her palanquin with the curtains drawn back, the bloodstained rip in her sleeve drawing all eyes, and faced down Lord Agelmar. "You will find the bowman or you will not, my son. Either way, my business in Tar Valon is as urgent as that of Ingtar on his quest. I leave now."

"But, Mother," Agelmar protested, "this attempt on your life changes everything. We still do not know who sent the man, or why. An hour more, and I will have the bowman and the answers for you."

The Amyrlin barked a laugh with no amusement in it. "You'll need slyer bait or finer nets to catch this fish, my son. By the time you have the man, it will be too late in the day for leaving. There are too many who would cheer to see me dead for me to worry overmuch about this one. You may send me news of what you find, if you find anything at all." Her eyes traveled around the towers overlooking the courtyard, and the ramparts and archers' balconies, still jammed with people, though silent now. The arrow had to have come from one of those places. "I think this bowman is already fled from Fal Dara."

"But, Mother—"

The woman in the palanquin cut him off with a sharp gesture of finality. Not even the Lord of Fal Dara could press the Amyrlin Seat too far. Her eyes came to rest on Egwene and Nynaeve, piercing eyes that seemed to Egwene to be seeing everything about herself that she wanted to keep secret. Egwene took a step back, then caught herself and dropped a curtsy, wondering if that were proper; no one had ever explained to her the protocol of meeting the Amyrlin Seat. Nynaeve kept her back straight and returned the Amyrlin's stare, but she fumbled for Egwene's hand and gripped as hard as Egwene did.

"So these are your two, Moiraine," the Amyrlin said. Moiraine gave the barest nod, and the other Aes Sedai turned to stare at the two women from Emond's Field. Egwene swallowed. They all looked as if they *knew* things, things other people did not, and it was no help at all to know that they truly did. "Yes, I sense a fine spark in each of them. But what will kindle from it? That's the question, isn't it?"

Egwene's mouth felt dry as dust. She had seen Master Padwhin, the carpenter back home, look at his tools much the same way as the Amyrlin was looking at the two of them. This one for this purpose, that one for that.

The Amyrlin said abruptly, "It is time we were gone. To horse. Lord Agelmar and I can say what needs be said without you all gawking like novices on a freeday. To horse!"

At her command the Warders scattered to their mounts, still wary, and the Aes Sedai, all but Leane, glided away from the palanquin to their own horses. As Egwene and Nynaeve turned to obey, a servant appeared at Lord Agelmar's shoulder with a silver chalice. Agelmar took it with a dissatisfied twist to his mouth.

"With this cup from my hand, Mother, take my wish that you fare well on this day, and every. . . ."

Whatever else they said was lost to Egwene as she scrambled onto Bela. By the time she had given the shaggy mare a pat, and arranged her skirts, the palanquin was already moving toward the open gates, its horses stepping without rein or lead. Leane rode beside the palanquin, her staff propped at her stirrup. Egwene and Nynaeve brought their horses along behind with the rest of the Aes Sedai.

Roars and cheers from the crowds lining the town streets greeted the procession, all but drowning the thunder of the drummers and the blare of the trumpeters. Warders led the column,

with the banner bearing the White Flame waving in ripples, and
rode guard around the Aes Sedai, keeping the mass of people
back; archers and pikemen, the Flame blazoned on their chests,
followed behind in precise ranks. The trumpets fell silent as the
column wound its way out of the town and turned southward, yet
the sounds of cheering from within the town followed still.
Egwene glanced back often, until trees and hills hid Fal Dara's
walls and towers.

Nynaeve, riding alongside, shook her head. "Rand will be all
right. He has Lord Ingtar and twenty lances with him. In any case,
there is nothing you can do about it. Nothing either of us can do."
She glanced toward Moiraine; the Aes Sedai's trim white mare
and Lan's tall black stallion made an odd pair off to one side by
themselves. "Not yet."

The column angled westward as it traveled, and it did not cover
the ground quickly. Even footmen in half armor could not move
fast through the Shienaran hills, not and maintain the pace for
long. Still, they pushed as hard as they could.

Camps came late each night, the Amyrlin allowing no stop
until barely enough light remained to pitch the tents, flattened
white domes just tall enough to stand in. Each pair of Aes Sedai
from the same Ajah had one, while the Amyrlin and the Keeper
had tents to themselves. Moiraine shared the tent of her two sisters of the Blue. The soldiers slept on the ground in their own
encampment, and the Warders wrapped themselves in their cloaks
near the tents of the Aes Sedai to whom they were bonded. The
tent shared by the Red sisters looked oddly lonely without any
Warders, while that of the Greens seemed almost festive, the two
Aes Sedai often sitting outside long past dark to talk with the four
Warders they had brought between them.

Lan came once to the tent Egwene shared with Nynaeve, taking
the Wisdom into the night a little distance away. Egwene peered

around the tent flap to watch. She could not hear what they said, except that Nynaeve eventually erupted in anger and came stalking back to wrap herself in her blankets and refuse to talk at all. Egwene thought her cheeks were wet, though she hid her face with a corner of her blanket. Lan stood watching the tent from the darkness for a long time before he went away. After that he did not come again.

Moiraine did not come near them, giving them only a nod in passing. She seemed to spend her waking hours speaking with the other Aes Sedai, all but the Red sisters, drawing them aside one by one as they rode. The Amyrlin allowed few stops for rest, and those short.

"Maybe she doesn't have time for us anymore," Egwene observed sadly. Moiraine was the one Aes Sedai she knew. Perhaps—though she did not like to admit it—the only one she was sure she could trust. "She found us, and we are on our way to Tar Valon. I suppose she has other things to concern her, now."

Nynaeve snorted softly. "I'll believe she is done with us when she's dead—or we are. She is sly, that one."

Other Aes Sedai came to their tent. Egwene almost jumped out of her skin that first night out of Fal Dara, when the tent flap was pushed aside and a plump, square-faced Aes Sedai, with graying hair and a vaguely distracted look in her dark eyes, ducked into their tent. She glanced at the lantern hanging at the highest point of the tent, and the flame rose a little higher. Egwene thought she felt something, thought she almost saw something about the Aes Sedai when the flame grew brighter. Moiraine had told her that one day—when she had more training—she would be able to *see* when another woman channeled, and to tell a woman who could channel even if she did nothing.

"I am Verin Mathwin," the woman said with a smile. "And you are Egwene al'Vere and Nynaeve al'Maera. From the Two Rivers, which was once Manetheren. Strong blood, that. It sings."

Egwene exchanged glances with Nynaeve as they got to their feet.

"Is this a summons to the Amyrlin Seat?" Egwene asked.

Verin laughed. The Aes Sedai had a smudge of ink on her nose. "Oh, my, no. The Amyrlin has more important things to deal with than two young women who are not even novices yet. Although, you never can tell. You both have considerable potential, especially you, Nynaeve. One day. . . ." She paused, rubbing a finger thoughtfully right atop the ink smudge. "But this is not one day. I am here to give you a lesson, Egwene. You have been poking in ahead of yourself, I fear."

Nervously, Egwene looked at Nynaeve. "What have I done? Nothing that I'm aware of."

"Oh, nothing wrong. Not exactly. Somewhat dangerous, perhaps, but not exactly wrong." Verin lowered herself to the canvas floor, folding her legs under her. "Sit, both of you. Sit. I don't mean to crane my neck." She shifted around until she had a comfortable position. "Sit."

Egwene settled cross-legged across from the Aes Sedai and did her best not to look at Nynaeve. *No need to look guilty until I know if I am. And maybe not then.* "What is it I've done that's dangerous but not exactly wrong?"

"Why, you've been channeling the Power, child."

Egwene could only gape. Nynaeve burst out, "That is ridiculous. Why are we going to Tar Valon, if not for that?"

"Moiraine has . . . I mean, Moiraine Sedai has been giving me lessons," Egwene managed.

Verin held up her hands for quiet, and they fell silent. She might seem vague, but she was Aes Sedai, after all. "Child, do you think Aes Sedai immediately teach every girl who says she wants to be one of us how to channel? Well, I suppose you are not exactly every girl, but just the same. . . ." She shook her head gravely.

"Then why did she?" Nynaeve demanded. There had been no

lessons for her, and Egwene was still not sure if it rankled Nynaeve or not.

"Because Egwene had already channeled," Verin said patiently.

"So. . . . So have I." Nynaeve did not sound happy about it.

"Your circumstances are different, child. That you are still alive shows you weathered the various crises, and did it on your own. I think you know how lucky you are. Of every four women forced to do what you did, only one survives. Of course, wilders—" Verin grimaced. "Forgive me, but I am afraid that *is* what we in the White Tower often call women who, without any training, have managed some rough control—random, and barely enough to be called control, usually, like you, but still control of a sort. Wilders have difficulties, it is true. Almost always they have built up walls to keep themselves from knowing what it was they were doing, and those walls interfere with conscious control. The longer those walls have to build, the harder it is to tear them down, but if they can be demolished—well, some of the most adept sisters ever have been wilders."

Nynaeve shifted irritably, and looked at the entrance as if thinking of leaving.

"I don't see what any of that has to do with me," Egwene said.

Verin blinked at her, almost as if wondering where she had come from. "With you? Why, nothing. Your problem is quite different. Most girls who want to become Aes Sedai—even most girls with the seed inside them, like you—are afraid of it, too. Even after they reach the Tower, even after they've learned what to do and how, for months they need to be led, step by step, by a sister, or by one of the Accepted. But not you. From what Moiraine tells me, you leaped into it as soon as you knew you could, fumbling your way through the dark with never a thought of whether there was a bottomless pit under your next step. Oh, there have been others like you; you are not unique. Moiraine was one herself. Once she knew what you had done, there was nothing for it but for her to begin teaching you. Did Moiraine never explain any of this to you?"

"Never." Egwene wished her voice was not so breathless. "She had . . . other matters to deal with." Nynaeve snorted softly.

"Well, Moiraine has never believed in telling anyone anything they did not need to know. Knowing serves no real purpose, but then, neither does not knowing. Myself, I always prefer knowing to not."

"Is there one? A pit, I mean?"

"Obviously not so far," Verin said, tilting her head. "But the next step?" She shrugged. "You see, child, the more you *try* to touch the True Source, the more you *try* to channel the One Power, the easier it becomes to actually do it. Yes, in the beginning, you stretch out to the Source and more often than not it is like grasping at air. Or you actually touch *saidar,* but even when you feel the One Power flowing through you, you find you can do nothing with it. Or you do something, and it isn't what you intended at all. That is the danger. Usually, with guidance and training—and the girl's own fear slowing her down—the ability to touch the Source and the ability to channel the Power come together with the ability to control what she is doing. But you began trying to channel without anyone there to teach you any control at all of what you do. I know you don't think you're very far along, and you are not, but you are like someone who has taught herself to run up hills—sometimes, at least—without ever learning how to run down the other side, or to walk. Sooner or later you are going to fall, if you don't learn the rest of it. Now, I am not talking about anything like what happens when one of those poor men begins channeling—you will not go mad; you won't die, not with sisters to teach and guide you—but what might you do entirely by accident, never meaning to?" For an instant the vagueness had dropped from Verin's eyes. For an instant, it seemed, the Aes Sedai's gaze had flicked from Egwene to

Nynaeve as sharply as the Amyrlin's had. "Your innate abilities are strong, child, and they will grow stronger. You must learn to control them before you harm yourself, or someone else, or a great many people. That is what Moiraine was trying to teach you. That is what I will try to help you with tonight, and what a sister will help you with every night until we put you into Sheriam's most capable hands. She is Mistress of Novices."

Egwene thought, *Can she know about Rand? It isn't possible. She'd never have let him leave Fal Dara if she even suspected.* But she was sure she had not imagined what she saw. "Thank you, Verin Sedai. I will try."

Nynaeve rose smoothly to her feet. "I will go sit by the fire and leave you two alone."

"You should stay," Verin said. "You could profit by it. From what Moiraine has told me, it should take only a little training for you to be raised to the Accepted."

Nynaeve hesitated only a moment before shaking her head firmly. "I thank you for the offer, but I can wait until we reach Tar Valon. Egwene, if you need me, I will be—"

"By any gauge," Verin cut in, "you are a woman grown, Nynaeve. Usually, the younger a novice, the better she does. Not with the training necessarily, but because a novice is expected to do as she is told, when she is told and without question. It is really only of use once the actual training has reached a certain point— a hesitation in the wrong place then, or a doubt of what you have been told to do, can have tragic consequences—but it is better to follow the discipline all the time. The Accepted, on the other hand, are expected to question things, as it is felt they know enough to know what questions to ask and when. Which do you think you would prefer?"

Nynaeve's hands tightened on her skirt, and she looked at the tent flap again, frowning. Finally she gave a short nod and settled back down on the floor. "I suppose I might as well," she said.

"Good," Verin said. "Now. You already know this part, Egwene, but for Nynaeve's sake I will take you through it step by step. In time, it will become second nature—you will do it all faster than you can think of it—but now it is best to go slowly. Close your eyes, please. It goes better in the beginning if you have no distractions at all." Egwene closed her eyes. There was a pause. "Nynaeve," Verin said, "please close your eyes. It will ready go better." Another pause. "Thank you, child. Now, you must empty yourself. Empty your thoughts. There is only one thing in your mind. The bud of a flower. Only that. Only the bud. You can see it in every detail. You can smell it. You can feel it. Every vein of every leaf, every curve of every petal. You can feel the sap pulsing. Feel it. Know it. Be it. You and the bud are the same. You are one. You are the bud."

Her voice droned on hypnotically, but Egwene no longer really heard; she had done this exercise before, with Moiraine. It was slow, but Moiraine had said it would come more quickly with practice. Inside herself, she was a rosebud, red petals curled tightly. Yet suddenly there was something else. Light. Light pressing on the petals. Slowly the petals unfolded, turning toward the light, absorbing the light. The rose and the light were one. Egwene and the light were one. She could feel the merest trickle of it seeping through her. She stretched for more, strained for more. . . .

In an instant it was all gone, rose and light. Moiraine had also said it could not be forced. With a sigh, she opened her eyes. Nynaeve had a grim look on her face. Verin was as calm as ever.

"You cannot *make* it happen," the Aes Sedai was saying. "You must *let* it happen. You must surrender to the Power before you can control it."

"This is complete foolishness," Nynaeve muttered. "I don't feel like a flower. If anything, I feel like a blackthorn bush. I think I will wait by the fire after all."

"As you wish," Verin said. "Did I mention that novices do

chores? They wash dishes, scrub floors, do laundry, serve at table, all sorts of things. I myself think the servants do a better job of it by far, but it is generally felt that such labor builds character. Oh, you are staying? Good. Well, child, remember that even a blackthorn bush has flowers sometimes, beautiful and white among the thorns. We will try it one at a time. Now, from the beginning, Egwene. Close your eyes."

Several times before Verin left, Egwene felt the flow of the Power through her, but it was never very strong, and the most she managed with it was to produce a stir in the air that made the tent flap stir slightly. She was sure a sneeze could have done as much. She had done better with Moiraine; sometimes, at least. She wished it was Moiraine doing the teaching.

Nynaeve never even felt a glimmer, or so she said. By the end her eyes were set and her mouth so tight that Egwene was afraid she was about to begin berating Verin as if the Aes Sedai were a village woman intruding on her privacy. But Verin simply told her to close her eyes once again, this time without Egwene.

Egwene was sitting, watching the other two between her yawns. The night had grown late, well past the time she would usually be asleep. Nynaeve wore a face like week-old death, her eyes clamped shut as if she never meant to open them and her hands white-knuckled fists in her lap. Egwene hoped the Wisdom's temper did not break loose, not after she had held it this long.

"Feel the flow through you," Verin was saying. Her voice did not change, but suddenly there was a gleam in her eyes. "Feel the flow. Flow of the Power. Flow like a breeze, a gentle stirring in the air." Egwene sat up straight. This was how Verin had guided her each time she had actually had the Power flowing through her. "A soft breeze, the slightest movement of air. Soft."

Abruptly the stacked blankets burst into flame like fatwood.

Nynaeve opened her eyes with a yell. Egwene was not sure if she screamed or not. All Egwene knew was that she was on her feet, trying to kick the burning blankets outside before they set the tent on fire. Before she managed a second kick, the flames vanished, leaving wispy smoke rising from a charred mass and the smell of burned wool.

"Well," Verin said. "Well. I did not expect to have to douse a fire. Don't faint on me, child. It's all right now. I took care of it."

"I—I was angry." Nynaeve spoke through trembling lips in a bloodless face. "I heard you talking about a breeze, telling me what to do, and fire just popped into my head. I—I didn't mean to burn anything. It was just a small fire, in—in my head." She shuddered.

"I suppose it was a small fire, at that." Verin barked a laugh that was gone with another look at Nynaeve's face. "Are you all right, child? If you feel ill, I can. . . ." Nynaeve shook her head, and Verin nodded. "Rest is what you need. Both of you. I've worked you too hard. You must rest. The Amyrlin will have us all up and away before first light." Standing, she toed the charred blankets. "I will have some more blankets brought to you. I hope this shows both of you how important control is. You must learn to do what you mean to do, and nothing more. Aside from harming someone else, if you draw more of the Power than you can safely handle—and you cannot handle much, yet; but it will grow—if you draw too much, you can destroy yourself. You can die. Or you can burn yourself out, destroy what ability you have." As if she had not told them they were walking a knife edge, she added a cheerful "Sleep well." With that, she was gone.

Egwene put her arms around Nynaeve and hugged her tight. "It is all right, Nynaeve. There is no need to be frightened. Once you learn to control—"

Nynaeve gave a croaking laugh. "I am not frightened." She glanced sideways at the smoking blankets and twitched her eyes away. "It takes more than a little fire to frighten me." But she did not look at the blankets again, even when a Warder came to take them away and leave new.

Verin did not come again, as she had said she would not. Indeed, as they journeyed on, south and west, day by day, as fast as the footmen could move, Verin paid the two women from Emond's Field no more mind than Moiraine did, than did any of the Aes Sedai. They were not precisely unfriendly, the Aes Sedai, but rather distant and aloof, as if preoccupied. Their coolness heightened Egwene's unease, and brought back all the tales she had heard as a child.

Her mother had always told her the tales about Aes Sedai were a lot of fool men's nonsense, but neither her mother nor any other woman in Emond's Field had ever met an Aes Sedai before Moiraine came there. She herself had spent a good deal of time with Moiraine, and Moiraine was proof to her that not all Aes Sedai were like the tales. Cold manipulators and merciless destroyers. Breakers of the World. She knew now that *those,* at least—the Breakers of the World—had been male Aes Sedai, when there were such, in the Age of Legends, but it did not help a great deal. Not *all* Aes Sedai were like the tales, but how many, and which?

The Aes Sedai who came to the tent each night were so mixed that they did not help at all in clearing her thoughts. Alviarin was as cool and businesslike as a merchant come to buy wool and tabac, surprised that Nynaeve was part of the lesson but accepting, sharp in her criticisms but always ready to try again. Alanna Mosvani laughed and spent as much time talking about the world, and men, as she did teaching. Alanna showed too much interest in Rand and Perrin and Mat for Egwene's comfort, though. Especially Rand. Worst of all was Liandrin, the only one who wore her shawl; the others had all packed them away before leaving Fal Dara. Liandrin sat fingering her red fringe and taught little, and reluctantly at that. She questioned Egwene and Nynaeve as if they had been accused of a crime, and her questions were all

about the three boys. She kept it up until Nynaeve threw her out—
Egwene was not sure why Nynaeve did so—and then she left with
a warning.

"Watch yourselves, my daughters. You are in your village no
longer. Now you dabble your toes where there are things to bite
you."

Finally the column reached the village of Medo, on the banks
of the Mora, which ran along the border between Shienar and
Arafel and so into the River Erinin.

Egwene was sure it was the Aes Sedai's questions about Rand
that had made her start dreaming of him, that and worrying about
him, about whether he and the others had had to follow the Horn
of Valere into the Blight. The dreams were always bad, but at first
they were just the ordinary sort of nightmare. By the night they
reached Medo, the dreams had changed, though.

"Pardon, Aes Sedai," Egwene asked diffidently, "but have you
seen Moiraine Sedai?" The slender Aes Sedai waved her away
and hurried on down the crowded, torchlit village street, calling
for someone to be careful with her horse. The woman was of the
Yellow Ajah, though not wearing her shawl now; Egwene knew
no more of her than that, not even her name.

Medo was a small village—though Egwene was shocked to
realize that what she now thought of as a "small village" was as
big as Emond's Field—and it was overwhelmed now with many
more outsiders than there were inhabitants. Horses and people
filled the narrow streets, jostling to the docks past villagers who
knelt whenever an unseeing Aes Sedai sped by. Harsh torchlight
lit everything. The two docks jutted out into the River Mora like
stone fingers, and each hosted a pair of small, two-masted ships.
There, horses were being hoisted on board by booms and cables
and canvas cradles under their bellies. More of the ships—
high-sided and stout, with lanterns topping their masts—crowded
the moon-streaked river, already loaded or waiting their turn. Row-

boats ferried out archers and pikemen, the raised pikes making the boats look like gigantic pricklebacks swimming on the surface.

On the left-hand dock Egwene found Anaiya, watching the loading and chivying those who were not moving fast enough. Though she had never said more than two words to Egwene, Anaiya seemed different from the others, more like a woman from home. Egwene could picture her baking in her kitchen; she could not see any of the others so. "Anaiya Sedai, have you seen Moiraine Sedai? I need to talk to her."

The Aes Sedai looked around with an absent frown. "What? Oh, it's you, child. Moiraine is gone. And your friend, Nynaeve, is already out on the *River Queen*. I had to bundle her onto a boat myself, shouting that she would not go without you. Light, what a scramble! You should be aboard, yourself. Find a boat going out to the *River Queen*. You two will be traveling with the Amyrlin Seat, so mind yourself once you're on board. No scenes or tantrums."

"Which ship is Moiraine Sedai's?"

"Moiraine isn't on a ship, girl. She's gone, two days gone, and the Amyrlin is in a taking over it." Anaiya grimaced and shook her head, though most of her attention was still on the workers. "First Moiraine vanishes with Lan, then Liandrin right on Moiraine's heels, and then Verin, none of them with so much as a word for anyone. Verin did not even take her Warder; Tomas is chewing nails with worry over her." The Aes Sedai glanced at the sky. The waxing moon shone without the hindrance of clouds. "We will have to call the wind again, and the Amyrlin will not be pleased with that, either. She says she wants us on our way to Tar Valon within an hour, and she will brook no delays. I would not want to be Moiraine, or Liandrin, or Verin, when she sees them next. They'll wish they were novices again. Why, child, what's the matter?"

Egwene drew a deep breath. *Moiraine gone? She can't be! I have to tell somebody, somebody who won't laugh at me.* She imagined Anaiya back in Emond's Field, listening to her daughter's problems; the woman fit the picture. "Anaiya Sedai, Rand is in trouble."

Anaiya gave her a considering look. "That tall boy from your village? Missing him already, are you? Well, I shouldn't be surprised if he *is* in trouble. Young men his age usually are. Though it was the other one—Mat?—who had the look of trouble. Very well, child. I don't mean to mock you or make light. What kind of trouble, and how do you know? He and Lord Ingtar must have the Horn and be back in Fal Dara by now. Or else they've had to follow it into the Blight, and there's nothing to do about that."

"I—I don't think they're in the Blight, or back in Fal Dara. I had a dream." She said it half defiantly. It sounded silly when she said it, but it had seemed so real. A nightmare for true, but real. First there had been a man with a mask over his face, and fire in place of his eyes. Despite the mask, she had thought he was surprised to see her. His look had frightened her till she thought her bones would break from shivering, but suddenly he vanished, and she saw Rand sleeping on the ground, wrapped in a cloak. A woman had been standing over him, looking down. Her face was in shadow, but her eyes seemed to shine like the moon, and Egwene had known she was evil. Then there was a flash of light, and they were gone. Both of them. And behind it all, almost like another thing altogether, was the feel of danger, as if a trap was just beginning to snap shut on an unsuspecting lamb, a trap with many jaws. As though time had slowed, and she could watch the iron jaws creep closer together. The dream had not faded with waking, the way dreams did. And the danger felt so strong she still wanted to look over her shoulder—only somehow she knew that it was aimed at Rand, not at her.

She wondered if she woman had been Moiraine, and upbraided herself for the thought. Liandrin fit that part better. Or perhaps Alanna; she had been interested in Rand, too.

She could not bring herself to tell Anaiya. Formally, she said, "Anaiya Sedai, I know it sounds foolish, but he is in danger. Great danger. I know it. I could feel it. I still can."

Anaiya wore a thoughtful look. "Well, now," she said softly, "that's a possibility I'll wager no one has considered. You may be a Dreamer. It is a small chance, child, but. . . . We haven't had one of those in—oh—four or five hundred years. And Dreaming is close linked to Foretelling. If you really can Dream, it may be that you can Foretell, as well. *That* would be a finger in the Reds' eye. Of course, it could be just an ordinary nightmare, brought on by a late night, and cold food, and us traveling so hard since we left Fal Dara. And you missing your young man. Much more likely. Yes, yes, child, I know. You are worried about him. Did your dream indicate what kind of danger?"

Egwene shook her head. "He just vanished, and I felt danger. And evil. I felt it even before he vanished." She shivered and rubbed her hands together. "I can still feel it."

"Well, we will talk about it more on the *River Queen*. If you *are* a Dreamer, I will see you have the training Moiraine should be here to. . . . You there!" the Aes Sedai barked suddenly, and Egwene jumped. A tall man, who had just sat down on a cask of wine, jumped, too. Several others quickened their step. "That's for loading aboard, not resting on! We will talk on the boat, child. No, you fool! You can't carry it by yourself! Do you want to hurt yourself?" Anaiya went striding off down the dock, giving the unfortunate villagers a rougher side of her tongue than Egwene would have suspected she had.

Egwene peered into the dark, toward the south. He was out there, somewhere. Not in Fal Dara, not in the Blight. She was sure of it. *Hold on, you wool-headed idiot. If you get yourself killed before I can get you out of this, I* will *skin you alive*. It did not occur to her to ask how she was going to get him out of anything, going to Tar Valon as she was.

Snugging her cloak around her, she set out to find a boat to the *River Queen*.

CHAPTER 13

From Stone to Stone

THE LIGHT OF THE RISING SUN WOKE RAND, and he wondered if he were dreaming. He sat up slowly, staring. Everything had changed, or almost everything. The sun and the sky were as he expected to see, if pallid and all but cloudless. Loial and Hurin still lay on either side of him, wrapped in their cloaks asleep, and their horses still stood hobbled a pace away, but everyone else was gone. Soldiers, horses, his friends, everyone and everything gone.

The hollow itself had changed, too, and they were in the middle of it now, no longer on the edge. At Rand's head rose a gray stone cylinder, every bit of three spans high and a full pace thick, covered with hundreds, perhaps thousands, of deeply incised diagrams and markings in some language he did not recognize. White stone paved the bottom of the hollow, as level as a floor, polished so smooth it almost glistened. Broad, high steps rose to the rim in concentric rings of different colored stone. And about the rim, the trees stood blackened and twisted as if a firestorm had roared through them. Everything seemed paler than it should be, just like the sun, more subdued, as if seen through mist. Only there was no mist. Just the three of them and the horses appeared truly solid. But when he touched the stone under him, it *felt* solid enough.

He reached out and shook Loial and Hurin. "Wake up! Wake up and tell me I'm dreaming. Please wake up!"

"Is it morning already?" Loial began, sitting up, then his mouth fell open, and his big, round eyes grew wider and wider.

Hurin woke with a start, then leaped to his feet, jumping like a flea on a hot rock to look this way, then that. "Where are we? What's happened? Where is everybody? Where are we, Lord Rand?" He sank to his knees, wringing his hands, but his eyes still darted. "What's happened?"

"I don't know," Rand said slowly. "I was hoping it was a dream, but. . . . Maybe it is a dream." He had had experience of dreams that were not dreams, experience he wanted neither to repeat nor to remember. He stood up carefully. Everything stayed as it was.

"I do not think so," Loial said. He was studying the column, and he did not appear happy. His long eyebrows sagged across his cheeks, and his tufted ears seemed to have wilted. "I think this is the same stone we went to sleep beside last night. I think I know what it is, now." For once, he sounded miserable about knowing.

"That's. . . ." *No.* That being the same stone was no more crazy than what he could see around him, Mat and Perrin and the Shienarans gone, and everything changed. *I thought I'd escaped, but it's started again, and there's no such thing as crazy anymore. Unless I am.* He looked at Loial and Hurin. They were not acting as if he were mad; they saw it, too. Something about the steps caught his eye, the different colors, seven rising from blue to red. "One for each Ajah," he said.

"No, Lord Rand," Hurin moaned. "No. Aes Sedai would not do this to us. They wouldn't! I walk in the Light."

"We all do, Hurin," Rand said. "The Aes Sedai won't hurt you." *Unless you get in the way.* Could this be Moiraine's doing somehow? "Loial, you said you know what the stone is. What is it?"

"I said I think I know, Rand. There was a piece of an old book, just a few pages, but one of them had a drawing of this stone, this Stone"—there was a distinct difference in the way he said it that marked importance—"or one very like it. And underneath, it said, 'From Stone to Stone run the lines of "if," between the worlds that might be.' "

"What does that mean, Loial? It doesn't make any sense."

The Ogier shook his massive head sadly. "It was only a few pages. Part of it said Aes Sedai in the Age of Legends, some of those who could Travel, the most powerful of them, could use these Stones. It did not say how, but I think, from what I could puzzle out, that perhaps those Aes Sedai used the Stones somehow to journey to those worlds." He glanced up at the seared trees and pulled his eyes down again quickly, as he did not want to think about what lay beyond the rim. "Yet even if Aes Sedai can use them, or could, we had no Aes Sedai with us to channel the Power, so I don't see how it can be."

Rand's skin prickled. *Aes Sedai used them. In the Age of Legends, when there were male Aes Sedai.* He had a vague memory of the void closing round him as he fell asleep, filled with that uneasy glow. And he remembered the room in the village, and the light he had reached for to escape. *If that was the male half of True Source. . . . No, it can't be. But what if it is? Light, I was wondering whether to run or not, and all the time it's right inside my head. Maybe I brought us here.* He did not want to think about it. "Worlds that might be? I don't understand, Loial."

The Ogier shrugged massively, and uneasily. "Neither do I, Rand. Most of it sounded like this. 'If a woman go left, or right,

does Time's flow divide? Does the Wheel then weave two Patterns? A thousand, for each of her turnings? As many as the stars?
Is one real, the others merely shadows and reflections?' You see, it
was not very clear. Mainly questions, most of which seemed to
contradict each other. And there just wasn't much of it." He went
back to staring at the column, but he looked as if he wished it
would go away. "There are supposed to be a good many of these
Stones, scattered all over the world, or there were, once, but I
never heard of anyone finding one. I never heard of anyone finding anything like this at all."

"My Lord Rand?" Now on his feet, Hurin seemed calmer, but
he clutched his coat at the waist with both hands, his face urgent.
"My Lord Rand, you'll get us back, won't you? Back where we
belong? I've a wife, my Lord, and children. Melia'd take it bad
enough, me dying, but if she doesn't even have my body to give to
the mother's embrace, she'll grieve to the end of her days. You
understand, my Lord. I can't leave her not knowing. You'll get us
back. And if I die, if you can't take her my body, you'll let her
know, so she has that, at least." He was no longer questioning at
the end. A note of confidence had crept into his voice.

Rand opened his mouth to say again he was not a lord, then
shut it without speaking. That was hardly important enough to
mention, now. *You got him into this.* He wanted to deny it, but he
knew what he was, knew he could channel, even if it always
seemed to happen all by itself. Loial said Aes Sedai used the
Stones, and that meant the One Power. What Loial said he knew,
you could be sure of—the Ogier never claimed to know if he did
not—and there was no one else nearby who could wield the
Power. *You got him into it, you have to get him out. You have
to try.*

"I will do my best, Hurin." And because Hurin was Shienaran,
he added, "By my House and honor. A shepherd's House and a
shepherd's honor, but I'll make them do as well as a lord's."

Hurin loosed his hold on his coat. The confidence reached his eyes, too. He bowed deeply. "Honor to serve, my Lord."

Guilt rippled through Rand. *He thinks you'll see him home, now, because Shienaran lords always keep their word. What are you going to do, Lord Rand?* "None of that, Hurin. There'll be no bowing. I'm not—" Suddenly he knew he could not tell the man again that he was not a lord. All that was holding the sniffer together was his belief in a lord, and he could not take that away, not now. Not here. "No bowing," he finished awkwardly.

"As you say, Lord Rand." Hurin's grin was almost as wide as when Rand first met him.

Rand cleared his throat. "Yes. Well, that's what I say."

They were both watching him, Loial curious, Hurin confident, both waiting to see what he would do. *I brought them here. I must have. So I have to get them back. And that means. . . .*

Drawing a deep breath, he walked across the white paving stones to the symbol-covered cylinder. Small lines of some language he did not know surrounded each symbol, odd letters that flowed in curves and spirals, suddenly turned to jagged hooks and angles, then flowed on. At least it was not Trolloc script. Reluctantly, he put his hands on the column. It looked like any dry, polished stone, but it felt curiously slick, like oiled metal.

He closed his eyes and formed the flame. The void came slowly, hesitantly. He knew his own fear was holding it back, fear of what he was trying. As fast as he fed fear into the flame, more came. *I can't do it. Channel the Power. I don't want to. Light, there has to be another way.* Grimly he forced the thoughts to stillness. He could feel sweat beading on his face. Determinedly he kept on, pushing his fears into the consuming flame, making it grow, and grow. And the void was there.

The core of him floated in emptiness. He could see the light—*saidin*—even with his eyes closed, feel the warmth of it, surrounding him, surrounding everything, suffusing everything. It wavered like a candle flame seen through oiled paper. Rancid oil. Stinking oil.

He reached for it—he was not sure *how* he reached, but it was something, a movement, a stretching toward the light, toward *saidin*—and caught nothing, as if running his hands through water. It felt like a slimy pond, scum floating atop clean water below, but he could not scoop up any of the water. Time and again it trickled through his fingers, not even droplets of the water remaining, only the slick scum, making his skin crawl.

Desperately, he tried to form an image of the hollow as it had been, with Ingtar and the lances sleeping by their horses, with Mat and Perrin, and the Stone lying buried except for one end. Outside the void he formed it, clinging to the shell of emptiness that enclosed him. He tried to link the image with the light, tried to force them together. The hollow as it had been, and he and Loial and Hurin there together. His head hurt. Together, with Mat and Perrin and the Shienarans. Burning, in his head. Together!

The void shattered into a thousand razor shards, slicing his mind.

Shuddering, he staggered back, wide-eyed. His hands hurt from pressing the Stone, and his arms and shoulders quivered with aching; his stomach lurched from the feel of filth covering him, and his head. . . . He tried to steady his breathing. That had never happened before. When the void went, it went like a pricked bubble, just gone, in a twinkling. Never broken like glass. His head felt numb, as if the thousand slashes had happened so quickly the pain had not yet come. But every cut had felt as real as if done with a knife. He touched his temple, and was surprised not to see blood on his fingers.

Hurin still stood there watching him, still confident. If anything, the sniffer seemed more sure by the minute. Lord Rand was doing something. That was what lords were for. They protected the land and the people with their bodies and their lives, and when something was wrong, they set it aright and saw fairness and justice done. As long as Rand was doing something, anything, Hurin would have confidence that it would all come right in the end. That was what lords did.

Loial had a different look, a slightly puzzled frown, but his eyes were on Rand, too. Rand wondered what he was thinking.

"It was worth a try," he told them. The rancid oil feel, inside his head—*Light, it's inside me! I don't want it inside me!*—was fading slowly, but he still thought he might vomit. "I will try again, in a few minutes."

He hoped he sounded confident. He had no idea how the Stones worked, if what he was doing had any chance of success. *Maybe there are rules for working them. Maybe you have to do something special. Light, maybe you can't use the same Stone twice, or. . . .* He cut off that line of thought. There was no good in thinking like that. He had to do it. Looking at Loial and Hurin, he thought he knew what Lan had meant about duty pressing down like a mountain.

"My Lord, I think. . . ." Hurin let his words trail off, looking abashed for a moment. "My Lord, maybe, if we find the Darkfriends, we can make one of them tell us how to get back."

"I would ask a Darkfriend or the Dark One himself if I thought I'd get a true answer back," Rand said. "But we are all there is. Just us three." *Just me. I'm the one who has to do it.*

"We could follow their trail, my Lord. If we catch them. . . ."

Rand stared at the sniffer. "You can still smell them?"

"I can, my Lord." Hurin frowned. "It's faint, pale-like, like everything else here, but I can smell the trail. Right up there." He pointed to the rim of the hollow. "I don't understand it, my Lord, but—Last night, I could have sworn the trail went right on by the hollow back—back where we were. Well, it's in the same place now, only here, and fainter, like I said. Not old, not faint like that, but. . . . I don't know, Lord Rand, except that it's there."

Rand considered. If Fain and the Darkfriends were here—wherever here was—they might know how to get back. They had to, if they had reached here in the first place. And they had the Horn, and the dagger. Mat had to have that dagger. For that if for nothing else, he had to find them. What finally decided him, he was ashamed so realize, was that he was afraid to try again. Afraid to try channeling the Power. He was less afraid of confronting Darkfriends and Trollocs with only Hurin and Loial than he was of that.

"Then we will go after the Darkfriends." He tried to sound sure, the way Lan would, or Ingtar. "The Horn must be recovered. If we can't puzzle out a way to take it from them, at least we will know where they are when we find Ingtar again." *If only they don't ask how we're going to find him again.* "Hurin, make sure it really is the trail we're after."

The sniffer leaped into his saddle, eager to be doing something himself, perhaps eager to be away from the hollow, and scrambled his horse up the broad, colored steps. The animal's hooves rang loudly on the stone, but they made not a mark.

Rand stowed Red's hobbles in his saddlebags—the banner was still there; he would not have minded if that had been left behind—then gathered his bow and quiver and climbed to the stallion's back. The bundle of Thom Merrilin's cloak made a mound behind his saddle.

Loial led his big mount over to him; with the Ogier standing on the ground, Loial's head came almost to Rand's shoulder, and him in his saddle. Loial still looked puzzled.

"You think we should stay here?" Rand said. "Try again to use the Stone? If the Darkfriends are here, in place, we have to find them. We can't leave the Horn of Valere in Darkfriend hands; you heard the Amyrlin. And we have to get that dagger back. Mat will die without it."

Loial nodded. "Yes, Rand, we do. But, Rand, the Stones. . . ."

"We will find another. You said they were scattered all over, and if they're all like this—all this stonework around them—it should not be too hard to find one."

"Rand, that fragment said the Stones came from an older Age than the Age of Legends, and even the Aes Sedai then did not understand them, though they used them, some of the truly powerful did. They used them with the One Power, Rand. How did you think to use this Stone to take us back? Or any other Stone we find?"

For a moment Rand could only stare at the Ogier, thinking faster than he ever had in his life. "If they are older than the Age of Legends, maybe the people who built them didn't use the Power. There must be another way. The Darkfriends got here, and they certainly couldn't use the Power. Whatever this other way is, I will find it out. I will get us back, Loial." He looked at the tall stone column with its odd markings, and felt a prickle of fear. *Light, if only I don't have to use the Power to do it.* "I will, Loial, I promise. One way or another."

The Ogier gave a doubtful nod. He swung up onto his huge horse and followed Rand up the steps to join Hurin among the blackened trees.

The land stretched out, low and rolling, sparsely forested here and there with grassland between, crossed by more than one stream. In the middle distance Rand thought he could see another burned patch. It was all pale, the colors washed. There was no sign of anything made by men except the stone circle behind them. The sky was empty, no chimney smoke, no birds, only a few clouds and the pale yellow sun.

Worst of all, though, the land seemed to twist the eye. What was close at hand looked all right, and what was seen straight ahead in the distance. But whenever Rand turned his head, things that appeared distant when seen from the corner of his eye seemed to rush toward him, to be nearer when he stared straight at them. It made for dizziness; even the horses whickered nervously and rolled their eyes. He tried moving his head slowly; the apparent movement of things that should have been fixed was still there, but it seemed to help a little.

"Did your piece of a book say anything about this?" Rand asked.

Loial shook his head, then swallowed hard as if he wished he had kept it still. "Nothing."

"I suppose there's nothing to do for it. Which way, Hurin?"

"South, Lord Rand." The sniffer kept his eyes on the ground.

"South, then." *There has to be a way back besides using the Power*. Rand heeled Red's flanks. He tried to make his voice light-hearted, as if he saw no difficulty at all in what they were about. "What was it Ingtar said? Three or four days to that monument to Artur Hawkwing? I wonder if that exists here, too, the way the Stones do. If this is a world that *could* be, maybe it's still standing. Wouldn't that be something to see, Loial?"

They rode south.

CHAPTER 14

Wolfbrother

"GONE?" INGTAR DEMANDED OF THE AIR. "AND my guards saw nothing. Nothing! They cannot just be gone!"

Listening, Perrin hunched his shoulders and looked at Mat, who stood a little way off frowning and muttering to himself. Arguing with himself was how Perrin saw it. The sun was peeking over the horizon, past time for them to have been riding. Shadows lay long across the hollow, stretched out and thinned, but still like the trees that made them. The packhorses, loaded and on their lead line, stamped impatiently, but everyone stood by his mount and waited.

Uno came striding up. "Not a goat-kissing track, my Lord." He sounded offended; failure touched on his skill. "Burn me, not so much as a flaming hoof scrape. They just bloody vanished."

"Three men and three horses do not just vanish," Ingtar

growled. "Go over the ground again, Uno. If anyone can find where they went, it's you."

"Maybe they just ran away," Mat said. Uno stopped and glared at him. *Like he'd cursed an Aes Sedai,* Perrin thought wonderingly.

"Why would they run away?" Ingtar's voice was dangerously soft. "Rand, the Builder, my sniffer—my sniffer!—why would any of them run, much less all three?"

Mat shrugged. "I don't know. Rand was. . . ." Perrin wanted to throw something at him, hit him, anything to stop him, but Ingtar and Uno were watching. He felt a flood of relief when Mat hesitated, then spread his hands and muttered, "I don't know why. I just thought maybe they had."

Ingtar grimaced. "Ran away," he growled as if he did not believe it for an instant. "The Builder can go as he will, but Hurin would not run away. And neither would Rand al'Thor. He would not; he knows his duty, now. Go on, Uno. Search the ground again." Uno gave a half bow and hurried away, sword hilt bobbing over his shoulder. Ingtar grumbled, "Why would Hurin leave like that, in the middle of the night, without a word? He knows what we're about. How am I to track this Shadow-spawned filth without him? I would give a thousand gold crowns for a pack of trail hounds. If I did not know better, I would say the Darkfriends managed this so they can slip east or west without me knowing. Peace, I don't know if I *do* know better." He stumped off after Uno.

Perrin shifted uneasily. The Darkfriends were doubtless getting further away with every minute. Getting further away, and with them the Horn of Valere—and the dagger from Shadar Logoth. He did not think that Rand, whatever he had become, whatever had happened to him, would abandon that chase. *But where* did *he go, and why?* Loial might go with Rand for friendship—but why Hurin?

"Maybe he did run away," he muttered, then looked around. No one appeared to have heard; even Mat was not paying him any mind. He scrubbed a hand through his hair. If Aes Sedai had been after him to be a false Dragon, he would have run, too. But worrying about Rand was doing nothing to help track the Darkfriends.

There was a way, perhaps, if he was willing to take it. He did not want to take it. He had been running away from it, but perhaps, now, he could no longer run. *Serves me right for what I told Rand. I wish I could run.* Even knowing what he could do to help—what he had to do—he hesitated.

No one was looking at him. No one would know what they were seeing even if they did look. Finally, reluctantly, he closed his eyes and let himself drift, let his thoughts drift, out, away from him.

He had tried denying it from the first, long before his eyes began to change from dark brown to burnished golden yellow. At that first meeting, that first instant of recognition, he had refused to believe, and he had run from the recognition ever since. He still wanted to run.

His thoughts drifted, feeling for what must be out there, what was always out there in country where men were few or far between, feeling for his brothers. He did not like to think of them that way, but they were.

In the beginning he had been afraid that what he did had some taint of the Dark One, or of the One Power—equally bad for a man who wanted nothing more than to be a blacksmith and live his life in the Light, and in peace. From that time, he knew something of how Rand felt, afraid of himself, feeling unclean. He was still not past that entirely. This thing he did was older than humans using the One Power, though, something from the birth of Time. Not the Power, Moiraine had told him. Something long vanished, now come again. Egwene knew, too, though he wished she did not. He wished no one did. He hoped she had not told anyone.

Contact. He felt them, felt other minds. Felt his brothers, the wolves.

Their thoughts came to him as a whirlpool blend of images and emotions. At first he had not been able to make out anything except the raw emotion, but now his mind put words to them. *Wolfbrother. Surprise. Two-legs that talks.* A faded image, dim with time, old beyond old, of men running with wolves, two packs hunting together. *We have heard this comes again. You are Long Tooth?*

It was a faint picture of a man dressed in clothes made of hides, with a long knife in his hand, but overlaid on the image, more central, was a shaggy wolf with one tooth longer than the rest, a steel tooth gleaming in the sunlight as the wolf led the pack in a desperate charge through deep snow toward the deer that would mean life instead of slow death by starvation, and the deer thrashing to run in powder to their bellies, and the sun glinting on the white until it hurt the eyes, and the wind howling down the passes, swirling the fine snow like mist, and. . . . Wolves' names were always complex images.

Perrin recognized the man. Elyas Machera, who had first introduced him to wolves. Sometimes he wished he had never met Elyas.

No, he thought, and tried to picture himself in his mind.

Yes. We have heard of you.

It was not the image he had made, a young man with heavy shoulders and shaggy, brown curls, a young man with an axe at his belt, who others thought moved and thought slowly. That man was there, somewhere in the mind picture that came from the wolves, but stronger by far was a massive, wild bull with curved horns of shining metal, running through the night with the speed and exuberance of youth, curly-haired coat gleaming in the moonlight, flinging himself in among Whitecloaks on their horses, with the air crisp and cold and dark, and blood so red on the horns, and. . . .

Young Bull.

For a moment Perrin lost the contact in his shock. He had not dreamed they had given him a name. He wished he could not remember how he had earned it. He touched the axe at his belt, with its gleaming, half-moon blade. *Light help me, I killed two men. They would have killed me even quicker, and Egwene, but. . . .*

Pushing all that aside—it was done and behind him; he had no wish to remember any of it—he gave the wolves the smell of Rand, of Loial and Hurin, and asked if they had scented the three. It was one of the things that had come to him with the change in his eyes; he could identify people by their smell even when he could not see them. He could see more sharply, too, see in anything but pitch-darkness. He was always careful to light lamps or candles, now, sometimes before anyone else thought they were needed.

From the wolves came a view of men on horses approaching the hollow in late day. That was the last they had seen or smelled of Rand or the other two.

Perrin hesitated. The next step would be useless unless he told Ingtar. *And Mat will die if we don't find that dagger. Burn you, Rand, why did you take the sniffer?*

The one time he had gone to the dungeon, with Egwene, the smell of Fain had made his hair stand on end; not even Trollocs smelled so foul. He had wanted to rip through the bars of the cell and tear the man apart, and finding that inside himself had frightened him more than Fain did. To mask Fain's smell in his own mind, he added the scent of Trollocs before he howled aloud.

From the distance came the cries of a wolfpack, and in the hollow horses stamped and whickered fearfully. Some of the soldiers fingered their long-bladed lances and eyed the rim of the hollow uneasily. Inside Perrin's head, it was much worse. He felt the rage of the wolves, the hate. There were only two things wolves hated.

All else they merely endured, but fire and Trollocs they hated, and they would go through fire to kill Trollocs.

Even more than the Trollocs, Fain's scent had put them into a frenzy, as if they smelled something that made Trollocs seem natural and right.

Where?

The sky rolled in his head; the land spun. East and west, wolves did not know. They knew the movements of sun and moon, the shift of seasons, the contours of the land. Perrin puzzled it out. South. And something more. An eagerness to kill the Trollocs. The wolves would let Young Bull share in the killing. He could bring the two-legs with their hard skins if he wanted, but Young Bull, and Smoke, and Two Deer, and Winter Dawn, and all the rest of the pack would hunt down the Twisted Ones who had dared come into their land. The inedible flesh and bitter blood would burn the tongue, but they must be killed. Kill them. Kill the Twisted Ones.

Their fury infected him. His lips peeled back in a snarl, and he took a step, to join them, run with them in the hunt, in the killing.

With an effort he broke the contact except for a thin sense that the wolves were there. He could have pointed to them across the intervening distance. He felt cold inside. *I'm a man, not a wolf. Light help me, I am a man!*

"Are you well, Perrin?" Mat said, moving closer. He sounded the way he always did, flippant—and bitter under it, too, of late— but he looked worried. "That is all I need. Rand run off, and then you get sick. I don't know where I'll find a Wisdom to look after you out here. I think I have some willowbark in my saddlebags. I can make you some willowbark tea, if Ingtar lets us stay that long. Serve you right if I make it too strong."

"I . . . I'm all right, Mat." Shaking off his friend, he went to find Ingtar. The Shienaran lord was scanning the ground on the rim with Uno, and Ragan, and Masema. The others frowned at him as he drew Ingtar aside. He made sure Uno and the rest were too far away to hear before he spoke. "I don't know where Rand or the others went, Ingtar, but Padan Fain and the Trollocs—and I guess the rest of the Darkfriends—are still heading south."

"How do you know this?" Ingtar said.

Perrin drew a deep breath. "Wolves told me." He waited, for what he was not sure. Laughter, scorn, an accusation of being a Darkfriend, of being mad. Deliberately, he tucked his thumbs behind his belt, away from the axe. *I will not kill. Not again. If he tries to kill me for a Darkfriend, I'll run, but I won't kill anybody else.*

"I have heard of things like this," Ingtar said slowly, after a moment. "Rumors. There was a Warder, a man called Elyas Machera, who some said could talk to wolves. He disappeared years ago." He seemed to catch something in Perrin's eyes. "You know him?"

"I know him," Perrin said flatly. "He's the one. . . . I don't want to talk about it. I didn't ask for it." *That's what Rand said. Light, I wish I were home working Master Luhhan's forge.*

"These wolves," Ingtar said, "they will track the Darkfriends and Trollocs for us?" Perrin nodded. "Good. I will have the Horn, whatever it takes." The Shienaran glanced around at Uno and the others still searching for tracks. "Better not to tell anyone else, though. Wolves are considered good luck in the Borderlands. Trollocs fear them. But still, better to keep this between us for the time. Some of them might not understand."

"I would as soon nobody else ever found out," Perrin said.

"I will tell them you think you have Hurin's talent. They know about that; they're easy with it. Some of them saw you wrinkling your nose back in that village, and at the ferry. I've heard jokes about your delicate nose. Yes. You keep us on the trail today, Uno will see enough of their tracks to confirm it *is* the trail, and before nightfall every last man will be sure you are a sniffer. I *will* have the Horn." He glanced at the sky, and raised his voice. "Daylight is wasting! To horse!"

To Perrin's surprise, the Shienarans seemed to accept Ingtar's story. A few of them looked skeptical—Masema went so far as to spit—but Uno nodded thoughtfully, and that was enough for most. Mat was the hardest to convince.

"A sniffer! You? You're going to track murderers by smell? Perrin, you are as crazy as Rand. I am the only sane one left from Emond's Field, with Egwene and Nynaeve trotting off to Tar Valon to become—" He cut himself short with an uneasy glance for the Shienarans.

Perrin took Hurin's place beside Ingtar as the small column rode south. Mat kept up a string of disparaging remarks, until Uno found the first tracks left by Trollocs and by men on horses, but Perrin paid him little mind. It was all he could do to keep the wolves from dashing on ahead to kill the Trollocs. The wolves cared only about killing the Twisted Ones; to them, Darkfriends were no different from any other two-legs. Perrin could almost see the Darkfriends scattering in a dozen directions while the wolves slew Trollocs, running away with the Horn of Valere. Running away with the dagger. And once the Trollocs were dead, he did not think he could interest the wolves in tracking the humans even if he had any idea which of them to track. He had a running argument with them, and sweat covered his forehead long before he got the first flash of images that turned his stomach.

He drew rein, stopping his horse dead. The others did the same, looking at him, waiting. He stared straight ahead and cursed softly, bitterly.

Wolves would kill men, but men were not a preferred prey. Wolves remembered the old hunting together, for one thing, and two-legs tasted bad, for another. Wolves were more particular about their food than he would have believed. They would not eat carrion, unless they were starving, and few would kill more than they could eat. What Perrin felt from the wolves could best be described as disgust. And there were the images. He could see them much more clearly than he wished. Bodies, men and women and children, heaped and tumbled about. Blood-soaked earth churned by hooves and frenzied attempts to escape. Torn flesh. Heads severed. Vultures flapping, their white wings stained red; bloody, featherless heads tearing and gorging. He broke loose before his stomach emptied itself.

Above some trees in the far distance he could just make out black specks whirling low, dropping then rising again. Vultures fighting over their meal.

"There's something bad up there." He swallowed, meeting Ingtar's gaze. How could he fit telling them into the story of being a sniffer? *I don't want to get close enough to look at that. But they'll want to investigate once they can see the vultures. I have to tell them enough so they'll circle around.* "The people from that village. . . . I think the Trollocs killed them."

Uno began cursing quietly, and some of the other Shienarans muttered to themselves. None of them seemed to take his announcement as odd, though. Lord Ingtar said he was a sniffer, and sniffers could smell killing.

"And there is someone following us," Ingtar said.

Mat turned his horse eagerly. "Maybe it's Rand. I knew he wouldn't run out on me."

Thin, scattered puffs of dust rose to the north; a horse was running across patches where the grass grew thin. The Shienarans spread out, lances ready, watching in all directions. It was no place to be casual about a stranger.

A speck appeared—a horse and rider; a woman, to Perrin's eyes, long before anyone else could discern the rider—and quickly drew closer. She slowed to a trot as she came up on them, fanning herself with one hand. A plump, graying woman, with her cloak tied behind her saddle, who blinked at them all vaguely.

"That's one of the Aes Sedai," Mat said disappointedly. "I recognize her. Verin."

"Verin Sedai," Ingtar said sharply, then bowed to her from his saddle.

"Moiraine Sedai sent me, Lord Ingtar," Verin announced with a satisfied smile. "She thought you might need me. Such a gallop I've had. I thought I might not catch you short of Cairhien. You saw that village, of course? Oh, that was very nasty, wasn't it? And that Myrddraal. There were ravens and crows all over the rooftops, but never a one went near it, dead as it was. I had to wave away the Dark One's own weight in flies, though, before I could make out what it was. A shame I did not have time to take it down. I've never had a chance to study a—" Suddenly her eyes narrowed, and the absent manner vanished like smoke. "Where is Rand al'Thor?"

Ingtar grimaced. "Gone, Verin Sedai. Vanished last night, without a trace. Him, the Ogier, and Hurin, one of my men."

"The Ogier, Lord Ingtar? And your sniffer went with him? What would those two have in common with . . .?" Ingtar gaped at her, and she snorted. "Did you think you could keep something like that secret?" She snorted again. "Sniffers. Vanished, you say?"

"Yes, Verin Sedai." Ingtar sounded unsettled. It was never easy discovering Aes Sedai knew the secrets you were trying to keep from them; Perrin hoped Moiraine had not told anyone about him. "But I have—I have a new sniffer." The Shienaran Lord gestured to Perrin. "This man seems to have the ability, also. I will find the Horn of Valere, as I swore to, have no fear. Your company will be welcome, Aes Sedai, if you wish to ride with us." To Perrin's surprise, he did not sound as if he entirely meant it.

Verin glanced at Perrin, and he shifted uneasily. "A new sniffer, just when you lose your old one. How . . . providential. You found no tracks? No, of course not. You said no trace. Odd. Last night." She twisted in her saddle, looking back north, and for a moment

Perrin almost thought she was going to ride back the way she had come.

Ingtar frowned at her. "You think their disappearance has something to do with the Horn, Aes Sedai?"

Verin settled back. "The Horn? No. No, I . . . think not. But it is odd. Very odd. I do not like odd things until I can understand them."

"I can have two men escort you back to where they disappeared, Verin Sedai. They will have no trouble taking you right to it."

"No. If you say they vanished without a trace. . . ." For a long moment she studied Ingtar, her face unreadable. "I will ride with you. Perhaps we will find them again, or they will find us. Talk to me as we ride, Lord Ingtar. Tell me everything you can about the young man. Everything he did, everything he said."

They started off in a jingle of harness and armor, Verin riding close beside Ingtar and questioning him closely, but too low to be overheard. She gave Perrin a look when he tried to maintain his place, and he fell back.

"It's Rand she's after," Mat murmured, "not the Horn."

Perrin nodded. *Wherever you've gotten to, Rand, stay there. It's safer than here.*

CHAPTER 15

Kinslayer

HE WAY THE STRANGELY FADED DISTANT
hills seemed to slide toward Rand when he looked
straight at them made his head spin, unless he wrapped
himself in the void. Sometimes the emptiness crept up on him
unawares, but he avoided it like death. Better to be dizzy than
share the void with that uneasy light. Better by far to stare at the
faded land. Still, he tried not to look at anything too far away
unless it lay right ahead of them.

Hurin wore a fixed look as he concentrated on sniffing the trail,
as if he were trying to ignore the land the trail crossed. When the
sniffer did notice what lay around them, he would give a start and
wipe his hands on his coat, then push his nose forward like a
hound, eyes glazing, excluding everything else. Loial rode
slumped in his saddle and frowned as he glanced around, ears
twitching uneasily, muttering to himself.

Again they crossed land blackened and burned, even the soil crunching under the horses' hooves as if it had been seared. The burned swathes, sometimes a mile wide, sometimes only a few hundred paces, all ran east and west as straight as an arrow's flight. Twice Rand saw the end of a burn, once as they rode over it, once as they passed nearby; they tapered to points at the ends. At least, the ends he saw were so, but he suspected they were all the same.

Once he had watched Whatley Eldin decorate a cart for Sunday, back home in Emond's Field, What painting the scenes in bright colors, and the intricate scrollwork that surrounded them. For the borders, What let the point of his brush touch the cart, making a thin line that grew thicker as he pressed harder, then thinner again as he eased up. That was how the land looked, as if someone had streaked it with a monstrous brush of fire.

Nothing grew where the burns were, though some burns, at least, had the feel of a thing long done. Not so much as a hint of char remained in the air there, not a whiff even when he leaned down to break off a black twig and smell it. Old, yet nothing had come in to reclaim the land. Black gave way to green, and green to black, along knife-edge lines.

In its own way, the rest of the land lay as dead as the burns, though grass covered the ground and leaves covered the trees. Everything had that faded look, like clothes too often washed and too long left in the sun. There were no birds or animals, not that Rand saw or heard. No hawk wheeling in the sky, no bark of a hunting fox, no bird singing. Nothing rustled in the grass or lit on a tree branch. No bees, or butterflies. Several times they crossed streams, the water shallow, though often it had dug itself a deep gulley with steep banks the horses had to scramble down and climb on the other side. The water ran clear except for the mud the horses' hooves stirred, but never a minnow or tadpole wriggled out of the roiling, not even a waterspider dancing across the surface, or a hovering lacewing.

The water was drinkable, which was just as well, since their waterbottles could not last forever. Rand tasted it first, and made Loial and Hurin wait to see if anything happened to him before he let them drink. He had gotten them into this; it was his responsibility. The water was cool and wet, but that was the best that could be said for it. It tasted flat, as if it had been boiled. Loial made a face, and the horses did not like it either, shaking their heads and drinking reluctantly.

There was one sign of life; at least, Rand thought it must be so. Twice he saw a wispy streak crawling across the sky like a line drawn with cloud. The lines were too straight to be natural, it seemed, but he could not imagine what might make them. He did not mention the lines to the others. Perhaps they did not see, Hurin intent on the trail as he was and Loial drawn in on himself. They said nothing of the lines, at any rate.

When they had ridden half the morning, Loial abruptly swung down from his huge horse without a word and strode to a stand of giantsbroom, their trunks splitting into many thick branches, stiff and straight, not a pace above the ground. At the top, all split again, into the leafy brush that gave them their name.

Rand pulled Red up and started to ask what he was doing, but something about the Ogier's manner, as if he himself were uncertain, kept Rand silent. After staring at the tree, Loial put his hands on a trunk and began to sing in a deep, soft rumble.

Rand had heard Ogier Treesong, once, when Loial had sung to a dying tree and brought it back to life, and he had heard of sung wood, objects wrought from trees by the Treesong. The Talent was fading, Loial said, he was one of the few who had the ability, now; that was what made sung wood even more sought after and treasured. When he had heard Loial sing before, it had been as if the earth itself sang, but now the Ogier murmured his song almost diffidently, and the land echoed it in a whisper.

It seemed pure song, music without words, at least none that

Rand could make out; if there were words, they faded into the music just as water pours into a stream. Hurin gasped and stared.

Rand was not sure what it was Loial did, or how; soft as the song was, it caught him up hypnotically, filling his mind almost the way the void did. Loial ran his big hands along the trunk, singing, caressing with his voice as well as his fingers. The trunk now seemed smoother, somehow, as if his stroking were shaping it. Rand blinked. He was sure the piece Loial worked on had had branches at its top just like the others, but now it stopped in a rounded end right above the Ogier's head. Rand opened his mouth, but the song quieted him. It seemed so familiar, that song, as if he should know it.

Abruptly Loial's voice rose to a climax—almost a hymn of thanks, it sounded—and ended, fading as a breeze fades.

"Burn me," Hurin breathed. He looked stunned. "Burn me, I never heard anything like. . . . Burn me."

In his hands Loial held a staff as tall as he was and as thick as Rand's forearm, smooth and polished. Where the trunk had been on the giantsbroom was a small stem of new growth.

Rand took a deep breath. *Always something new, always something I didn't expect, and sometimes it isn't horrible.*

He watched Loial mount, resting the staff across his saddle in front of him, and wondered why the Ogier wanted a staff at all, since they were riding. Then he saw the thick rod, not as big as it was, but in relation to the Ogier, saw the way Loial handled it. "A quarterstaff," he said, surprised. "I didn't know Ogier carried weapons, Loial."

"Usually we do not," the Ogier replied almost curtly. "Usually. The price has always been too high." He hefted the huge quarterstaff and wrinkled his broad nose with distaste. "Elder Haman would surely say I am putting a long handle on my axe, but I am not just being hasty or rash, Rand. This place. . . ." He shivered, and his ears twitched.

"We'll find our way back soon," Rand said, trying to sound confident.

Loial spoke as if he had not heard. "Everything is . . . linked, Rand. Whether it lives or not, whether it thinks or not, everything that *is,* fits together. The tree does not think, but it is part of the whole, and the whole has a—a feeling. I can't explain any more than I can explain what being happy is, but. . . . Rand, this land was glad for a weapon to be made. Glad!"

"The Light shine on us," Hurin murmured nervously, "and the Creator's hand shelter us. Though we go to the last embrace of the mother, the Light illumine our way." He kept repeating the catechism as if it had a charm to protect him.

Rand resisted the impulse to look around. He definitely did not look up. All it would take to break them all was another of those smoky lines across the sky right at that moment. "There's nothing here to hurt us," he said firmly. "And we'll keep a good watch and make sure nothing does."

He wanted to laugh at himself, sounding so certain. He was not certain about anything. But watching the others—Loial with his tufted ears drooping, and Hurin trying not to look at anything—he knew one of them had to seem to be sure, at least, or fear and uncertainty would break them all apart. *The Wheel weaves as the Wheel wills.* He squeezed that thought out. *Nothing to do with the Wheel. Nothing to with ta'veren, or Aes Sedai, or the Dragon. It's just the way it is, that's all.*

"Loial, are you done here?" The Ogier nodded, regretfully rubbing the quarterstaff. Rand turned to Hurin. "Do you still have the trail?"

"I do, Lord Rand. I do that."

"Then let's keep on with it. Once we find Fain and the Darkfriends, why, we'll go home heroes, with the dagger for Mat, and the Horn of Valere. Lead out, Hurin." *Heroes? I'll settle for all of us getting out of here alive.*

"I do not like this place," the Ogier announced flatly. He held the quarterstaff as if he expected to have to use it soon.

"As well we don't mean to stay here, then, isn't it?" Rand said. Hurin barked a laugh as if he had made a joke, but Loial gave him a level look.

"As well we don't, Rand."

Yet as they rode on southward, he could see that his casual assumption that they would get home had picked them both up a little. Hurin sat a bit straighter in his saddle, and Loial's ears did not seem so wilted. It was no time or place to let them know he shared their fear, so he kept it to himself, and fought it by himself.

Hurin kept his humor through the morning, murmuring, "As well we don't mean to stay," then chuckling, until Rand felt like telling him to be quiet. Toward midday, the sniffer did fall silent, though, shaking his head and frowning, and Rand found he wished the man was still repeating his words and laughing.

"Is there something wrong with the trail, Hurin?" he asked.

The sniffer shrugged, looking troubled. "Yes, Lord Rand, and then again no, as you might say."

"It must be one or the other. Have you lost the trail? No shame if you have. You said it was weak to start. If we can't find the Darkfriends, we will find another Stone and get back that way." *Light, anything but that.* Rand kept his face smooth. "If Darkfriends can come here and leave, so can we."

"Oh, I haven't lost it, Lord Rand. I can still pick out the stink of them. It isn't that. It's just. . . . It's. . . ." With a grimace, Hurin burst out, "It's like I'm remembering it, Lord Rand, instead of smelling it. But I'm not. There's dozens of trails crossing it all the time, dozens and dozens, and all sorts of smells of violence, some of them fresh, almost, only washed out like everything else. This morning, right after we left the hollow, I could have sworn there were hundreds slaughtered right under my feet, just minutes before, but there weren't any bodies, and not a mark on the grass but our own hoofprints. A thing like that couldn't happen without the ground being torn up and bloodied, but there wasn't a mark. It's all like that, my Lord. But I am following the trail. I am. This place just has me all on edge. That's it. That must be it."

Rand glanced at Loial—the Ogier did come up with the oddest knowledge, at times—but he looked as puzzled as Hurin. Rand made his voice more confident than he felt. "I know you are doing your best, Hurin. We are all of us on edge. Just follow as best you can, and we'll find them."

"As you say, Lord Rand." Hurin booted his horse forward. "As you say."

But by nightfall, there was still no sign of the Darkfriends, and Hurin said the trail was fainter still. The sniffer kept muttering to himself about "remembering."

There had been no sign. Really no sign. Rand was not as good a tracker as Uno, but any boy in the Two Rivers was expected to track well enough to find a lost sheep, or a rabbit for dinner. He had seen nothing. It was as if no living thing had ever disturbed the land before they came. There should have been something if the Darkfriends were ahead of them. But Hurin kept following the trail he said he smelled.

As the sun touched the horizon they made camp in a stand of trees untouched by the burn, eating from their saddlebags. Flatbread and dried meat washed down with flat-tasting water; hardly a filling meal, tough and far from tasty. Rand thought they might have enough for a week. After that. . . . Hurin ate slowly, determinedly, but Loial gulped his down with a grimace and settled back with his pipe, the big quarterstaff close at hand. Rand kept their fire small and well hidden in the trees. Fain and his Darkfriends and Trollocs might be close enough to see a fire, for all of Hurin's worries about the oddness of their trail.

It seemed odd to him that he had begun to think of them as Fain's Darkfriends, Fain's Trollocs. Fain was just a madman. *Then why did they rescue him?* Fain had been part of the Dark One's scheme to find him. Perhaps it had something to do with that. *Then why is he running instead of chasing me? And what killed that Fade? What happened in that room full of flies? And those eyes, watching me in Fal Dara. And that wind, catching me like a beetle in pine sap. No. No, Ba'alzamon has to be dead.* The Aes Sedai did not believe it. Moiraine did not believe it, nor the Amyrlin. Stubbornly, he refused to think about it any longer. All he had to think about now was finding that dagger for Mat. Finding Fain, and the Horn.

It's never over, al'Thor.

The voice was like a thin breeze whispering in the back of his head, a thin, icy murmur working its way into the crevices of his mind. He almost sought the void to escape it, but remembering what waited for him there, he pushed down the desire.

In the half dark of twilight, he worked the forms with his sword, the way Lan had taught, though without the void. Parting the Silk. Hummingbird Kisses the Honeyrose. Heron Wading in the Rushes, for balance. Losing himself in the swift, sure movements, forgetting for a time where he was, he worked until sweat covered him. Yet when he was done, it all came back; nothing was changed. The weather was not cold, but he shivered and pulled his cloak around him as he hunched by the fire. The others caught his mood, and they finished eating quickly and in silence. No one complained when he kicked dirt over the last fitful flames.

Rand took the first watch himself, walking the edges of the copse with his bow, sometimes easing his sword in its scabbard. The chill moon was almost full, standing high in the blackness, and the night was as silent as the day had been, as empty. Empty was the right word. The land was as empty as a dusty milk crock. It was hard to believe there was anyone in the whole world, in this world, except for the three of them, hard to believe even the Darkfriends were there, somewhere ahead.

To keep himself company, he unwrapped Thom Merrilin's

cloak, exposing the harp and flute in their hard leather cases atop the many-colored patches. He took the gold-and-silver flute from its case, remembering the gleeman teaching him as he fingered it, and played a few notes of "The Wind That Shakes the Willow," softly so as not to wake the others. Even soft, the sad sound was too loud in that place, too real. With a sigh he replaced the flute and did up the bundle again.

He held the watch long into the night, letting the others sleep. He did not know how late it was when he suddenly realized a fog had risen. Close to the ground it lay, thick, making Hurin and Loial indistinct mounds seeming to hump out of clouds. Thinner higher up, it still shrouded the land around them, hiding everything except the nearest trees. The moon seemed viewed through watered silk. Anything at all could come right up to them unseen. He touched his sword.

"Swords do no good against me, Lews Therin. You should know that."

The fog swirled around Rand's feet as he spun, the sword coming into his hands, heron-mark blade upright before him. The void leaped up inside him; for the first time, he barely noticed the tainted light of *saidin*.

A shadowy figure drew nearer through the mist, walking with a tall staff. Behind it, as if the shadow's shadow were vast, the fog darkened till it was blacker than night. Rand's skin scrawled. Closer the figure came, until it resolved into the shape of a man, clothed and gloved in black, with a black silk mask covering his face, and the shadow came with it. His staff was black, too, as if the wood had been charred, yet smooth and shining like water by moonlight. For an instant the eyeholes of the mask glowed, as if fires stood behind them rather than eyes, but Rand did not need that to know who it was.

"Ba'alzamon," he breathed. "This is a dream. It has to be. I fell asleep, and—"

Ba'alzamon laughed like the roar of an open furnace. "You always try to deny what is, Lews Therin. If I stretch out my hand, I can touch you, Kinslayer. I can always touch you. Always and everywhere."

"I am not the Dragon! My name is Rand al'—!" Rand clamped his teeth shut to stop himself.

"Oh, I know the name you use now, Lews Therin. I know every name you have used through Age after Age, long before you were even the Kinslayer." Ba'alzamon's voice began to rise in intensity; sometimes the fires of his eyes flared so high that Rand could see them through the openings in the silk mask, see them like endless seas of flame. "I know you, know your blood and your line back to the first spark of life that ever was, back to the First Moment. You can never hide from me. Never! We are tied together as surely as two sides of the same coin. Ordinary men may hide in the sweep of the Pattern, but *ta'veren* stand out like beacon fires on a hill, and you, *you* stand out as if ten thousand shining arrows stood in the sky to point you out! You are mine, and ever in reach of my hand!"

"Father of Lies!" Rand managed. Despite the void, his tongue wanted to cleave to the roof of his mouth. *Light, please let it be a dream.* The thought skittered outside the emptiness. *Even one of those dreams that isn't a dream. He can't* really *be standing in front of me. The Dark One is sealed in Shayol Ghul, sealed by the Creator at the moment of Creation. . . .* He knew too much of the truth for it to help. "You're well named! If you could just take me, why haven't you? Because you cannot. I walk in the Light, and you cannot touch me!"

Ba'alzamon leaned on his staff and looked at Rand a moment, then moved to stand over Loial and Hurin, peering down at them. The vast shadow moved with him. He did not disturb the fog, Rand saw—he moved, the staff swung with his steps, but the gray mist did not swirl and eddy around his feet as it did around

Rand's. That gave him heart. Perhaps Ba'alzamon really was *not* there. Perhaps it *was* a dream.

"You find odd followers," Ba'alzamon mused. "You always did. These two. The girl who tries to watch over you. A poor guardian and weak, Kinslayer. If she had a lifetime to grow, she would never grow strong enough for you to hide behind."

Girl? Who? Moiraine is surely not a girl. "I don't know what you are talking about, Father of Lies. You lie, and lie, and even when you tell the truth, you twist it to a lie."

"Do I, Lews Therin? You know what you are, who you are. I have told you. And so have those women of Tar Valon." Rand shifted, and Ba'alzamon gave a laugh, like a small thunderclap. "They think themselves safe in their White Tower, but my followers number even some of their own. The Aes Sedai called Moiraine told you who you are, did she not? Did she lie? Or is she one of mine? The White Tower means to use you like a hound on a leash. Do I lie? Do I lie when I say you seek the Horn of Valere?" He laughed again; calm of the void or no, it was all Rand could do not to cover his ears. "Sometimes old enemies fight so long that they become allies and never realize it. They think they strike at you, but they have become so closely linked it is as if you guided the blow yourself."

"You don't guide me," Rand said. "I deny you."

"I have a thousand strings tied to you, Kinslayer, each one finer than silk and stronger than steel. Time has tied a thousand cords between us. The battle we two have fought—do you remember any part of that? Do you have any glimmering that we have fought before, battles without number back to the beginning of Time? I know much that you do not! That battle will soon end. The Last Battle is coming. The last, Lews Therin. Do you really think you can avoid it? You poor, shivering worm. You will serve me or die! And this time the cycle will not begin anew with your death. The grave belongs to the Great Lord of the Dark. This time if you die, you will be destroyed utterly. This time the Wheel will be broken whatever you do, and the world remade to a new mold. Serve me! Serve Shai'tan, or be destroyed forever!"

With the utterance of that name, the air seemed to thicken. The darkness behind Ba'alzamon swelled and grew, threatening to swallow everything. Rand felt it engulfing him, colder than ice and hotter than coals both at the same time, blacker than death, sucking him into the depths of it, overwhelming the world.

He gripped his sword hilt till his knuckles hurt. "I deny you, and I deny your power. I walk in the Light. The Light preserves us, and we shelter in the palm of the Creator's hand." He blinked. Ba'alzamon still stood there, and the great darkness still hung behind him, but it was as if all the rest had been illusion.

"Do you want to see my face?" It was a whisper.

Rand swallowed. "No."

"You should." A gloved hand went to the black mask.

"No!"

The mask came away. It was a man's face, horribly burned. Yet between the black-edged, red crevices crossing those features, the skin looked healthy and smooth. Dark eyes looked at Rand; cruel lips smiled with a flash of white teeth. "Look at me, Kinslayer, and see the hundredth part of your own fate." For a moment eyes and mouth became doorways into endless caverns of fire. "This is what the Power unchecked can do, even to me. But I heal, Lews Therin. I know the paths to greater power. It will burn you like a moth flying into a furnace."

"I will not touch it!" Rand felt the void around him, felt *saidin*. "I won't."

"You cannot stop yourself."

"Leave—me—ALONE!"

"Power." Ba'alzamon's voice became soft, insinuating. "You can have power again, Lews Therin. You are linked to it now, this moment. I know it. I can see it. Feel it, Lews Therin. Feel the glow inside you. Feel the power that could be yours. All you must do is reach out for it. But the Shadow is there between you and it. Madness and death. You need not die, Lews Therin, not ever again."

"No," Rand said, but the voice went on, burrowing into him.

"I can teach you to control that power so that it does not destroy you. No one else lives who can teach you that. The Great Lord of the Dark can shelter you from the madness. The power can be yours, and you can live forever. Forever! All you must do in return is serve. Only serve. Simple words—I am yours, Great Lord—and power will be yours. Power beyond anything those women of Tar Valon dream of, and life eternal, if you will only offer yourself up and serve."

Rand licked his lips. *Not to go mad. Not to die.* "Never! I walk in the Light," he grated hoarsely, "and you can never touch me!"

"Touch you, Lews Therin? Touch you? I can consume you! Taste it and know, as I knew!"

Those dark eyes became fire again, and that mouth, flame that blossomed and grew until it seemed brighter than a summer sun. Grew, and suddenly Rand's sword glowed as if just drawn from the forge. He cried out as the hilt burned his hands, screamed and dropped the sword. And the fog caught fire, fire that leaped, fire that burned everything.

Yelling, Rand beat at his clothes as they smoked and charred and fell in ashes, beat with hands that blackened and shriveled as naked flesh cracked and peeled away in the flames. He screamed. Pain beat at the void inside him, and he tried to crawl deeper into the emptiness. The glow was there, the tainted light just out of sight. Half mad, no longer caring what it was, he reached for *saidin,* tried to wrap it around him, tried to hide in it from the burning and the pain.

As suddenly as the fire began, it was gone. Rand stared wonderingly at his hand sticking out of the red sleeve of his coat. There was not so much as a singe on the wool. *I imagined it all.*

Frantically, he looked around. Ba'alzamon was gone. Hurin shifted in his sleep; the sniffer and Loial were still only two mounds sticking up out of the low fog. *I did imagine it.*

Before relief had a chance to grow, pain stabbed his right hand, and he turned it up to look. There across the palm was branded a heron. The heron from the hilt of his sword, angry and red, as neatly done as though drawn with an artist's skill.

Fumbling a kerchief from his coat pocket, he wrapped it around his hand. The hand throbbed, now. The void would help with that—he was *aware* of pain in the void, but he did not *feel* it—but he put the thought out of his head. Twice now, unknowing—and once on purpose; he could not forget that—he had tried to channel the One Power while he was in the void. It was with that that Ba'alzamon wanted to tempt him. It was that that Moiraine and the Amyrlin Seat wanted him to do. He would not.

CHAPTER 16

In the Mirror of Darkness

"YOU SHOULD NOT HAVE DONE IT, LORD Rand," Hurin said when Rand woke the others just at daybreak. The sun yet hid below the horizon, but there was light enough to see. The fog had melted away while dark still held, fading reluctantly. "If you use yourself up to spare us, my Lord, who will see to getting us home?"

"I needed to think," Rand said. Nothing showed the fog had ever been, or Ba'alzamon. He fingered the kerchief wrapped around his right hand. There was that to prove Ba'alzamon had been there. He wanted to be away from this place. "Time to be in the saddle if we are going to catch Fain's Darkfriends. Past time. We can eat flatbread while we ride."

Loial paused in the act of stretching, his arms reaching as high as Hurin could have standing on Rand's shoulders. "Your hand, Rand. What happened?"

"I hurt it. It's nothing."

"I have a salve in my saddlebags—"

"It is nothing!" Rand knew he sounded harsh, but one look at the brand would surely bring questions he did not want to answer. "Time's wasting. Let us be on our way." He set about saddling Red, awkwardly because of his injured hand, and Hurin jumped to his own horse.

"No need to be so touchy," Loial muttered.

A track, Rand decided as they set out, would be something natural in that world. There were too many unnatural things there. Even a single hoofprint would be welcome. Fain and the Darkfriends and the Trollocs had to leave some mark. He concentrated on the ground they passed over, trying to make out any trace that could have been made by another living thing.

There was nothing, not a turned stone, not a disturbed clod of earth. Once he looked at the ground behind them, just to reassure himself that the land did take hoofprints; scraped turf and bent grass marked their passage plainly, yet ahead the ground was undisturbed. But Hurin insisted he could smell the trail, faint and thin, but still heading south.

Once again the sniffer put all his attentions on the trail he followed, like a hound tracking deer, and once again Loial rode lost in his own thoughts, muttering to himself and rubbing the huge quarterstaff held across his saddle in front of him.

They had not been riding more than an hour when Rand saw the spire ahead. He was so busy watching for tracks that the tapering column already stood thick and tall above the trees in the middle distance when he first noticed it. "I wonder what that is." It lay directly in their path.

"I don't know what it can be, Rand," Loial said.

"If this—if this was our own world, Lord Rand. . . ." Hurin shifted uncomfortably in his saddle. "Well, that monument Lord Ingtar was talking about—the one to Artur Hawkwing's victory over the Trollocs—it was a great spire. But it was torn down a thousand years ago. There's nothing left but a big mound, like a hill. I saw it, when I went to Cairhien for Lord Agelmar."

"According to Ingtar," Loial said, "that is still three or four days ahead of us. If it is here at all. I don't know why it should be. I don't think there are any people here at all."

The sniffer put his eyes back on the ground. "That's just it, isn't it, Builder? No people, but there it is ahead of us. Maybe we ought to keep clear of it, my Lord Rand. No telling what it is, or who's there, in a place like this."

Rand drummed his fingers on the high pommel of his saddle for a moment, thinking. "We have to stick as close to the trail as we can," he said finally. "We don't seem to be getting any closer to Fain as it is, and I don't want to lose more time, if we can avoid it. If we see any people, or anything out of the ordinary, then we'll circle around until we pick it up again. But until then, we keep on."

"As you say, my Lord." The sniffer sounded odd, and he gave Rand a quick, sidelong look. "As you say."

Rand frowned for a moment before he understood, and then it was his turn to sigh. Lords did not explain to those who followed them, only to other lords. *I didn't ask him to take me for a bloody lord. But he did,* a small voice seemed to answer him, *and you let him. You made the choice; now the duty is yours.*

"Take the trail, Hurin," Rand said.

With a flash of relieved grin, the sniffer heeled his horse onward.

The weak sun climbed as they rode, and by the time it was overhead, they were only a mile or so from the spire. They had reached one of the streams, in a gully a pace deep, and the intervening trees were sparse. Rand could see the mound it was built on, like a round, flat-topped hill. The gray spire itself rose at least a hundred spans, and he could just make out now that the top was carved in the likeness of a bird with outstretched wings.

"A hawk," Rand said. "It *is* Hawkwing's monument. It must be.

There were people here, whether there are now or not. They just built it in another place here, and never tore it down. Think of it, Hurin. When we get back, you'll be able to tell them what the monument really looked like. There will only be three of us in the whole world who have ever seen it."

Hurin nodded. "Yes, my Lord. My children would like to hear that tale, their father seeing Hawkwing's spire."

"Rand," Loial began worriedly.

"We can gallop the distance," Rand said. "Come on. A gallop will do us good. This place may be dead, but we're alive."

"Rand," Loial said, "I don't think that is a—"

Not waiting to hear, Rand dug his boots into Red's flanks, and the stallion sprang forward. He splashed across the shallow ribbon of water in two strides, then scrabbled up the far side. Hurin launched his horse right behind him. Rand heard Loial calling behind them, but he laughed, waved for the Ogier to follow, and galloped on. If he kept his eyes on one spot, the land did not seem to slip and slide so badly, and the wind felt good on his face.

The mound covered a good two hides, but the grassy slope rose at an easy slant. The gray spire reared into the sky, squared and broad enough despite its height to seem massive, almost squat. Rand's laughter died, and he pulled Red up, his face grim.

"Is that Hawkwing's monument, Lord Rand?" Hurin asked uneasily. "It doesn't look right, somehow."

Rand recognized the harsh, angular script that covered the face of the monument, and he recognized some of the symbols chiseled on the breadth, chiseled as tall as a man. The horned skull of the Dha'vol Trollocs. The iron fist of the Dhai'mon. The trident of the Ko'bal, and the whirlwind of the Ahf'frait. There was a hawk, too, carved near the bottom. With a wingspan of ten paces, it lay on its back, pierced by a lightning bolt, and ravens pecked at its eyes. The huge wings atop the spire seemed to block the sun.

He heard Loial galloping up behind him.

"I tried to tell you, Rand," Loial said. "It is a raven, not a hawk. I could see it clearly." Hurin turned his horse, refusing even to look at the spire any longer.

"But how?" Rand said. "Artur Hawkwing won a victory over the Trollocs here. Ingtar said so."

"Not here," Loial said slowly. "Obviously not here. 'From Stone to Stone run the lines of it, between the worlds that might be.' I've been thinking on it, and I believe I know what the 'the worlds that might be' are. Maybe I do. Worlds our world might have been if things had happened differently. Maybe that's why it is all so . . . washed-out looking. Because it's an 'if,' a 'maybe.' Just a shadow of the real world. In this world, I think, the Trollocs won. Maybe that's why we have not seen any villages or people."

Rand's skin crawled. Where Trollocs won, they did not leave humans alive except for food. If they had won across an entire world. . . . "If the Trollocs had won, they would be everywhere. We'd have seen a thousand of them by now. We'd be dead since yesterday."

"I do not know, Rand. Perhaps, after they killed the people, they killed one another. Trollocs live to kill. That is all they do; that is all they are. I just don't know."

"Lord Rand," Hurin said abruptly, "something moved down there."

Rand whirled his horse, ready to see charging Trollocs, but Hurin was pointing back the way they had come, at nothing. "What did you see, Hurin? Where?"

The sniffer let his arm drop. "Right at the edge of that clump of trees there, about a mile. I thought it was . . . a woman . . . and something else I couldn't make out, but. . . ." He shivered. "It's so hard to make out things that aren't under your nose. Aaah, this place has my guts all awhirl. I'm likely imagining things, my Lord. This is a place for queer fancies." His shoulders hunched as if he felt the spire pressing on them. "No doubt it was just the wind, my Lord."

Loial said, "There's something else to consider, I'm afraid." He sounded troubled again. He pointed southward. "What do you see off there?"

Rand squinted against the way things far off seemed to slide toward him. "Land like what we've been crossing. Trees. Then some hills, and mountains. Nothing else. What do you want me to see?"

"The mountains," Loial sighed. The tufts on his ears drooped, and the ends of his eyebrows were down on his cheeks. "That has to be Kinslayer's Dagger, Rand. There aren't any other mountains they could be, unless this world is completely different from ours. But Kinslayer's Dagger lies more than a hundred leagues south of the Erinin. A good bit more. Distances are hard to judge in this place, but. . . . I think we will reach them before dark." He did not have to say any more. They could not have covered over a hundred leagues in less than three days.

Without thinking, Rand muttered, "Maybe this place is like the Ways." He heard Hurin moan, and instantly regretted not keeping a rein on his tongue.

It was not a pleasant thought. Enter a Waygate—they could be found just outside Ogier *stedding,* and in Ogier groves—enter and walk for a day, and you could leave by another Waygate a hundred leagues from where you started. The Ways were dark, now, and foul, and to travel them meant to risk death or madness. Even Fades feared to travel the Ways.

"If it is, Rand," Loial said slowly, "can a misstep kill us here, too? Are there things we have not yet seen that can do worse than kill us?" Hurin moaned again.

They had been drinking the water, riding along as if they had not a concern in the world. Unconcern would kill quickly in the Ways. Rand swallowed, hoping his stomach would settle.

"It is too late for worrying about what is past," he said. "From here on, though, we will watch our step." He glanced at Hurin. The sniffer's head had sunk between his shoulders, and his eyes darted as if he wondered what would leap at him, and from where. The man had run down murderers, but this was more than he had ever bargained for. "Hold on to yourself, Hurin. We are not dead, yet, and we won't be. We will just have to be careful from here on. That's all."

It was at that moment they heard the scream, thin with distance.

"A woman!" Hurin said. Even this much that was normal seemed to rouse him a little. "I knew I saw—"

Another scream came, more desperate than the first.

"Not unless she can fly," Rand said. "She's south of us." He kicked Red to a dead run in two strides.

"Be careful you said!" Loial shouted after him. "Light, Rand, remember! Be careful!"

Rand lay low on Red's back, letting the stallion run. The screams drew him on. It was easy to say be careful, but there was terror in that woman's voice. She did not sound as if she had time for him to be careful. On the edge of another stream, in a sheer-banked channel deeper than most, he drew rein; Red skidded in a shower of stones and dirt. The screams were coming. . . . *There!*

He took it all in at a glance. Perhaps two hundred paces away, the woman stood beside her horse in the stream, both of them backed against the far bank. With a broken length of branch, she was fending off a snarling . . . something. Rand swallowed, stunned for a moment. If a frog were as big as a bear, or if a bear had a frog's gray-green hide, it might look like that. A big bear.

Not letting himself think about the creature, he leaped to the ground, unlimbering his bow. If he took the time to ride closer, it might be too late. The woman was barely keeping the . . . thing . . . at the edge of the branch. It was a fair distance—he kept blinking as he tried to judge it; the distance seemed to change by spans every time the thing moved—yet a big target. His bandaged hand made drawing awkward, but he had an arrow loosed almost before his feet were set.

The shaft sank into the leathery hide for half its length, and the creature spun to face Rand. Rand took a step back despite the distance. That huge, wedge-shaped head had never been on any animal he could imagine, nor that wide, horny-lipped beak of a mouth, hooked for ripping flesh. And it had three eyes, small, and fierce, and ringed by hard-looking ridges. Gathering itself, the thing bounded toward him down the stream in great, splashing leaps. To Rand's eye, some of the leaps seemed to cover twice as much distance as others, though he was sure they were all the same.

"An eye," the woman called. She sounded surprisingly calm, considering her screams. "You must hit an eye to kill it."

He drew the fletching of another arrow back to his ear. Reluctantly, he sought the void; he did not want to, but it was for this that Tam had taught him, and he knew he could never make the shot without it. *My father,* he thought with a sense of loss, and emptiness filled him. The quavering light of *saidin* was there, but he shut it away. He was one with the bow, with the arrow, with the monstrous shape leaping toward him. One with the tiny eye. He did not even feel the arrow leave the bowstring.

The creature rose in another bound, and at the peak, the arrow struck its central eye. The thing landed, fountaining another huge splash of water and mud. Ripples spread out from it, but it did not move.

"Well shot, and bravely," the woman called. She was on her horse, riding to meet him. Rand felt vaguely surprised that she had not run once the thing's attention was diverted. She rode past the bulk, still surrounded by the ripples of its dying, without even a downward glance, scrambled her horse up the bank and dismounted. "Few men would stand to face the charge of a *grolm,* my Lord."

She was all in white, her dress divided for riding and belted in silver, and her boots, peeking out from under her hems, were tooled in silver, too. Even her saddle was white, and silver-mounted. Her snowy mare, with its arched neck and dainty step, was almost as tall as Rand's bay. But it was the woman herself—she was perhaps Nynaeve's age, he thought—who held his eyes. She was tall, for one thing; a hand taller and she could almost look him in the eyes. For another, she was beautiful, ivory-pale skin contrasting sharply with long, night-dark hair and black eyes. He had seen beautiful women. Moiraine was beautiful, if cool, and so was Nynaeve, when her temper did not get the better of her. Egwene, and Elayne, the Daughter-Heir of Andor, were each enough to take a man's breath. But this woman. . . . His tongue stuck to the roof of his mouth; he felt his heart start beating again.

"Your retainers, my Lord?"

Startled, he looked around. Hurin and Loial had joined them. Hurin was staring the way Rand knew he had been, and even the Ogier seemed fascinated. "My friends," he said. "Loial, and Hurin. My name is Rand. Rand al'Thor."

"I have never thought of it before," Loial said abruptly, sounding as if he were talking to himself, "but if there is such a thing as perfect human beauty, in face and form, then you—"

"Loial!" Rand shouted. The Ogier's ears stiffened in embarrassment. Rand's own ears were red; Loial's words had been too close to what he himself was thinking.

The woman laughed musically, but the next instant she was all regal formality, like a queen on her throne. "I am called Selene," she said. "You have risked your life, and saved mine. I am yours, Lord Rand al'Thor." And, to Rand's horror, she knelt before him.

Not looking at Hurin or Loial, he hastily pulled her to her feet. "A man who will not die to save a woman is no man." Immediately he disgraced himself by blushing. It was a Shienaran saying, and he knew it sounded pompous before it was out of his mouth, but her manner had infected him, and he could not stop it. "I mean. . . . That is, it was. . . ." *Fool, you can't tell a woman saving her life was nothing.* "It was my honor." That sounded vaguely Shienaran and formal. He hoped it would do; his mind was as blank of anything else to say as if he were still in the void.

Suddenly he became conscious of her eyes on him. Her expression had not changed, but her dark eyes made him feel as if he were naked. Unbidden, the thought came of Selene with no clothes. His face went red again. "Aaah! Ah, where are you from, Selene? We have not seen another human being since we came here. Is your town nearby?" She looked at him thoughtfully, and he stepped back. Her look made him too aware of how close to her he was.

"I'm not from this world, my Lord," she said. "There are no people here. Nothing living except the *grolm* and a few other creatures like them. I am from Cairhien. And as to how I came here, I don't know, exactly. I was out riding, and I stopped to nap, and when I woke, my horse and I were here. I can only hope, my Lord, that you can save me again, and help me go home."

"Selene, I am not a . . . that is, please call me Rand." His ears felt hot again. *Light, it won't hurt anything if she thinks I'm a lord. Burn me, it won't hurt anything.*

"If you wish it . . . Rand." Her smile made his throat tighten. "You will help me?"

"Of course, I will." *Burn me, but she's beautiful. And looking at me like I'm a hero in a story.* He shook his head to clear it of foolishness. "But first we have to find the men we are following. I'll try to keep you out of danger, but we must find them. Coming with us will be better than staying here alone."

For a moment she was silent, her face blank and smooth; Rand had no idea what she was thinking, except that she seemed to be studying him anew. "A man of duty," she said finally. A small smile touched her lips. "I like that. Yes. Who are these miscreants you follow?"

"Darkfriends and Trollocs, my Lady," Hurin burst out. He made an awkward bow to her from his saddle. "They did murder in Fal Dara keep and stole the Horn of Valere, my Lady, but Lord Rand will fetch it back."

Rand stared at the sniffer ruefully; Hurin gave a weak grin. *So much for secrecy.* It did not matter here, he supposed, but once back in their world. . . . "Selene, you must not say anything of the Horn to anyone. If it gets out, we'll have a hundred people on our heels trying to get the Horn for themselves."

"No, it would never do," Selene said, "for *that* to fall into the wrong hands. The Horn of Valere. I could not tell you how often I've dreamed of touching it, holding it in my hands. You must promise me, when you have it, you will let me touch it."

"Before I can do that, we have to find it. We had better be on our way." Rand offered his hand to help her mount; Hurin scrambled down to hold her stirrup. "Whatever that thing was I killed— a *grolm?*—there may be more of them around." Her hand was firm—there was surprising strength in her grip—and her skin was. . . . Silk? Something softer, smoother. Rand shivered.

"There always are," Selene said. The tall white mare frisked and bared her teeth once at Red, yet Selene's touch on the reins quieted her.

Rand slung his bow across his back and climbed onto Red. *Light, how could anyone's skin be so soft?* "Hurin, where's the trail? Hurin? Hurin!"

The sniffer gave a start, and left off staring at Selene. "Yes, Lord Rand. Ah . . . the trail. South, my Lord. Still south."

"Then let's ride." Rand gave an uneasy look at the gray-green bulk of the *grolm* lying in the stream. It had been better believing they were the only living things in that world. "Take the trail, Hurin."

Selene rode alongside Rand at first, talking of this and that, asking him questions and calling him lord. Half a dozen times he started to tell her he was no lord, only a shepherd, and every time, looking at her, he could not get the words out. A lady like her would not talk the same way with a shepherd, he was sure, even one who had saved her life.

"You will be a great man when you've found the Horn of Valere," she told him. "A man for the legends. The man who sounds the Horn will make his own legends."

"I don't want to sound it, and I don't want to be part of any legend." He did not know if she was wearing perfume, but there seemed to be a scent to her, something that filled his head with her. Spices, sharp and sweet, tickling his nose, making him swallow.

"Every man wants to be great. You could be the greatest man in all the Ages."

It sounded too close to what Moiraine had said. The Dragon Reborn would certainly stand out through the Ages. "Not me," he said fervently. "I'm just"—he thought of her scorn if he told her now that he was only a shepherd after letting her believe he was a lord, and changed what he had been going to say—"just trying to find it. And to help a friend."

She was silent a moment, then said, "You've hurt your hand."

"It is nothing." He started to put his injured hand inside his coat—it throbbed from holding the reins—but she reached out and took it.

He was so surprised he let her, and then there was nothing to do except either jerk away rudely or else let her unwrap the kerchief. Her touch felt cool and sure. His palm was angrily red and puffy, but the heron still stood out, plainly and clearly.

She touched the brand with a finger, but made no comment on it, not even to ask how he had come by it. "This could stiffen your hand if it's untended. I have an ointment that should help." From a pocket inside her cloak she produced a small stone vial, unstopped it, and began gently rubbing a white salve on the burn as they rode.

The ointment felt cold at first, then seemed to melt away warmly into his flesh. And it worked as well as Nynaeve's ointments sometimes did. He stared in amazement as the redness faded and the swelling went down under her stroking fingers.

"Some men," she said, not raising her eyes from his hand, "choose to seek greatness, while others are forced to it. It is always better to choose than to be forced. A man who's forced is never completely his own master. He must dance on the strings of those who forced him."

Rand pulled his hand free. The brand looked a week old or more, all but healed. "What do you mean?" he demanded.

She smiled at him, and he felt ashamed of his outburst. "Why, the Horn, of course," she said calmly, putting away her salve. Her mare, stepping along beside Red, was tall enough that her eyes were only a little below Rand's. "If you find the Horn of Valere, there will be no avoiding greatness. But will it be forced on you, or will you take it? That's the question."

He flexed his hand. She sounded so much like Moiraine. "Are you Aes Sedai?"

Selene's eyebrows lifted; her dark eyes glittered at him, but her voice was soft. "Aes Sedai? I? No."

"I didn't mean to offend you. I'm sorry."

"Offend me? I am not offended, but I'm no Aes Sedai." Her lip curled in a sneer; even that was beautiful. "They cower in what they think is safety when they could do so much. They serve when they could rule, let men fight wars when they could bring order to the world. No, never call me Aes Sedai." She smiled and laid her hand on his arm to show she was not angry—her touch made him swallow—but he was relieved when she let the mare drop back beside Loial. Hurin bobbed his head at her like an old family retainer.

Rand was relieved, but he missed her presence, too. She was only two spans away—he twisted in his saddle to stare at her, riding by Loial's side; the Ogier was bent half double in his saddle so he could talk with her—but that was not the same as being right there beside him, close enough for him to smell her heady scent, close enough to touch. He settled back angrily. It was not that he wanted to touch her, exactly—he reminded himself that he loved Egwene; he felt guilty at the need for reminding—but she was beautiful, and she thought he was a lord, and she said he could be a great man. He argued sourly with himself inside his head. *Moiraine says you can be great, too; the Dragon Reborn. Selene is not Aes Sedai. That's right; she's a Cairhienin noblewoman, and you're a shepherd. She doesn't know that. How long do you let her believe a lie? It's only till we get out of this place. If we get out. If.* On that note, his thoughts subsided to sullen silence.

He tried to keep a watch on the country through which they rode—if Selene said there were more of those things . . . those *grolm* . . . about, he believed her, and Hurin was too intent on smelling the trail to notice anything else; Loial was too wrapped up in his talk with Selene to see anything until it bit him on the heel—but it was hard to watch. Turning his head too quickly made his eyes water; a hill or a stand of trees could seem a mile off when seen from one angle and only a few hundred spans when seen from another.

The mountains were growing closer, of that much he was sure. Kinslayer's Dagger, looming against the sky now, a sawtooth expanse of snow-capped peaks. The land around them already rose in foothills heralding the coming of the mountains. They would reach the edge of the mountains proper well before dark, perhaps in only another hour or so. *More than a hundred leagues in less than three days. Worse than that. We spent most of a day south of the Erinin in the real world. Over a hundred leagues in less than two days, here.*

"She says you were right about this place, Rand."

Rand gave a start before he realized Loial had ridden up beside him. He looked for Selene and found her riding with Hurin; the sniffer was grinning and ducking his head and all but knuckling his forehead at everything she said. Rand glanced sideways at the Ogier. "I'm surprised you could let her go, the way you two had your heads together. What do you mean, I was right?"

"She is a fascinating woman, isn't she? Some of the Elders don't know as much as she does about history—especially the Age of Legends—and about—oh, yes. She says you were right about the Ways, Rand. The Aes Sedai, some of them, studied worlds like this, and that study was the basis of how they grew the Ways. She says there are worlds where it is time rather than distance that changes. Spend a day in one of those, and you might come back to find a year has passed in the real world, or twenty. Or it could be the other way round. Those worlds—this one, all the others—are reflections of the real world, she says. This one seems pale to us because it is a weak reflection, a world that had little chance of ever being. Others are almost as likely as ours. Those are as solid as our world, and have people. The same people, she says, Rand. Imagine it! You could go to one of them and meet yourself. The Pattern has infinite variation, she says, and every variation that can be, will be."

Rand shook his head, then wished he had not as the landscape flickered back and forth and his stomach lurched. He took a deep breath. "How does she know all that? You know about more things than anybody I ever met before, Loial, and all you knew about this world amounted to no more than a rumor."

"She's Cairhienin, Rand. The Royal Library in Cairhien is one of the greatest in the world, perhaps the greatest outside Tar Valon. The Aiel spared it deliberately, you know, when they burned Cairhien. They will not destroy a book. Did you know that they—"

"I don't care about Aielmen," Rand said hotly. "If Selene knows so much, I hope she read how to get us home from here. I wish Selene—"

"You wish Selene what?" The woman laughed as she joined them.

Rand stared at her as if she had been gone months; that was how he felt. "I wish Selene would come ride with me some more," he said. Loial chuckled, and Rand felt his face burn.

Selene smiled, and looked at Loial. "You will excuse us, *alantin*."

The Ogier bowed in his saddle and let his big horse fall back, the tufts on his ears drooping with reluctance.

For a time Rand rode in silence, enjoying Selene's presence. Now and again he looked at her out of the corner of his eye. He wished he could get his feelings about her straight. Could she be an Aes Sedai, despite her denial? Someone sent by Moiraine to push him along whatever path he was meant to follow in the Aes Sedai's plans? Moiraine could not have known he would be taken to this strange world, and no Aes Sedai would have tried to fend off that beast with a stick when she could strike it dead or send it running with the Power. Well. Since she took him for a lord and no one in Cairhien knew different, he might keep on letting her think it. She was surely the most beautiful woman he had ever seen, intelligent and learned, and she thought he was brave; what more could a man ask from a wife? *That's crazy, too. I'd marry Egwene if I could marry anyone, but I can't ask a woman to marry a man who's going to go mad, maybe hurt her.* But Selene was so beautiful.

She was studying his sword, he saw. He readied the words in his head. No, he was not a blademaster, but his father had given him the sword. *Tam. Light, why couldn't you really be my father?* He squashed the thought ruthlessly.

"That was a magnificent shot," Selene said.

"No, I'm not a—" Rand began, then blinked. "A shot?"

"Yes. A tiny target, that eye, moving, at a hundred paces. You've a wonderful hand with that bow."

Rand shifted awkwardly. "Ah . . . thank you. It's a trick my father taught me." He told her about the void, about how Tam had taught him how to use it with the bow. He even found himself telling her about Lan and his sword lessons.

"The Oneness," she said, sounding satisfied. She saw his questioning look and added, "That is what it is called . . . in some places. The Oneness. To learn the full use of it, it is best to wrap it around you continuously, to dwell in it at all times, or so I've heard."

He did not even have to think about what lay waiting for him in the void to know his answer to that, but what he said was, "I'll think about it."

"Wear this void of yours all the time, Rand al'Thor, and you'll learn uses for it you never suspected."

"I said I will think about it." She opened her mouth again, but he cut her off. "You know all these things. About the void—the Oneness, you call it. About this world. Loial reads books all the time; he's read more books than I've ever seen, and he's never seen anything but a fragment about the Stones."

Selene drew herself up straight in her saddle. Suddenly she reminded him of Moiraine, and of Queen Morgase, when they were angry.

"There was a book written about these worlds," she said tightly. "*Mirrors of the Wheel*. You see, the *alantin* has not seen *all* the books that are."

"What is this *alantin* you call him? I've never heard—"

"The Portal Stone beside which I woke is up there," Selene said, pointing into the mountains, off to the east of their path. Rand found himself wishing for her warmth again, and her smiles. "If you take me to it, you can return me to my home, as you promised. We can reach it in an hour."

Rand barely looked where she pointed. Using the Stone—Portal Stone, she called it—meant wielding the Power, if he were to take her back to the real world. "Hurin, how is the trail?"

"Fainter than ever, Lord Rand, but still there." The sniffer spared a quick grin and bob of his head for Selene. "I think it's starting to angle off to the west. There's some easier passes there, toward the tip of the Dagger, as I recall from when I went to Cairhien that time."

Rand sighed. *Fain, or one of his Darkfriends, has to know another way to use the Stones. A Darkfriend couldn't use the Power.* "I have to follow the Horn, Selene."

"How do you know your precious Horn is even in this world? Come with me, Rand. You'll find your legend, I promise you. Come with me."

"You can use the Stone, this Portal Stone, yourself," he said angrily. Before the words were out of his mouth he wanted them back. *Why does she have to keep talking about legends?* Stubbornly, he forced himself to go on. "The Portal Stone didn't bring you here by itself. You did it, Selene. If you made the Stone bring you here, you can make it take you back. I'll take you to it, but then I must go on after the Horn."

"I know nothing about using the Portal Stones, Rand. If I did anything, I don't know what it was."

Rand studied her. She sat her saddle, straight-backed and tall, just as regally as before, but somehow softer, too. Proud, yet vulnerable, and needing him. He had put Nynaeve's age to her—a handful of years older than himself—but he had been wrong, he realized. She was more his own age, and beautiful, and she needed him. The thought, just the thought, of the void flickered through his head, and of the light. *Saidin.* To use the Portal Stone, he must dip himself back into that taint.

"Stay with me, Selene," he said. "We'll find the Horn, and Mat's dagger, and we'll find a way back. I promise you. Just stay with me."

"You always. . . ." Selene drew a deep breath as if to calm herself. "You always are so stubborn. Well, I can admire stubbornness in a man. There is little to a man who's too easily biddable."

Rand colored; it was too much like the things Egwene some-times said, and they had all but been promised in marriage since they were children. From Selene, the words, and the direct look that went with them, were a shock. He turned to tell Hurin to press on with the trail.

From behind them came a distant, coughing grunt. Before Rand could whirl Red to look, another bark sounded, and three more on its heels. At first he could make out nothing as the land-scape seemed to waver in his eyes, but then he saw them through the widespread stands of trees, just topping a hill. Five shapes, it seemed, only half a mile distant, a bare thousand paces at most, and coming in thirty-foot bounds.

"Grolm," Selene said calmly. "A small pack, but they have our scent, it seems."

CHAPTER 17

Choices

"**W**E'LL RUN FOR IT," RAND SAID. "HURIN, can you gallop and still follow the trail?"

"Yes, Lord Rand."

"Then push on. We will—"

"It won't do any good," Selene said. Her white mare was the only one of their mounts not dancing at the gruff barks coming from the *grolm*. "They don't give up, not ever. Once they have your scent, *grolm* keep coming, day and night, until they run you down. You must kill them all, or find a way to go elsewhere. Rand, the Portal Stone can take us elsewhere."

"No! We *can* kill them. I can. I already killed one. There are only five. If I can just find. . . ." He cast around for the spot he needed, and found it. "Follow me!" Digging his heels in, he set Red to a gallop, confident before he heard their hooves that the others would come.

The place he had chosen was a low, round hill, bare of trees. Nothing could come close without him seeing. He swung down from his saddle and unlimbered his longbow. Loial and Hurin joined him on the ground, the Ogier hefting his huge quarterstaff, the sniffer with his short sword in his fist. Neither quarterstaff nor sword would be of much use if the *grolm* closed with them. *I won't let them get close.*

"This risk is not necessary," Selene said. She barely looked toward the *grolm,* bending from her saddle to concentrate on Rand. "We can easily reach the Portal Stone ahead of them."

"I will stop them." Hastily Rand counted the arrows remaining in his quiver. Eighteen, each as long as his arm, ten of them with points like chisels, designed to drive through Trolloc armor. They would do as well for *grolm* as for Trollocs. He stuck four of those upright in the ground in front of him; a fifth he nocked to the bow. "Loial, Hurin, you can do no good down here. Mount and be ready to take Selene to the Stone if any get through." He wondered whether he could kill one of the things with his sword, if it came to that. *You* are *mad! Even the Power is not as bad as this.*

Loial said something, but he did not hear; he was already seeking the void, as much to escape his own thoughts as for need. *You know what's waiting. But this way I don't have to touch it.* The glow was there, the light just out of sight. It seemed to flow toward him, but the emptiness was all. Thoughts darted across the surface of the void, visible in that tainted light. *Saidin. The Power. Madness. Death.* Extraneous thoughts. He was one with the bow, with the arrow, with the things topping the next rise.

The *grolm* came on, overreaching one another in their leaps, five great, leathery shapes, triple-eyed, with horny maws gaping. Their grunting calls rebounded from the void, barely heard.

Rand was not aware of raising his bow, or drawing the fletching against his cheek, to his ear. He was one with the beasts, one with the center eye of the first. Then the arrow was gone. The first *grolm* died; one of its companions leaped on it as it fell, beak of a mouth ripping gobbets of flesh. It snarled at the others, and they circled wide. But they came on, and as if compelled, it abandoned its meal and leaped after them, its horny maw already bloody.

Rand worked smoothly, unconsciously, nock and release. Nock and release.

The fifth arrow left his bow, and he lowered it, still deep in the void, as the fourth *grolm* fell like a huge puppet with its strings cut. Though the final arrow still flew, somehow he knew there was no need for another shot. The last beast collapsed as if its bones had melted, a feathered shaft jutting from its center eye. Always the center eye.

"Magnificent, Lord Rand," Hurin said. "I . . . I've never seen shooting like that."

The void held Rand. The light called to him, and he . . . reached . . . toward it. It surrounded him, filled him.

"Lord Rand?" Hurin touched his arm, and Rand gave a start, the emptiness filling up with what was around him. "Are you all right, my Lord?"

Rand brushed his forehead with fingertips. It was dry; he felt as if it should have been covered with sweat. "I. . . . I'm fine, Hurin."

"It grows easier each time you do it, I've heard," Selene said. "The more you live in the Oneness, the easier."

Rand glanced at her. "Well, I won't need it again, not for a while." *What happened? I wanted to. . . .* He still wanted to, he realized with horror. He *wanted* to go back into the void, wanted to feel that light filling him again. It had seemed as if he were truly alive then, sickliness and all, and now was only an imitation. No, worse. He had been almost alive, knowing what "alive" would be like. All he had to do was reach out to *saidin. . . .*

"Not again," he muttered. He gazed off at the dead *grolm,* five monstrous shapes lying on the ground. Not dangerous anymore. "Now we can be on our—"

A coughing bark, all too familiar, sounded beyond the dead *grolm,* beyond the next hill, and others answered it. Still more came, from the east, from the west.

Rand half raised his bow.

"How many arrows do you have left?" Selene demanded. "Can you kill twenty *grolm?* Thirty? A hundred? We *must* go to the Portal Stone."

"She is right, Rand," Loial said slowly. "You do not have any choice now." Hurin was watching Rand anxiously. The *grolm* called, a score of barks overlapping.

"The Stone," Rand agreed reluctantly. Angrily he threw himself back into his saddle, slung the bow on his back. "Lead us to this Stone, Selene."

With a nod she turned her mare and heeled it to a trot. Rand and the others followed, they eagerly, he holding back. The barks of *grolm* pursued them, hundreds it seemed. It sounded as if the *grolm* were ranged in a semicircle around them, closing in from every direction but the front.

Swiftly and surely Selene led them through the hills. The land rose in the beginning of mountains, slopes steepening so the horses scrambled over washed-out–looking rocky outcrops and the sparse, faded-looking brush that clung to them. The way became harder, the land slanting more and more upward.

We're not going to make it, Rand thought, the fifth time Red slipped and slid backwards in a shower of stone. Loial threw his quarterstaff aside; it would be of no use against *grolm,* and it only slowed him. The Ogier had given up riding; he used one hand to haul himself up, and pulled his tall horse behind him with the other. The hairy-fetlocked animal made heavy going, but easier than with Loial on its back. *Grolm* barked behind them, closer now.

Then Selene drew rein and pointed to a hollow nestled below them in the granite. It was all there, the seven wide, colored stairs around a pale floor, and the tall stone column in the middle.

She dismounted and led her mare into the hollow, down the stairs to the column. It loomed over her. She turned to look back up at Rand and the others. The *grolm* gave their grunting barks, scores of them, loud. Near. "They will be on us soon," she said. "You must use the Stone, Rand. Or else find a way to kill all the *grolm.*"

With a sigh, Rand got down from his saddle and led Red into the hollow. Loial and Hurin followed hastily. He stared at the symbol-covered column, the Portal Stone, uneasily. *She must be able to channel, even if she doesn't know it, or it couldn't have brought her here. The Power doesn't harm women.* "If this brought you here," he began, but she interrupted him.

"I know what it is," she said firmly, "but I do not know how to use it. You must do what must be done." She traced one symbol, a little larger than the others, with a finger. A triangle standing on its point inside a circle. "This stands for the true world, our world. I believe it will help if you hold it in your mind while you. . . ." She spread her hands as if unsure exactly what it was he was supposed to do.

"Uh . . . my Lord?" Hurin said diffidently. "There isn't much time." He glanced over his shoulder at the rim of the hollow. The barking was louder. "Those things will be here in minutes, now." Loial nodded.

Drawing a deep breath, Rand put his hand on the symbol Selene had pointed out. He looked at her to see if he was doing it right, but she merely watched, not even the slightest frown of worry wrinkling her pale forehead. *She's confident you can save her. You have to.* The scent of her filled his nostrils.

"Uh . . . my Lord?"

Rand swallowed, and sought the void. It came easily, springing up around him without effort. Emptiness. Emptiness except for the light, wavering in a way that turned his stomach. Emptiness except for *saidin.* But even the queasiness was distant. He was one with the Portal Stone. The column felt smooth and slightly oily under his hand, but the triangle-and-circle seemed warm against the brand on his palm. *Have to get them to safety. Have to get them home.* The light drifted toward him, it seemed, surrounded him, and he . . . embraced . . . it.

Light filled him. Heat filled him. He could see the Stone, see the others watching him—Loial and Hurin anxiously, Selene showing no doubt that he could save her—but they might as well not have been there. The light was all. The heat and the light, suffusing his limbs like water sinking into dry sand, filling him. The symbol burned against his flesh. He tried to suck it all in, all the heat, all the light. All. The symbol. . . .

Suddenly, as if the sun had gone out for the blink of an eye, the world flickered. And again. The symbol was a live coal under his hand; he drank in the light. The world flickered. Flickered. It made him sick, that light; it was water to a man dying of thirst. Flicker. He sucked at it. It made him want to vomit; he wanted it all. Flicker. The triangle-and-circle seared him; he could feel it charring his hand. Flicker. He wanted it all! He screamed, howling with pain, howling with wanting.

Flicker . . . flicker . . . flickerflickerflicker. . . .

Hands pulled at him; he was only vaguely aware of them. He staggered back; the void was slipping away, the light, and the sickness that twisted at him. The light. He watched it go regretfully. *Light, that's crazy to want it. But I was so* full *of it! I was so.* . . . Dazed, he stared at Selene. It was she who held his shoulders, stared wonderingly into his eyes. He raised his hand in front of his face. The heron brand was there, but nothing else. No triangle-and-circle burned into his flesh.

"Remarkable," Selene said slowly. She glanced at Loial and Hurin. The Ogier looked stunned, his eyes as big as plates; the sniffer was squatting with one hand on the ground, as if unsure he could support himself else. "All of us here, and all of our horses. And you do not even know what you did. Remarkable."

"Are we . . .?" Rand began hoarsely, and had to stop to swallow.

"Look around you," Selene said. "You've brought us home." She gave a sudden laugh. "You brought all of us home."

For the first time Rand became aware of his surroundings again. The hollow surrounded them without any stairs, though here and there lay a suspiciously smooth piece of stone, colored red, or blue. The column lay against the mountainside, half buried in the loose rock of a fall. The symbols were unclear, here; wind and water had worked long on them. And everything looked real. The colors were solid, the granite a strong gray, the brush green and brown. After that other place, it seemed almost too vivid.

"Home," Rand breathed, and then he was laughing, too. "We're home." Loial's laughter sounded like a bull bellowing. Hurin danced a caper.

"You did it," Selene said, leaning closer, until her face filled Rand's eyes. "I knew that you could."

Rand's laughter died. "I—I suppose I did." He glanced as the fallen Portal Stone and managed a weak laugh. "I wish I knew what it was I did, though."

Selene looked deep into his eyes. "Perhaps one day you will know," she said softly. "You are surely destined for great things."

Her eyes seemed as dark and deep as night, as soft as velvet. Her mouth. . . . *If I kissed her.* . . . He blinked and stepped back hurriedly, clearing his throat. "Selene, please don't tell anyone about this. About the Portal Stone, and me. I don't understand it, and neither will anybody else. You know how people are about things they don't understand."

Her face wore no expression at all. Suddenly he wished very much that Mat and Perrin were there. Perrin knew how to talk to girls, and Mat could lie with a straight face. He could manage neither very well.

Suddenly Selene smiled, and dropped a half-mocking curtsy. "I will keep your secret, my Lord Rand al'Thor."

Rand glanced at her, and cleared his throat again. *Is she angry with me? She'd certainly be angry if I had tried to kiss her. I think.* He wished she would not look at him as she was, as if she knew what he was thinking. "Hurin, is there any chance the Darkfriends used this Stone before us?"

The sniffer shook his head ruefully. "They were angling to the west of here, Lord Rand. Unless these Portal Stone things are more common than I've seen, I'd say they're still in that other world. But it wouldn't take me an hour to check it. The land's the same here as there. I could find the place here where I lost the trail there, if you see what I mean, and see if they've already gone by."

Rand glanced at the sky. The sun—a wonderfully strong sun, not pale at all—sat low to the west, stretching their shadows out across the hollow. Another hour would bring full twilight. "In the morning," he said. "But I fear we've lost them." *We can't lose that dagger! We can't!* "Selene, if that's the case, in the morning we will take you on to your home. Is it in the city of Cairhien itself, or . . .?"

"You may not have lost the Horn of Valere yet," Selene said slowly. "As you know, I do know a *few* things about those worlds."

"Mirrors of the Wheel," Loial said.

She gave him a look, then nodded. "Yes. Exactly. Those worlds truly are mirrors in a way, especially the ones where there are no people. Some of them reflect only great events in the true world, but some have a shadow of that reflection even before the event occurs. The passage of the Horn of Valere would certainly be a great event. Reflections of what will be are fainter than reflections of what is or what was, just as Hurin says the trail he followed was faint."

Hurin blinked incredulously. "You mean to say, my Lady, I've been smelling where those Darkfriends are *going* to be? The Light help me, I wouldn't like that. It's bad enough smelling where violence *has* been, without smelling where it *will* be, too. There can't be many spots where there won't be *some* kind of violence, *some* time. It would drive me crazy, like as not. That place we just left nearly did. I could smell it all the time, there, killing and hurting, and the vilest evil you could think of. I could even smell it on us. On all of us. Even on you, my Lady, if you'll forgive me for saying so. It was just that place, twisting me the way it twisted your eye." He gave himself a shake. "I'm glad we're out of there. I can't get it out of my nostrils yet, all the way."

Rand rubbed absently at the brand on his palm. "What do you think, Loial? Could we really be ahead of Fain's Darkfriends?"

The Ogier shrugged, frowning. "I don't know, Rand. I don't know anything about any of this. I think we are back in our world. I think we are in Kinslayer's Dagger. Beyond that. . . ." He shrugged again.

"We should be seeing you home, Selene," Rand said. "Your people will be worried about you."

"A few days will see if I'm right," she said impatiently. "Hurin can find where he left the trail; he said so. We can watch over it. The Horn of Valere cannot be much longer reaching here. The Horn of Valere, Rand. Think of it. The man who sounds the Horn will live in legend forever."

"I don't want anything to do with legends," he said sharply. *But if the Darkfriends get by you. . . . What if Ingtar lost them? Then the Darkfriends have the Horn of Valere forever, and Mat dies.* "All right, a few days. At the worst, we will probably meet Ingtar and the others. I can't imagine they've stopped or turned back just because we . . . went away."

"A wise decision, Rand," Selene said, "and well thought out." She touched his arm and smiled, and he found himself again thinking of kissing her.

"Uh . . . we need to be closer to where they'll come. If they do come. Hurin, can you find us a camp before dark, somewhere we can watch the place where you lost the trail?" He glanced at the Portal Stone and thought about sleeping near it, thought of the way the void had crept up on him in sleep the last time, and the light in the void. "Somewhere well away from here."

"Leave it in my hands, Lord Rand." The sniffer scrambled to his saddle. "I vow, I'll never sleep again without first I see what kind of stone there is nearby."

As Rand rode Red up out of the hollow, he found himself watching Selene more than he did Hurin. She seemed so cool and self-possessed, no older than he, yet queenly, but when she smiled at him, as she did just then. . . . *Egwene wouldn't have said I was wise. Egwene would have called me a woolhead.* Irritably, he heeled Red's flanks.

CHAPTER 18

To the White Tower

EGWENE BALANCED ON THE HEELING DECK AS the *River Queen* sped down the wide Erinin under cloud-dark skies, sails full-bellied, White Flame banner whipping furiously at the mainmast. The wind had risen as soon as the last of them was aboard the ships, back in Medo, and it had not failed or flagged for an instant since, day or night. The river had begun to race in flood, as it still did, slapping the ships about while it drove them onward. Wind and river had not slowed, and neither had the ships, all clustered together. The *River Queen* led, only right for the vessel that carried the Amyrlin Seat.

The helmsman held his tiller grimly, feet planted and spread, and sailors padded barefoot at their work, intent on what they did; when they glanced at the sky or the river, they tore their eyes away with low mutters. A village was just fading from view behind, and a boy raced along the bank; he had kept up with the ships for a short distance, but now they were leaving him behind. When he vanished, Egwene made her way below.

In the small cabin they shared, Nynaeve glared up at her from her narrow bed. "They say we'll reach Tar Valon today. The Light help me, but I'll be glad to put foot on land again even if it is in Tar Valon." The ship lurched with wind and current, and Nynaeve swallowed. "I'll never step on a boat again," she said breathlessly.

Egwene shook the river spray out of her cloak and hung it on a peg by the door. It was not a big cabin—there were no big cabins on the ship, it seemed, not even the one the Amyrlin had taken over from the captain, though that was larger than the rest. With its two beds built into the walls, shelves beneath them and cabinets above, everything lay close to hand.

Except for keeping her balance, the movements of the ship did not bother her the way they did Nynaeve; she had given up offering Nynaeve food after the third time the Wisdom threw the bowl at her. "I'm worried about Rand," she said.

"I'm worried about all of them," Nynaeve replied dully. After a moment, she said, "Another dream last night? The way you've been staring at nothing since you got up. . . ."

Egwene nodded. She had never been very good at keeping things from Nynaeve, and she had not tried with the dreams. Nynaeve had tried to dose her at first, until she heard one of the Aes Sedai was interested; then she began to believe. "It was like the others. Different, but the same. Rand is in some kind of danger. I know it. And it is getting worse. He's done something, or he's going to do something, that puts him in. . . ." She dropped down on her bed and leaned toward the other woman. "I just wish I could make some sense of it."

"Channeling?" Nynaeve said softly.

Despite herself, Egwene looked around to see if anyone was there to hear. They were alone, with the door closed, but still she spoke just as softly. "I don't know. Maybe." There was no telling what Aes Sedai could do—she had seen enough already to make her believe every story of their powers—and she would not risk eavesdropping. *I won't risk Rand. If I did right, I'd tell them, but Moiraine knows, and she hasn't said anything. And it's Rand! I can't.* "I don't know what to do."

"Has Anaiya said anything more about these dreams?" Nynaeve seemed to make it a point never to add the honorific Sedai, even when the two of them were alone. Most of the Aes Sedai appeared not to care, but the habit had earned a few strange looks, and some hard ones; she was going to train in the White Tower, after all.

"'The Wheel weaves as the Wheel wills,'" Egwene quoted Anaiya. "'The boy is far away, child, and there's nothing we can do until we know more. I will see to testing you myself once we reach the White Tower, child.' Aaagh! She *knows* there is something in these dreams. I can tell she does. I like the woman, Nynaeve; I do. But she won't *tell* me what I want to know. And I can't tell her everything. Maybe if I could. . . ."

"The man in the mask again?"

Egwene nodded. Somehow, she was sure it was better not to tell Anaiya about him. She could not imagine why, but she was sure. Three times the man whose eyes were fire had been in her dreams each time when she dreamed a dream that convinced her Rand was in danger. He always wore a mask across his face; sometimes she could see his eyes, and sometimes she could only see fire where they should be. "He laughed at me. It was so . . . contemptuous. As though I were a puppy he was going to have to push out of his way with his foot. It frightens me. He frightens me."

"Are you sure it has anything to do with the other dreams, with Rand? Sometimes a dream is just a dream."

Egwene threw up her hands. "And sometimes, Nynaeve, you sound just like Anaiya Sedai!" She put a special emphasis on the title, and was pleased to see Nynaeve grimace.

"If I ever get out of this bed, Egwene—"

A knock at the door cut off whatever Nynaeve had been going to say. Before Egwene could speak or move, the Amyrlin herself came in and shut the door behind her. She was alone, for a wonder; she seldom left her cabin, and then always with Leane at her side, and maybe another of the Aes Sedai.

Egwene sprang to her feet. The room was a little crowded, with three of them in it.

"Both of you feeling well?" the Amyrlin said cheerily. She tilted her head at Nynaeve. "Eating well, too, I trust? In good temper?"

Nynaeve struggled to a sitting position, with her back against the wall. "My temper is just fine, thank you."

"We are honored, Mother," Egwene began, but the Amyrlin waved her to silence.

"It's good to be on the water again, but it grows boring as a mill pond after a while with nothing to do." The ship heeled, and she shifted her balance without seeming to notice. "I will give you your lesson today." She folded herself onto the end of Egwene's bed, feet tucked under her. "Sit, child."

Egwene sat, but Nynaeve began trying to push herself to her feet. "I think I will go on deck."

"I said, sit!" The Amyrlin's voice cracked like a whip, but Nynaeve kept rising, wavering. She still had both hands on the bed, but she was almost upright. Egwene held herself ready to catch her when she fell.

Closing her eyes, Nynaeve slowly lowered herself back to the bed. "Perhaps I will stay. It is no doubt windy up there."

The Amyrlin barked a laugh. "They told me you had a temper in you like a fisher-bird with a bone in its throat. Some of them, child, say you'd do well for some time as a novice, no matter how old you are. I say, if you have the ability I hear of, you deserve to be one of the Accepted." She gave another laugh. "I always believe in giving people what they deserve. Yes. I suspect you will learn a great deal once you reach the White Tower."

"I'd rather one of the Warders taught me how to use a sword," Nynaeve growled. She swallowed convulsively, and opened her eyes. "There is someone I'd like to use it on." Egwene looked at her sharply; did Nynaeve mean the Amyrlin—which was stupid, and dangerous besides—or Lan? She snapped at Egwene every time Lan was mentioned.

"A sword?" the Amyrlin said. "I never thought swords were much use—even if you have the skill, child, there are always men who have as much, and a deal more strength—but if you want a sword. . . ." She held up her hand—Egwene gasped, and even Nynaeve's eyes bulged—and there was a sword in it. With blade and hilt of an odd bluish white, it looked somehow . . . cold. "Made from the air, child, with Air. It's as good as most steel blades, better than most, but still not much use." The sword became a paring knife. There was no shrinking; it just was one thing, then the other. "This, now, is useful." The paring knife turned to mist, and the mist faded away. The Amyrlin put her empty hand back in her lap. "But either takes more effort than it is worth. Better, easier, simply to carry a good knife with you. You have to learn when to use your ability, as well as how, and when it's better to do things the way any other woman would. Let a blacksmith make knives for gutting fish. Use the One Power too often and too freely, and you can come to like it too much. That way lies danger. You begin to want more of it, and sooner or later you run the risk of drawing more than you've learned to handle. And that can burn you out like a guttered candle, or—"

"If I must learn all this," Nynaeve broke in stiffly, "I would as soon learn something useful. All this—this . . . 'Make the air stir, Nynaeve. Light the candle, Nynaeve. Now put it out. Light it again,' Paah!"

Egwene closed her eyes for a moment. *Please, Nynaeve. Please keep a check on your temper.* She bit her lip to keep from saying it out loud.

The Amyrlin was silent for a moment. "Useful," she said at last. "Something useful. You wanted a sword. Suppose a man came at me with a sword. What would I do? Something useful, you can be sure. This, I think."

For an instant, Egwene thought she saw a glow around the woman at the other end of her bed. Then the air seemed to thicken; nothing changed that Egwene could see, but she could surely feel it. She tried to lift her arm; it did not budge any more than if she were buried to her neck in thick jelly. Nothing could move except her head.

"Release me!" Nynaeve grated. Her eyes glared, and her head jerked from side to side, but the rest of her sat as rigidly as a statue. Egwene realized that she was not the only one held. "Let me go!"

"Useful, wouldn't you say? And it is nothing but Air." The Amyrlin spoke in a conversational tone, as if they were all chatting over tea. "Big man, with his muscles and his sword, and the sword does him as much good as the hair on his chest."

"Let me go, I say!"

"And if I don't like where he is, why, I can pick him up." Nynaeve squawked furiously as she slowly rose, still in a sitting position, until her head almost touched the ceiling. The Amyrlin smiled. "I've often wished I could use this to fly. The records say Aes Sedai *could* fly, in the Age of Legends, but they aren't clear on how, exactly. Not this way, though. It doesn't work like that. You might reach out with your hands and pick up a chest that weighs as much as you do; you look strong. But take hold of yourself however you will, you cannot pick yourself up."

Nynaeve's head jerked furiously, but not another muscle of her twitched. "The Light burn you, let me go!"

Egwene swallowed hard and hoped she was not also to be lifted.

"So," the Amyrlin continued, "big, hairy man, and so forth. He can do nothing to me, while I can do anything at all to him. Why, if I had a mind to"—she leaned forward, her eyes intent on Nynaeve; suddenly her smile did not seem very friendly—"I could turn him upside down and paddle his bottom. Just like—" Suddenly the Amyrlin flew backwards so hard her head rebounded from the wall, and there she stayed, as if something were pressing against her.

Egwene stared, her mouth dry. *This isn't happening. It isn't.*

"They were right," the Amyrlin said. Her voice sounded strained, as though she found it hard to breathe. "They said you learned quickly. And they said it took your temper burning to get to the heart of what you can do." She took a struggling breath. "Shall we release each other together, child?"

Nynaeve, floating in the air with her eyes ablaze, said, "You let me go right now, or I'll—" Abruptly a look of amazement came over her face, a look of loss. Her mouth worked silently.

The Amyrlin sat up, working her shoulders. "You don't know everything yet, do you, child? Not the hundredth part of everything. You did not suspect I could cut you off from the True Source. You can still feel it there, but you can't touch it any more than a fish can touch the moon. When you learn enough to be raised to full sisterhood, no one woman will be able to do that to you. The stronger you become, the more Aes Sedai it will take to shield you against your will. Do you think, now, you want to learn?" Nynaeve pressed her mouth shut in a thin line and stared her in the eye grimly. The Amyrlin sighed. "If you had a hair less potential than you do, child, I would send you to the Mistress of Novices and tell her to keep you the rest of your life. But you will get what you deserve."

Nynaeve's eyes widened, and she had just time to start a yell before she dropped, hitting her bed with a loud thud. Egwene winced; the mattresses were thin, and the wood beneath hard. Nynaeve's face stayed frozen as she shifted the way she sat, just a fraction.

"And now," the Amyrlin said firmly, "unless you would like

further demonstration, we will get on with your lesson. Continue
your lesson, we might say."

"Mother?" Egwene said faintly. She still could not twitch
below her chin.

The Amyrlin looked at her questioningly, then smiled. "Oh. I am
sorry, child. Your friend was occupying my attention, I'm afraid."
Suddenly Egwene could move again; she raised her arms, just to
convince herself that she could. "Are you both ready to learn?"

"Yes, Mother," Egwene said quickly.

The Amyrlin raised an eyebrow at Nynaeve.

After a moment, Nynaeve said in a tight voice, "Yes, Mother."

Egwene heaved a sigh of relief.

"Good. Now, then. Empty your thoughts of everything but a
flower bud."

Egwene was sweating by the time the Amyrlin left. She had
thought some of the other Aes Sedai had been hard teachers, but
that smiling, plain-faced woman coaxed out every last drop of
effort, drew it out, and when there was nothing left, she seemed to
reach into you and pulled it out. It had gone well, though. As the
door closed behind the Amyrlin, Egwene raised one hand; a tiny
flame sprang to life, balanced a hairbreadth above the tip of her
forefinger, then danced from fingertip to fingertip. She was not
supposed to do this without a teacher—one of the Accepted, at the
very least—to watch over her, but she was too excited at her
progress to pay any mind to that.

Nynaeve bounded to her feet and threw her pillow at the closing door. "That—that vile, contemptible, miserable—hag! The
Light burn her! I'd like to feed *her* to the fish. I'd like to dose her
with things that would turn her green for the rest of her life! I
don't care if she's old enough to be my mother, if I had her in
Emond's Field, she wouldn't sit down comfortably for. . . ." Her
teeth ground so loudly that Egwene jumped.

Letting the flame die, Egwene put her eyes firmly on her lap.

She wished she could think of a way to sneak out of the room without catching Nynaeve's eye.

The lesson had not gone well for Nynaeve, because she had held her temper on a tight lead until the Amyrlin was gone. She never could do very much unless she was angry, and then it all burst out of her. After failure upon failure, the Amyrlin had done everything she could to rouse her again. Egwene wished Nynaeve could forget she had been there to see or hear any of it.

Nynaeve stalked stiffly to her bed and stood staring at the wall behind it, her fist clenched at her side. Egwene looked longingly at the door.

"It was not your fault," Nynaeve said, and Egwene gave a start.

"Nynaeve, I—"

Nynaeve turned to look down at her. "It was not your fault," she repeated, sounding unconvinced. "But if you ever breathe one word, I'll—I'll. . . ."

"Not a word," Egwene said quickly. "I don't even remember anything to breathe a word about."

Nynaeve stared at her a moment longer, then nodded. Abruptly she grimaced. "Light, I did not think *anything* tasted worse than raw sheepstongue root. I'll remember that, the next time you act the goose, so watch yourself."

Egwene winced. That had been the first thing the Amyrlin had done trying to rouse Nynaeve's anger. A dark glob of something that glistened like grease and smelled vile had suddenly appeared and, while the Amyrlin held Nynaeve with the Power, had been forced into the Wisdom's mouth. The Amyrlin had even held her nose to make her swallow. And Nynaeve remembered things, if she had seen them done once. Egwene did not think there was any way of stopping her if she took it into her mind to do it; for all her own success in making a flame dance, *she* could never have held the Amyrlin against a wall. "At least being on the ship isn't making you sick anymore."

Nynaeve grunted, then gave a short, sharp laugh. "I'm too angry to be sick." With another mirthless laugh, she shook her head. "I'm too miserable to be sick. Light, I feel as if I've been dragged through a knothole backwards. If that is what novice training is like, you will have incentive to learn quickly."

Egwene scowled at her knees. Compared to Nynaeve, the Amyrlin had only coaxed her, smiled at her successes, sympathized with her failures, then coaxed again. But all the Aes Sedai had said things would be different in the White Tower; harder, though they would not say how. If she had to go through what Nynaeve had, day after day, she did not think she could stand it.

Something changed in the motion of the ship. The rocking eased, and feet thumped on the deck above their heads. A man shouted something Egwene could not quite make out.

She looked up at Nynaeve. "Do you think. . . . Tar Valon?"

"There is only one way to find out," Nynaeve replied, and determinedly took her cloak from its peg.

When they reached the deck, sailors were running everywhere, heaving at lines, shortening sail, readying long sweeps. The wind had died to a breeze, and the clouds were scattering, now.

Egwene rushed to the rail. "It is! It is Tar Valon!" Nynaeve joined her with an expressionless face.

The island was so big it looked more as if the river split in two than contained a bit of land. Bridges that seemed to be made of lace arched from either bank to the island, crossing marshy ground as well as the river. The walls of the city, the Shining Walls of Tar Valon, glistened white as the sun broke through the clouds. And on the west bank, its broken top leaking a thin wisp of smoke, Dragonmount reared black against the sky, one mountain standing among flat lands and rolling hills. Dragonmount, where the Dragon had died. Dragonmount, made by the Dragon's dying.

Egwene wished she did not think of Rand when she looked at the mountain. *A man channeling. Light, help him.*

The *River Queen* passed through a wide opening in a tall, circular wall that thrust out into the river. Inside, one long wharf surrounded a round harbor. Sailors furled the last sails and used sweeps alone to move the ship stern-first to its docking. Around the long wharf, the other ships that had come downriver were now being snugged into their berths among the ships already there. The White Flame banner set workers scurrying along the already busy wharf.

The Amyrlin came on deck before the shore lines were tied off, but dockworkers ran a gangplank aboard as soon as she appeared. Leane walked at her side, flame-tipped staff in hand, and the other Aes Sedai on the ship followed them ashore. None of them so much as glanced at Egwene or Nynaeve. On the wharf a delegation greeted the Amyrlin—shawled Aes Sedai, bowing formally, kissing the Amyrlin's ring. The wharf bustled, between ships unloading and the Amyrlin Seat arriving; soldiers formed up on disembarking, men set booms for cargo; trumpet flourishes rang from the walls, competing with cheers from the onlookers.

Nynaeve gave a loud sniff. "It seems they've forgotten us. Come along. We'll see to ourselves."

Egwene was reluctant to leave her first sight of Tar Valon, but she followed Nynaeve below to gather their things. When they came back topside, bundles in their arms, soldiers and trumpets were gone—and Aes Sedai, too. Men were swinging back hatches along the deck and lowering cables into the holds.

On the deck, Nynaeve caught a dockman's arm, a burly fellow in a coarse brown shirt with no sleeves. "Our horses," she began.

"I'm busy," he growled, pulling free. "Horses'll all be took to the White Tower." He looked them up and down. "If you've business with the Tower, best you take yourselves on. Aes Sedai don't hold with newlings being tardy." Another man, wrestling with a bale being swung out of the hold on a cable, shouted to him, and he left the women without a backwards glance.

Egwene exchanged looks with Nynaeve. It seemed they really were on their own.

Nynaeve stalked off the ship with grim determination on her face, but Egwene made her way dejectedly down the gangplank and through the tarry smell that hung over the wharf. *All that talk about wanting us here, and now they don't seem to care.*

Broad stairs led up from the dock to a wide arch of dark redstone. On reaching it, Egwene and Nynaeve stopped to stare.

Every building seemed a palace, though most of those close to the arch seemed to contain inns or shops, from the signs over the doors. Fanciful stonework was everywhere, and the lines of one structure seemed designed to complement and set off the next, leading the eye along as if everything were part of one vast design. Some structures did not look like buildings at all, but like gigantic waves breaking, or huge shells, or fanciful, wind-sculpted cliffs. Right in front of the arch lay a broad square, with a fountain and trees, and Egwene could see another square further on. Above everything rose the towers, tall and graceful, some with sweeping bridges between them, high in the sky. And over all rose one tower, higher and wider than all the rest, as white as the Shining Walls themselves.

"Fair takes the breath at first sight," said a woman's voice behind them. "At tenth sight, for that. And at hundredth."

Egwene turned. The woman was Aes Sedai; Egwene was sure of it, though she wore no shawl. No one else had that ageless look; and she held herself with an assurance, a confidence that seemed to confirm it. A glance at her hand showed the golden ring, the serpent biting its own tail. The Aes Sedai was a little plump, with a warm smile, and one of the oddest-appearing women Egwene had ever seen. Her plumpness could not hide high cheekbones, her eyes had a tilt to them and were the clearest, palest green, and her hair was almost the color of fire. Egwene barely stopped herself from goggling at that hair, those slightly slanted eyes.

"Ogier built, of course," the Aes Sedai went on, "and their best work ever, some say. One of the first cities built after the Breaking. There weren't half a thousand people here altogether then— no more than twenty sisters—but they built for what would be needed."

"It is a lovely city," Nynaeve said. "We are supposed to go to the White Tower. We came here for training, but no one seems to care if we go or stay."

"They care," the woman said, smiling. "I came here to meet you, but I was delayed speaking with the Amyrlin. I am Sheriam, the Mistress of Novices."

"I am not to be a novice," Nynaeve said in a firm voice, but a little too quickly. "The Amyrlin herself said I was to be one of the Accepted."

"So I was told." Sheriam sounded amused. "I have never heard of it being done so before, but they say you are . . . exceptional. Remember, though, even one of the Accepted can be called to my study. It requires more breaking of the rules than for a novice, but it has been known to happen." She turned to Egwene as if she had not seen Nynaeve frown. "And you are our new novice. It is always good to see a novice come. We have too few, these days. You will make forty. Only forty. And no more than eight or nine of those will be raised to the Accepted. Though I don't think you will have to worry about that too much, if you work hard and apply yourself. The work is hard, and even for one with the potential they tell me you have, it will not be made any easier. If you cannot stick to it, no matter how hard it is, or if you will break under the strain, better we find it out now, and let you go on your way, than wait until you are a full sister and others are depending on you. An Aes Sedai's life is not easy. Here, we will prepare you for it, if you have in you what is required."

Egwene swallowed. *Break under the strain?* "I will try, Sheriam Sedai," she said faintly. *And I will not break.*

Nynaeve looked at her worriedly. "Sheriam. . . ." She stopped and took a deep breath. "Sheriam Sedai"—she seemed to force the honorific out—"does it have to be so hard on her? Flesh and blood can only take so much. I know . . . something . . . of what novices must go through. Surely there's no need to try to break her just to find out how strong she is."

"You mean what the Amyrlin did to you today?" Nynaeve's back stiffened; Sheriam looked as though she were trying to keep amusement from her face. "I told you I spoke with the Amyrlin. Rest your worries for your friend. Novice training is hard, but not that hard. That is for the first few weeks of being one of the Accepted." Nynaeve's mouth fell open; Egwene thought the Wisdom's eyes were going to come right out of her head. "To catch the few who might have slipped through novice training when they should not have. We cannot risk having one of our number—a full Aes Sedai—who will break under the stress of the world outside." The Aes Sedai gathered them both up, an arm around the shoulders of each. Nynaeve hardly seemed to realize where she was going. "Come," Sheriam said, "I will see you settled in your rooms. The White Tower awaits."

CHAPTER 19

Beneath the Dagger

NIGHT ON THE EDGE OF KINSLAYER'S DAGGER was cold, as nights in the mountains are always cold. The wind whipped down from the high peaks carrying the iciness of the snowcaps. Rand shifted on the hard ground, tugging at his cloak and blanket, and only half asleep. His hand went to his sword, lying beside him. *One more day,* he thought drowsily. *Just one more, and then we go. If no one comes tomorrow, Ingtar or Darkfriends one, I'll take Selene to Cairhien.*

He had told himself that before. Every day they had been there on the mountainside, watching the place where Hurin said the trail had been, in that other world—where Selene said the Darkfriends would surely appear in this world—he told himself it was time to leave. And Selene talked of the Horn of Valere, and touched his arm, and looked into his eyes, and before he knew it he had agreed to yet another day before they went on.

He shrugged against the chill of the wind, thinking of Selene touching his arm and looking into his eyes. *If Egwene saw that, she'd shear me for a sheep, and Selene, too. Egwene could already be in Tar Valon by now, learning to be an Aes Sedai. The next time she sees me, she'll probably try to gentle me.*

As he shifted over, his hand slid past the sword and touched the bundle holding Thom Merrilin's harp and flute. Unconsciously, his fingers tightened on the gleeman's cloak. *I was happy then, I think, even running for my life. Playing the flute for my supper. I was too ignorant to know what was going on. There's no turning back.*

Shivering, he opened his eyes. The only light came from the waning moon, not far past full and low in the sky. A fire would give them away to those for whom they watched. Loial muttered in his sleep, a low rumble. One of the horses stamped a hoof. Hurin had the first watch, from a stone outcrop a little way up the mountain; he would be coming to wake Rand for his turn, soon.

Rand rolled over . . . and stopped. In the moonlight he could see the shape of Selene, bending over his saddlebags, her hands on the buckles. Her white dress gathered the faint light. "Do you need something?"

She gave a jump, and stared toward him. "You—you startled me."

He rolled to his feet, shedding the blanket and wrapping the cloak around himself, and went to her. He was sure he had left the saddlebags right by his side when he lay down; he always kept them close. He took them from her. All the buckles were fastened, even those on the side that held the damning banner. *How can my life depend on keeping it? If anybody sees it and knows what it is, I'll die for having it.* He peered at her suspiciously.

Selene stayed where she was, looking up at him. The moon glistened in her dark eyes. "It came to me," she said, "that I've been wearing this dress too long. I could brush it, at least, if I had something else to wear while I did. One of your shirts, perhaps."

Rand nodded, feeling a sudden relief. Her dress looked as clean to him as when he first saw her, but he knew that if a spot appeared on Egwene's dress, nothing would do but that she cleaned it immediately. "Of course." He opened the capacious pocket into which he had stuffed everything except the banner and pulled out one of the white silk shirts.

"Thank you." Her hands went behind her back. To the buttons, he realized.

Eyes wide, he spun away from her.

"If you could help me with these, it would be much easier."

Rand cleared his throat. "It would not be proper. It isn't as if we were promised, or. . . ." *Stop thinking about that! You can never marry anyone.* "It just wouldn't be proper."

Her soft laugh sent a shiver down his back, as if she had run a finger along his spine. He tried not to listen to the rustlings behind him. He said, "Ah . . . tomorrow . . . tomorrow, we'll leave for Cairhien."

"And what of the Horn of Valere?"

"Maybe we were wrong. Maybe they are not coming here at all. Hurin says there are a number of passes through Kinslayer's Dagger. If they went only a little further west, they do not have to come into the mountains at all."

"But the trail we followed came here. They will come here. The Horn will come here. You may turn around, now."

"You say that, but we don't know. . . ." He turned, and the words died in his mouth. Her dress lay across her arm, and she wore his shirt, hanging in baggy folds on her. It was a long-tailed shirt, made for his height, but she was tall for a woman. The bottom of it came little more than halfway down her thighs. It was not as if he had never seen a girl's legs before; girls in the Two Rivers always tied up their skirts to go wading in Waterwood ponds. But they stopped doing it well before they were old enough to braid their hair, and this was in the dark, besides. The moonlight seemed to make her skin glow.

"What is it you don't know, Rand?"

The sound of her voice unfroze his joints. With a loud cough, he whirled to face the other way. "Ah . . . I think . . . ah . . . I . . . ah. . . ."

"Think of the glory, Rand." Her hand touched his back, and he almost shamed himself with a squeak. "Think of the glory that will come to the one who finds the Horn of Valere. How proud I'll be to stand beside him who holds the Horn. You have no idea the heights we will scale together, you and I. With the Horn of Valere in your hand, you can be a king. You can be another Artur Hawkwing. You. . . ."

"Lord Rand!" Hurin panted into the campsite. "My Lord, they. . . ." He skidded to a halt, suddenly making a gurgling sound. His eyes dropped to the ground, and he stood wringing his hands. "Forgive me, my Lady. I didn't mean to. . . . I. . . . Forgive me."

Loial sat up, his blanket and cloak falling away. "What's happening? Is it my turn to watch already?" He looked toward Rand and Selene, and even in the moonlight the widening of his eyes was plain.

Rand heard Selene sigh behind him. He stepped away from her, still not looking at her. *Her legs are so white, so smooth.* "What is it, Hurin?" He made his voice more moderate; was he angry with Hurin, himself, or Selene? *No reason to be angry with her.* "Did you see something, Hurin?"

The sniffer spoke without raising his eyes. "A fire, my Lord, down in the hills. I didn't see it at first. They made it small, and hid it, but they hid it from somebody following them, not somebody ahead, and up above. Two miles, Lord Rand. Less than three, for sure."

"Fain," Rand said. "Ingtar would not be afraid of anyone

following him. It must be Fain." Suddenly he did not know what to do, now. They had been waiting for Fain, but now that the man was only a mile or so away, he was uncertain. "In the morning. . . . In the morning, we will follow. When Ingtar and the others catch up, we'll be able to point right to them."

"So," Selene said. "You will let this Ingtar take the Horn of Valere. And the glory."

"I don't want. . . ." Without thinking, he turned, and there she was, legs pale in the moonlight, and as unconcerned that they were bare as if she were alone. *As if we were alone,* the thought came. *She wants the man who finds the Horn.* "Three of us cannot take it away from them. Ingtar has twenty lances with him."

"You don't know you cannot take it. How many followers does this man have? You don't know that, either." Her voice was calm, but intent. "You don't even know if these men camped down there do have the Horn. The only way is to go down yourself and see. Take the *alantin;* his kind have sharp eyes, even by moonlight. And he has the strength to carry the Horn in its chest, if you make the right decision."

She's right. You do not know for sure if it's Fain. A fine thing it would be to have Hurin casting about for a trail that was not there, all of them out in the open if the real Darkfriends did finally come. "I will go alone," he said. "Hurin and Loial will stand guard for you."

Laughing, Selene came to him so gracefully it almost seemed she danced. Moonshadows veiled her face in mystery as she looked up at him, and mystery made her even more beautiful. "I am capable of guarding myself, until you return to protect me. Take the *alantin.*"

"She is right, Rand," Loial said, rising. "I can see better by moonlight than you. With my eyes, we may not need to go as close as you would alone."

"Very well." Rand strode over to his sword and buckled it at his waist. Bow and quiver he left where they lay; a bow was not of much use in the dark, and he intended to look, not fight. "Hurin, show me this fire."

The sniffer led him scrambling up the slope to the outcrop, like a huge stone thumb thrust out of the mountain. The fire was only a speck—he missed it the first time Hurin pointed. Whoever had made it did not mean for it to be seen. He fixed it in his head.

By the time they returned to the camp, Loial had saddled Red and his own horse. As Rand climbed to the bay's back, Selene caught his hand. "Remember the glory," she said softly. "Remember." The shirt seemed to fit her better than he recalled, molding itself to her form.

He drew a deep breath and took his hand back. "Guard her with your life, Hurin. Loial?" He heeled Red's flanks gently. The Ogier's big mount plodded along behind.

They did not try to move quickly. Night shrouded the mountainside, and moon-cast shadows made footing uncertain. Rand could not see the fire any longer—no doubt it was better hidden from eyes on the same level—but he had its location in his mind. For someone who had learned to hunt in the tangle of the Westwood, in the Two Rivers, finding the fire would be no great difficulty. *And what then?* Selene's face loomed before him. *How proud I'll be to stand beside him who holds the Horn.*

"Loial," he said suddenly, trying to clear his thoughts, "what's this *alantin* she calls you?"

"It's the Old Tongue, Rand." The Ogier's horse picked its way uncertainly, but he guided it almost as surely as if it were daylight. "It means Brother, and is short for *tia avende alantin.* Brother to the Trees. Treebrother. It is very formal, but then, I've heard the Cairhienin are formal. The noble Houses are, at least. The common people I saw there were not very formal at all."

Rand frowned. A shepherd would not be very acceptable to a formal Cairhienin noble House. *Light, Mat's right about you.*

You're crazy, and with a big head to boot. But if I could marry. . . .

He wished he could stop thinking, and before he realized it, the void had formed within him, making thoughts distant things, as if part of someone else. *Saidin* shone at him, beckoned to him. He gritted his teeth and ignored it; it was like ignoring a burning coal inside his head, but at least he could hold it at bay. Barely. He almost left the void, but the Darkfriends were out there in the night, and closer, now. And the Trollocs. He needed the emptiness, needed even the uneasy calm of the void. *I don't have to touch it. I don't.*

After a time, he reined in Red. They stood at the base of a hill, the wide-scattered trees on its slopes black in the night. "I think we must be close by now," he said softly. "Best we go the rest of the way on foot." He slid from the saddle and tied the bay's reins to a branch.

"Are you all right?" Loial whispered, climbing down. "You sound odd."

"I'm fine." His voice sounded tight, he realized. Stretched. *Saidin* called to him. *No!* "Be careful. I can't be sure exactly how far it is, but that fire should be somewhere just ahead of us: On the hilltop, I think." The Ogier nodded.

Slowly Rand stole from tree to tree, placing each foot carefully, holding his sword tight so it did not clatter against a tree trunk. He was grateful for the lack of undergrowth. Loial followed like a big shadow; Rand could not see much more of him than that. Everything was moonshadows and darkness.

Suddenly some trick of the moonlight resolved the shadows ahead of him, and he froze, touching the rough bole of a leatherleaf. Dim mounds on the ground became men wrapped in blankets, and apart from them a group of larger mounds. Sleeping Trollocs. They had doused the fire. One moonbeam, moving through the branches, caught a shine of gold and silver on the ground, halfway between the two groups. The moonlight seemed to brighten; for an instant he could see clearly. The shape of a sleeping man lay close by to the gleam, but that was not what held his eye. *The chest. The Horn.* And something atop it, a point of red flashing in the moonbeam. *The dagger! Why would Fain put . . .?*

Loial's huge hand settled over Rand's mouth, and a good part of his face besides. He twisted to look at the Ogier. Loial pointed off to his right, slowly, as if motion might attract attention.

At first Rand could not see anything, then a shadow moved, not ten paces away. A tall, bulky shadow, and snouted. Rand's breath caught. A Trolloc. It lifted its snout as if sniffing. Some of them hunted by scent.

For an instant the void wavered. Someone stirred in the Darkfriend camp, and the Trolloc turned to peer that way.

Rand froze, letting the calm of emptiness envelope him. His hand was on his sword, but he did not think of it. The void was all. Whatever happened, happened. He watched the Trolloc without blinking.

A moment longer the snouted shadow watched the Darkfriend camp, then, as if satisfied, folded itself down beside a tree. Almost immediately a low sound, like coarse cloth ripping, drifted from it.

Loial put his mouth close to Rand's ear. "It's asleep," he whispered incredulously.

Rand nodded. Tam had told him Trollocs were lazy, apt to give up any task but killing unless fear kept them to it. He turned back to the camp.

All was still and quiet there again. The moonbeam no longer shone on the chest, but he knew now which shadow it was. He could see it in his mind, floating beyond the void, glittering golden, chased with silver, in the glow of *saidin*. The Horn of Valere and the dagger Mat needed, both almost within reach of his hand. Selene's face drifted with the chest. They could follow Fain's party in the morning, and wait until Ingtar joined them. If Ingtar did come, if he still followed the trail without his sniffer.

No, there would never be a better chance. All within reach of his hand. Selene was waiting on the mountain.

Motioning for Loial to follow, Rand dropped to his belly and crawled toward the chest. He heard the Ogier's muffled gasp, but his eyes were fixed on that one shadowed mound ahead.

Darkfriends and Trollocs lay to left and right of him, but once he had seen Tam stalk close enough to a deer to put his hand on its flank before the animal bounded off; he had tried to learn from Tam. *Madness!* The thought flew by dimly, almost out of reach. *This is madness! You—are—going—mad!* Dim thoughts; someone else's thoughts.

Slowly, silently, he slithered to that one special shadow, and put out a hand. Ornate traceries worked in gold met his touch. It *was* the chest that held the Horn of Valere. His hand touched something else, on the lid. The dagger, bare-bladed. In the dark, his eyes widened. Remembering what it had done to Mat, he jerked back, the void shifting with his agitation.

The man sleeping nearby—no more than two paces from the chest; no one else lay so close by spans—groaned in his sleep and thrashed at his blankets. Rand allowed the void to sweep thought and fear away. Murmuring uneasily in his sleep, the man stilled.

Rand let his hand go back to the dagger, not quite touching it. It had not harmed Mat in the beginning. Not much, at least; not quickly. In one swift motion he lifted the dagger, stuck it behind his belt, and pulled his hand away, as if it might help to minimize the time it touched his bare skin. Perhaps it would, and Mat would die without the dagger. He could feel it there, almost a weight pulling him down, pressing against him. But in the void sensation was as distant as thought, and the feel of the dagger faded quickly to something he was used to.

He wasted only a moment more staring at the shadow-wrapped chest—the Horn had to be inside, but he did not know how to open it and he could not lift it by himself—then he looked around for Loial. He found the Ogier crouched not far behind him, massive head swiveling as he peered back and forth from sleeping human Darkfriends to sleeping Trollocs. Even in the night it was plain Loial's eyes were as wide as they could go; they looked as big as saucers in the light of the moon. Rand reached out and took Loial's hand.

The Ogier gave a start and gasped. Rand put a finger across his lips, set Loial's hand on the chest, and mimed lifting. For a time— it seemed forever, in the night, with Darkfriends and Trollocs all around; it could not have been more than heartbeats—Loial stared. Then, slowly, he put his arms around the golden chest and stood. He made it seem effortless.

Ever so carefully, even more carefully than he had come in, Rand began to walk out of the camp, behind Loial and the chest. Both hands on his sword, he watched the sleeping Darkfriends, the still shapes of the Trollocs. All those shadowed figures began to be swallowed deeper in the darkness as they drew away. *Almost free. We've done it!*

The man who had been sleeping near the chest suddenly sat up with a strangled yell, then leaped to his feet. "It's gone! Wake, you filth! It's gooonnne!" Fain's voice; even in the void Rand recognized it. The others scrambled erect, Darkfriends and Trollocs, calling to know what was happening, growling and snarling. Fain's voice rose to a howl. "I know it is you, al'Thor! You're hiding from me, but I know you are out there! Find him! Find him! Al'Thoooor!" Men and Trollocs scattered in every direction.

Wrapped in emptiness, Rand kept moving. Almost forgotten in entering the camp, *saidin* pulsed at him.

"He cannot see us," Loial whispered low. "Once we reach the horses—"

A Trolloc leaped out of the dark at them, cruel eagle's beak in a man's face where mouth and nose should have been, scythe-like sword already whistling through the air.

Rand moved without thought. He was one with the blade. Cat Dances on the Wall. The Trolloc screamed as it fell, screamed again as it died.

"Run, Loial!" Rand commanded. *Saidin* called to him. "Run!" He was dimly aware of Loial lumbering to an awkward gallop, but another Trolloc loomed from the night, boar-snouted and tusked, spiked axe raised. Smoothly Rand glided between Trolloc and Ogier; Loial must get the Horn away. Head and shoulders taller than Rand, half again as wide, the Trolloc came at him with a silent snarl. The Courtier Taps His Fan. No scream, this time. He walked backwards after Loial, watching the night. *Saidin* sang to him, such a sweet song. *The Power could burn them all, burn Fain and all the rest to cinders. No!*

Two more Trollocs, wolf and ram, gleaming teeth and curling horns. Lizard in the Thornbush. He rose smoothly from one knee as the second toppled, horns almost brushing his shoulder. The song of *saidin* caressed him with seduction, pulled him with a thousand silken strings. *Burn them all with the Power. No. No! Better dead than that. If I were dead, it would be done with.*

A knot of Trollocs came into sight, hunting uncertainly. Three of them, four. Suddenly one pointed to Rand and raised a howl the rest answered as they charged.

"Let it be done with!" Rand shouted, and leaped to meet them.

For an instant surprise slowed them, then they came on with guttural cries, gleeful, bloodthirsty, swords and axes raised. He danced among them to the song of *saidin.* Hummingbird Kisses the Honeyrose. So cunning that song, filling him. Cat on Hot Sand. The sword seemed alive in his hands as it had never been before, and he fought as if a heron-mark blade could keep *saidin* from him. The Heron Spreads Its Wings.

Rand stared at the motionless shapes on the ground around him. "Better to be dead," he murmured. He raised his eyes, back up the hill toward where the camp lay. Fain was there, and Darkfriends, and more Trollocs. Too many to fight. Too many to face and live. He took a step that way. Another.

"Rand, come on!" Loial's urgent, whispered call drifted through the emptiness to him. "For life and the Light, Rand, come on!"

Carefully, Rand bent to wipe his blade on a Trolloc's coat. Then, as formally as if Lan were watching him train, he sheathed it.

"Rand!"

As though he knew of no urgency, Rand joined Loial by the horses. The Ogier was tying the golden chest atop his saddle with straps from his saddlebags. His cloak was stuffed underneath to help balance the chest on the rounded saddle seat.

Saidin sang no more. It was there, that stomach-turning glow, but it held back as if he truly had fought it off. Wonderingly, he let the void vanish. "I think I am going mad," he said. Suddenly realizing where they were, he peered back the way they had come. Shouts and howls came from half a dozen different directions; signs of search, but none of pursuit. Yet. He swung up onto Red's back.

"Sometimes I do not understand half of what you say," Loial said. "If you must go mad, could it at least wait until we are back with the Lady Selene and Hurin?"

"How are you going to ride with that in your saddle?"

"I will run!" The Ogier suited his words by breaking into a quick trot, pulling his horse behind him by the reins. Rand followed.

The pace Loial set was as fast as a horse could trot. Rand was sure the Ogier could not keep it for long, but Loial's feet did not flag. Rand decided that his boast of once outrunning a horse might really be true. Now and again Loial looked behind them as he ran, but the shouts of Darkfriends and howls of Trollocs faded with distance.

Even when the ground began to slope upwards more sharply, Loial's pace barely slowed, and he trotted into their campsite on the mountainside with only a little hard breathing.

"You have it." Selene's voice was exultant as her gaze rested on the ornately worked chest on Loial's saddle. She was wearing her own dress again; it looked as white as new snow to Rand. "I knew you would make the right choice. May I . . . have a look at it?"

"Did any of them follow, my Lord?" Hurin asked anxiously. He stared at the chest with awe, but his eyes slid off into the night, down the mountain. "If they followed, we'll have to move quick."

"I do not think they did. Go to the outcrop and see if you can see anything." Rand climbed down from his saddle as Hurin hurried up the mountain. "Selene, I don't know how to open the chest. Loial, do you?" The Ogier shook his head.

"Let me try. . . ." Even for a woman of Selene's height, Loial's saddle was high above the ground. She reached up to touch the finely wrought patterns on the chest, ran her hands across them, pressed. There was a click, and she pushed the lid up, let it fall open.

As she stretched on tiptoe to put a hand inside, Rand reached over her shoulder and lifted out the Horn of Valere. He had seen it once before, but never touched it. Though beautifully made, it did not look a thing of great age, or power. A curled golden horn, gleaming in the faint light, with inlaid silver script flowing around the mouth of the bell. He touched the strange letters with a finger. They seemed to catch the moon.

"Tia mi aven Moridin isainde vadin," Selene said. " 'The grave is no bar to my call.' You *will* be greater than Artur Hawkwing ever was."

"I am taking it to Shienar, to Lord Agelmar." *It should go to Tar Valon,* he thought, *but I'm done with Aes Sedai. Let Agelmar or Ingtar take it to them.* He set the Horn back in the chest; it cast back the moonlight, pulled the eye.

"That is madness," Selene said.

Rand flinched at the word. "Mad or not, it is what I'm doing. I told you, Selene, I want no part of greatness. Back there, I thought I did. For a while, I thought I wanted things. . . ." *Light, she's so beautiful. Egwene. Selene. I'm not worthy of either of them.* "Something seemed to take hold of me." *Saidin came for me, but I fought it off with a sword. Or is that mad, too?* He breathed deeply. "Shienar is where the Horn of Valere belongs. Or if not there, Lord Agelmar will know what to do with it."

Hurin appeared from up the mountain. "The fire's there again, Lord Rand, and bigger than ever. And I thought I heard shouting. It was all down in the hills. I don't think they've come upon the mountain, yet."

"You misunderstand me, Rand," Selene said. "You cannot go

back, now. You are committed. Those Friends of the Dark will not simply go away because you've taken the Horn from them. Far from it. Unless you know some way to kill them all, they will be hunting you now as you hunted them before."

"No!" Loial and Hurin looked surprised at Rand's vehemence. He softened his tone. "I don't know any way to kill them all. They can live forever for all of me."

Selene's long hair shifted in waves as she shook her head. "Then you cannot go back, only onward. You can reach the safety of Cairhien's walls long before you could return to Shienar. Does the thought of a few more days in my company seem so onerous?"

Rand stared at the chest. Selene's company was far from burdensome, but near her he could not help thinking things he should not. Still, trying to ride back north meant risking Fain and his followers. She was right in that. Fain would never give up. Ingtar would not give up, either. If Ingtar came on southward, and Rand knew of no reason for him to turn aside, he would arrive at Cairhien, soon or late.

"Cairhien," he agreed. "You will have to show me where you live, Selene. I've never been to Cairhien." He reached to close the chest.

"You took something else from the Friends of the Dark?" Selene said. "You spoke earlier of a dagger."

How could I forget? He left the chest as it was and pulled the dagger from his belt. The bare blade curved like a horn, and the quillons were golden serpents. Set in the hilt, a ruby as big as his thumbnail winked like an evil eye in the moonlight. Ornate as it was, tainted as he knew it was, it felt no different from any other knife.

"Be careful," Selene said. "Do not cut yourself."

Rand felt a shiver inside. If simply carrying it was dangerous, he did not want to know what a cut from it would do. "This is from Shadar Logoth," he told the others. "It will twist whoever carries it for long, taint them to the bone the way Shadar Logoth is tainted. Without Aes Sedai Healing, that taint will kill, eventually."

"So that is what ails Mat," Loial said softly. "I never suspected." Hurin stared at the dagger in Rand's hand and wiped his own hands on the front of his coat. The sniffer did not look happy.

"None of us must handle it any more than is necessary," Rand went on. "I will find some way to carry it—"

"It is dangerous." Selene frowned at the blade as if the snakes were real, and poisonous. "Throw it away. Leave it, or bury it if you wish to keep it from other hands, but be rid of it."

"Mat needs it," Rand said firmly.

"It is too dangerous. You said so yourself."

"He needs it. The Am . . . the Aes Sedai said he would die without it to use in Healing him." *They still have a string on him, but this blade will cut it. Until I'm rid of it, and the Horn, they have a string on me, but I'll not dance however much they pull.*

He set the dagger in the chest, inside the curl of the Horn—there was just room for it—and pulled the lid down. It locked with a sharp snap. "That should shield us from it." He hoped it would. Lan said the time to sound most sure was when you were least certain.

"The chest will surely shield us," Selene said in a tight voice. "And now I mean to finish what is left of my night's sleep."

Rand shook his head. "We are too close. Fain seems able to find me, sometimes."

"Seek the Oneness if you are afraid," Selene said.

"I want to be as far from those Darkfriends come morning as we can be. I will saddle your mare."

"Stubborn!" She sounded angry, and when he looked at her, her mouth curved in a smile that never came close to her dark eyes. "A stubborn man is best, once. . . ." Her voice trailed off, and that worried him. Women often seemed to leave things unsaid, and in his limited experience it was what they did not say that proved the most trouble. She watched in silence as he slung her saddle onto the white mare's back and bent to fashion the girths.

"GATHER THEM ALL in!" Fain snarled. The goat-snouted Trolloc backed away from him. The fire, piled high with wood now, lit the hilltop with flickering shadows. His human followers huddled near the blaze, fearful to be out in the dark with the rest of the Trollocs. "Gather them, every one that still lives, and if any think to run, let them know they'll get what that one got." He gestured to the first Trolloc that had brought him word al'Thor was not to be found. It still snapped at ground muddied with its own blood, hooves scraping trenches as they jerked. "Go," Fain whispered, and the goat-snouted Trolloc ran into the night.

Fain glanced contemptuously at the other humans—*They'll have their uses still*—then turned to stare into the night, toward Kinslayer's Dagger. Al'Thor was up there, somewhere, in the mountains. With the Horn. His teeth grated audibly at the thought. He did not know where, exactly, but something pulled him toward the mountains. Toward al'Thor. That much of the Dark One's . . . gift . . . remained to him. He had hardly thought of it, had tried not to think of it, until suddenly, after the Horn was gone—*Gone!*— al'Thor was there, drawing him as meat draws a starving dog.

"I am a dog no longer. A dog no longer!" He heard the others shifting uneasily around the fire, but he ignored them. "You will pay for what was done to me, al'Thor! The world will pay!" He cackled at the night with mad laughter. "The world will pay!"

CHAPTER 20

Saidin

RAND KEPT THEM MOVING THROUGH THE night, allowing only a brief stop at dawn, to rest the horses. And to allow Loial rest. With the Horn of Valere in its gold-and-silver chest occupying his saddle, the Ogier walked or trotted ahead of his big horse, never complaining, never slowing them. Sometime during the night they had crossed the border of Cairhien.

"I want to see it again," Selene said as they halted. She dismounted and strode to Loial's horse. Their shadows, long and thin, pointed west from the sun just peeking over the horizon. "Bring it down for me, *alantin*." Loial began to undo the straps. "The Horn of Valere."

"No," Rand said, climbing down from Red's back. "Loial, no." The Ogier looked from Rand to Selene, his ears twitching doubtfully, but he took his hands away.

"I want to see the Horn," Selene demanded. Rand was sure she was no older than he, but at that moment she suddenly seemed as old and as cold as the mountains, and more regal than Queen Morgase at her haughtiest.

"I think we should keep the dagger shielded," Rand said. "For all I know, looking at it may be as bad as touching it. Let it stay where it is until I can put it in Mat's hands. He—he can take it to the Aes Sedai." *And what price will they demand for that Healing? But he hasn't any choice.* He felt a little guilty over feeling relief that he, at least, was through with Aes Sedai. *I am done with them. One way or another.*

"The dagger! All you seem to care about is that dagger. I told you to be rid of it. The Horn of Valere, Rand."

"No."

She came to him, a sway in her walk that made him feel as if he had something caught in his throat. "All I want is to see it in the light of day. I won't even touch it. You hold it. It would be something for me to remember, you holding the Horn of Valere in your hands." She took his hands as she said it; her touch made his skin tingle and his mouth go dry.

Something to remember—when she had gone. . . . He could close the dagger up again as soon as the Horn was out of the chest. It would be something to hold the Horn in his hands where he could see it in the light.

He wished he knew more of the Prophecies of the Dragon. The one time he heard a merchant's guard telling a part of it, back in Emond's Field, Nynaeve had broken a broom across the man's shoulders. None of the little he had heard mentioned the Horn of Valere.

Aes Sedai trying to make me do what they want. Selene was still gazing intently into his eyes, her face so young and beautiful that he wanted to kiss her despite what he was thinking. He had never seen an Aes Sedai act the way she did, and she looked young, not ageless. *A girl my age couldn't be Aes Sedai. But. . . .*

"Selene," he said softly, "*are* you an Aes Sedai?"

"Aes Sedai," she almost spat, flinging his hands away. "Aes Sedai! Always you hurl that at me!" She took a deep breath and smoothed her dress, as if gathering herself. "I am what and who I am. And I am no Aes Sedai!" And she wrapped herself in a silent coldness that made even the morning sun seem chill.

Loial and Hurin bore it all with as good a grace as they could manage, trying to make conversation and hiding their embarrassment when she froze them with a look. They rode on.

By the time they made camp that night beside a mountain stream that provided fish for their supper, Selene seemed to have regained some of her temper, chatting with the Ogier about books, speaking kindly to Hurin.

She barely spoke to Rand, though, unless he spoke first, either that evening or the following day as they rode through mountains that reared on either side of them like huge, jagged gray walls, ever climbing. But whenever he looked at her, she was watching him and smiling. Sometimes it was the sort of smile that made him smile back, sometimes the sort that made him clear his throat and blush at his own thoughts, and sometimes the mysterious, knowing smile that Egwene sometimes wore. It was a kind of smile that always put his back up—but at least it was a smile.

She can't *be Aes Sedai.*

The way began to slope downwards, and with the promise of twilight in the air, Kinslayer's Dagger at last gave way to hills, rolling and round, with more brush than trees, more thickets than forest. There was no road, just a dirt track, such as might be used by a few carts now and again. Fields carved some of the hills into terraces, fields full of crops but empty of people at this hour. None of the scattered farm buildings lay close enough to the path they rode for Rand to make out more than that they were all made of stone.

When he saw the village ahead, lights already twinkled in a few windows against the coming of night.

"We'll sleep in beds tonight," he said.

"That I will enjoy, Lord Rand." Hurin laughed. Loial nodded agreement.

"A village inn," Selene sniffed. "Dirty, no doubt, and full of unwashed men swilling ale. Why can't we sleep under the stars again? I find I enjoy sleeping under the stars."

"You would not enjoy it if Fain caught up with us while we slept," Rand said, "him and those Trollocs. He's coming after me, Selene. After the Horn, too, but it is me he can find. Why do you think I've kept such a close watch these past nights?"

"If Fain catches us, you will deal with him." Her voice was coolly confident. "And there could be Darkfriends in the village, too."

"But even if they knew who we are, they can't do much with the rest of the villagers around. Not unless you think everyone in the village is a Darkfriend."

"And if they discover you carry the Horn? Whether you want greatness or not, even farmers dream of it."

"She is right, Rand," Loial said. "I fear even farmers might want to take it."

"Unroll your blanket, Loial, and throw it over the chest. Keep it covered." Loial complied, and Rand nodded. It was obvious there was a box or chest beneath the Ogier's striped blanket, but nothing suggested it was more than a travel chest. "My Lady's chest of clothes," Rand said with a grin and a bow.

Selene met his sally with silence and an unreadable look. After a moment, they started on again.

Almost immediately, off to Rand's left, a glitter from the setting sun reflected from something on the ground. Something large. Something very large, by the light it threw up. Curious, he turned his horse that way.

"My Lord?" Hurin said. "The village?"

"I just want to see this first," Rand said. *It's brighter than sunlight on water. What can it be?*

His eyes on the reflection, he was surprised when Red suddenly stopped. On the point of urging the bay on, he realized that they stood on the edge of a clay precipice, above a huge excavation. Most of the hill had been dug away to a depth of easily a hundred paces. Certainly more than one hill had vanished, and maybe some farmers' fields, for the hole was at least ten times as wide as it was deep. The far side appeared to have been packed hard to a ramp. There were men on the bottom, a dozen of them, getting a fire started; down there, night was already descending. Here and there among them armor turned the light, and swords swung at their sides. He hardly glanced at them.

Out of the clay at the bottom of the pit slanted a gigantic stone hand holding a crystal sphere, and it was this that shone with the last sunlight. Rand gaped at the size of it, a smooth ball—he was sure not so much as a scratch marred its surface—at least twenty paces through.

Some distance away from the hand, a stone face in proportion had been uncovered. A bearded man's face, it thrust out of the soil with the dignity of vast years; the broad features seemed to hold wisdom and knowledge.

Unsummoned, the void formed, whole and complete in an instant, *saidin* glowing, beckoning. So intent was he on the face and the hand that he did not even realize what had happened. He had once heard a ship captain speak of a giant hand holding a huge crystal sphere; Bayle Domon had claimed it stuck out of a hill on the island of Tremalking.

"This is dangerous," Selene said. "Come away, Rand."

"I believe I can find a way down there," he said absently. *Saidin* sang to him. The huge ball seemed to glow white with the light of the sinking sun. It seemed to him that in the depths of the crystal, light swirled and danced in time to the song of *saidin*. He wondered why the men below did not appear to notice.

Selene rode close and took hold of his arm. "Please, Rand, you must come away." He looked at her hand, puzzled, then followed her arm up to her face. She seemed genuinely worried, perhaps even afraid. "If this bank doesn't give way beneath our horses and break our necks with the fall, those men are guards, and no one puts guards on something they wish every passerby to examine. What good will it do you to avoid Fain, if some lord's guards arrest you? Come away."

Suddenly—a drifting, distant thought—he realized that the void surrounded him. *Saidin* sang, and the sphere pulsed—even without looking, he could *feel* it—and the thought came that if he sang the song *saidin* sang, that huge stone face would open its mouth and sing with him. With him and with *saidin*. All one.

"Please, Rand," Selene said. "I will go to the village with you. I won't mention the Horn again. Only come away!"

He released the void . . . and it did not go. *Saidin* crooned, and the light in the sphere beat like a heart. Like his heart. Loial, Hurin, Selene, they all stared at him, but they seemed oblivious to the glorious blaze from the crystal. He tried to push the void away. It held like granite; he floated in an emptiness as hard as stone. The song of *saidin,* the song of the sphere, he could feel them quivering along his bones. Grimly, he refused to give in, reached deep inside himself . . . *I will not. . . .*

"Rand." He did not know whose voice it was.

. . . reached for the core of who he was, the core of what he was . . .

. . . *will not . . .*

"Rand." The song filled him, filled the emptiness.

. . . touched stone, hot from a pitiless sun, cold from a merciless night. . . .

. . . *not . . .*

Light filled him, blinded him.

"Till shade is gone," he mumbled, "till water is gone . . ."

Power filled him. He was one with the sphere.

". . . into the Shadow with teeth bared . . ."

The power was his. The Power was his.

". . . to spit in Sightblinder's eye . . ."

Power to Break the World.

". . . on the last day!" It came out as a shout, and the void was gone. Red shied at his cry; clay crumbled under the stallion's hoof, spilling into the pit. The big bay went to his knees. Rand leaned forward, gathering the reins, and Red scrambled to safety, away from the edge.

They were all staring at him, he saw. Selene, Loial, Hurin, all of them. "What happened?" *The void.* . . . He touched his forehead. The void had not gone when he released it, and the glow of *saidin* had grown stronger, and. . . . He could not remember anything more. *Saidin.* He felt cold. "Did I . . . do something?" He frowned, trying to remember. "Did I say something?"

"You just sat there stiff as a statue," Loial said, "mumbling to yourself no matter what anyone said. I couldn't make out what you were saying, not until you shouted 'day!' loud enough to wake the dead and nearly put your horse over the edge. Are you ill? You're acting more and more oddly every day."

"I'm not sick," Rand said harshly, then softened it. "I am all right, Loial." Selene watched him warily.

From the pit came the sound of men calling, the words indistinguishable.

"Lord Rand," Hurin said, "I think those guards have finally noticed us. If they know a way up this side, they could be here any minute."

"Yes," Selene said. "Let us leave here quickly."

Rand glanced at the excavation, then away again, quickly. The great crystal held nothing except reflected light from the evening sun, but he did not want to look at it. He could almost remember . . . *something* about the sphere. "I don't see any reason to wait for them. We didn't do anything. Let's find an inn." He turned Red toward the village, and they soon left pit and shouting guards behind.

As many villages did, Tremonsien covered the top of a hill, but like the farms they had passed, this hill had been sculpted into terraces with stone retaining walls. Square stone houses sat on precise plots of land, with exact gardens behind, along a few straight streets that crossed each other at right angles. The necessity of a curve to streets going around the hill seemed begrudged.

Yet the people seemed open and friendly enough, pausing to nod to each other as they hurried about their last chores before nightfall. They were a short folk—none taller than Rand's shoulder, and few as tall as Hurin—with dark eyes and pale, narrow faces, and dressed in dark clothes except for a few who wore slashes of color across the chest. Smells of cooking—oddly spiced, to Rand's nose—filled the air, though a handful of goodwives still hung over their doors to talk; the doors were split, so the top could stand open while the bottom was closed. The people eyed the newcomers curiously, with no sign of hostility. A few stared a moment longer at Loial, an Ogier walking alongside a horse as big as a Dhurran stallion, but never more than a moment longer.

The inn, at the very top of the hill, was stone like every other building in the town, and plainly marked by a painted sign hanging over the wide doors. The Nine Rings. Rand swung down with a smile and tied Red to one of the hitching posts out front. "The Nine Rings" had been one of his favorite adventure stories when he was a boy; he supposed it still was.

Selene still seemed uneasy when he helped her dismount. "Are you all right?" he asked. "I didn't frighten you back there, did I? Red would never fall over a cliff with me." He wondered what had really happened.

"You terrified me," she said in a tight voice, "and I do not frighten easily. You could have killed yourself, killed. . . ." She smoothed her dress. "Ride with me. Tonight. Now. Bring the Horn, and I will stay by your side forever. Think of it. Me by your side, and the Horn of Valere in your hands. And that will only be the beginning, I promise. What more could you ask for?"

Rand shook his head. "I can't, Selene. The Horn. . . ." He looked around. A man looked out his window across the way, then twitched the curtains closed; evening darkened the street, and there was no one else in sight now except Loial and Hurin. "The Horn is not mine. I told you that." She turned her back on him, her white cloak walling him off as effectively as bricks.

CHAPTER 21

The Nine Rings

AND EXPECTED THE COMMON ROOM TO BE empty, since it was nearly suppertime, but half a dozen men crowded one table, dicing among their jacks of ale, and another sat by himself over a meal. Though the dicers carried no weapons in sight and wore no armor, only plain coats and breeches of dark blue, something about the way they held themselves told Rand they were soldiers. His eyes went to the solitary man. An officer, with the tops of his high boots turned down, and his sword propped against the table beside his chair. A single slash of red and one of yellow crossed the chest of the officer's blue coat from shoulder to shoulder, and the front of his head was shaved, though his black hair hung long in the back. The soldiers' hair was clipped short, as if it all had been cut under the same bowl. All seven turned to look as Rand and the others came in.

The innkeeper was a lean woman with a long nose and graying hair, but her wrinkles seemed part of her ready smile more than anything else. She came bustling up, wiping her hands on a spotless white apron. "Good even to you"—her quick eyes took in Rand's gold-embroidered red coat, and Selene's fine white dress—"my Lord, my Lady. I am Maglin Madwen, my Lord. Be welcome to The Nine Rings. And an Ogier. Not many of your kind come this way, friend Ogier. Would you be up from Stedding Tsofu, then?"

Loial managed an awkward half bow under the weight of the chest. "No, good innkeeper. I come the other way, from the Borderlands."

"From the Borderlands, you say. Well. And you, my Lord? Forgive me for asking, but you've not the look of the Borderlands, if you don't mind my saying it."

"I'm from the Two Rivers, Mistress Madwen, in Andor." He glanced at Selene—she did not seem to admit he existed; her level look barely admitted that the room existed, or anyone in it. "The Lady Selene is from Cairhien, from the capital, and I am from Andor."

"As you say, my Lord." Mistress Madwen's glance flickered to Rand's sword; the bronze herons were plain on scabbard and hilt. She frowned slightly, but her face was clear again in a blink. "You'll be wanting a meal for yourself and your beautiful Lady, and your followers. And rooms, I expect. I'll have your horses seen to. I've a good table for you, right this way, and pork with yellow peppers on the fire. Would you be hunting the Horn of Valere, then, my Lord, you and your Lady?"

In the act of following her, Rand almost stumbled. "No! Why would you think we were?"

"No offense, my Lord. We've had two through here already, all polished to look like heroes—not to suggest anything of the kind about you, my Lord—in the last month. Not many strangers come here, except traders up from the capital to buy oats and barley. I'd not suppose the Hunt has left Illian, yet, but maybe some don't think they really need the blessing, and they'll get a jump on the others by missing it."

"We are not hunting the Horn, mistress." Rand did not glance at the bundle in Loial's arms; the blanket with its colorful stripes hung bunched over the Ogier's thick arms and disguised the chest well. "We surely are not. We are on our way to the capital."

"As you say, my Lord. Forgive me for asking, but is your Lady well?"

Selene looked at her, and spoke for the first time. "I am quite well." Her voice left a chill in the air that stifled talk for a moment.

"You're not Cairhienin, Mistress Madwen," Hurin said suddenly. Burdened down with their saddlebags and Rand's bundle, he looked like a walking baggage cart. "Pardon, but you don't sound it."

Mistress Madwen's eyebrows rose, and she shot a glance at Rand, then grinned. "I should have known you'd let your man speak freely, but I've grown used to—" Her glance darted toward the officer, who had gone back to his own meal. "Light, no, I'm not Cairhienin, but for my sins, I married one. Twenty-three years I lived with him, and when he died on me—the Light shine on him—I was all ready to go back to Lugard, but he had the last laugh, he did. He left me the inn, and his brother the money, when I was sure it would be the other way round. Tricksome and scheming, Barin was, like every man I've ever known, Cairhienin most of all. Will you be seated, my Lord? My Lady?"

The innkeeper gave a surprised blink when Hurin sat at table with them—an Ogier, it seemed, was one thing, but Hurin was clearly a servant in her eyes. With another quick look at Rand, she bustled off to the kitchens, and soon serving girls came with their meal, giggling and staring at the lord and the lady, and the Ogier, till Mistress Madwen chased them back to their work.

At first, Rand stared at his food doubtfully. The pork was cut in small bits, mixed with long strips of yellow peppers, and peas, and a number of vegetables and things he did not recognize, all in some sort of clear, thick sauce. It smelled sweet and sharp, both at the same time. Selene only picked at hers, but Loial was eating with a will.

Hurin grinned at Rand over his fork. "They spice their food oddly, Cairhienin do, Lord Rand, but for all that, it's not bad."

"It won't bite you, Rand," Loial added.

Rand took a hesitant mouthful, and almost gasped. It tasted just as it smelled, sweet and sharp together, the pork crisp on the outside and tender inside, a dozen different flavors, spices, all blending and contrasting. It tasted like nothing he had ever put in his mouth before. It tasted wonderful. He cleaned his plate, and when Mistress Madwen returned with the serving girls to clear away, he nearly asked for more the way Loial did. Selene's was still half full, but she motioned curtly for one of the girls to take it.

"A pleasure, friend Ogier." The innkeeper smiled. "It takes a lot to fill up one of you. Catrine, bring another helping, and be quick." One of the girls darted away. Mistress Madwen turned her smile on Rand. "My Lord, I had a man here who played the bittern, but he married a girl off one of the farms, and she has him strumming reins behind a plow, now. I couldn't help noticing what looks like a flute case sticking out of your man's bundle. Since my musician's gone, would you let your man favor us with a little music?"

Hurin looked embarrassed.

"He doesn't play," Rand explained. "I do."

The woman blinked. It appeared lords did not play the flute, at least not in Cairhien. "I withdraw the request, my Lord. Light's own truth, I meant no offense, I assure you. I'd never ask one such as yourself to be playing in a common room."

Rand hesitated only a moment. It had been too long since he had practiced the flute rather than the sword, and the coins in his pouch would not last forever. Once he was rid of his fancy clothes—once he turned the Horn over to Ingtar and the dagger over to Mat—he would need the flute to earn his supper again while he searched for somewhere safe from Aes Sedai. *And safe from myself? Something* did *happen back there. What?*

"I don't mind," he said. "Hurin, hand me the case. Just slide it out." There was no need to show a gleeman's cloak; enough unspoken questions shone in Mistress Madwen's dark eyes as it was.

Worked gold chased with silver, the instrument looked the sort a lord might play, if lords anywhere played the flute. The heron branded on his right palm did not interfere with his fingering. Selene's salves had worked so well he hardly thought of the brand unless he saw it. Yet it was in his thoughts now, and unconsciously he began to play "Heron on the Wing."

Hurin bobbed his head to the tune, and Loial beat time on the table with a thick finger. Selene looked at Rand as if wondering what he was—*I'm not a lord, my Lady. I'm a shepherd, and I play the flute in common rooms*—but the soldiers turned from their talk to listen, and the officer closed the wooden cover of the book he had begun reading. Selene's steady gaze struck a stubborn spark inside Rand. Determinedly he avoided any song that might fit in a palace, or a lord's manor. He played "Only One Bucket of Water" and "The Old Two Rivers Leaf," "Old Jak's Up a Tree" and "Goodman Priket's Pipe."

With the last, the six soldiers began to sing in raucous tones, though not the words Rand knew.

> "We rode down to River Iralell
> just to see the Tairen come.
> We stood along the riverbank
> with the rising of the sun.
> Their horses blacked the summer plain,
> their banners blacked the sky.

> But we stood our ground on the banks
>   of River Iralell.
> Oh, we stood our ground.
> Yes, we stood our ground.
> Stood our ground along the river in the
>   morning."

It was not the first time that Rand had discovered a tune had different words and different names in different lands, sometimes even in villages in the same land. He played along with them until they let the words die away, slapping each other's shoulders and making rude comments on one another's singing.

When Rand lowered the flute, the officer rose and made a sharp gesture. The soldiers fell silent in mid-laugh, scraped back their chairs to bow to the officer with hand on breast—and to Rand— and left without a backwards look.

The officer came to Rand's table and bowed, hand to heart; the shaven front of his head looked as if he had dusted it with white powder. "Grace favor you, my Lord. I trust they did not bother you, singing as they did. They are a common sort, but they meant no insult, I assure you. I am Aldrin Caldevwin, my Lord. Captain in His Majesty's Service, the Light illumine him." His eyes slid over Rand's sword; Rand had the feeling Caldevwin had noticed the herons as soon as he came in.

"They didn't insult me." The officer's accent reminded him of Moiraine's, precise and every word pronounced to its full. *Did she really let me go? I wonder if she's following me. Or waiting for me.* "Sit down, Captain. Please." Caldevwin drew a chair from another table. "Tell me, Captain, if you don't mind. Have you seen any other strangers recently? A lady, short and slender, and a fighting man with blue eyes. He's tall, and sometimes he wears his sword on his back."

"I have seen no strangers at all," he said, lowering himself stiffly to his seat. "Saving yourself and your Lady, my Lord. Few of the nobility ever come here." His eyes flicked toward Loial with a minute frown; Hurin he ignored for a servant.

"It was only a thought."

"Under the Light, my Lord, I mean no disrespect, but may I hear your name? We have so few strangers here that I find I wish to know every one."

Rand gave it—he claimed no title, but the officer seemed not to notice—and said as he had to the innkeeper, "From the Two Rivers, in Andor."

"A wondrous place I have heard, Lord Rand—I may call you so?—and fine men, the Andormen. No Cairhienin has ever worn a blademaster's sword so young as you. I met some Andormen, once, the Captain-General of the Queen's Guards among them. I do not remember his name; an embarrassment. Perhaps you could favor me with it?"

Rand was conscious of the serving girls in the background, beginning to clean and sweep. Caldevwin seemed only to be making conversation, but there was a probing quality to his look. "Gareth Bryne."

"Of course. Young, to hold so much responsibility."

Rand kept his voice level. "Gareth Bryne has enough gray in his hair to be your father, Captain."

"Forgive me, my Lord Rand. I meant to say that he came to it young." Caldevwin turned to Selene, and for a moment he only stared. He shook himself, finally, as if coming out of a trance. "Forgive me for looking at you so, my Lady, and forgive me for speaking so, but Grace has surely favored you. Will you give me a name to put to such beauty?"

Just as Selene opened her mouth, one of the serving girls let out a cry and dropped a lamp she was taking down from a shelf. Oil splattered, and caught in a pool of flame on the floor. Rand leaped to his feet along with the others at the table, but before any of them could move, Mistress Madwen appeared, and she and the girl smothered the flames with their aprons.

"I have told you to be careful, Catrine," the innkeeper said, shaking her now-smutty apron under the girl's nose. "You'll be burning the inn down, and yourself in it."

The girl seemed on the point of tears. "I *was* being careful, Mistress, but I had such a twinge in my arm."

Mistress Madwen threw up her hands. "You always have some excuse, and you still break more dishes than all the rest. Ah, it's all right. Clean it up, and don't burn yourself," The innkeeper turned to Rand and the others, all still standing around the table. "I hope none of you take this amiss. The girl really won't burn down the inn. She's hard on the dishes when she starts mooning over some young fellow, but she's never mishandled a lamp before."

"I would like to be shown to my room. I do not feel well after all." Selene spoke in careful tones, as though uncertain of her stomach, but despite that she looked and sounded as cool and calm as ever. "The journey, and the fire."

The innkeeper clucked like a mother hen. "Of course, my Lady. I have a fine room for you and your Lord. Shall I fetch Mother Caredwain? She has a fine hand with soothing herbs."

Selene's voice sharpened. "No. And I wish a room by myself."

Mistress Madwen glanced at Rand, but the next moment she was bowing Selene solicitously toward the stairs. "As you wish, my Lady. Lidan, fetch the Lady's things like a good girl, now." One of the serving girls ran to take Selene's saddlebags from Hurin, and the women disappeared upstairs, Selene stiff-backed and silent.

Caldevwin stared after them until they were gone, then shook himself again. He waited until Rand had seated himself before taking his chair again. "Forgive me, my Lord Rand, for staring so at your Lady, but Grace has surely favored you in her. I mean no insult."

"None taken," Rand said. He wondered if every man felt the way he did when they looked at Selene. "As I was riding to the village, Captain, I saw a huge sphere. Crystal, it seemed. What is it?"

The Cairhienin's eyes sharpened. "It is part of the statue, my Lord Rand," he said slowly. His gaze flickered toward Loial; for an instant he seemed to be considering something new.

"Statue? I saw a hand, and a face, too. It must be huge."

"It is, my Lord Rand. And old." Caldevwin paused. "From the Age of Legends, so I am told."

Rand felt a chill. The Age of Legends, when use of the One Power was everywhere, if the stories could be believed. *What happened there? I know there was something.*

"The Age of Legends," Loial said. "Yes, it must be. No one has done work so vast since. A great piece of work to dig that up, Captain." Hurin sat silently, as if he not only was not listening, but was not there at all.

Caldevwin nodded reluctantly. "I have five hundred laborers in camp beyond the diggings, and even so it will be past summer's end before we have it clear. They are men from the Foregate. Half my work is to keep them digging, and the other half to keep them out of this village. Foregaters have a fondness for drinking and carousing, you understand, and these people lead quiet lives." His tone said his sympathies were all with the villagers.

Rand nodded. He had no interest in Foregaters, whoever they were. "What will you do with it?" The captain hesitated, but Rand only looked back at him until he spoke.

"Galldrian himself has ordered that it be taken to the capital."

Loial blinked. "A very great piece of work, that. I am not sure how something that big could be moved so far."

"His Majesty has ordered it," Caldevwin said sharply. "It will be set up outside the city, a monument to the greatness of Cairhien and of House Riatin. Ogier are not the only ones who know how to move stone." Loial looked abashed, and the captain visibly calmed himself. "Your pardon, friend Ogier. I spoke in haste, and rudely." He still sounded a little gruff. "Will you be staying in Tremonsien long, my Lord Rand?"

"We leave in the morning," Rand said. "We are going to Cairhien."

"As it happens, I am sending some of my men back to the city tomorrow. I must rotate them; they grow stale after too long watching men swing picks and shovels. You will not mind if they ride in your company?" He put it as a question, but as if acceptance were a foregone conclusion. Mistress Madwen appeared on the stairs, and he rose. "If you will excuse me, my Lord Rand, I must be up early. Until the morning, then. Grace favor you." He bowed to Rand, nodded to Loial, and left.

As the doors closed behind the Cairhienin, the innkeeper came to the table.

"I have your Lady settled, my Lord. And I've good rooms prepared for you and your man, and you, friend Ogier." She paused, studying Rand. "Forgive me if I overstep myself, my Lord, but I think I can speak freely to a lord who lets his man speak up. If I'm wrong . . . well, I mean no insult. For twenty-three years Barin Madwen and I were arguing when we weren't kissing, so to speak. That's by way of saying I have some experience. Right now, you're thinking your Lady never wants to see you again, but it's my way of thinking that if you tap on her door tonight, she'll be taking you in. Smile and say it was your fault, whether it was or not."

Rand cleared his throat and hoped his face was not turning red. *Light, Egwene would kill me if she knew I'd even thought of it. And Selene would kill me if I did it. Or would she?* That did make his cheeks burn. "I . . . thank you for your suggestion, Mistress Madwen. The rooms. . . ." He avoided looking at the blanket-covered chest by Loial's chair; they did not dare leave it without someone awake and guarding it. "We three will all sleep in the same room."

The innkeeper looked startled, but she recovered quickly. "As you wish, my Lord. This way, if you please."

Rand followed her up the stairs. Loial carried the chest under its blanket—the stairs groaned under the weight of him and the chest together, but the innkeeper seemed to think it was just an Ogier's bulk—and Hurin still carried all the saddlebags and the bundled cloak with the harp and flute.

Mistress Madwen had a third bed brought in and hastily assembled and made up. One of the beds already there stretched nearly from wall to wall in length, and had obviously been meant for Loial from the start. There was barely room to walk between the beds. As soon as the innkeeper was gone, Rand turned to the others. Loial had pushed the still-covered chest under his bed and was trying the mattress. Hurin was setting out the saddlebags.

"Do either of you know why that captain was so suspicious of us? He was, I'm sure of it." He shook his head. "I almost think he thought we might steal that statue, the way he was talking."

"*Daes Dae'mar,* Lord Rand," Hurin said. "The Great Game. The Game of Houses, some call it. This Caldevwin thinks you must be doing something to your advantage or you wouldn't be here. And whatever you're doing might be to his disadvantage, so he has to be careful."

Rand shook his head. " 'The Great Game'? What game?"

"It isn't a game at all, Rand," Loial said from his bed. He had pulled a book from his pocket, but it lay unopened on his chest. "I don't know much about it—Ogier don't do such things—but I have heard of it. The nobles and the noble Houses maneuver for advantage. They do things they think will help them, or hurt an enemy, or both. Usually, it's all done in secrecy, or if not, they try to make it seem as if they're doing something other than what they are." He gave one tufted ear a puzzled scratch. "Even knowing what it is, I don't understand it. Elder Haman always said it would take a greater mind than his to understand the things humans do, and I don't know many as intelligent as Elder Haman. You humans are odd."

Hurin gave the Ogier a slanted look, but he said, "He has the right of *Daes Dae'mar,* Lord Rand. Cairhienin play it more than most, though all southerners do."

"These soldiers in the morning," Rand said. "Are they part of Caldevwin playing this Great Game? We can't afford to get mixed in anything like that." There was no need to mention the Horn. They were all too aware of its presence.

Loial shook his head. "I don't know, Rand. He's human, so it could mean anything."

"Hurin?"

"I don't know, either." Hurin sounded as worried as the Ogier looked. "He could be doing just what he said, or. . . . That's the way of the Game of Houses. You never know. I spent most of my time in Cairhien in the Foregate, Lord Rand, and I don't know much about Cairhienin nobles, but—well, *Daes Dae'mar* can be dangerous anywhere, but especially in Cairhien, I've heard." He brightened suddenly. "The Lady Selene, Lord Rand. She'll know better than me or the Builder. You can ask her in the morning."

But in the morning, Selene was gone. When Rand went down to the common room, Mistress Madwen handed him a sealed parchment. "If you'll forgive me, my Lord, you should have listened to me. You should have tapped on your Lady's door."

Rand waited until she went away before he broke the white wax seal. The wax had been impressed with a crescent moon and stars.

I must leave you for a time. There are too many people here, and I do not like Caldevwin. I will await you in Cairhien. Never think that I am too far from you. You will be in my thoughts always, as I know that I am in yours.

It was not signed, but that elegant, flowing script had the look of Selene.

He folded it carefully and put it in his pocket before going outside, where Hurin had the horses waiting.

Captain Caldevwin was there, too, with another, younger officer and fifty mounted soldiers crowding the street. The two officers were bare-headed, but wore steel-backed gauntlets, and gold-worked breastplates strapped over their blue coats. A short staff was fastened to the harness on each officer's back, bearing a small, stiff blue banner above his head. Caldevwin's banner bore a single white star, while the younger man's was crossed by two white bars. They were a sharp contrast to the soldiers in their plain armor and helmets that looked like bells with metal cut away to expose their faces.

Caldevwin bowed as Rand came out of the inn. "Good morning to you, my Lord Rand. This is Elricain Tavolin, who will command your escort, if I may call it that." The other officer bowed; his head was shaved as Caldevwin's was. He did not speak.

"An escort will be welcome, Captain," Rand said, managing to sound at ease. Fain would not try anything against fifty soldiers, but Rand wished he could be certain they were only an escort.

The captain eyed Loial, on his way to his horse with the blanket-covered chest. "A heavy burden, Ogier."

Loial almost missed a step. "I never like to be far from my books, Captain." His wide mouth flashed teeth in a self-conscious grin, and he hurried to strap the chest onto his saddle.

Caldevwin looked around, frowning. "Your Lady is not down yet. And her fine animal is not here."

"She left already," Rand told him. "She had to go on to Cairhien quickly, during the night."

Caldevwin's eyebrows lifted. "During the night? But my men. . . . Forgive me, my Lord Rand." He drew the younger officer aside, whispering furiously.

"He had the inn watched, Lord Rand," Hurin whispered. "The Lady Selene must have gotten past them unseen somehow."

Rand climbed to Red's saddle with a grimace. If there had been any chance Caldevwin did not suspect them of something, it seemed Selene had finished it. "Too many people, she says," he muttered. "There'll be more people by far in Cairhien."

"You said something, my Lord?"

Rand looked up as Tavolin joined him, mounted on a tall, dust-colored gelding. Hurin was in his saddle, too, and Loial stood beside his big horse's head. The soldiers were formed up in ranks. Caldevwin was nowhere to be seen.

"Nothing is happening the way I expect," Rand said.

Tavolin gave him a brief smile, hardly more than a twitch of his lips. "Shall we ride, my Lord?"

The strange procession headed for the hard-packed road that led to the city of Cairhien.

GLOSSARY

A Note on Dates in This Glossary. Three systems of recording dates have been in general use since the Breaking of the World. The first recorded years After the Breaking (AB). Since the years of the Breaking and immediately after were years of almost total chaos, and since this calendar was adopted a good hundred years after the end of the Breaking, its starting point was arbitrarily assigned. At the end of the Trolloc Wars many records had been lost, so much so that there was argument about the exact year under the old system. A new calendar was therefore established, dating from the end of the Wars and celebrating the supposed freedom of the world from the Trolloc threat. This second calendar recorded each year as Free Year (FY). After the disruption, death, and destruction caused by the War of the Hundred Years, a third calendar came into being. This calendar, of the New Era (NE), is currently in use.

a'dam *(AYE-dam):* A device, consisting of a collar and a bracelet linked by a silvery metal leash, that may be used to control, against her will, any woman who can channel. The collar is worn by the *damane,* the bracelet by the *sul'dam. See also damane; sul'dam.*

Aes Sedai (EYEZ seh-DEYE): Wielders of the One Power. Since the Time of Madness, all surviving Aes Sedai are women. Widely distrusted and feared, even hated, they are blamed by many for the Breaking of the World, and are thought to meddle in the affairs of nations. At the same time, few rulers will be without an Aes Sedai advisor, even in lands where the existence of such a connection must be kept secret. *See also* Ajah; Amyrlin Seat; Time of Madness.

Agelmar; Lord Agelmar of House Jagad *(AGH-el-mar;* JAH-gad): Lord of Fal Dara. His sign is three running red foxes.

Age of Legends: The Age ended by the War of the Shadow and the Breaking of the World. A time when Aes Sedai performed wonders now only dreamed of. *See also* Wheel of Time; Breaking of the World; War of the Shadow.

Aiel (eye-EEL): The people of the Aiel Waste. Fierce and hardy. Also called Aielmen. They veil their faces before they kill, giving rise to the saying "acting like a black-veiled Aiel" to describe someone who is being violent. Deadly warriors with weapons or with nothing but their bare hands, they will not touch a sword. Their pipers play them into battle with the music of dances, and Aielmen call battle "the Dance." *See also* Aiel warrior societies; Aiel Waste.

Aiel warrior societies: Aiel warriors are all members of one of the warrior societies, such as the Stone Dogs, the Red Shields, or the Maidens of the Spear. Each society has its own customs, and sometimes specific duties. For example, Red Shields act as police. Stone Dogs often vow not to retreat once battle has been joined, and will die to the last man if necessary to fulfill this vow. The clans of the Aiel frequently fight among themselves, but members of the same society will not fight one another even if their clans are doing so. In this way, there are always lines of contact between the clans even when they are in open warfare. *See also* Aiel; Aiel Waste; *Far Dareis Mai.*

Aiel Waste: The harsh, rugged, and all-but-waterless land east of the Spine of the World. Few outsiders venture there, not only because water is almost impossible to find for one not born there, but because the Aiel consider themselves at war with all other peoples and do not welcome strangers.

Ajah (AH-jah): Societies among the Aes Sedai to which all Aes Sedai except the Amyrlin Seat belong. They are designated by colors: Blue, Red, White, Green, Brown, Yellow, and Gray. Each follows a specific philosophy of the use of the One Power and the purposes of the Aes Sedai. For example, the Red Ajah bends all its energies to finding men who are attempting to wield the Power and to gentling them. The Brown Ajah, on the other hand, forsakes involvement with the mundane world and dedicates itself to seeking knowledge. There are rumors (hotly denied, and never safely mentioned in front of any Aes Sedai) of a Black Ajah, dedicated to serving the Dark One.

Alanna Mosvani (ah-LAN-nah mos-VANH-nie): An Aes Sedai of the Green Ajah.

alantin *(ah-LANH-tin):* In the Old Tongue, "Brother;" short for *tia avende alantin,* "Brother to the Trees;" "Treebrother."

Alar (AYE-lahr): Eldest of the Elders of Stedding Tsofu.

Aldieb (ahl-DEEB): In the Old Tongue, "West Wind," the wind that brings the spring rains.

al'Meara, Nynaeve (ahl-MEER-ah, NIGH-neev): A woman from Emond's Field, in the Two Rivers district of Andor (AN-door).

al'Thor, Rand (ahl-THOR, RAND): A young man from Emond's Field, once a shepherd.

al'Vere, Egwene (ahl-VEER, eh-GWAIN): A young woman from Emond's Field.

Amalisa, Lady (ah-mah-LEE-sah): Shienaran of House Jagad; Lord Agelmar's sister.

Amyrlin Seat (AHM-ehr-lin SEAT): (1) The title of the leader of the Aes Sedai. Elected for life by the Hall of the Tower, the highest council of the Aes Sedai, which consists of three representatives (called Sitters) from each of the seven Ajahs. The Amyrlin Seat has, theoretically at least, almost supreme authority among the Aes Sedai, and ranks socially as the equal of a king or queen. A slightly less formal usage is simply the Amyrlin. (2) The throne upon which the leader of the Aes Sedai sits.

Anaiya (ah-NYE-yah): An Aes Sedai of the Blue Ajah.

angreal (anh-gree-AHL): A very rare object that allows anyone capable of channeling the One Power to handle a greater amount of the Power than would be safely possible unaided. Remnants of the Age of Legends, the means of their making is no longer known. Few remain in existence. *See also sa'angreal; ter'angreal.*

Arad Doman (AH-rahd do-MAHN): A nation on the Aryth Ocean.

Arafel (AH-rah-fehl): One of the Borderlands.

Avendesora *(AH-vehn-deh-SO-rah):* In the Old Tongue, "the Tree of Life." Mentioned in many stories and legends.

Aybara, Perrin (ay-BAHR-ah, PEHR-rihn): A young man from Emond's Field, formerly a blacksmith's apprentice.

Ba'alzamon (bah-AHL-zah-mon): In the Trolloc tongue, "Heart of the Dark." Believed to be the Trolloc name for the Dark One. *See also* Dark One; Trollocs.

Barthanes, Lord, of House Damodred (bahr-THAN-nehs): Cairhienin lord, second only to the king in power. His personal sign is the Charging Boar. The sign of House Damodred is the Crown and Tree.

Bel Tine (BEHL TINE): Spring festival celebrating the end of winter, the first sprouting of crops, and the birth of the first lambs.

Betrayer of Hope: See Ishamael.

Birgitte (ber-GEET-teh): Golden-haired heroine of legend and a hundred gleemen's tales, she had a silver bow and silver arrows, with which she never missed.

bittern (BIHT-tehrn): A musical instrument that may have six, nine, or twelve strings, and is held flat on the knees and played by plucking or strumming.

Blasted Lands: Desolated lands surrounding Shayol Ghul, beyond the Great Blight.

Blight, the: *See* Great Blight, the.

Borderlands, the: The nations bordering the Great Blight. Saldaea, Arafel, Kandor, and Shienar.

Bornhald, Geofram (BOHRN-hahld, JEHF-rahm): A Lord Captain of the Children of the Light.

Breaking of the World, the: During the Time of Madness, male Aes Sedai who had gone insane, and who could wield the One Power to a degree now unknown, changed the face of the earth. They caused great earthquakes, leveled old mountain ranges and raised new mountains, lifted dry land where seas had been and made the ocean rush in where dry land had been. Many parts of the world were completely depopulated, and the survivors were scattered like dust on the wind. This destruction is remembered in stories, legends, and history as the Breaking of the World. *See also* Time of Madness.

Byar, Jaret (BY-ahr, JAH-ret): An officer of the Children of the Light.

Caemlyn (KAYM-lihn): The capital city of Andor.

Cairhien (KEYE-ree-EHN): Both a nation along the Spine of the World and the capital city of that nation. The city was burned and looted during the Aiel War (976–978 NE). The sign of Cairhien is a many-rayed golden sun rising from the bottom of a field of sky blue.

Caralain (KAH-rah-layn): One of the nations wrung from Artur Hawkwing's empire during the War of the Hundred Years. It weakened thereafter, and the last traces vanished about 500 NE.

Cauthon, Mat (CAW-thon, MAT): A young man from the Two Rivers. Full name: Matrim (MAT-rihm) Cauthon.

channel: (verb) To control the flow of the One Power. *See also* One Power.

Children of the Light: A society holding strict ascetic beliefs, dedicated to the defeat of the Dark One and the destruction of all Darkfriends. Founded during the War of the Hundred Years by Lothair Mantelar (LOH-thayr MAHN-tee-LAHR) to proselytize against the increasing numbers of Darkfriends, they evolved during the war into a completely military organization, extremely rigid in their beliefs, and completely certain that only they know the truth and the right. They hate Aes Sedai, considering them, and any who support or befriend them, Darkfriends. They are known disparagingly as Whitecloaks. Their sign is a golden sunburst on a field of white.

Chronicles, Keeper of the: Second in authority to the Amyrlin Seat among the Aes Sedai, she also acts as secretary to the Amyrlin. Chosen for life by the Hall of the Tower, and usually of the same Ajah as the Amyrlin. *See also* Amyrlin Seat; Ajah.

Corenne *(koh-REEN-neh):* In the Old Tongue, "Return," or "the Return.

Covenant of the Ten Nations: A union formed in the centuries after the Breaking of the World when nations were first re-created (circa 300 AB). Dedicated to the defeat of the Dark One. Broken apart by the Trolloc Wars. *See also* Trolloc Wars.

cuendillar (CWAIN-der-yar): Also known as heartstone. *See* heartstone.

Daes Dae'mar (DAH-ess day-MAR): The Great Game, also known as the Game of Houses. Name given the scheming, plots, and manipulations for advantage by the noble Houses. Great value is given to subtlety, to aiming at one thing while seeming to aim at another, and to achieving ends with the least visible effort.

Dai Shan (DYE SHAN): A title in the Borderlands meaning Diademed Battle Lord. *See also* Borderlands.

damane (dah-MAHN-ee): In the Old Tongue, "Leashed Ones." Women who can channel who are held prisoner by *a'dam* and used by the Seanchan for many purposes, chiefest of these being as weapons in battle. *See also* Seanchan; *a'dam; sul'dam.*

Damodred, Lord Galadedrid (DAHM-oh-drehd, gah-LAHD-eh-drihd): Half-brother to Elayne and Gawyn. His sign is a winged silver sword, point down.

Darkfriends: Those who follow the Dark One and believe they will gain great power and rewards, and even immortality, when he is freed from his prison.

Dark One: Most common name, used in every land, for Shai'tan. The source of evil, antithesis of the Creator. Imprisoned by the Creator at the moment of Creation in a prison at Shayol Ghul. An attempt to free him from that prison brought about the War of the

Shadow, the tainting of *saidin,* the Breaking of the World, and the end of the Age of Legends.

Dark One, naming the: Saying the true name of the Dark One (Shai'tan) draws his attention, inevitably bringing ill fortune at best, disaster at worst. For that reason, many euphemisms are used, among them the Dark One, Father of Lies, Sightblinder, Lord of the Grave, Shepherd of the Night, Heartsbane, Heartfang, Grassburner, and Leafblighter. Someone who seems to be inviting ill fortune is often said to be "naming the Dark One."

Daughter-Heir: Title of the heir to the throne of Andor. The eldest daughter of the queen succeeds her mother on the throne. Without a surviving daughter, the throne goes to the nearest female blood relation of the queen.

Daughter of the Night: *See* Lanfear.

Dome of Truth: Great audience hall of the Children of the Light, located in Amador (AH-mah-door), the capital of Amadicia (AH-mah-DEE-cee-ah). There is a King of Amadicia, but the Children rule in all but name. *See also* Children of the Light.

Do Miere A'vron (DOH me-EHR a-VRAWN): *See* Watchers Over the Waves.

Domon, Bayle (DOH-mon, BAIL): The captain of the *Spray,* who collects old things.

Draghkar (DRAGH-kahr): A creature of the Dark One, made originally by twisting human stock. A Draghkar appears to be a large man with bat-like wings, whose skin is too pale and whose eyes are too large. The Draghkar's song can draw its prey to it, suppressing the victim's will. There is a saying: "The kiss of the Draghkar is death." It does not bite, but its kiss will consume first the soul of its victim, and then its life.

Dragon, false: Occasionally men claim to be the Dragon Reborn, and sometimes one of them gains following enough to require an army to put it down. Some have begun wars that involved many nations. Over the centuries most of these have been men unable to channel the One Power, but a few could do so. All, however, either disappeared or were captured or killed without fulfilling any of the Prophecies concerning the Rebirth of the Dragon. These men are called false Dragons. Among those who could channel, the most powerful were Raolin Darksbane (335–36AB), Yurian Stonebow (circa 1300–1308 AB), Davian (FY 351), Guaire Amalasan (FY 939–43), and Logain (997 NE). *See also* Dragon Reborn.

Dragon, Prophecies of the: Little known and seldom spoken of, the Prophecies, given in *The Karaethon Cycle,* foretell that the Dark One will be freed again to touch the world. And that Lews Therin Telamon, the Dragon, Breaker of the World, will be reborn to fight Tarmon Gai'don, the Last Battle against the Shadow. *See also* Dragon, the.

Dragon, the: The name by which Lews Therin Telamon was known during the War of the Shadow. In the madness that overtook all male Aes Sedai, Lews Therin killed every living person who carried any of his blood, as well as everyone he loved, thus earning the name Kinslayer. *See also* Dragon Reborn; Dragon, Prophecies of the.

Dragon Reborn: According to prophecy and legend the Dragon will be born again at mankind's greatest hour of need to save the world. This is not something people look forward to, both because the Prophecies say the Dragon Reborn will bring a new Breaking to the world and because Lews Therin Kinslayer, the Dragon, is a name to make men shudder, even more than three thousand years after his death. *See also* Dragon, the; Dragon, false; Dragon, Prophecies of the.

Dragon's Fang, the: *A* stylized mark in the shape of a teardrop balanced on its point. Scrawled on a door or a house, it is an accusation of evil against the people inside, or an attempt to bring the Dark One's attention, and thus harm, to them.

Dreadlords: Those men and women who, able to channel the One Power, went over to the Shadow during the Trolloc Wars, acting as commanders of the Trolloc forces.

Elaida (eh-LY-da): An Aes Sedai of the Red Ajah who advises Queen Morgase of Andor. She sometimes has the Foretelling. *See also* Foretelling.

Elayne (ee-LAIN): Queen Morgase's daughter, the Daughter-Heir to the Throne of Andor. Her sign is a golden lily.

Fain, Padan (FAIN, PAHD-ahn): A man imprisoned as a Darkfriend in Fal Dara keep.

Far Dareis Mai *(FAHR DAH-rize MY):* Literally. "Maidens of the Spear." A warrior society of the Aiel, which, unlike any of the others, admits women and only women. A Maiden may not marry and remain in the society, nor may she fight while carrying a child. Any child born to a Maiden is given to another woman to raise, in such a way that no one knows who the child's mother was. ("You may belong to no man, nor may any man belong to you, nor any child. The spear is your lover, your child, and your life.") These children are treasured, for it is prophesied that a child born of a Maiden will unite the clans and return the Aiel to the greatness they knew during the Age of Legends. *See also* Aiel; Aiel warrior societies.

Five Powers, the: There are threads to the One Power, and each person who can channel can usually grasp some threads better than others. These threads are named according to the sorts of things that can be done using them—Earth, Air, Fire, Water, and Spirit—and are called the Five Powers. Any wielder of the Power will have a greater degree of strength with one, or possibly two, of these, and lesser strength in the others. Some few may have great strength with three, but since the Age of Legends no one has had great strength with all five. Even then this was extremely rare. The degree of strength can vary greatly between individuals, so that some who can channel are much stronger than others. Performing certain acts with the One Power requires ability in one of more of the Five Powers. For example, starting or controlling a fire requires Fire, and affecting the weather requires Air and Water, while Healing requires Water and Spirit. While Spirit was found equally in men and in women, great ability with Earth and/or Fire was found much more often among men; with Water and/or Air among women. There were exceptions, but it was so often so that Earth and Fire came to be regarded as male Powers, Air and Water as female. Generally, no ability is considered stronger than any other, though there is a saying among Aes Sedai: "There is no rock so strong that water and wind cannot wear it away, no fire so fierce that water cannot quench it or wind snuff it out." It should be noted this saying came into use long after the last male Aes Sedai was dead. Any equivalent saying among male Aes Sedai is long lost.

Flame of Tar Valon: The symbol of Tar Valon, the Amyrlin Seat, and the Aes Sedai. A stylized representation of a flame; a white teardrop with the point upward.

Forsaken, the: Name given to thirteen of the most powerful Aes Sedai ever known, who went over to the Dark One during the War of the Shadow in return for the promise of immortality. According to both legend and fragmentary records, they were imprisoned along with the Dark One when his prison was resealed. Their names are still used to frighten children.

Gaidin (GYE-deen): Literally, "Brother to Battles." A title used by Aes Sedai for the Warders. *See also* Warder.

Galad (gah-LAHD): *See* Damodred, Lord Galadedrid.

Galldrian su Riatin Rie (GAHL-dree-ahn soo REYE-ah-tin REE): Literally, Galldrian of House Riatin, King. King of Cairhien. *See also* Cairhien.

Game of Houses, the: See Daes Dae'mar.

Gawyn (GAH-wihn): Queen Morgase's son, and Elayne's brother. His sign is a white boar.

gentling: The act, performed by Aes Sedai, of shutting off a man who can channel from the One Power. This is necessary because any man who learns to channel will go insane from the taint on *saidin* and will almost certainly do horrible things with the Power in his madness. A man who has been gentled can still sense the True Source, but he cannot touch it. Whatever madness has come before gentling is arrested by the act of gentling but not cured by it, and if it is done soon enough death can be averted. *See also* One Power, the; stilling.

gleeman: A traveling storyteller, musician, juggler, tumbler, and all-around entertainer. Known by their trademark cloaks of many-colored patches, they perform mainly in the villages and smaller towns.

Goaban (GO-ah-banh): One of the nations wrung from Artur Hawkwing's empire during the War of the Hundred Years. It weakened, and faded away approximately 500 NE. *See also* Artur Hawkwing; War of the Hundred Years.

Great Blight, the: A region in the far north, entirely corrupted by the Dark One. A haunt of Trollocs, Myrddraal, and other creatures of the Shadow.

Great Game, the: See Daes Dae'mar.

Great Hunt of the Horn, The: A cycle of stories concerning the legendary search for the Horn of Valere, in the years between the end of the Trolloc Wars and the beginning of the War of the Hundred Years. If told in its entirety, the cycle would take many days.

Great Lord of the Dark: The name by which Darkfriends refer to the Dark One, claiming that to use his true name would be blasphemous.

Great Serpent: A symbol for time and eternity, ancient before the Age of Legends began, consisting of a serpent eating its own tail. A ring in the shape of the Great Serpent is awarded to women who have been raised to the Accepted among the Aes Sedai.

Hailene *(heye-LEE-neh):* In the Old Tongue, "Those Who Come Before," or "Forerunners."
Halfman: *See* Myrddraal.

Hardan: One of the nations wrung from Artur Hawkwing's empire, now long forgotten. It lay between Cairhien and Shienar.

Hawkwing, Artur: A legendary king (ruled FY 943–994) who united all the lands west of the Spine of the World. He even sent armies across the Aryth Ocean (FY 992), but all contact with these was lost at his death, which set off the War of the Hundred Years. His sign was a golden hawk in flight. *See also* War of the Hundred Years.

heartstone: An indestructible substance created during the Age of Legends. Any force used in an attempt to break it is absorbed, making heartstone stronger.

hide: A unit of area for measuring land, equal to 100 paces by 100 paces.

Horn of Valere (vah-LEER): The legendary object of the Great Hunt of the Horn. The Horn supposedly can call back dead heroes from the grave to fight against the Shadow.

Hundred Companions, the: One hundred male Aes Sedai, among the most powerful of the Age of Legends, who, led by Lews Therin Telamon, launched the final stroke that ended the War of the Shadow by sealing the Dark One back into his prison. The Dark One's counterstroke tainted *saidin;* the Hundred Companions went mad and began the Breaking of the World. *See also* Time of Madness; Breaking of the World; True Source; One Power.

Hurin (HEW-rhin): A Shienaran who has the ability to smell where violence has been done, and to follow the scent of those who did it. Called a "sniffer," he serves the King's justice in Fal Dara, in Shienar.

Illian (IHL-lee-ahn): A great port on the Sea of Storms, capital city of the nation of the same name.

Ingtar, Lord, of House Shinowa (IHNG-tahr); (shih-NOH-wah): A Shienaran warrior. His sign is the Gray Owl.

Ishamael (ih-SHAH-may-EHL): In the Old Tongue, "Betrayer of Hope." One of the Forsaken. Name given to the leader of the Aes Sedai who went over to the Dark One in the War of the Shadow. It is said that even he forgot his true name. *See also* Forsaken.

Karaethon Cycle, The (ka-rah-AY-thon): *See* Dragon, Prophecies of the.

kith: Close friends and acquaintances.

Laman (LAY-mahn): A king of Cairhien, of House Damodred, who lost his throne and life in the Aiel War.

Lan; al'Lan Mandragoran (AHL-LAN man-DRAG-or-an): A Warder, bonded to Moiraine. Uncrowned King of Malkier, Dai Shan, and the last surviving Malkieri lord. *See also* Warder; Moiraine; Malkier; Dai Shan.

Lanfear (LAN-fear): In the Old Tongue, "Daughter of the Night." One of the Forsaken, perhaps the most powerful next to Ishamael. Unlike the other Forsaken, she chose this name herself.

She is said to have been in love with Lews Therin Telamon. *See also* Forsaken; Dragon, the.

league: See Length, units of.

Leane (lee-AHN-eh): An Aes Sedai of the Blue Ajah, and Keeper of the Chronicles. *See also* Ajah; Chronicles, Keeper of the.

Leashed Ones: See damane.

Length, units of: 10 inches = 3 hands = 1 foot; 3 feet = 1 pace; 2 paces = 1 span; 1000 spans = 1 mile; 4 miles = 1 league.

Lews Therin Telamon; Lews Therin Kinslayer: See Dragon, the.

Liandrin (lee-AHN-drihn): An Aes Sedai of the Red Ajah, from Tarabon.

Logain (loh-GAYN): A false Dragon, gentled by the Aes Sedai.

Loial (LOY-ahl): An Ogier from Stedding Shangtai.

Luc; Lord Luc of House Mantear (LUKE; MAN-tee-ahr): Tigraine's brother. His disappearance in the Great Blight (971 NE) is believed to be connected to Tigraine's later disappearance. His sign was an acorn.

Luthair: See Mondwin, Luthair Paendrag.

Malkier (mahl-KEER): A nation, once one of the Borderlands, now consumed by the Blight. The sign of Malkier was a golden crane in flight.

Manetheren (mahn-EHTH-ehr-ehn): One of the Ten Nations that made the Second Covenant, and also the capital city of that nation. Both city and nation were utterly destroyed in the Trolloc Wars.

marath'damane *(MAH-rahth'dah-MAHN-ee):* In the Old Tongue, "Those Who Must Be Leashed." Term used by the Seanchan for women who can channel, but who have not yet been captured and collared. *See also damane; a'dam;* Seanchan.

Masema (mah-SEE-mah): A Shienaran soldier who hates Aiel.

mashiara *(mah-shee-AH-rah):* In the Old Tongue, "beloved," but meaning a love that is lost beyond redeeming.

Merrilin, Thom (MER-rih-lihn, TOM): A gleeman.

mile: *See* Length, units of.

Min (MIN): A young woman with the ability to read the auras she sometimes sees surrounding people.

Moiraine (mwah-RAIN): An Aes Sedai of the Blue Ajah.

Mondwin, Luthair Paendrag (LEW-thair PAY-ehn-DRAG MON-dwihn): Son of Artur Hawkwing, he commanded the armies Hawkwing sent across the Aryth Ocean. His banner was a golden, spread-winged hawk clutching lightning bolts. *See also* Hawkwing, Artur.

Mordeth (MOOR-death): Councilor who turned the city of Aridhol to use Darkfriends' ways against the Darkfriends, thus bringing its destruction and earning it a new name, Shadar Logoth

("Where the Shadow Waits"). Only one thing survives in Shadar Logoth beside the hate that killed it, and that is Mordeth himself, bound in the ruins for two thousand years, waiting for someone to come whose soul he can consume and so take on new flesh.

Morgase (moor-GAYZ): Queen of Andor, High Seat of House Trakand (TRAHK-ahnd).

Myrddraal (MUHRD-draal): Creatures of the Dark One, commanders of the Trollocs. Twisted offspring of Trollocs in which the human stock used to create the Trollocs has resurfaced, but tainted by the evil that made the Trollocs. Physically they are like men except they have no eyes, but can see like eagles in light or dark. They have certain powers stemming from the Dark One, including the ability to cause paralyzing fear with a look and the ability to vanish wherever there are shadows. One of their few known weaknesses is that they are reluctant to cross running water. In different lands they are known by many names, among them Halfmen, the Eyeless, Shadowmen, Lurks, and Fades.

Niall, Pedron (NEYE-awl, PAY-drohn): Lord Captain Commander of the Children of the Light. *See also* Children of the Light.

Nisura, Lady (nih-SOO-rah): A Shienaran noblewoman, and one of the Lady Amalisa's attendants.

One Power, the: The power drawn from the True Source. The vast majority of people are completely unable to learn to channel the One Power. A very small number can be taught to channel, and an even tinier number have the ability inborn. For these few there is no need to be taught; they will touch the True Source and channel the Power whether they want to or not, perhaps without even realizing what they are doing. This inborn ability usually manifests itself in late adolescence or early adulthood. If control is not taught, or self-learned (extremely difficult, with a success rate of only one in four), death is certain. Since the Time of Madness, no man has been able to channel the Power without eventually going completely, horribly mad, and then, even if he has learned some control, dying from a wasting sickness that causes the sufferer to rot alive, a sickness caused, as is the madness, by the Dark One's taint on *saidin.* For a woman the death that comes without control of the Power is less horrible, but it is death just the same. Aes Sedai search for girls with the inborn ability as much to save their lives as to increase Aes Sedai numbers, and for men with it in order to stop the terrible things they inevitably do with the Power in their madness. *See also* channel; Time of Madness; True Source.

Pattern of an Age: The Wheel of Time weaves the threads of human lives into the Pattern of an Age, often called simply the Pattern, which forms the substance of reality for that Age. *See also ta'veren.*

Powers, the Five: See Five Powers.

Questioners, the: An order within the Children of the Light. Their avowed purposes are to discover the truth in disputations and to uncover Darkfriends. In the search for truth and the Light, their normal method of inquiry is by torture; their normal attitude that they know the truth already and must only make their victim confess to it. The Questioners refer to themselves as the Hand of the Light, the Hand that digs out truth, and at times act as if they were entirely separate from the Children and the Council of the Anointed, which commands the Children. The head of the Questioners is the High Inquisitor, who sits on the Council of the Anointed. Their sign is a blood-red shepherd's crook.

Ragan (rah-GAHN): A Shienaran warrior.

Red Shields: *See* Aiel warrior societies.

Renna (REEN-nah): A Seanchan woman; *a sul'dam. **See also*** Seanchan; *sul'dam.*

Rhyagelle *(rheye-ah-GEHL):* In the Old Tongue, "Those Who Come Home," or "Homecomers."

sa'angreal (SAH-ahn-GREE-ahl): Any one of a number of objects that allow an individual to channel much more of the One Power than would otherwise be possible or safe. *A sa'angreal* is like unto, but much more powerful than, an *angreal.* The amount of the Power that can be wielded with a *sa'angreal* compares to the amount of the Power that can be handled with an *angreal* as the power wielded with the aid of an *angreal* does to the amount of the Power that can be handled unaided. Remnants of the Age of Legends, the means of making *sa'angreal* is no longer known. Only a handful remain, far fewer even than *angreal.*

saidar *(sah-ih-DAHR):* **saidin** (sah-ih-DEEN): *See* True Source.

Saldaea (sahl-DAY-ee-ah): One of the Borderlands.

Sanche, Siuan (SAHN-chay, swahn): An Aes Sedai formerly of the Blue Ajah. Raised to the Amyrlin Seat 988 NE. The Amyrlin Seat is of all Ajahs, and of none.

Sea Folk: More properly, the Atha'an Miere (a-tha-AHN mee-AIR), the People of the Sea. Inhabitants of islands in the Aryth (AH-rihth) Ocean and the Sea of Storms, they spend little time on those islands, living most of their lives on their ships. Most seaborne trade is carried by the Sea Folk's ships.

Seanchan (SHAWN-CHAN): (1) Descendants of the armies Artur Hawkwing sent across the Aryth Ocean, who have returned to reclaim the lands of their forefathers. (2) The land from which the Seanchan come. *See also Hailene; Corenne; Rhyagelle.*

Seandar (shawn-DAHR): Capital city of Seanchan, where the Empress sits on the Crystal Throne in the Court of the Nine Moons.

Selene (seh-LEEN): A woman met on the journey to Cairhien.

Seta (SEE-tah): A Seanchan woman; a *sul'dam. See also* Seanchan; *sul'dam.*

Shadar Lagoth (SHAH-dahr LOH-goth): A city abandoned and shunned since the Trolloc Wars. It is tainted ground, and not a pebble of it is safe. *See also* Mordeth.

Shai'tan (SHAY-ih-TAN): *See* Dark One.

Shayol Ghul (SHAY-ol GHOOL): A mountain in the Blasted Lands, the site of the Dark One's prison.

Sheriam (SHEER-ee-ahm): An Aes Sedai of the Blue Ajah. The Mistress of Novices in the White Tower.

Shienar (shy-NAHR): One of the Borderlands. The sign of Shienar is a stooping black hawk.

shoufa *(SHOO-fah):* A garment of the Aiel, a cloth, usually the color of sand or rock, that wraps around the head and neck, leaving only the face bare.

span: *See* Length, units of.

Spine of the World, the: A towering mountain range, with only a few passes, which separates the Aiel Waste from the lands to the west.

stedding (STEHD-ding): An Ogier (OH-geer) homeland. Many *stedding* have been abandoned since the Breaking of the World. They are shielded in some way, no longer understood, so that within them no Aes Sedai can channel the One Power, nor even sense that the True Source exists. Attempts to wield the One Power from outside a *stedding* have no effect inside a *stedding* boundary. No Trolloc will enter a *stedding* unless driven, and even a Myrddraal will do so only at the greatest need and then with the greatest reluctance and distaste. Even Darkfriends, if truly dedicated, feel uncomfortable within a *stedding*.

stilling: the act, performed by Aes Sedai, of shutting off a woman who can channel from the One Power. A woman who has been stilled can sense the True Source, but she cannot touch it.

Stone Dogs: *See* Aiel warrior societies.

sul'dam *(SUHL-DAHM):* A woman who has passed the tests to show that she can wear the bracelet of an *a'dam* and thus control a *damane*. *See also* a'dam; damane.

Sunday: A feastday and festival in midsummer, celebrated in many parts of the world.

sung wood: *See* Treesinger.

Suroth, High Lady (SUE-roth): A Seanchan noblewoman of high degree.

Tai'shar *(TIE-SHAHR):* In the Old Tongue, "True blood of."

ta'maral'ailen *(tah-MAHR-ahl-EYE-lehn):* In the Old Tongue, "Web of Destiny." A great change in the Pattern of an Age, centered around one or more people who are *ta'veren. See also* Pattern of an Age; *ta'veren.*

Tanreall, Artur Paendrag (tahn-REE-ahl, AHR-tuhr PAY-ehn-DRAG): *See* Hawkwing, Artur.

Tarmon Gai'don (TAHR-mohn GAY-dohn): The Last Battle. *See also* Dragon, Prophecies of the; Horn of Valere.

Tar Valon (TAHR VAH-lon): A city on an island in the River Erinin. The center of Aes Sedai power, and location of the White Tower.

ta'veren *(tah-VEER-ehn):* A person around whom the Wheel of Time weaves all surrounding life-threads, perhaps *all* life-threads, to form a Web of Destiny. *See also* Pattern of an Age.

Tear (TEER): A great seaport on the Sea of Storms.

Telamon, Lews Therin (TEHL-ah-mon, LOOZ THEH-rihn): *See* Dragon, the.

ter'angreal *(TEER-ahn-GREE-ahl):* Any one of a number of remnants of the Age of Legends that use the One Power. Unlike *angreal* and *sa'angreal,* each *ter'angreal* was made to do a particular thing. For example, one makes oaths taken holding it binding. Some are used by Aes Sedai, but their original purposes are largely unknown. Some will kill or destroy the ability to channel of any woman who uses them. *See also angreal; sa'angreal.*

tia avende alantin (TEE-ah ah-VEN-day ah-LANH-tin): "Brother to the Trees."

Tia mi aven Moridin isainde vadin: In the Old Tongue, "The grave is no bar to my call." Inscription on the Horn of Valere. *See also* Horn of Valere.

Tigraine (tee-GRAIN): As Daughter-Heir of Andor, she married Taringail Damodred and bore his son Galadedrid. Her disappearance in 972 NE, shortly after her brother Luc vanished in the Blight, led to the struggle in Andor called the Succession, and caused the events in Cairhien that eventually brought on the Aiel War. Her sign was a woman's hand gripping a thorny rose stem with a white blossom.

Time of Madness: The years after the Dark One's counterstroke tainted the male half of the True Source, when male Aes Sedai went mad and Broke the World. The exact duration of this period is unknown, but it is believed to have lasted nearly one hundred years. It ended completely only with the death of the last male Aes Sedai. *See also* Hundred Companions; True Source; One Power; Breaking of the World.

Tinkers: *See* Tuatha'an.

Traveling People: *See* Tuatha'an.

Tree, the: See Avendesora.

Treekillers: An Aiel name for the Cairhienin, always said in tones of horror and disgust.

Treesinger: An Ogier who has the ability to sing to trees (called "Treesong"), either healing them, or helping them to grow and flower, or making things from the wood without damaging the tree. Objects made in this manner are called "sung wood" and are highly prized. Few Ogier remain who are Treesingers; the Talent seems to be dying out.

Treesong: See Treesinger.

Trollocs (TRAHL-lohks): Creatures of the Dark One, created during the War of the Shadow. Huge in stature, they are a twisted blend of animal and human stock. Vicious by nature, they kill for the pure pleasure of killing. Deceitful in the extreme, they cannot be trusted unless coerced by fear. They are divided into tribe-like bands, among them the Dha'vol, the Ko'bal, and the Dhai'mon.

Trolloc Wars: A series of wars, beginning about 1000 AB and lasting more than three hundred years, during which Trolloc armies ravaged the world. Eventually the Trollocs were slain or driven back into the Great Blight, but some nations ceased to exist, while others were almost depopulated. All records of the time are fragmentary. *See also* Covenant of the Ten Nations.

True Source: The driving force of the universe, which turns the Wheel of Time. It is divided into a male half *(saidin)* and a female half *(saidar),* which work at the same time with and against each other. Only a man can draw on *saidin,* only a woman on *saidar.* Since the beginning of the Time of Madness, *saidin* has been tainted by the Dark One's touch. *See also* One Power.

Tuatha'an (too-AH-thah-AHN): A wandering folk, also known as the Tinkers and as the Traveling People, who live in brightly painted wagons and follow a totally pacifist philosophy called the Way of the Leaf. Things mended by Tinkers are often better than new. They are among the few who can cross the Aiel Waste unmolested, for the Aiel strictly avoid all contact with them.

Turak, High Lord of House Aladon (TOO-rak; AL-ah-dohn): A Seanchan of high degree, commander of the *Hailene*. *See also* Seanchan; *Hailene*.

Verin (VEHR-ihn): An Aes Sedai of the Brown Ajah.

Warder: A warrior bonded to an Aes Sedai. The bonding is a thing of the One Power, and by it he gains such gifts as quick healing, the ability to go long periods without food, water, or rest, and the ability to sense the taint of the Dark One at a distance. So long as a Warder lives, the Aes Sedai to whom he is bonded knows he is alive however far away he is, and when he dies she will know the moment and manner of his death. While most Ajahs believe an Aes Sedai may have one Warder bonded to her at a time, the Red Ajah refuses to bond any Warders at all, while the Green Ajah believe an Aes Sedai may bond as many Warders as she wishes. Ethically the Warder must accede to the bonding, but it has been known to be done involuntarily. What the Aes Sedai gain from the bonding is a closely held secret. *See also* Aes Sedai.

War of Power: See War of the Shadow.

War of the Hundred Years: A series of overlapping wars among constantly shifting alliances, precipitated by the death of Artur Hawkwing and the resulting struggle for his empire. It lasted from FY 994 to FY 1117. The war depopulated large parts of the lands between the Aryth Ocean and the Aiel Waste, from the Sea of Storms to the Great Blight. So great was the destruction that only fragmentary records of the time remain. The empire of Artur Hawkwing was pulled apart in the wars, and the nations of the present day were formed. *See also* Hawkwing, Artur.

War of the Shadow: Also known as the War of Power, it ended the Age of Legends. It began shortly after the attempt to free the Dark One, and soon involved the whole world. In a world where even the memory of war had been forgotten, every facet of war was rediscovered, often twisted by the Dark One's touch on the world, and the One Power was used as a weapon. The war was ended by the resealing of the Dark One into his prison. *See also* Hundred Companions, the; Dragon, the.

Watchers Over the Waves: A group who believe that the armies Artur Hawkwing sent across the Aryth Ocean will one day return, and so keep watch from the town of Falme (FAHL-may) on Toman Head.

Web of Destiny: See ta'maral'ailen.

Weight, units of: 10 ounces = 1 pound; 10 pounds = 1 stone; 10 stone = 1 hundredweight; 10 hundredweight = 1 ton.

Wheel of Time, the: Time is a wheel with seven spokes, each spoke an Age. As the Wheel turns, the Ages come and go, each leaving memories that fade to legend, then to myth, and are forgotten by the time that Age comes again. The Pattern of an Age is slightly different each time an Age comes, and each time it is subject to greater change, but each time it is the same Age.

Whitecloaks: See Children of the Light.

White Tower: The palace of the Amyrlin Seat in Tar Valon, and the place where Aes Sedai are trained.

Wisdom: In villages, a woman chosen by the Women's Circle for her knowledge of such things as healing, and foretelling the weather, as well as for common good sense. A position of great responsibility and authority, both actual and implied. She is generally considered the equal of the mayor, just as the Women's Circle is the equal of the Village Council. Unlike the mayor, the Wisdom is chosen for life, and it is very rare for a Wisdom to be removed from office before her death. Depending on the land, she may instead have another title, such as Guide, Healer, Wise Woman, or Reader.

ABOUT THE AUTHOR

Robert Jordan was born in 1948 in Charleston, South Carolina, where he now lives with his wife, Harriet, in a house built in 1797. He taught himself to read when he was four with the incidental aid of a twelve-year-older brother, and was tackling Mark Twain and Jules Verne by five. He is a graduate of The Citadel, the Military College of South Carolina, with a degree in physics. He served two tours in Vietnam with the U.S. Army; among his decorations are the Distinguished Flying Cross, the Bronze Star with 'V' and two Vietnamese Crosses of Gallantry. A history buff, he has also written dance and theater criticism. He enjoys the outdoor sports of hunting, fishing and sailing, and the indoor sports of poker, chess, pool and pipe collecting. He has been writing since 1977 and intends to continue until they nail shut his coffin.

Book Six: *Lord of Chaos*

0-812-51375-4 • $7.99 ($10.99 CAN) / in hardcover: 0-312-85428-5 • $29.95 ($39.95 CAN)

"A great read.... Some surprising new developments.... I can't recommend starting anywhere but at the beginning, but the volumes only get richer as they go along." —*Locus*

Book Seven: *A Crown of Swords*

0-812-55028-5 • $7.99 ($10.99 CAN) / in hardcover: 0-312-85767-5 • $29.95 ($41.95 CAN)

"Jordan's preeminent saga [has] remained remarkably rich....Will not disappoint." —*Booklist*

Book Eight: *The Path of Daggers*

0-812-55029-3 • $7.99 ($10.99 CAN) / in hardcover: 0-312-85769-1 • $27.95 ($38.95 CAN)

"For sheer imagination and storytelling skill . . . *The Wheel of Time* rivals Tolkien's *The Lord of the Rings*."
—*Publishers Weekly* (starred review)

Book Nine: *Winter's Heart*

0-812-57558-X • $7.99 ($10.99 CAN) / in hardcover: 0-312-86425-6 • $29.95 ($39.95 CAN)

"The plot continues to thicken and intrigue, as always, runs rampant." —*Booklist*

Book Ten: *Crossroads of Twilight*

0-812-57133-9 • $7.99 ($10.99 CAN) / in hardcover: 0-312-86459-0 • $29.95 ($41.95 CAN)

"For those who like to keep themselves in a fantasy world, it's hard to beat the complex, detailed world created here."
—*Locus*

All these books are available in both hardcover and paperback. If you do not see them on display, ask your bookseller to order them for you.